FRACTURES, DREAMS AND SECOND CHANCES

To Donna,

I hope you enjoy the book

All te best

July 2021

FRACTURES, DREAMS AND SECOND CHANCES

STEPHEN ANTHONY BROTHERTON

The Book Guild Ltd

First published in Great Britain in 2021 by
The Book Guild Ltd
9 Priory Business Park
Wistow Road, Kibworth
Leicestershire, LE8 0RX
Freephone: 0800 999 2982
www.bookguild.co.uk
Email: info@bookguild.co.uk
Twitter: @bookguild

Typeset in Minion Pro

Printed and bound in Great Britain by CPI Group (UK) Ltd, Croydon, CR0 4YY

ISBN 978 1913551 896

British Library Cataloguing in Publication Data.
A catalogue record for this book is available from the British Library.

For a fractured seven-year-old boy
who found a way to survive.

Part One

Let's Dance

The jangling brass doorway bell heralded my arrival at the coffee shop. Several of the regulars looked up, but they quickly returned to their gossipy chatter about families, friends and neighbours, hushed voices backdropped by the sound of a gushing steamer, grinding beans and clattering crockery.

'Skimmed milk latte,' said the waitress, already pouring the red-top milk into the jug.

It used to make me feel special, the fact that they knew me, knew what I wanted, but it had soured with repetition. I'd become my drink order – that's what it felt like. But it was okay. People watching in this place made me feel part of the world, got me away from the house for a few hours.

And it was here she came back to me.

I hadn't seen her for three decades and suddenly there she was, standing next to my table.

'Hello, Freddie.'

Freddie – November 1979

She walked across Max's nightclub dance floor towards me as Blondie's 'Dreaming' started up.

'I thought you'd never ask,' she said.

I wouldn't. What would have been the point? She was first division and I was Sunday pub league. I stood in silence, mouth open, waiting for the punchline, waiting for my mate, Jack, to burst out laughing. Piss-take of the century.

'I'll take that as a no then,' she said, turning to walk away, jolting me back to my senses.

'Wait. Dance. Yes.'

Monosyllabic, but at least I'd found my voice.

Freddie – July 2015

It felt like I'd messed up the coffee shop reunion by breaking my five-second-hug rule and clinging on for too long. I remembered a time when holding each other for all eternity wouldn't have been enough.

I scooped up the newspapers from the second seat and dropped them to the floor. 'Sit down,' I said. 'I can't believe it's you.'

'You're looking well, Freddie,' she said.

'And you. It's been a long time.'

An awkward silence fell as we met each other's eyes – her line of nose freckles reminding me of the mole above her bellybutton and triggering an age-old desire to join the dots. I could feel the regulars staring, trying to work out who the stranger was. She looked nervously around the room, china cats and dogs staring down at her from a Welsh dresser.

'What are you doing here, Jo-Jo?'

She reached across the table and squeezed my hand.

'I'm looking for you,' she said.

Freddie – November 1979

We didn't dance to Blondie. I spent most of the record explaining why it wasn't a good idea for a gangly man to do disco dancing. I expected her to get bored, to walk away, but she stayed and nodded, looking up at me as though I was explaining the theory of DNA.

'I'm Jo-Jo,' she said.

'Right,' I said. 'Jo-Jo. Freddie. I mean, that's me. My name's Freddie.'

Dr Hook came to my rescue. 'More Like the Movies'.

'I can do this one,' I said.

We walked hand in hand onto the dance floor.

For the next three and a half minutes I was more conscious of my body's proximity to another human being than I'd ever been before in my life. I had this voice inside my head reminding me of my rules – *Don't hold her too close. Keep your hand flat in the middle of her back. Don't tread on her feet. Don't sing.* I relaxed, closed my eyes, went with the sway from side to side, opened my eyes, smiled at her, she was real, she smiled back. And then – I could have kissed him – the DJ played the Commodores, 'Still', followed by Exile, 'Kiss You All Over'. Three in a row. Ten glorious minutes of holding her as close as I dared, intoxicated by her white musk perfume. The lights came on. We handed in our tickets and collected our coats. I waved goodbye to Jack, left him searching for his sister, and offered to walk Jo-Jo home.

'Where do you live, Freddie?'

'Lower Farm,' I said.

'But that's in the opposite direction.'

I shrugged and she laughed. I'd never made anyone like her laugh before.

We crunched through the icy night. I was wearing my cousin's blue cord jacket and a pair of Pod shoes that had cost me most of a week's pay packet. I was distracted by the shoes, hoping the snow wasn't shredding them to pieces. She asked what I did. I told her I was on a YOP scheme, working at a timber yard. She told me she worked at a hairdresser's as a Saturday girl.

We reached a patch of green in the middle of a council estate, a big oak tree growing in its centre. She stopped walking. 'That's my house there,' she said.

She looked at me, her lips glistening with what I hoped was strawberry lip gloss. I wanted to kiss her, but I froze. After a few seconds she smiled and touched my cheek. 'You're sweet,' she said. 'I'll call you.'

She reached her front door and waved.

I turned up my coat collar and headed home.

Freddie – July 2015

'Morning.'

Tom Stone, retired headmaster, unelected leader of the coffee shop brigade, had sidled up to the table and was looking at me, waiting for his formal introduction.

'Tom,' I said. 'This is…'

'I'm an old friend,' said Jo-Jo, giving him a hard stare.

He looked at her, the smile disappearing from his face.

'Perhaps we can talk later,' I said. 'We're just in the middle of something.'

'Of course. I can see you're busy.'

He leaned lightly on his walking stick and limped back to his table. He sat down, shook his head and said something to his wife. They both looked over.

'Nosy old sods,' said Jo-Jo, still holding my hand.

'They're okay,' I said.

'You're too soft, Freddie. You always were.'

'Jo-Jo, it's been over thirty years. Why are you looking for me now?'

'Because it's the right time.'

'The right time for what?'

She hesitated, reached inside her coat pocket, which she'd draped over the back of her chair, and pulled out a black and white passport-sized photograph.

'To give you this,' she said.

On the walk home from the nightclub, I reasoned through what had happened. She'd fancied a change from her *Saturday Night Fever* blokes, I'd caught her eye and half an hour later she'd regretted it. She wouldn't call. Why would she?

Two days later, she called.

'Hi, it's me.'

For some bizarre reason, and I blame the Steve McQueen film on telly that night, I decided to play it cool. 'Hello, me,' I said.

She went quiet for a few seconds. 'Is that you, Freddie?'

'Sure is.'

'It's Jo-Jo.'

The stutter of insecurity in her voice shifted my brain into gear.

'Jo-Jo,' I said. 'I didn't think you'd call.'

'I nearly hung up. Perhaps I shouldn't have called.'

'I was hoping you'd call. I enjoyed our dance.'

'Me too.'

'It was bloody freezing walking home though.'

'I told you not to walk me back.'

'I'll wear my thermals next time.'

She laughed.

'So you work on a Saturday,' I said.

'Yeah, but I can't wait to leave that cow at the hairdresser's. What about you?'

'Me?'

'Yeah. How's things with you? What have you been up to?'

I could have told her about spending the previous evening with Jack, sorting out my postcard collection of World War Two fighter planes. I had them in date order of manufacture, and we'd reordered them into number of missions flown in combat.

'Oh, nothing much,' I said. 'Same old stuff.'

Silence.

'Do you fancy meeting up?' I said.

Freddie – July 2015

I could feel Tom and his wife still looking at us as I took the photograph from Jo-Jo.

'Do you remember where that was taken?' she said.

'Blackpool,' I said. 'God, we were so young.'

'Look at your hair. It's on your shoulders. You'd just bought that car.'

I studied the picture, resurfacing the memory of how she'd smartened me up in a black pork-pie hat, Chelsea boots and hugging trousers she'd tapered herself. She was wearing a red beret, a pink cheesecloth shirt and a mod jacket with the collar turned up. She'd bought the beret from one of the market stalls in town, said it made her look like Marianne Faithfull.

'It's wonderful,' I said. 'But you haven't come all this way to bring me a photograph.'

Freddie – May 1980

I turned into Jo-Jo's street and dropped the speed of my second-hand Chrysler Avenger down to twenty miles per hour, a Springsteen cassette on cue to provide the backing track for our first weekend away together. We'd spent the previous evening in Jo-Jo's bedroom plotting every detail. 'Isn't this a bit obsessive, Freddie?' she'd said, looking at my list. 'Do we really need to know where we're eating every meal?'

I pulled up outside her house and beeped the horn. Her face appeared briefly at the lounge window and then she was coming through the front door, clutching a tweed carpet bag. She threw the bag on the back seat and jumped in the passenger side.

'You got it. I can't believe you bought it.'

'Thank my mum. She lent me the money.'

'I'd rather thank you,' she said, dropping her arms around my neck and kissing me full on the lips.

I eased her gently away. 'Shall we go?' I said.

'Ready when you are. Turn the music up and get us there as fast as you can.'

I slammed the car into gear and screeched away from the kerb. Jo-Jo fell back in the passenger seat laughing, her loose auburn hair flinging itself around her tanned face. 'Easy tiger,' she said, putting her hand on my thigh. 'I would like to get there in one piece.'

I grinned and pushed in the tape. 'Growin Up' brought the stereo to life.

Freddie – July 2015

The brass bell jangled. We both looked over at the shop doorway. It was Dora, another of the regulars. She was clutching her toy poodle, Alfie.

'You'll have to keep him on your lap,' said the waitress.

'I know,' said Dora.

Jo-Jo took a sip of her coffee. 'There is something else, Freddie.'

I felt a rising panic in my stomach. 'What?' I said.

'I'm emigrating,' she said, gently placing her coffee cup back in its saucer. 'My husband, Jason, died last year and I'm off to join my daughter, Amy, in New Zealand. She's got two kids. Can you imagine me a granny? It's ridiculous.'

Husband. Daughter. She'd had a life – a life without me. 'I'll miss you,' I said.

She looked at me quizzically. 'We haven't seen each other for years.'

I felt the blood rush to my cheeks, conscious of having said something really stupid. 'Another country seems different,' I said. 'And it's so far away.'

'I know what you mean,' she said. 'I'm still getting used to the idea. It's all happened so quickly.'

'And you came to tell me? After all this time.'

'It sounds silly, but I didn't want to go without seeing you again.'

'How did you know I'd be here?'

'That mate of yours, Jack. We got chatting at a dementia charity event. His name jumped out from the delegate list.'

I smiled. Jo-Jo laughed.

'Poor Jack,' I said. 'He was really pissed off when that film came out. Threatened to sue Johnny Depp.'

'He was loving it at the conference. Had a big name badge with 'Jack Sparrow' emblazoned across his chest. You two stayed in touch then?'

'Yep. Don't know what I'd do without him. He's as straight as they come.'

'Not that straight,' she said.

'You worked that one out then.'

'First thing he said to me. "You've probably heard I'm queer, darling." I thought he was winding me up.'

'That's Jack,' I said. 'Says it as it is.'

She was looking at me, stroking my hand. I wanted her to say something, anything.

'It's strange to think of you married,' I said.

It was too hot to run but that hadn't stopped us tying our hair in ponytails, putting on matching trainers, tracksuit bottoms and tee-shirts, all found by Jo-Jo on our last shopping trip to town, and setting off on what had become our regular Sunday morning jog down the lane; past Sam the gypsy and his greyhounds, all sitting outside his battered and rusty caravan, and then back along the side of the canal. Twenty minutes in, we reached our field, dropped into the grass and stared at the sky.

'I can't see it.'

'It's there,' she said, pointing upwards.

'I can see the cloud, but it's nothing like a face.'

'That's Cat Stevens. Trust me. I'm good at this sort of stuff.'

'There's no way that's a face.'

She looked across at me, a piece of grass hanging from her mouth, her nose freckles raised by the sun. 'You're hopeless. No imagination. I don't know why I put up with you.'

'My wit, charm and personality?' I offered.

She put her head on my chest and cuddled close. 'Yeah, maybe. Either that or your new car.'

I closed my eyes and let the sun soak into my face.

'What do you want to do with your life, Freddie?'

'Not thought about it.'

'You should. I want to get my degree, start my own business, travel, have a family – all sorts of things. Life's for living. My dad taught me that.'

'We should go,' I said. 'Mum will have cooked the dinner.'

She sighed. 'Just five more minutes.'

The second-hand 1600 GL Avenger cost me five hundred and forty pounds from Newtown Service Station. It had a rev counter with red digits next to the speedo. I stuck a Freddie and Jo-Jo sun-strip across the front windscreen, bought a leather top for the gearstick and fitted a Sony radio cassette player, with two speakers set up on the rear window shelf. Jo-Jo filled the back seat with cuddly lions, dogs and cats. We used to park up down the lane next to Sam's caravan, three o'clock in the morning, fresh out of Max's, climb in the back seat and make love to Barbra Streisand's *Guilty* album. One night, Jo-Jo got drunk and slow-danced naked in front of the car headlights. I watched from the driver's seat, storing the memory for the rest of my life.

Freddie – July 2015

The coffee shop lunchtime crowd had assembled for their toasted sandwiches and homemade cakes. Some of the regulars were on their third cappuccino with chocolate sprinkles. The waitress came over and asked if we wanted more drinks. We shook our heads and she moved on around the tables.

'Gets busy here,' said Jo-Jo.

'Every day,' I said. 'We should have had another drink really.'

'They don't seem that bothered. Anyway, I haven't finished this one yet. You still haven't told me about your family.'

'Not much to tell.'

'Did you marry?'

'I came close. I have a daughter, Becky. She's grown up now. I don't see her much.'

'Jack said you live on your own.'

'Sounds like he gave you chapter and verse.'

'I might have asked,' she said.

I looked around the room. My eyes fell on two watercolours of a medieval church. Stella, the coffee shop owner, had bought them from a local artist. I picked up one of the paper napkins and turned it over in my hand. 'Jack's always been an old gossip,' I said. 'He wouldn't have needed much encouragement. Tell me about your daughter.'

'We're close, always have been.'

'What does she do?'

'She's a lawyer, got her own practice. Nicky, my grandson, he's ten and Sophia, my gorgeous granddaughter, is thirteen. She's fallen in love already. I told her, "Take your time. There's no rush".'

'Sounds wonderful. I can see why you want to be with them.'

'I don't go until the end of the month,' she said. 'Perhaps we could meet up, go for a meal, a bottle of wine.' She reached inside her bag and handed over a slip of paper. 'I've written down my address and phone number. Just in case you want to keep in touch. No pressure.'

'Of course,' I said. 'I will. I'll call.'

*

The chair opposite me was empty. I looked again at the photo Jo-Jo had left behind. Thirty-five years. The lane and the field would still be there, but the Avenger was long gone. And Sam. And his greyhounds. And the pork-pie hat. I finger traced Jo-Jo's photographic image, bringing her back to me. We were sitting in a photo booth. I was leaning in from the side. It had taken us ages to fix the stool at the right height, standing opposite each other, me turning it clockwise, Jo-Jo anticlockwise. 'That's right. Leave it alone.' 'It isn't. It needs to come down more.' And then the wait outside. Spitting with rain. My anxiety. My anticipation.

Would they come out okay? Our first pictures together, proof of a connection. The photos dropping into the metal grid; us waiting ten seconds while they dried. I'd tried not to smile too widely, embarrassed by my chipped front tooth. Jo-Jo was holding up two fingers in a peace sign, the camera had caught her glancing sideways at me. Her auburn hair. Her nose freckles. Why didn't I kiss her when she left the coffee shop?

'You okay, Freddie?'

Tom. He was at my table again, his wife smiling anxiously across the room.

'I'm fine, Tom. Thanks for asking.'

'It's just that... well, we couldn't help noticing.'

The waitress came over. 'Another skimmed milk latte?' she said.

Everything had gone quiet, eyes at every table were looking at me – closing in on me. I shook my head, stood up and walked out of the shop.

Jo-Jo – July 2015

I turned right out of the coffee shop and walked along the high street to the pub car park where I'd left my panther-black Mazda convertible. I pressed the key fob. The lights on the car flickered twice and I sat in the driver's seat, staring out at the playing fields. Freddie. I'd wanted him to hug me for longer, but he'd pulled away after a few seconds. He'd blushed when I'd kissed him on the cheek, his neck turning florid as though we'd been caught out in some major indecency. I smiled at the thought. Sweet. I'd said it thirty-five years ago and I'd been right.

The passenger side door opened. Amy dropped in the seat next to me.

'Everything okay, Mum? Was he there?'

I nodded.

'What's he like? Was he pleased to see you?'

A noise from the park. A boy and a girl about seven years of age were being pushed on the swings by their mother. 'Higher, Mummy,' the girl shouted. 'I want to go higher.'

I pressed the power button and dabbed the accelerator with my right foot. The engine ignited. 'Put your seatbelt on,' I said.

'Mum. What did he say?'

'He said he'd ring.'

Amy shook her head, pulled the seatbelt across her body and clicked it in place.

Jo-Jo – A Memory

Amy is seven. I watch from the landing as she conducts a marriage ceremony for Sindy and Action Man in her bedroom. The Action Man belongs to her cousin, Thomas. It's the Eagle Eyes version whose creepy gaze follows you around the room. She places both dolls on the bed, standing them against her My Little Pony cushions. Sindy is dressed in a ballerina outfit with blue dancing slippers, white tights, a light blue leotard and a pink tutu skirt. Eagle Eyes is wearing full khaki combat dress with an American officer's cap placed on his head. Amy kneels on the floor in front of them.

'Do you, Eagle Eyes, take the beautiful and gorgeous Sindy, to be your lawfully wedded wife?'

'I do,' says Amy in a deep, gruff voice.

She turns Action Man's eyes to face his soon to be bride. 'Let's get on with it. I've got a battle to fight.'

I put my hand to my mouth.

Amy tuts. 'Typical man, Mummy,' she says.

I nod, trying desperately not to laugh.

'We need to make you look presentable,' she says to Sindy, smoothing down the doll's blonde nylon hair. 'Do you, Sindy, take the rugged and handsome Eagle Eyes to be your lawfully wedded husband?'

'I do. I do. I do.'

Amy picks up both dolls.

'You may kiss the bride,' she declares, bringing Eagle Eyes and Sindy's faces together and looking up at me.

'They love each other, Mummy. They'll be together forever.'

Jo-Jo – February 1980

Freddie and I were sitting side by side on a squishy white leather sofa in Max's games area. Freddie liked to get to the club early and play space invaders on the table-top Pac-Man before the crowds arrived. He was top scorer.

'Shouldn't we be going?' I said, stretching to look over the balcony at the dance floor. 'I want to eat before the Beatles Night starts.'

'In a minute,' he said, his eyes still fixed on the beeping screen.

I took a sip of my Pernod crème de menthe and flopped back in the chair, my black and white polka-dot Twiggy dress riding up my bare thighs.

'Do you like my dress?' I said.

He grunted.

'Dad gave me the money.'

Another grunt.

'And the Go-Go boots,' I said, putting my feet up on the Pac-Man.

He looked at the yellow boots and then at my thighs.

'You're blushing, Freddie.'

He took a quick look around the room, put his hand on my knee and traced a line up my right leg with his forefinger. He was grinning like a mischievous little boy who'd stolen a toffee. He stopped just under the hemline of my dress, leaned down and kissed me on the lips. 'You're beautiful,' he said.

I lightly pinched his sideburns. His breath smelt of aniseed. 'These are coming on. We'll soon have you looking like Ray Davies.' I tilted my head to one side and looked up at him, my eyes covered in thick black pencil liner and mascara. 'Can we eat now?'

'What do you fancy?' he said.

I pulled his head down and gave him a long, hard searching kiss.

Jo-Jo – July 2015

The Mazda purred effortlessly along the countryside lanes, acres and acres of fields streaming past the window, birdsong filling the car through the open roof. I thought of Dad and our endless day trips to dirty rain seaside towns: Borth, Rhyl, Aberystwyth. We did them all in his hearse-like brown Volvo; me and my younger brother, Josh, flicking at each other in the back seat, Dad giving us his rear-view mirror glare, Mum passing round cheese and onion quarter-cut sandwiches and orange pop in plastic cups to calm everyone down.

'Has he changed much?' said Amy.

'Not really,' I said. 'He's still Freddie.'

I turned on the radio. Jeremy Vine was interviewing a politician. 'So when exactly will that take place, Minister?' Amy switched the radio off.

'Tell me what you said to him, Mum.'

'I told him I was emigrating.'

'That must have shook him up.'

'Why? We haven't exactly kept in touch.'

'I bet he phones.'

'Maybe,' I said. 'We'll see.'

'You still care for him, don't you?'

'I'm not sure. We always just...'

'You're not going to say clicked, are you?'

'I was going to say fitted.'

'Like comfy slippers,' she said. 'That's good. Now Dad's gone. Now you're...'

'If you say old, you're walking to the hotel.'

'I was going to say mature.'

'That's worse. Makes me sound like a smelly cheese.'

'I'm just saying, I get it. No one wants comfy slippers at eighteen. You want a pair of Jimmy Choo's. Fluorescent ones with five-inch heels. But as you get older...'

'I might slap you in a minute.'

'He'll phone,' she said.

Jo-Jo – May 1974

We were all packed inside Dad's Volvo on our way to Aberystwyth. Drizzling rain had woken up the vegetation, leaving a freshly laundered sheen on the world. Mum had pointed out the sheep and cows in the fields like they were exotic herds roaming the land, Josh and I grunting acknowledgements from the back seat. I'd read my *Jackie* magazine over and over and we'd eaten two packets of Marks and Spencer mint humbugs. Dad had spent most of the journey singing his way through the Beatles greatest hits and we'd all joined in with the choruses.

'There's the sea,' said Dad.

I craned my neck to look.

'I can see it,' said Josh.

'No you can't,' I said.

'You'll both be able to see in a minute,' said Mum.

We turned a corner and there it was. I'd built it up in my head as an azure water carpet stretching out to the horizon, but it was more battleship grey with dirty white flecks on the tips of the waves. I felt sad to see the end of the land, the end of our journey.

Dad parked the Volvo and pushed some coins into one of the parking meters. 'That'll give us a couple of hours,' he said. Mum stood me and Josh in front of her, pulled the Parka hoods over our heads and zipped the coats tight under our chins. 'Don't take them off,' she warned us. 'You'll catch your death. And put your gloves on.'

Mum and Dad walked in front of us along the seafront, Dad holding their umbrella, me holding ours. I hummed 'A Hard Day's Night' and Dad joined in. Mum tutted and I looked at Josh. He shrugged and ran into one of the open-fronted arcades, bells and flashing lights beating out from every direction, a faint odour of sweat and dirty coins. An unshaven man with uncombed hair, grass-stained tracksuit bottoms and a hooded sweat-top, slapped the side of a fruit machine in frustration. 'Oi, mate,' boomed a voice. I looked around. The change counter woman, standing inside a Perspex box, leaned into her mike. 'Do that again,' she said, 'and you're out.' The man smiled, kicked the front of the machine and ran out of the arcade. 'Dick,' said the woman.

Josh sat down behind the steering wheel of the Grand Prix machine and looked hopefully at Mum. She walked over and pushed a two-pence coin into the slot. The screen lit up.

Dad and I closed the umbrellas. We walked over to the machine and watched in silence as Josh turned the wheel, laughing and steering his way around a Formula One track, the sounds of tyre screeches and exhaust acceleration coming from the simulated Lotus.

Mum rubbed the back of Josh's head. 'Well done, darling,' she said.

I looked at Dad and raised my eyebrows. He smiled and squeezed my hand.

Jo-Jo – January 1972

I blew out the pink candles on my princess birthday cake and Dad handed me a long rectangular box, which he'd wrapped the night before in Snoopy wrapping paper. I read the card.

> *'To our darling daughter, Jo-Jo.*
> *Happy Birthday*
> *All our love*
> *Mum and Dad* .
> *XXXX'*

'I don't know why you've bought her that,' said Mum. 'She won't use it.'

'I will,' I said, tearing at the wrapping paper. 'What is it?'

'It's a telescope,' said Josh.

Dad glared at him. 'And it's meant to be a surprise.'

I looked at the uncovered box. It had a picture of the night sky with shooting stars, moons, rushing meteors and 'Stargazer' written across its full length in gold lettering.

'We can set it up in your room,' said Dad. 'It's got its own tripod.'

I opened the box and pulled out the white telescope.

'She hates it,' said Mum.

'I love it,' I said.

Dad grinned and handed me a second present. It was a hardback book entitled, *Exploring the Universe*. 'It tells us what to look for,' he said.

I kissed him on the cheek. 'Thank you, Dad.'

Jo-Jo – August 1972

We were at my cousin Denise's wedding. Waltz music started up. Dad put his arm around my waist and twirled me across the dance floor.

'One, two, three. One, two, three.'

I could feel Mum watching, and Josh.

'One, two, three. One, two, three.'

Dad spun me faster and faster. My first pair of high-heeled shoes were slipping off my feet and I had to concentrate really hard to keep up with him. 'Don't let him down,' I told myself. I held my head back and closed my eyes. I opened my eyes. The mirror balls, the laughter from everyone around us, the smell of Dad's tangy Aramis aftershave. The music changed. We stopped dancing. The room carried on spinning.

'That was great, Dad.'

'You're a natural,' he said. 'We'll get you some classes sorted.'

'Really? When? When can we start?'

Mum walked over and hugged me.

'Dad's going to teach me to dance. Aren't you, Dad?'

Jo-Jo – February 1980

We had to make our way down two spiral staircases to reach Max's basement restaurant. A gang of lads at the bar stared at us as we came down the first flight. I smiled at them, praying all the time to stay upright in the Go-Go boots. Freddie kept his eyes fixed on the steel steps. He was wearing the outfit I'd chosen for him: a slim-cut black suit; highly polished Chelsea boots; a sky-blue Oxford shirt with a button-down collar, and a tightly knotted pencil tie. I'd gone with him the previous afternoon to get his hair cut, pointing out John Lennon's mop-top style from a copy of *Face* magazine. 'That one,' I'd said. 'That's the one he wants.'

The waiter hurried over as we walked through the saloon-style swing doors. He showed us to our table, and we gave him our order. Freddie rearranged his cutlery.

'Why do you do that?' I said.

'My mum's left-handed.'

'But you're right-handed.'

'Apart from using a knife and fork.'

The Muscadet arrived.

'Would madam like to taste?' said the waiter.

I took a sip and nodded.

'I always expect you to send that back,' said Freddie.

'One of these days, I will.'

'I'd die,' he said. 'I'd rather pay for it.'

The food arrived.

'Don't,' I said.

'What?'

'You're about to say what you always say. It drives me mad.'

'I was just wondering how you can eat steak like that.'

'Like what?'

'Your plate's full of blood. It's soaking into your chips.'

I forked a piece of the T-bone into my mouth and began to slowly chew. 'It's yummy,' I said. 'You don't know what you're missing.'

'Blood, mainly, by the looks of it.'

'No point in having a steak if you're going to cook all the good out of it. That's what my dad tells me. How's your chicken?'

'My *chicken chasseur* is fine. At least it's cooked.'

'Do you want to try my steak?'

'No thanks.'

I forked another piece of meat and waved it under his nose. 'Go on. Get some proper food inside you.'

'I think you're a vampire,' he said.

I bared my teeth and growled at him. 'You'd like that wouldn't you?'

'What?'

'Me dressed as a vampire and biting you.'

He poured some wine into my glass. 'Maybe,' he said.

I laughed. 'Try this piece of steak and I might think about it.'

Jo-Jo – July 2015

I turned the Mazda into the conifer-framed entrance of the Hotel Rushmore, dropped the car into second gear and crept along the narrow privet-hedged lane. Flashes of sunlight streaked through the trees, reflecting off the windscreen. The car was moving from dark to light, dark to light. I wanted to sneeze, but I pushed the thought away and concentrated on avoiding any overhanging branches. I didn't want to scratch the car. It was the only thing I'd bought for myself out of Jason's insurance money.

'You'd think they'd have better access,' I said, my eyes fixed on the tarmac.

'Strange name for a hotel,' said Amy.

The car hit a pothole and bounced to the right. I jerked the steering wheel to correct it.

'What?' I said.

'The hotel. The receptionist told me the owner wanted a reminder of her holiday in New York.'

'But Mount Rushmore's in Dakota.'

'I think she just wanted something American.'

We pulled out of the lane and into the driveway sweep in front of the Georgian house. I parked up in one of the guest spaces and unclicked my seatbelt.

'I'm not sure I'll be that bothered if he doesn't phone,' I said.

'Stop worrying, Mum. I think you're the best thing that's ever happened to him.'

I looked at her. 'What a strange thing to say.'

'Does he have a family?' she said.

'A daughter. He doesn't see her.'

'And this Jack fellow's his only mate?'

'You make him sound really sad.'

'All I'm saying is, he'll phone. I bet there's a message at reception.'

'And then what?'

'I don't know, Mum. Whatever you want.'

Jo-Jo – April 1980

The fairground was humming with conversation, the smell of frying doughnuts and hot dogs with onions laced the air, and the Boomtown Rats' 'I Don't Like Mondays' was blasting out through the music system. I grabbed Freddie's arm and pulled him through the crowd to the waltzers.

We dropped into one of the cars and I snuggled into his chest. One of the ride attendants jumped on the back and grinned down at us. He had a gold sovereign ring on his right hand and a red-faced pirate tattoo on his forearm. 'You two okay?' he said. We looked up at him and nodded. Freddie pulled a crumpled one-pound note from his trouser pocket and handed it over. The attendant gave him a fifty-pence piece out of his money bag. 'Nice hat,' he said, before jumping to the waltzer next door.

'See,' I said.

'He was taking the piss,' said Freddie. 'I'm taking it off.'

'You can't. It was a present. You look good. Sexy.'

'Really?'

'Really.'

He grinned. The ride started. Freddie pressed the Mod hat down on his head.

'Make sure it doesn't blow off,' I said.

Jo-Jo – July 2015

We climbed the hotel steps and entered the reception area, me wearily following Amy. She strode across the lobby's thick pile carpet, her heels leaving a trail of indentations in the beige wool. I saw the nervy young male receptionist spot her heading his way. He straightened up in his chair and beamed out his best greeting smile like a defence shield. He looked like he was about to be held up at gunpoint. 'Good morning, madam,' he stuttered. 'Can I help you?'

'You have a message for my mother,' she said. 'Mrs Coulman. Room 242.'

'Of course,' he said. 'I'll check.'

Amy drummed her fingers on the desk as he tapped away at the keyboard in front of him. I gave her a glare and she stopped.

'I'm sorry,' said the receptionist. 'There's no message.'

'Can you check again?'

He looked back at his computer screen. 'No,' he said. 'There's nothing against that name. Were you told there was?'

'No,' I said. 'We just thought there might be. Thank you for looking.'

Amy turned to me and shrugged. 'He'll call later,' she said. 'What do you want to do this afternoon, Mum?'

'I'm going up to have a lie down. Do you mind? I feel exhausted.'

She touched my arm, gave me a sympathetic look. 'Of course not. You go and have a rest. We'll meet up in a couple of hours.'

'What about you?'

'I might give Dan a call. See how the kids are.'

'You can't phone now. It's after midnight over there.'

She pulled an iPhone out of her Gucci handbag and walked towards the conservatory. 'Later, Mum,' she said, putting her hand in the air.

'I wish I had that confidence,' said the receptionist.

I looked at him. He blushed and looked back at his screen.

'She gets it off her father,' I said.

'Would you like to book a call for four o'clock, madam?'

I smiled. 'Yes,' I said. 'Thank you. A call's a good idea.'

Jo-Jo – April 1980

We stood still for a few seconds to regain our balance. The attendant had perched himself on the back of our car and spun us all the way through the waltzer ride. 'I think he was trying to knock your hat off,' I said.

'Still here though,' said Freddie, lifting up his hat in salute.

I grabbed his hand and nodded towards the Shoot a Duck stall. 'Come on. You can win me one of those bears.'

He groaned. 'Jo-Jo, they're fixed.'

'I thought you were good at that stuff, Mr Pac-Man-Top-Scorer.'

'That's different.'

'Well, if you're not up to it...'

'I didn't say that.'

We ran over to the stall. Freddie handed over his money.

'What you after?' said the stallholder, picking up his greasy beefburger and taking a bite.

'He's going to win me the bear,' I said, pointing at the three-foot-high white teddy bear perched on the top shelf. The bear had a gold star pinned to his chest with 'Star Prize' written in red felt-tip pen.

The Shoot a Duck man stopped chewing and looked at Freddie, who was already taking aim through the sights of the rifle. 'You need all six on target to win a bear, mate.'

'He knows,' I said.

Ten minutes later, we walked away from the stall, me clutching a five-inches high brown teddy bear, Freddie with a scowl across his face.

'I told you it was fixed,' he said.

'You got all six ducks.'

'Yeah, and then he pulls that, "Sign says win a bear. It don't say which bear," routine.'

'You're still my hero,' I said, kissing the bear. 'And now, Mr Rifleman, you owe me a candyfloss. A pink one.'

Jo-Jo – July 2015

My mum gave me the oriental carpet bag on my sixteenth birthday. She came into the kitchen, still in her dressing gown, and dropped it in the middle of the dining table. 'Look after it,' she said. 'It was your granny's.' It was edged with gold stitching and had a satin image of two geisha girls standing in a garden of eucalyptus trees, bowing serenely at the world. When I went to Blackpool with Freddie it held my Sony Walkman and transistor radio; in the Hotel Rushmore it held my iPod and Kindle.

I pulled the bag down from the top shelf of the wardrobe, unzipped one of the side pockets and retrieved a red leather photograph album. Three pages in, I found Jason's list. He'd written it with a 15 carat gold fountain pen given to him by the university when he retired. Josh used to tease him, saying he must be the last person in England to use real ink.

Things I love about Jo-Jo

1. Our holidays in the Indian Ocean
2. Watching you sleep
3. Watching you catwalk through La Rambla Boulevard in your red evening dress
4. Our dances – me holding you closer and closer
5. Talcum powdered sheets
6. Meals on the beach
7. All the men staring in envy at me
8. You decorating the Christmas tree, everything co-ordinated

I'd read the list over and over since his death, but I still couldn't work out why he'd written it. Wishful thinking, romanticism of what he really wanted but could never achieve. 'That's so sweet,' Amy had said when we'd found it in his desk drawer. It was all lies. He thought the beach meals were chilly, the red dress was showy, and he was far too self-conscious to enjoy our dances. 'I bet they think you're my nurse,' he'd say when we were out together. He used to sit for hours with his head buried in a book, paralysed by his own inadequacies, real life passing him by at express train speed. 'If only,' was his mantra. 'If only I was twenty years younger.' 'You said that twenty years ago,' I'd answer. He gave me security, stability and, eventually, Amy. I got used to the rest.

1. Saturday night Monopoly with our neighbours, Alex and Julie – Jason the Top Hat, me the Iron, him the Banker and Sommelier, me the nibbles and things on sticks provider.

2. Sunday lunch at the Horse and Jockey, him beef, me pork (the look on his face when I announced my conversion to vegetarianism), two bottles of Merlot limit (any more would be reckless), his raised eyebrows when I moved on to gin and tonics, him studiously reading the broadsheets, critiquing the state of the nation, me pressing his buttons by bringing him up-to-date with the gossip columns – 'Can't you read that rubbish quietly?'

3. Tea on the table at five thirty, even after he'd retired – 'It gives us a chance to get ready for the news.'

4. Him retiring to his office to audit our joint bank account, ticking off every item, filing them away in date order, separate folders for each financial year, after year, after year, waving statements in my face, questioning me about every purchase – 'What did you draw another twenty pounds out for?' 'Can't you take sandwiches to work?'

Jo-Jo – July 1976

Miss Giles, our English teacher, had let us leave school early and I was back at home, watching Dad through the kitchen window. I was counting down from ten, giving Dad's declared sixth sense a chance to kick itself into action. I reached six before he looked up from his rose pruning and grinned. I ran outside and within seconds I was lifted skywards in his muscular arms, sucking in the leathery tang of his gardening-day sweat.

'How did you know I was here?'

'I always know,' he said, putting me back on planet earth and ruffling my hair. 'How was school? It was English today wasn't it?'

'I'll do well to get the O level, Dad.'

'Oh, you'll get it. You're going to write a book. I can feel it in my bones.'

I looked back towards the house. 'Where's Mum?'

'In bed,' he muttered, the smile disappearing from his face. 'She's had a bad day. Go and see her.'

'I've got homework to do.'

'Jo-Jo, you know she watches the clock until you get home. Just go and say hello.'

'Do I have to? I never know what to say.'

He turned me around and pushed me gently up the garden. 'Go now,' he said. 'I'll get the tea on.'

I trudged up the path and into the kitchen, shedding motivation with every step as I walked into the hallway and started up the stairs. I stopped and looked up at the landing, pictures of long-dead relatives hanging along the flocked wallpaper route. 'For God's sake, Jo-Jo,' I said to myself. 'You're only going to say hello to Mum.'

'Hello, Mum.'

'Is that you, Jo-Jo?'

I was leaning against the open door to Mum's room, her infantile voice creeping out from under a duck feather duvet. Two years she'd been ill. What was wrong with her? Schizophrenia, Dad called it. 'Jesus, Mum. It's like a sauna in here.'

'I feel the cold,' she said. 'You know I feel the cold.'

I walked into the bedroom and yanked the curtains open, dust shimmering into the room, sunlight exploding onto the bed. Mum screamed. 'Oh my God, close the curtains. Please close the curtains.'

I pulled the curtains back together.

'What wrong, Mum?' I said, sitting down on the bed. 'It's a lovely day. I can't see how lying in the dark is going to help.'

'I'm sorry, sweetheart,' she said, sweat beads glistening on her forehead.

'Let me turn the heating down. You're wringing wet.'

'No, darling. Just sit and talk to me.'

I lifted a flannel from the bowl of water Dad kept by the side of the bed, squeezed it out, and gently wiped Mum's brow. I looked across at the curtains, double checking they were closed. I must try harder, I told myself. I must try to understand.

'She'll be okay. I'm going to the doctor's tomorrow.'

Dad was filling the space in the doorway. I guessed that Mum's scream had brought him sprinting upstairs. 'But you're at work tomorrow,' I said.

'They'll understand. I'll make it up at the weekend.'

'You're working at the weekend,' said Mum. 'What about the shopping, Joseph? Who's going to do the shopping? I can't do it. You know I can't do it. Please don't ask me to do it.'

He walked over to the bed and took Mum's hand. 'Calm down, love. I'm going to the shop after work.'

'What about the tea? Who's going to get Jo-Jo's tea?'

'I'll get my own tea,' I said. 'I'm not the one who's useless, and it sounds like Dad's got enough to do.'

'Get out,' screamed Mum. 'Just go, leave me alone. Both of you leave me alone. You don't understand. I'm not well. I need rest. Leave me alone.'

'Fine,' I said. 'I've got homework to do anyway.'

I'd walked into town to get some fresh air, taking a break from revising for my O level mock exams. I came out of the newsagents, where I'd stopped off to buy a can of Pepsi, and saw Dad striding through the green entrance gates of the park. He stopped at one of the wooden benches, sat down and placed his Dunlop golfing umbrella at his side. He stood up again almost immediately and put up his hand in greeting. A woman, walking towards him, waved back. Dad walked towards her, leaving his umbrella on the bench. They came together, hugged, and then kissed a thirty-seconds kiss on the lips. Dad touched the woman's cheek, looked into her eyes and said something. The woman nodded. They held hands and walked back to the bench. The woman said something to Dad, and he laughed. They reached the bench, sat down, still holding hands, still talking, still smiling, still laughing.

I walked across the road and into the park. Dad saw me as I came through the gates and he jumped up off the bench. The woman looked at him with concerned eyes and then looked at me.

'Hello, Dad.'

'Jo-Jo. What are you doing here?'

'I thought you were at your evening class.'

'It was cancelled.'

I held out my hand towards the woman. 'I'm his daughter. I don't think we've met.'

She stood up and kissed Dad on the cheek. 'I think it's best if I go, Joseph. Give me a call later.' He nodded and she walked away, out of the park. Dad watched her go and then picked up his umbrella. 'I don't want to talk about this, Jo-Jo,' he said, staring at the bench.

'Who is she?'

'A friend.'

'She looked like more than a friend. Is it serious?'

'Jo-Jo, you're fifteen, old enough to understand. I needed some company and she was there.'

'Does Mum know?'

'No. But I don't think she'd care if she did.'

'I can't believe this, Dad. This isn't you.'

He pulled me close and kissed the top of my head. 'I love you, Jo-Jo,' he said.

I pushed him away. 'What about Mum?'

'I'll always love your mother...'

'Are you going to leave us?' I said, tears welling in my eyes.

'Leave you? Of course I'm not going to leave you.'

Jo-Jo – July 2015

Back in my room at the Hotel Rushmore, I lay on the bed and stared at the L.S. Lowry print on the bedroom wall. A picture of a man standing on a beach, looking out at a cloudless sky and calm sea. He had his hands shoved into his suit trouser pockets and two black and white terrier dogs were facing up to each other behind him.

I remembered Dad watching the tide come in, the waves encroaching slowly up the beach, consuming the sandy moats and turrets that he'd spent all afternoon building with me and Josh. Mum used to lie on her sun lounger and shout instructions – 'That end needs to be higher.' 'You need more of a mound there.' We'd ask her to join in. 'I'm here to look glamorous,' she'd say. 'Like Brigitte bloody Bardot,' Dad would answer, making Mum laugh.

Dad taught me and Josh the symptoms of schizophrenia and the side effects of Mum's tablets. Josh used to run around our front room with a sheet over him making spooky ghost noises. 'Ooh... Mum's voices have got me. The voices... ooh... I can't stand the voices.' If Dad caught him, he'd cuff him lightly across the back of his head. 'Show some bloody respect,' he'd say, but he'd wink at me as he was doing it. Dad made Mum get up, get dressed and come downstairs. She always protested. 'I can't, Joseph. You know I can't.' 'Yes you can, love. Today's a good day and you can.'

The phone rang at the side of the bed, making me jump. I reached over and picked up the receiver. 'Hello.'

'Mrs Coulman?'

I recognised the shy receptionist's hesitant voice. 'Yes,' I said.

'I'm sorry to disturb you, madam, but there is a message for you. It had been put in the wrong box. You see all the rooms have their own mailbox...'

'What's the message?' I said.

Freddie's Morning Regime

1. I wake up early, turn on my side, pull the mustard-coloured candlewick bedspread under my chin and watch the red digits on the bedside clock tick over to alarm time, forcing myself to stay in bed until Springsteen's 'Thunder Road' starts the day.

2. I listen out for Georgie, my neighbour's basset hound. No howling means she isn't in the house. I imagine her out on her morning walk, sniffing down a scent in the local park, her ears trailing a path through the dew-covered grass. The image makes me smile. She'll be back soon, re-energised by the fresh air, ready to face another day on her own while Tracey, her owner, is out at work in the local

care home. Georgie's howling doesn't bother me. It interrupts the various moods of loneliness that possess every room in my mum's three-bedroom semi like uninvited guests.

3. Bruce's harmonica breaks the silence, triggering me to get up, open the curtains, walk downstairs and let the cats out – the only other heartbeats in the house since Mum's death. All four of them appear from their various sleeping places and head for the back door.

4. I shower, dress and go through my leaving the house ritual, starting in the kitchen, moving from room to room, checking the plugs are out, running my hand under all the taps, making sure there's an even spread of curtain on each side of the windows, locking and unlocking the back door, counting out loud, one, two, three, four, moving the handle up and down after each turn of the key, repeating the routine with the front door – out in the street, exposed.

Freddie – October 1986

H.I.V. tombstone adverts, the world getting over macho man Rock Hudson dying of AIDS, Boy George having a lifestyle meltdown with his new beau, Marilyn, and the chief constable of Greater Manchester Police describing gay men as 'swirling in a cesspit of their own making'. This was the year Jack came out. It was like he looked at the headlines and thought, *Fuck it.*

He told his mum and dad over a pot of tea and a Mr Kipling Victoria sandwich. His mum kissed him on the forehead, told him to be careful. His dad didn't say a word. 'I'll never forget the look of disappointment on his face,' Jack told me.

Jack took his mouthy sister, Jackie, to the Mason's Arms and bought her a G & T – 'I knew she'd tell the others before I got back to the house,' he said. The rest of his siblings took the piss: 'Fancy our kid being a big poof.' 'Hey, Jackie, hide your dresses. He'll be after them.' In the pub someone shouted 'Fairy' and Jack's brother, Malcolm, walked over and punched the bloke in the face. 'You call it him,' said the barman. 'That's different,' said Malcolm, the whole pub looking at him. 'We're family. You lot leave him alone.'

Jack told me over a pint of Guinness and a game of darts.

'Gay?'

'Yeah. You know what that means, Freddie?'

'Sort of.'

'It doesn't mean I fancy you.'

Freddie – July 2015

When Jack and I were kids, I used to singsong the names of his fifteen siblings in age order. My mum used to let him have his tea at our house – 'It'll save him getting in the queue over there.' She'd give him my old socks, which he was forever losing – 'Our Malcolm pinched them, Mrs B.' 'Never mind, lad. Go and get yourself another pair out of Freddie's drawer.' At fourteen, we started wagging days off school, hiding away in my house to plot our big ideas. We were going to form a band, sail around the world, write a best seller. We also made lists of girls we fancied. Jack used to lie on my mum's leather settee and I'd sit in the armchair with my feet up on a footstool, both of us wearing Ian Dury flat caps and flared Levi's, chewing on BIC biros and staring at our hardback notebooks.

'Sharon Barber. She should be on your list.'

'Why?'

'She likes you.'

'This is stupid, Freddie. I've got twenty-five names on here.'

'Once we've got a list we can come up with a strategy. See how that goes.'

'It's not a battle plan.'

'Preparation's everything, my friend.'

'You know Wilkes has got a girl now?'

'Smelly Wilkes?'

'Yeah.'

'Who'd go out with him?'

'Yvonne Mason.'

'Proves my point. No plan and you end up with buck teeth and glasses.'

'Yeah, well. At least he's not making bloody lists.'

I walked to Jack's house from the coffee shop. We only lived three streets apart, but he'd insisted on a schedule for keeping in touch – a curry at the Saleem Bagh on the last Friday of the month and a weekly Wednesday night catch-up on the phone. 'I love you to bits, Freddie, but I need some space.' 'You make it sound like we're married.' 'You mean we're not?' I knew his rules were flexible, though, and I could always break them in an emergency.

I pressed the front doorbell. Jack's tomcat, Boris, who was dozing on the front lawn, opened his one eye and looked at me with suspicion, daring me to disturb his morning. A silver Ford Fiesta pulled up at the house opposite. A nurse in uniform got out of the car and ran up the path. She was a midwife visiting Jack's neighbour, Sandra, who was expecting her third child.

Jack opened his door. 'Freddie,' he said. 'Come in.'

I followed him down the hallway. 'I've just seen Jo-Jo,' I said. 'Why didn't you tell me you'd met up with her?'

'I forgot. It was only last week. I've just made coffee. Do you want some?'

We walked into his lounge and sat down opposite each other in his blue leather bucket seats from Next. Paul Weller's

'Wild Wood' was humming away in the corner from a Bose sound dock. The room had no ornaments, pictures or mirrors. Stainless steel spotlights were fixed at uniform gaps across the white ceiling. 'What were you doing at a charity event?' I said.

'I do have a life beyond you, Freddie.'

I handed him the picture. 'She gave me that.'

He wolf whistled. 'Nice hair. That cut was always underrated.'

'You had it as well,' I said. 'Before you turned all Erasure on us.'

He grinned, turned the picture over and read aloud the inscription on the back: 'Freddie and Me. Blackpool. 1980. DTR.' He looked at me. 'DTR?'

'She used to rate her pictures. DTR: Days to Remember or DTF: Days to Forget.'

'Well, at least you got top billing, darling.'

He only ever called me darling when he was being sarcastic, and I didn't want him taking the piss out of the picture. I held out my hand and he passed it back to me. 'She brought me this photo,' I said. 'And then told me she was emigrating.'

'I don't see the problem.'

'It's a bit odd, don't you think, turning up after thirty-five years. She wants me to phone her and meet up for a meal.'

He pushed the plunger down on his Café Bohème cafetière, which was positioned in the centre of a glass-topped coffee table. 'Give her a call,' he said. 'What have you got to lose?'

Freddie – July 1997

It was the third night of our stay in Sitges and we were on the terrace of the Hotel Romántico, the Catalonia air laced with a fruity aroma of lemon and lime trees, a droning background soundtrack of chirping male cicadas looking for a mate. Jack and the four guys we'd met two hours earlier in the bar were sitting around a large bamboo table. I was lying on a sun lounger, listening in on their conversation. We were slowly working our way through four carafes of the bar manager's sangria special.

'How did you two meet?' said Jack, directing his question at Bob, the short, plump one with a receding hairline who'd told us he was a teacher.

'You tell them,' Bob said to his partner, Terry. 'You're the star man.'

'Don't build him up too much,' said Patrick. 'He doesn't look like top billing material to me.'

Patrick was the hotel's karaoke star. He dressed up every night in a ball gown and tiara to give his rendition of Freddie Mercury's 'God Save the Queen'. His cheeks were still covered in red rouge, but he was now wearing a white sweat-vest bearing a cartoon image of fornicating hedgehogs and the legend, 'Be Careful of the Pricks'. He responded to Bob's hard glare by holding up his hands, palms outwards. 'Sorry,' he said. 'I'll not say another word.'

'Yeah, right,' said Terry.

Patrick went to reply, but his partner, Mickey, put a hand on his arm. 'Just let him tell the bloody story,' he said.

Terry took a sip of his sangria. 'Not much to tell. I was fifty-five, had a wife, kids, and grandkids, and then he turned up.' He nodded at Bob. 'I'd been watching him for months before I asked him out for a coffee. Next thing I know, I'm announcing us to the world.'

'That must have been tough,' said Jack.

'It was a relief to be honest. I'd got sick of living the lie.'

'Do you still see your kids?' I said.

All five of them turned and faced me. I think they'd forgotten I was there.

Terry shook his head. 'Jemma, my daughter, writes, but my two sons have blanked me. They won't let me see the grandkids.'

'You will,' said Bob. 'They'll come round.'

'No chance,' said Patrick, stirring the fruit in his sangria with an umbrella cocktail stick. 'They'll be too busy crucifying you.'

Terry stood up and walked into the bar. Bob followed him.

'You're an insensitive prat sometimes,' said Mickey.

'What? It's true.'

'Yeah, but you don't always have to say it.'

*

6 p.m. the following evening. I was sitting in the piano bar, sipping an ice-cold San Miguel. Jack was out on a trip to Barcelona and I'd spent the day by the pool, reading J.K. Rowling's *Harry Potter and the Philosopher's Stone*. It was early, and the bar was empty. Terry walked in, saw me and put up his hand. He walked over and sat down on the stool next to me. 'I'll have one of those,' he said to the barman, pointing at my chill-frosted glass.

'How's it going?' I said.

He swallowed a gulp of beer. 'God, that's good,' he said, lifting up his glass in my direction. We clinked our glasses together. 'Grimsby,' he said. We both laughed.

'Where's your mate?' said Terry.

'He's off seeing the sights. Where's Bob?'

'Glamming himself up. He'll be down in a minute.'

We took a sip of our beers. He wiped his mouth with the back of his hand. 'Sorry about last night,' he said.

'Nothing to be sorry for. Patrick's a prat.'

He nodded. 'Maybe, but he's right. They are going to crucify me.'

I took another sip of beer and stared at the yellow and red horizontal stripes painted on the wall behind the bar. There were two black and white pictures of a 1930s bullfight on each side of the stripes. They showed a matador with one hand behind his back, facing up to a bull in different "olé" poses. The bull had his head bowed and looked as though he was scraping at the dusty ground and snorting out his frustration.

'Do you mind if I ask you a question?' I said.

'Ask away.'

'Do you regret leaving them?'

'If you mean my family, they left me.'

'I mean your wife. You left her for Bob.'

'The only regret I have is hurting the kids and not being honest with myself years ago. It's nothing to do with Bob.'

'But you love him, right?'

He laughed. 'Yeah,' he said. 'Whatever that means.' He tore the beer mat in half. 'You ever been in love?'

'Once,' I said.

'Are you still together?'

I shook my head. 'We split up when we were kids, wanted different things. She went off to university.'

'And?' he said.

'And nothing. We lost contact. It fizzled out.'

*

It was after midnight when Jack and I walked back to the hotel along the harbour front, returning from our nightly residence in the Blue Oyster nightclub in the centre of Sitges. I'd been drinking pints of San Miguel since meeting Terry in the bar, but Jack was having one of his orange juice nights – 'It helps to clear out the system, darling.'

I suddenly had an urge to jump up on the seafront wall.

'What are doing, Freddie? Get down.'

I looked up at the night sky and sucked in the sea air. 'If we died now, Jack, I'd be happy.'

'That's because you're drunk.'

I held my arms out to my sides, tightrope-walker style, and stepped carefully along the wall. 'See. I can walk the line. That means I'm perfectly sober.'

'Yeah, right. And I'm the Queen's granny.'

'You need to lighten up, Jack. You're getting old. You can't stand the pace.'

'You'll be sick in a minute, Freddie. Just after you fall off that wall.'

I gave him a sideways glance, stumbled, adjusted my balance and then glared at him.

'What?' he said. 'It's true. You're always sick.'

'That's because I'm a sensitive soul. If you paid me more attention you'd know.'

He laughed and held out his hand. 'All right. You've made your point. Now get down off that bloody wall before you do some damage.'

I grabbed his hand and jumped down in front of him. 'Why aren't you nicer to me, Jack?' I looked straight into his eyes. 'How come you never make a pass at me?'

His eyes dropped. 'Not this again, Freddie.'

I touched his unshaven cheek, lifted his chin and gently traced my forefinger around his lips. 'Kiss me,' I said. 'Just once. I want to know what it feels like.'

He pulled his hand out of my grasp and walked away.

'What's wrong with me?' I said, sitting down on the wall.

He turned back to face me. 'You're not gay, Freddie. You're drunk and lonely.'

'I love you, Jack,' I shouted.

He smiled, walked back to me and ruffled my hair. 'No you don't,' he said. 'But it's sweet of you to think you do.' He pulled me to my feet, put his arm around my waist and we started to walk.

'I think I'm going to be sick,' I said.

'Course you are,' he said, guiding me back towards the wall.

I closed my eyes and let Weller's throaty vocals fill my head. 'Wild Wood' had morphed into 'Shout to the Top' by the Style Council.

'What about if it's a sympathy thing?' I said, opening my eyes.

Jack sat back in the bucket seat. 'What?' he said.

'The redundancy, living on my own. She probably thinks I'm some sort of sad loser in need of her charity.'

'Aren't you?'

'Piss off,' I said.

He leaned forward in his chair. 'Did you tell her about the redundancy?'

'No. But I bet you did.'

'The point is, she was already looking for you. She didn't know anything about your life, but she was looking for you. Doesn't that say something?'

'Maybe.'

'You can be such a wanker sometimes. She's asked you out for a goodbye meal. She doesn't want to marry you or have your babies.' He picked up his iPhone and threw it into my lap. 'Call her. Use my phone.'

I turned the phone over in my hand.

'I swear to God, Freddie, I'll call her if you don't. And that'll make you look a right prick.'

He stood up and walked into the kitchen. I followed him. He put the coffee cups into the Belfast sink and threw a paisley tea towel in my direction. 'You're drying,' he said. I ignored him, sat down on one of the breakfast stools and started flicking through the culture section of the *Guardian* newspaper. The front door opened. Bob walked down the hallway. He was wearing a light-brown corduroy suit, desert boots and a red Panama hat, which he'd taken to after watching the first *Indiana Jones* film. I knew Bob visited, but I didn't know Jack had given him a key.

'Morning,' said Bob, dropping his hat on the breakfast bar and pulling out a packet of More menthol cigarettes from his jacket pocket. He shook the packet in Jack's direction.

Jack sighed, opened the cupboard door under the sink and fetched out an amber-coloured bubble glass ashtray in the shape of a duck, which he handed to Bob. 'I can't believe I let you smoke those things in here,' he said.

Bob took the ashtray, lit his cigarette and nodded at the kettle. 'Any chance of a coffee?' he said. 'Don't forget I'm back on sugar.'

*

Jack made Bob put out his cigarette in the kitchen and we walked back into the lounge. Bob and I were carrying a mug of coffee and Jack was carrying a cup of liquorice tea. I smiled as we sat down on the bucket chairs. It really did feel like Jack was offering therapy appointments. Jackie used to tell him off. 'You shouldn't let people dump all their problems on you,' she'd say, and then she'd tell him about her latest love crisis. 'He's left me. Gone back to his wife.'

'How's Terry?' I said.

'He doesn't recognise me,' said Bob.

'Any sign of the family?' said Jack.

'The daughter phones but nothing else.'

I thought of Patrick's prophecy all those years ago. Jack was one of the first people Bob called when Terry had his stroke. 'You're a social worker. What do we do?' They'd found him a care home twenty minutes away.

Jack took a sip of his liquorice tea and grimaced.

'You look like you're enjoying that,' said Bob.

'It's good for your iron levels,' said Jack.

Bob lifted his coffee mug to his face and rested his right cheek against its warmth. He held it there for a few seconds and then pulled it away. I'd seen him do it before. I assumed it was a comfort thing. 'How's things with you, Freddie?' he said. 'Don't know how you cope in that house with all those cats. It'd drive me mad.'

'He manages,' said Jack.

I put my mug on the coffee table, stood up and walked over to the bay window. It had started to drizzle with rain. I could hear Jack and Bob chatting behind me. They seemed to be getting on better than ever. Jack was saying he had a cupboard full of gluten free food. Bob said he only smoked menthol cigarettes to clear his sinuses.

'You okay, Freddie?' said Jack.

'I'm fine,' I said.

Freddie – January 2014

I went with Bob to visit Terry in the care home. A member of staff met us in the reception area, told us her name was Angela. She wore a navy blue trouser suit uniform with a white badge pinned to the smock top. The badge said 'Key Worker'. 'Follow me,' she said.

'I know the way,' said Bob.

'We have to escort you, sir. Health and safety.'

We followed her in silence, down a never-ending corridor with spillage-proof flooring and wipe-easy walls. There was a pervading smell of bleach and stale breath. It felt like the sort of route that needed a mortuary as its end point. We walked past closed and open bedroom doors, some with black and white pictures of residents Blu-tacked on the oak veneer. The pictures had all been taken in the reception area. No one was smiling.

Occasionally we walked past a room with a television on, Noel Edmonds opening boxes on *Deal or No Deal*.

Angela stopped outside bedroom number twenty-eight. 'Here we are,' she said.

'I know,' said Bob.

We opened the door and walked into the bedroom.

Terry was sitting in a chair by the window, a restraining belt fixed tightly around his waist, his glassy eyes staring vacantly around the room. Gloopy streams of saliva dripped from his mouth, soaking into his food-stained lumberjack shirt and black tracksuit bottoms. He looked wedged in the chair, like someone had dropped him from a great height.

'The chair keeps him safe,' said Bob. 'He falls if he tries to stand.'

'Hello, Terry,' I said, sitting down on the bed and taking his hand. I felt a tiny amount of pressure returned, which made me feel desperately sad. 'He squeezed my hand,' I said.

Bob knelt down in front of the chair and wiped Terry's mouth with a paper tissue. 'It's the only way we know you're in there, isn't it, old friend?' He threw the tissue in the wastepaper bin and took Terry's other hand.

Jo-Jo – July 2015

I found Amy in the far corner of the hotel conservatory. She was standing next to a yucca tree, her iPhone pressed to her ear. She put up her hand. I walked over and sat down in one of the cottage suite chairs. I could only hear her side of the conversation, but it was obvious she was talking to Dan.

'Were you in bed?'

'Oh, it was just something Mum said. Made me feel a bit guilty.'

She held the phone closer to her mouth.

'She's not said much, but I think she really cares about him.'

'What's that mean?'

'Well, it's better than being Mr Fate Will Decide.'

She turned back towards me and raised her eyebrows.

'I know. I'll be back next week.'

'Yeah, Mum's coming with me.'

She faced the window.

'You liar. I bet you're sprawled over my side.'

'Ditto.'

Jo-Jo – May 1980

Blackpool. I'd convinced Freddie to swap Springsteen for Michael Jackson's *Off the Wall*. Three weeks earlier we'd camped out in my lounge and I'd made him listen to the whole album – two o'clock in the morning curled up on the floor under a duvet, drinking tea and eating thick-cut toast covered in Marmite.

Freddie stroked the steering wheel of the Avenger like it was the most sumptuous fur he'd ever come across, his chipped front tooth beaming out through the joyous grin super-glued to his face.

'It's wonderful,' I said. 'I feel like I'm on the Monte Carlo rally. I'm going to get our names across the windscreen, some cuddly toys on the back seat.'

He squeezed my thigh. We raced past a motorway service station.

'Are we stopping soon?'

He shook his head. 'I want to get booked in early.'

'Suits me,' I said. 'We can go and look at the sea.'

'I want it to be perfect,' he said.

I put my hand on top of his, which was resting idly on the gearstick. I turned back towards the open window, the wind blowing in my face, the M6 streaming by at seventy miles per hour.

*

It took us an hour to find the street and another twenty minutes to find a place to park. We stood on the pavement looking up at the semi-detached house of the Bed and Breakfast.

'There must be somewhere better down by the front,' said Freddie.

'Let's at least have a look inside.'

'Let's not. We're miles from the sea.'

I started to walk up the driveway. 'I'm going to have a look,' I said.

'Okay,' he said, holding up his hands and following me.

We walked across the crumbling tarmac and reached the flaking red paint of the front door. I rang the bell. 'There's no place like home' chimed out of the tiny speaker.

'You can say that again,' said Freddie.

We laughed.

I looked at the neighbouring houses. 'It does look a bit rough round here.'

Freddie dropped on one knee, took hold of my hand and gazed up at me. 'I'll protect you,' he said. 'No one messes with the woman of an Avenger driver.'

I slapped his arm. 'Idiot. Get up. People might be watching.'

He stood up and pulled me close. 'Try the bell again,' he said, nodding towards the front door.

I pressed the button a second time. There was still no reply.

'This is definitely it,' he said, fumbling in his back pocket and pulling out a crumpled letter. 'Look. It's this address. Three nights booking confirmed.'

I double checked. It all tallied. I pressed the bell for a third time, this time keeping my finger on the button.

'All right, all right, I'm coming. Give me a chance.'

The front door opened, but it caught on a safety chain. A bald-headed man stared out at us. 'Yes,' he said. 'What do you want?'

'Mr Lewis?' said Freddie.

'Yes.'

'We've got a room booked. Mr and Mrs Charlton.'

The man mumbled something, and we heard the chain drop out of its catch. The front door opened wide. 'Come in. Come in,' he said, standing to one side and ushering us over the threshold. He had owl-like eyes and a mile-wide toothy grin.

'We'd like to see the room,' I said.

He looked behind us. 'Where are your cases?'

'In the car. But we want to see the room before deciding whether to stay.'

'Not stay?'

'Well, you are quite a way from the sea.'

'It's a five-minute walk through the back garden,' said Mr Lewis. 'You'll pay twice as much near the front. And you'll be lucky to get anything this week, with the weather being so nice.'

'We'd still like to see the room.'

He sighed and started to limp up the stairs, holding the bottom of his back. 'Okay,' he said. 'Follow me.'

'You all right?' said Freddie.

'Oh, don't worry about me, son. It's just me arthritis in me back… and me knees… and me hip…'

Freddie grinned at me and I sniggered. Mr Lewis looked back at us. 'You really named Charlton?'

'Yes,' said Freddie. 'What are you suggesting?'

'Nothing, son,' he said, turning away and resuming his limp up the stairs. 'It's just, you'd be surprised how many of the World Cup team I get stay here. Mr and Mrs Hurst. Mr and Mrs Moore. They've stayed twice this year.'

49

We laughed.

He faced us again. 'How old are you two?'

'Old enough to pay your rent,' I said.

Thirty minutes later Freddie came panting back into the attic room. 'Do you know how many stairs there are in this place?' he said, dropping the bags on the floor and flopping down on the bed.

I looked at him quizzically from the window. 'Why would I know that?'

'The answer is too many, especially when I'm carrying that bloody carpet thing of yours. What have you got in it? We're only here for three nights.'

'Woman stuff. Stop moaning and come and look at the view. You can see the sea from here.'

He groaned, dragged himself off the bed and walked over to the window. 'Where?' he said.

I pointed at the horizon. 'Over there.'

'That's just the sky.'

'No. Look. It's the sea.'

'It can't be,' he said. 'This room's facing the wrong way. I think the sea's behind us.'

'No. It's definitely the sea,' I said.

Jo-Jo – July 2015

Amy closed her phone, walked over to the cottage chairs and sat down. 'I told you he never goes to bed before two,' she said.

I smiled. 'How are the kids?'

'Sophia's had another row with her boyfriend, says she hates him.'

'They'll make up.'

'Maybe. Dan says she's been staring at her phone all day.'

A waitress came over, carrying a silver tray. 'Cream tea,' she said. 'I've charged it to your room.'

Amy pointed at the small coffee table between the two chairs. 'I shouldn't really,' she said. 'It's my second this week. Did you want something, Mum?'

I shook my head. The waitress put the tray on the table and walked away in the direction of the restaurant. Amy spread a scone with strawberry jam. 'They're freshly baked you know, Mum. And the jam's homemade. You should try one.'

I looked out of the conservatory window. I could see the gravel car park and its surrounding border of neatly pruned conifers. I scanned my eyes across the line of parked cars and felt a sense of relief when I saw the Mazda. I wondered whether to mention the ditto line from Amy's telephone conversation with Dan. I'd told her so many times. 'I thought you were meant to be a die-hard romantic. Tell him you love him.' I always got the same response. 'Mind your own business, Mum. He knows what ditto means.'

'You okay?' said Amy. 'You look a bit flushed. I thought you were having a lie down.'

'Freddie phoned,' I said. 'He wants me to call him back.'

'That's great,' she said, licking a blob of clotted cream off her finger. 'I told you he would. So why the anxious face? Oh, Mum, if you're worried about Dad, he'd have been happy for you.'

'It's nothing to do with your father.'

'What then?'

'It's just… well, perhaps it's best to leave the past where it belongs.'

'You're only going for a meal.'

'It was always different with Freddie. I don't want to spoil the memory.'

'You think it'll still be the same, after all this time?'

'No, of course not.'

'I never really understood why you wanted to look for him in the first place.'

'Curiosity,' I said. 'Ghosts. Thinking about what might have been... something.'

'Mum. It's a meal. You don't have to sleep with him.' She held out her phone. 'Call him,' she said.

Freddie – July 2015

When I was twelve, I wrote my list of the ten best ways to commit suicide. It was all Fat Nigel's fault. He was in our class at school and nearly starved himself to death, went down to four and a half stone, had to be put on a drip. No one noticed. He must have been throwing his food away for weeks, but he carried on wearing the same size clothes. Everyone, including the teachers, carried on calling him Fat Nigel.

Jack tried to help with the list. 'What about shooting yourself? Or hanging. Hanging would be good.'

'Where would you get a gun, Jack? Do you know how to tie a knot?'

We used to dare each other to stand right at the edge of the kerb as the bus raced past. He always stepped back, but I stayed absolutely still, the wind making me gasp for breath. When Dave Cooper moved into a flat on the thirteenth floor we used to visit him just to look out at the world from his balcony. I'd stand out there talking to them through the open French door. 'It'd be like flying if you jumped from here. Come and have a look.'

I thought about going back to the coffee shop from Jack's but decided to go home instead. Under Jack's supervision, I'd called Jo-Jo's number and left a message with the hotel receptionist. The only thing I could do now was wait for her to call back. Maybe she wouldn't call. Maybe I wouldn't have to worry about meeting her again. I still couldn't work out why she'd wanted to find me in the first place.

I walked into my street and felt the usual sense of urgency to get inside the house. I wanted to break into a run. I needed to find out if everything was exactly as I'd left it. Perhaps I'd left the gas on or the taps running, perhaps I hadn't locked the door properly, maybe there'd been a break-in. I forced myself to get my keys slowly out of my pocket, trying all the time to remember that people were watching.

Freddie – April 1970

Jack and I were sitting on top of my dad's whitewashed gates, pitching conkers at each other. Dad had shown me how to soak the conkers in vinegar and bake them in the oven, said it would make them indestructible. 'Strings,' shouted Jack as the conkers tangled together.

I inspected my conker – the insides were peeping out through a split across its centre. 'It's busted,' I said.

'Hold it up,' he said. 'I get another go. That's the game.'

I hung my conker out, my whole body stiffening up. I wondered what had gone wrong with Dad's plan.

Crack.

'That makes mine a sixer,' he said.

'You were lucky,' I said, picking bits of conker from the grubby string. 'Come on, let's get the ball, they'll be here soon.'

We jumped down from the gate.

'My mum says your dad's dead,' he said, kicking a stone into the road.

I shrugged and ran up my path to fetch the Casey ball from the shed.

Mum had placed her emergency candles around the lounge. 'Bloody strikes,' she said. 'Put some coal on the fire, son.'

I jumped off the settee and walked over to the bucket at the side of the hearth.

'Not too much.'

'I know, Mum. Two big lumps at the back and the little ones at the front.'

I watched as she walked around the room. She was striking matches from a Swan Vesta box and lighting her candles. It reminded me of Dad trying to light his pipe, holding a match to his Old Holborn tobacco and puff, puff, puffing away, the veins on his forearms throbbing out through his anchor tattoos from his merchant navy days. Mum walked over to our oak-veneered sideboard, which she'd had since her wedding day, and lit one of the candles next to Dad's pink dish. It had a dancing nymph statue as its centrepiece. 'That's his guilt dish,' she'd tell everyone. 'Bought it after he'd been out drinking with his mates.'

She was eighteen when she married Dad – a proper man she called him. I never heard her shout, but she could sulk for England. I fell in a pond on a day trip when I was five. Dad pulled me out in seconds, but Mum wrapped me in a blanket, packed up the picnic and made him take us home. She didn't speak to him for weeks. 'How is it my fault?' he said, but she just looked at him as if it was the stupidest question she'd ever heard. I've got a picture of Mum scowling at the camera on a day trip to London. Dad used to get the picture out every so often. 'Here's your mother enjoying herself,' he'd say. She cooked, knitted and sewed her way through life. Bread and butter puddings, egg custards, steak and kidney pies. She knitted Dad a green jumper. It stretched in the wash, the arms touching the floor when she hung it on the line. 'You're ruining that kid,' Dad would say every time I sat on her lap. She'd pull me close and glare at him.

She caught me looking at her and smiled. 'You're a good boy,' she said.

I flopped on the carpet in front of the fire, listening to the slack as it crackled away, watching the yellow and blue flames being pulled up the chimney. The warmth felt as though it was burning my cheeks. Dad's porcelain dogs looked down on me from the mantelpiece. Mum came and sat next to me. She touched my face. 'You okay, Freddie? You warm enough?'

I nodded.

'Brush my hair,' she said, holding out a blue plastic hairbrush.

I knelt behind her and she pulled out her tightly pinned hairclips. She shook her head. Her jet-black hair tumbled down her back and I brushed. 'That's nice,' she said. 'Your dad used to do this for me.'

Freddie – June 1970

I ran across the damp grass and crossed the ball to Jack. He headed it back to one of the kids from the next estate who toe-punted it past the goalie. We all jumped on the scorer and hugged him.

Rob, who lived three doors away from me, fetched the ball from Mr Perry's hedge. 'It's burst,' he said. 'Where'd you get it? It's crap.'

'I think Mum got it from the market.'

'Tell her to get us another one.'

'I'll ask her tonight,' I said.

He stepped towards me and pushed me in the chest. 'Tell her now. Go on. Go now.' He looked around at the other lads and then back at me. 'You're a Mummy's Boy,' he said. 'Your dad's dead and you're a Mummy's Boy.' He started clapping. 'Mummy's Boy, Mummy's Boy,' he chanted. He turned back to the others, encouraging them to join in. They all circled me, pushing me backwards and forwards, wide eyes and stupid grins leering at me. I looked for Jack. 'He's not going to help you. No one helps a Mummy's Boy.' Someone pushed me from behind. I swung round and threw a punch. It missed. Rob laughed and crashed his fist into my nose. I fell to the ground, face down on the grass. 'Get up, Mummy's Boy. Get up and fight.'

'Freddie! Freddie! Your tea's done.'

'Mummy's calling you, Mummy's Boy. Off you go for your tea.'

I wiped my face with the back of my hand. Tears, blood and snot smeared across my cheek.

Freddie – July 2015

As I put my key in the lock, I wondered if I should have stayed at Jack's. My head felt like it was full of syrup, milky floaters were swimming across my vision. I was sweating and shivering at the same time. I closed my front door, walked into the kitchen and got a bottle of water from the fridge. I poured some of the water into a glass, took two of my beta blockers and sat down at the kitchen table, waiting for the drugs to take effect.

I didn't take the beta blockers every day, they were there more as a comfort blanket, but I still cashed the script every month, stockpiling the surplus. I had a year's supply stored away in a battered copper chest, which I kept in the loft. My stash. My exit plan. I'd sit up there in an evening and count out the button-size purple tablets, trying to work out how many it would take. My plan was to tip them all into a bucket and push handfuls at a time into my mouth, taking swigs of Vodka to wash them down.

The phone rang. I answered it on the second ring. 'Hello.'

'Freddie. It's Jo-Jo.'

'Jo-Jo. How are you?'

'I'm okay. Not changed much since you saw me this morning.'

'Sorry. I meant did you get back okay?'

'Is that why you called?'

'What?'

'To ask me if I'd got back okay.'

'No. I… Where are you staying?'

'About ten miles away from where I left you.'

Silence.

'Are you still there, Freddie?'

'I didn't call to see if you'd got back okay.'

'No?'

'I wanted to check that as well, of course.'

'That's good. And we've established that I did.'

A voice inside my head was saying, 'Ask her. Ask her. Ask her.' I still couldn't believe I was talking to her. 'I would like to meet up. If you meant it.'

'Why wouldn't I have meant it?'

I felt my cheeks flush again. 'It's what people say, isn't it?'

'I meant it,' she said.

*

I looked at the bedside clock. 4 a.m. Tai, my little black cat, was snoring away on the vacant side of my double bed. I was massaging her head, which always sent her into a deep sleep. Jo-Jo. The meal. Tonight. What would we talk about? The coffee shop was different. I hadn't known she was coming, hadn't had time to think. She'd given me the photo. She'd told me about her family. Maybe I should phone her and say I couldn't make it. I turned over and punched the pillow. Tai opened her one eye. Jack was right. I could be such a wanker.

A couple we'd seen at dinner the previous evening came into the conservatory. They stood out because of their difference in height, him over six foot with a bushy grey beard and a cap that made him look the spitting image of Captain Birdseye; her a foot shorter, with a stooped gait that made her look even smaller. They were holding hands as always. I'd told Amy off for saying they looked like a ventriloquist and his dummy on a works outing. We'd nicknamed them Hansel and Gretel. People watching was good but giving them fictional names made it more fun. They looked over and caught me staring. I handed Amy back her iPhone.

'That seemed like hard work, Mum.'

'Yes,' I said.

'He is okay, isn't he?'

'What do you mean?'

'You know, mentally?'

'He's shy, Amy. That doesn't make him mad.'

'I'm just saying, you haven't seen him for years. You never really told me why you split up.'

'It got complicated. Where's that waitress? I could do with a cup of tea.'

'Complicated in what way?'

'University started. I went away. We lost touch.'

'But if you felt so strongly about each other?'

'It wasn't that simple.'

'Why?'

'The distance for a start.'

'I thought you went to Lincoln.'

'I did.'

'Right.'

'What?'

'Well, it's not that far.'

'It wasn't just that.'

The waitress reappeared. I called her over and ordered a pot of Earl Grey.

Jo-Jo – September 1980

Freddie was sitting in the wicker chair and I was lying on my single bed underneath a poster of Starsky and Hutch. They were pretending to arm wrestle across the bonnet of Starsky's cherry-red Ford Gran Torino. It had large white vector stripes on either side; the striped tomato, Hutch called it.

'We would like to offer you an unconditional place... Can you believe that, Freddie?'

'Great,' he said.

I patted the bed. 'Come and give me a cuddle.'

He walked over and lay down next to me.

'Tell me you're happy for me,' I said.

'Lincoln,' he said. 'It's so far away.'

'It's only for three years. And there's the holidays. We can write, talk on the phone. You can visit. It'll fly by.'

'I'm not good at writing.'

'It'll be good practice for you then.'

'It won't be the same.'

'I know, but I have to do this.'

'We've only just started, Jo-Jo.'

'And this needn't get in the way. It'll be different, exciting.'

'You'll soon forget about me.'

'For God's sake, Freddie. It's Lincoln.'

'Look, Mum, if you don't want to tell me why you split up, that's fine.'

'There wasn't really a reason. We just drifted apart.'

'So when did you last see him?'

'Before I went to university.'

'And that was it?'

I nodded.

'He didn't call you?'

'No. He didn't call me.'

'I thought he loved you.'

Jo-Jo – September 1980

I was in the outdoor of the Saddler's Arms. We used to go in there every Friday night to buy microwaved steak and kidney pies and bottles of Vimto, taking them back to my house to watch *Pot Black* with my dad. The old woman, Elsie, was in her usual spot at the oak-panelled bar, staring at the froth in her half-pint of stout like it contained the secrets of the universe. Tony Kelly, the leather-clad biker bully, was standing by the cigarette machine, nursing a pint of Banks's mild. He used to ride around the estate on his Kawasaki motorbike, looking for school kids to torment. If he found any, he'd fire a catapult of his dad's fishing maggots at them and then ride away laughing. He asked me out once and then spat at me when I said no. He looked up from his beer. I turned my back and leaned closer into the payphone receiver. Freddie's voice said 'hello' and then I heard the pips. I pushed a two-pence piece into the slot. 'It's me,' I said.

'Have you phoned them?'

He made his question sound urgent, like it was the only thing that mattered.

'No, Freddie. You know I haven't. I told you last night.'

Silence.

'Are you not going to talk to me?'

'I don't want you to go,' he said.

'I want to. It's all arranged.'

'You could go next year.'

'Let's not do this again. I'm going next week.'

Silence.

'I've got no more money, Freddie. Are you coming round?'

Jo-Jo – July 2015

'Oh my God,' said Amy. 'I've just realised.'

'Realised what?' I said.

'You don't know? That's why you're not saying. He said he'd call you and he didn't. Why didn't you call him?'

I sat back in the chair and crossed my legs. 'It was all a long time ago. It doesn't matter now.'

'Pride,' she said. 'That's it. Isn't it?'

'And I suppose you'd have called Dan?'

'Probably not.'

'Definitely not,' I said.

'Is that why you wanted to see him? To find out why?'

'Partly.'

'Been the first thing I'd have said to him. Depending on his answer, it might have been the last.'

'It wasn't the only reason.'

'You still love him, don't you?'

She reached across the table and squeezed my hands. She

had tears in her eyes. 'Oh, sweetheart,' I said. 'What's wrong? It's okay. I'm just being silly. A silly old fool.'

She looked up at me. 'If you tell Dan about me crying, I will assassinate you.'

I laughed.

'I'm not joking,' she said.

I hugged her. 'I know, my darling. I know.'

Jo-Jo – July 2015

The beach is deserted as I walk along the shoreline hand in hand with Dad. A black mass of cloud anchors itself on the horizon. Something bursts out from its centre and flies towards us.

'What is it, Dad?'

'It's a dragon, sweetheart.'

The creature reaches the beach and hovers above our heads. I can see its fleshy underbelly and green spiky back scales, fitting together like intricate jigsaw pieces.

'Dragons aren't real, Dad.'

'This one is.'

The dragon lands with a thud on the sand, making me drop my ice-cream. It has red puckered lips and long black mascaraed lashes sitting on top of award-winning come-to-bed eyes. Dad lets go of my hand, walks over and climbs on its back.

'Come back, Dad,' I shout, but he ignores me, leans over and whispers something in the dragon's ear.

The dragon laughs and flies off in the direction of the clouds.

My eyes flashed open.

Daylight was streaming across the bed through a crack in the hotel curtains, 4 a.m. flashing at me from the bedside clock. I looked again at the Lowry. Suit man was still staring out to sea, the dogs waiting patiently behind him.

Freddie.

I was eighteen, leaving home, leaving Dad, and Freddie's seal-pup eyes were looking up at me, waiting for me to decide, waiting for me to tell him it was all going to be okay. I asked him once why he loved me. 'It's obvious,' he said. And to him it was. He'd placed me on a skyscraper pedestal like I was the brightest, most talented star in a billion-dollar Broadway show – that's how he made me feel. He was the man who promised to phone, the man who hadn't held me for long enough in the coffee shop, the man who'd stayed rooted in my head from the moment Debbie Harry had brought him into my life. I'd tried to explain the attraction to Amy, but it had come out all wrong, made him sound desperate, needy. Maybe he was. Maybe I was.

Freddie – July 2015

I drove Jack's Mini Cooper to the hotel. The table was booked for seven thirty, but I wanted to get there early and find somewhere to park. The car was two months old and still had that new car smell. Jack had bought it as a reward for passing his Best Interest Assessor course. A yellow Mickey Mouse air freshener, hanging from one of the vents, bounced against the dashboard as I rolled carefully over the speed bumps on the outskirts of the village. Mum drifted into my thoughts.

She'd expected to die in her own bed. She'd bought it with Dad when they got married and kept it for the rest of her life. The steel frame had to be bolted together with a special spanner and tied up with pieces of string at each corner. She came home after her diagnosis. There were no clues it would end so quickly. She'd have her usual lie down in the afternoons, her "turns" she called them – ever since Dad's death she'd had her turns. But the jaundice spread, covering her skin and filling the whites of her eyes. 'I've got the big C,' she told me, trying to sound like John Wayne – who my dad loved.

I was holding Mum's hand when she died. She hadn't been conscious for a couple of days and her breathing had turned into a suck and blow rasp, which reverberated around the house. She'd inhale and then not exhale for a few seconds. I'd hold my breath and she'd start breathing again. I waited and waited after her last breath, squeezing her hand, staring at her mouth.

A few spots of rain fell on the windscreen, triggering the automatic wipers, saving my desperate search for the right switch or lever. *Had I locked the front door?* landed as a thought inside my head. I took a deep breath and told myself to relax, the hypnotic swish, swish, swish of the wipers helping me to calm down.

Freddie – May 1980

I'd worked out the quickest route to the sea front and we'd run Mr Lewis' five-minute walk in a ten-minute jog. We made our way down the nearest set of steps and along the beach to a sheltered spot not far from the pier. Jo-Jo stepped out of her pink Crocs and crunched her toes into the malted milk-coloured sand. She unrolled two Charlie Brown beach towels and handed one to me. We laid them out on the beach, side by side. I took off my Adidas tee-shirt and put on my Foster Grant sunglasses. Jo-Jo frowned at me.

'What?'

'They're huge,' she said. 'They make you look old, like you're trying to hide the bags.'

'I like them.'

'Yeah, but you've got no taste, Freddie. The John Lennon ones are in my carpet bag. We'll bring those tomorrow.'

I straightened out the edges of my towel and lay down. Grains of sand itched against my back. I looked up at the walkway. A row of people were standing above us eating 99 ice-creams or staring out at the horizon through the penny a go telescopes. I could hear 'Teddy Bears' Picnic' tinkling out of a rocking yellow play bus, a little girl yanking hard at its steering wheel, giggling with excitement, her mother standing to the side, smiling encouragement. Ted and Alison, a couple from our B and B, were leaning on the green metal railings and looking down at us. They waved. I waved back. Ted said something to Alison.

'They come from Walsall,' said Jo-Jo, sitting down on her towel. 'Just up the road from us.'

'Yeah.'

'Don't you think that's odd?'

'What?'

'Living so close and ending up in the same B and B.'

'Not really.'

'It's fate,' she said.

'You don't believe in that stuff, do you?'

'Don't you?'

'Why would we be destined to meet them?'

'We don't know yet, Freddie. That's how it works.'

*

We skipped Mr Lewis' cod and chips tea and found one of the restaurants on my list. Jo-Jo declared Malibu and ice as our drink for the evening – 'No one gets drunk on Malibu,' she said. Three hours later we did the "I'm not drunk" walk out of the bar.

It was past midnight when we got back to the B and B. I closed the front door behind us. A Tiffany-shade table lamp lit up the hallway and a second lamp lit up the landing, guiding the route to our bedroom. Jo-Jo stood on the first step of the stairs and pulled me towards her. 'I told you he was nice,' she said. 'He's left the lights on for us.'

'Come on,' I said. 'Let's go to bed.'

'I want you to carry me.'

'There's no way I'm carrying you up those stairs.'

'If you love me, you will.'

I looked up at the landing.

'It's not that far,' she said. 'Not for a big, strong man like you.'

'You're really drunk, aren't you?'

'Yes,' she said, closing her eyes and nodding. 'I'm really drunk.'

I lifted her in my arms and started to walk up the stairs. She put her finger to her lips and made a shushing noise. I tripped up a step and she laughed. 'Quiet, Mr Charlton,' she said. 'Someone will hear us.'

One of the bedroom doors opened and Alison peered down at us over the bannister. She was wearing a pink flannelette dressing gown and holding a Ruth Rendell novel. Ted appeared next to her in his paisley pyjamas. 'What's going on?' he said. 'Oh, hello. Are you two okay?'

Jo-Jo stroked my cheek. 'He's my hero,' she said.

*

We'd made it to the bed. I was awake. Jo-Jo was asleep. I kissed her forehead. She muttered something and turned over, the back of her head now facing me. I sniffed her hair. It smelt of strawberry shampoo. She pulled the white Egyptian cotton sheet up around her shoulders. I'd pushed the sheets and blanket back on my side, but Jo-Jo had kept herself covered, said it made her feel safe. She muttered something else. It sounded like peas. I smiled and thought about what she'd said on the beach, about fate, about Ted and Alison. I couldn't think of a single thing we had in common with them. Ted wore a brown corduroy jacket with leather patches on each elbow and Alison laughed like a hyena at everything he said. I pulled Jo-Jo into my body and squeezed her close.

*

We are in a wood, walking hand in hand. I can hear birdsong, Elvis Costello singing 'Alison'. And then we are in the middle of town, standing outside Midland Educational, still holding hands. I can hear pigeons cooing. It sounds like they're calling over and over, 'do it now, do it now; do it now.'

Someone pinched the end of my nose. I opened one eye. Jo-Jo was smiling at me. 'Your turn to make the tea,' she said.

'In a minute,' I said, turning over.

She kissed the back of my neck. I turned back towards her.

'I'm thirsty,' she said.

'I'm not surprised.'

'You shouldn't let me drink so much.'

She put her head on my chest and pulled at my chest hairs. I could feel her warm skin through her silk nightdress, her bare thighs touching mine. She slid her hand across my stomach and under the waistband of my boxer shorts. 'I thought you were tired,' she said.

Freddie – August 1980

Jo-Jo's bedroom, cuddling up on her single bed. Her mum and dad out shopping, Josh in his room, listening to his latest Genesis album. 'Let's get married,' I said.

'I'm not ready for that, Freddie.'

'We're good together. I'll find a vicar, someone we can talk to.'

'Not yet.'

'Why? I love you.'

'I know.'

'But you're still going?'

'It's three years. And it's Lincoln. If it's real, we'll survive.'

'Do you love me?'

'What?'

'You've never said you love me.'

'I struggle with that. You know I do.'

'Maybe that's the problem. All that stuff with your dad.'

'Maybe the problem is you want it too much.'

'What?'

'You. It's all about you. I know your mum's...'

'It's nothing to do with my mum.'

Freddie – July 2015

I could see the diners through the Mini's rain-splattered windscreen. They were gathered in the hotel's conservatory, a yellow glow from the central chandelier enveloping them like a protective cloak. Two couples were sitting in wicker chairs, a bottle of wine in an ice bucket placed in the centre of their tables; further along, a man, a woman and two children, and, at the table next to them, an older couple, the man reading a broadsheet, the woman looking in her handbag.

I unfastened my seatbelt. The Mini's engine was still running. It had taken me four or five goes to park evenly between the white lines, equidistance on each side of the car.

A knock on the passenger side window made me jump. There was a pocked-faced, moustachioed man staring in at me. He was wearing a high-visibility jacket and a black cap with Security Guard written across the front in yellow letters. He gestured for me to wind the window down. I pressed a switch on the dashboard, opening the window by about six inches.

'Are you staying in the hotel, sir?'

'No. I'm here to meet a friend. We're having dinner.'

'Ah, you'll need to move the car then. This area is for hotel guests only. The restaurant parking is on the other side.'

He gestured to the far side of the car park, no more than a hundred metres away.

I nodded and pressed the switch again, closing the window.

I watched him walk over to the three industrial-size grey dustbins on the edge of the car park. He stood, hands on hips, watching me. He touched the peak of his cap and pointed again towards the non-resident parking spaces.

Freddie – December 1980

Yoko cremated John. I'd never heard of anyone being cremated. Mum told me it was pagan. I wrote to Yoko, told her I had a band, which I didn't, told her how John inspired us all, which he did. I cut the 'You may say I'm a dreamer...' quote out of *Melody Maker*, Blu-tacking it on my bedroom wall; bought *Double Fantasy*, learned every word, and listened religiously to the Andy Peebles interviews on a Sunday teatime.

Forty-eight hours after the interview, Lennon was gone.

Mark Chapman shot him, but Yoko had him burned.

'Happy Christmas, John.' 'Happy Christmas, Yoko.'

Freddie – May 1980

Back on the beach, lying on the towels, me wearing Jo-Jo's sunglasses and tracking a fat brain-coloured cloud, willing it to crawl faster across the sky. 'He really loves Yoko,' I said.

'Who?'

'John Lennon. Who'd you think?'

'He calls her mother. That's just wrong.'

'It's a pet name.'

'It's weird. She controls him, even his love affairs.'

'What?'

'May Pang, that eighteen months lost weekend. Yoko arranged it all.'

'Shows how much she loves him.'

'Shows his weakness. A little boy. That's what he is.'

I touched the bridge of the sunglasses.

Jo-Jo sat up and ran her hand through her hair. 'A little, little boy,' she repeated.

Freddie – July 2015

I re-parked the car in one of the non-resident spaces, pulled on the handbrake and turned off the engine. I was facing the hotel's exit. I couldn't see the conservatory, but I could see the security man through the rear-view mirror. He was still standing by the bins, still watching me.

I reached in the back seat for my jacket. For the first time in three years I was wearing my Jeff Banks pinstriped suit that I'd bought second-hand off eBay. The fastened-up top button of my Van Heusen shirt was pinching at my throat. I undid the button, loosened my silk tie, took in a deep breath and looked out of the window. All of the conifers were slide rule-pruned, the lawns mowed and trimmed to perfection. We'd be having proper wine and food menus. I'd have to work out the knives and forks.

I thought about the coffee shop, about Jo-Jo turning up after all this time, all of our connections three decades old. I wondered if she liked cats. A roll of anxiety turned in my stomach and I fumbled inside my jacket pocket for the strip of beta blockers that I'd brought with me.

Jo-Jo – April 1981

We stood in the front row of the church, waiting for Dad's coffin to be carried in by the top-hatted pall bearers, Mum staring straight ahead at a stained glass image of Christ in mid-crucifixion, Josh and I each side of her, gripping her hands. Someone gasped. I turned my head and looked down the aisle. The procession was still stepping out towards us. I found out later that Uncle Arthur, Dad's eldest brother, had tripped himself up on the bottom of his new suit trousers. The coffin had slipped off his shoulder, but he'd caught it mid-fall and lifted it back in place without breaking his stride.

Josh had found Dad in the back garden, but it was two months after the funeral before we talked about it.

'You never said what happened.'

'Not something I want to relive, sis.'

'I'd still like to know, Josh.'

'I came home from college and there he was, face down on the lawn.'

'And he was already dead?'

'I think so.'

'Where was Mum?'

'In bed. She came down in her nightie, kept shaking him.'

The Student's Union, me eating the chilli special, Mr Averis, my dissertation supervisor, walking into the canteen, looking around, seeing me, bowing his head, coming over to my table, kneeling down in front of me, dandruff on his blue velvet sports jacket collar, patches of grey beard on his cheeks and under his nose.

'It's your father, Jo-Jo.'

'My father?'

'Shall we go somewhere more private?'

The church door creaked open. I turned and looked down the aisle.

Dad's woman from the park.

Jo-Jo – May 1980

We'd been sunbathing for two hours. I couldn't see Freddie's eyes behind the John Lennon sunglasses, but I knew he was asleep. A copy of Norman Mailer's *The Naked and the Dead* lay open on his chest. It had a picture of a tin-hatted American soldier, holding a hand grenade and screaming something obscene out of a muddy trench. Jack had recommended the book, but I could see from the way it lay that Freddie had only managed to struggle through a couple of chapters before he'd nodded off. I yawned and sat up on my elbows. The beach was packed, but there was a free patch of sand directly in front of us. I pinched Freddie's arm.

'Wake up, lazy bones. I want you to build me a sandcastle.'

He lifted his sunglasses. 'A what?'

'A sandcastle. You do know what a sandcastle is?'

He sat up and rubbed his eyes. The book slid off his chest. 'I wasn't asleep.'

'Yeah, right. I believe you.'

'What time is it?'

I reached into the beach bag for my watch. 'Twelve thirty.'

'Lunchtime,' said Freddie, dropping the glasses back over his eyes and lying back down on the towel.

I turned towards him and started curling the hairs on his chest. 'No lunch until I get my sandcastle,' I said.

He looked at me. 'A sandcastle?'

I nodded.

'What am I meant to build it with?'

I grinned and held up a yellow plastic bucket and spade set, still inside its red net bag. 'I bought it from the shop at the top of the steps,' I said. 'While you were asleep.'

'Okay. I'll build you a sandcastle.'

'Four turrets,' I said. 'And don't forget the moat.'

Jo-Jo – July 2015

Mum had a photograph of Uncle Arthur, taken just before the war. He looked like a young Errol Flynn, with a pencil moustache. He used to drive around in highly waxed saloon cars with walnut dashboards and leather seats, taking Josh and me for rides in the country. I was frightened to move in case I dirtied anything. When they were teenagers, his brothers, including Dad, used to tease him when he wiped the pub seat with his white handkerchief before he sat down – 'Clean enough for you now, Arthur? Wouldn't want you catching anything.'

Arthur married twice. His first wife sold everything in the house and left him while he was away in India; his second wife, Peggy, had a stroke and he looked after her on his own for years, refusing any offer of help. He was seventy-three when he moved to Birmingham to live with another woman after Peggy died. But he kept his flat in Bloxwich – his bolthole, he called it.

I'd been at the table for ten minutes when I saw Freddie walking up to the reception desk. He said something to the receptionist who pointed towards the conservatory. Freddie turned, saw me, bowed his head for a split second and then looked at me again. I waved. He put his hands in his pockets and walked over to my table. 'Jo-Jo,' he said.

I noticed he was wearing thick-framed, designer glasses, Joe 90 style. I didn't remember him having them on in the coffee shop. They looked good, accentuated his grey blue eyes. 'I didn't think you'd come,' I said.

He ran his fingers through his hair. 'I nearly lost it in the car park.'

'Lost it?'

'I'm okay. It's just nerves.'

'Nothing to be nervous of.'

He sat down and swapped over his knives and forks.

I laughed. 'You still do that then?'

He gave me a puzzled look.

'With the cutlery, swap them over.'

'Oh, yes. Sorry. It's instinctive. Shall I put them back?'

'No. It's nice. Reassuring.'

The waitress came over. 'Would you like to see the wine menu?' she said.

Freddie and I smiled at each other.

Jo-Jo – April 1981

Dad carried on seeing his park woman, disappearing for evenings out with imaginary friends from his schooldays. No one questioned him, except me. 'Leave it, Jo-Jo. I don't want to talk about it.' I used to watch him with Mum, looking for a change, waiting for his big announcement, convinced he'd leave us. There was no point relying on Mum. I was the eldest. I had to be ready. But he carried on being Dad. I wondered if he ever felt guilty, if he ever felt the need to tell her, to confess, to come clean. I wanted to tell her. I felt guilty. I felt dirtied by his grubby little secret. And then he died.

The vicar was over six-foot tall, had a bulbous belly and a totally grey Brian Blessed beard. His voice boomed out to every corner of the church and everyone, even the children, went quiet when he stood up to start the service. 'How Great Thou Art,' my choice, was the first hymn. I couldn't take my eyes off Dad's coffin. It was light oak with a brass plaque in the centre of the lid. The thought that he was in there, listening to us, filled my head. The funeral director gave me and Josh a choice of coffins. We'd tried to get Mum involved, but she'd left it to us. 'Just get the one that's going to last him,' she'd said. 'And nice lining. It has to have nice lining.'

'Devoted husband... loving father... loved his garden...' The vicar said lots of nice words and we all walked serenely out of the church. 'They did him proud,' someone said. 'Nice sermon, Vicar,' another called out. Everyone offered their condolences to Mum, but she didn't answer. Josh thanked them. I looked for Dad's woman. I thought she'd gone and then I saw her, standing by the coffin, both hands resting on the lid. I looked at Mum, but she hadn't noticed. Josh had. He gave me a quizzical look. I shook my head. Mum and Josh walked outside. I walked back up the aisle.

'Hello,' I said.

'It wasn't just an affair, you know. We loved each other.'

She was staring at the coffin, looking as though she was talking to Dad. I didn't know what to say, how to react. I could see her hands were trembling. I expected her to burst into tears. 'You should be grateful for all the time you had with him,' she said.

And then she walked past me and out of the church.

I went up to the coffin and touched the lid. 'Goodbye, Dad,' I said.

Jo-Jo – July 2015

I took a sip of the Muscadet. Freddie was still smiling at me. 'It's fine,' I said.

The waitress nodded and filled my glass. She turned to Freddie.

'I'll stick with water,' he said, pouring himself a drink from the jug in the centre of the table.

She put the bottle in the ice bucket and walked away towards the kitchen.

'Water?' I said.

'I never drink and drive,' he said.

'That sounds like one of your rules.'

'My rules?'

'You had rules for everything. Don't you remember?'

'I remember you always threatening to send the wine back.'

'I never did though.'

'No,' he said. 'I don't think you ever did.'

We picked up the food menus. The man at the next table had finished reading his newspaper. 'Where's that waitress?' the man said. 'I'm ready for my starter.' The woman with him looked around the restaurant.

'I know what you're having,' said Freddie.

'You do?' I said.

'Steak,' he declared, looking like a child who'd just got one over on the grown-ups. 'Rare, with the blood still running. I'm right aren't I?'

I could tell by the way he was looking at me how much energy his confidence had taken. I shook my head. It made me feel sad.

'You're not having steak?' he said.

'I'm vegetarian, Freddie. Have been for the last twenty years.'

Jo-Jo – September 1980

Digbeth Coach Station. Freddie and I were sitting on blue plastic seats at terminal twenty-four. I had my carpet bag on my lap and Dad's brown leather suitcase at my feet. The coach was parked in front of us.

I looked at my watch. 'He's cutting it fine,' I said.

'Still got five minutes,' said Freddie. 'Here he is now.'

The driver walked across the road from the canteen, an Express Coaches badge pinned to his jacket lapel. 'Morning,' he said, throwing the butt of his cigarette in the gutter. 'You two off to sunny Lincoln?'

'Just me,' I said, standing up and nodding at my suitcase. 'Can you store that one? I'll keep the bag with me.'

'No problem,' said the driver, touching his cap. He looked at Freddie and then back at me.

A man and a woman stood up from the plastic seats further along the concourse. The man picked up a suede holdall from the pavement and put it over his shoulder. He went to pick up a second holdall, but the driver, now holding my suitcase, rushed over. 'I'll get that for you, sir,' he said.

'Thank you,' said the woman, brushing down the back of her coat. 'Isn't that kind, Frank?'

The man nodded and, looking relieved, put the first holdall back on the floor. 'You couldn't take this one as well, could you?'

The driver opened up the luggage flaps on the side of the coach and pushed the bags inside. My suitcase went in first.

A younger couple, about the same age as me, each wearing a backpack, climbed the steps of the coach. 'You two going to Lincoln?' said the driver. 'That's right, mate,' said the girl, neither of them breaking stride as they ran laughing down the coach towards the back seat. The driver tutted at the older couple. 'Young love,' he said. 'I suppose they'll be giggling all the way.' He looked at me and then quickly went back to his bag duty.

'This is it then,' said Freddie.

'You should have come with me. I don't start until Monday. You could have helped me settle in.'

He shrugged. 'It's better this way.'

I pulled him towards me. 'I'll see you in a few weeks?'

He nodded. 'I'll book the Friday off and come up at the weekend.'

I kissed him on the lips. 'Stop looking so sad. It'll fly by.'

The driver, who was now sitting behind the steering wheel, started the engine. 'You coming, love?' he shouted.

I threw the carpet bag over my shoulder and kissed Freddie again. 'I'll see you soon. Don't forget to phone.'

'I promise,' he said.

I turned, climbed the steps and walked along to the middle of the coach. I put my bag in the overhead storage and sat down next to the window. Freddie put up his hand. He mouthed 'I love you' as the coach pulled away. I looked back, but he was already walking towards the exit, his hands in his pockets.

'Ob-la-di, Ob-la-da. Life goes on…'

I looked down the coach for the source of the singing. The backpack couple were now part of a group of six, three couples. One of the girls pulled a stack of multi-coloured plastic cups and a bottle of Bacardi out of a Marks and Spencer carrier bag. She gave the cups to the lad sitting next to her. 'Come on, Jess,' said the lad on the end. 'We're dying of thirst here.'

She unscrewed the cap on the Bacardi bottle and filled the cups, which the lad next to her was holding out one by one. With the cups half-filled, he handed them round to the group.

I looked at the driver. He was watching the back seats in his rear-view mirror.

'Excuse me.'

I looked up. There was a man standing in the aisle. He was wearing a navy blue Crombie coat and a black bowler hat, which he touched at the brim in greeting. I put his age at mid-thirties and, apart from the hat, the other striking thing about him was his Union Jack nose stud. I wondered why I hadn't seen him get on the coach.

'Do you mind if I sit here?' he said, tugging nervously at his two-tone, mostly ginger but with patches of black, goatee beard.

I smiled. 'No,' I said.

He sat down. I realised I was staring at him and I turned to look out of the window.

'I was trying to read,' he said, waving a crumpled paperback book in my direction. 'But that song gets inside your head.'

I looked at his book: *The Collected Works of Shelley*.

'My dad loves him,' I said.

'It's prep for my course,' he said.

'You're going to the university?'

'You sound surprised.'

'No, it's just, well...'

'It's just, I'm a little old to be a student.' He tapped the book. 'I want to study these guys before it's too late.'

'The rest of the guys in the band,' I said.

He looked at me quizzically.

'The Romantics. Shelley and the rest of the guys in the band. That's what my dad calls them.'

Jo-Jo – July 2015

Dad learned Shelley's moonbeams and kisses poem off by heart, reciting it at every opportunity. I'd close my eyes and listen, entranced with the thought that you could love someone that much. I used to dream about Dad flying across a starry night sky on a magic carpet, searching for Mum, risking everything for a single kiss. I wanted to find my own Shelley. Dad met his woman in the park, but he stayed with Mum, sacrificed everything to look after her. Sunlight, moonbeams and kisses versus loyalty and commitment. What a choice.

Josh married his first girlfriend, Glenda, who worked in a bank. He waited ten years before having his first child, had another the year after, and then no more. He'd paid off his

79

mortgage by the time he was forty. Mum moved into a sheltered housing scheme after Dad died and Josh would phone her every night after *Coronation Street* or *Heartbeat*, depending on the day. Sometimes she'd ignore his call, getting it into her head it was a duty call. He'd phone back every half an hour until she answered. Every Sunday he'd take her to his house for lunch and they'd watch old westerns and Jimmy Cagney films – 'Top of the world, Ma.' Some weeks she'd say she wasn't going, telling him on the Saturday night. 'Okay, Mum,' he'd say and then turn up the next day to pick her up. She was always ready. One night, someone set fire to the landing in her block of flats. It was the middle of the night and Mum phoned my brother: 'Okay, Mum,' he said. 'I'm on my way.' He rang the fire brigade.

The starters arrived. Freddie had ordered the liver paté and I'd asked for the green salad. I was conscious of having sipped my way through my glass of wine. I wanted to refill the glass, but I fought the urge and poured myself a glass of water.

'It's okay,' he said. 'Don't feel you have to avoid the wine for me.'

'I'm not,' I said, a little too sharply. 'I'm thirsty.'

I carried on eating my salad. He put down his knife and then picked it up again. He looked as though he was going to say something, but he didn't. He looked at the table. I felt guilty for snapping. 'So, thirty-five years,' I said.

He was looking nervously around the room, wringing his hands, beads of sweat on his forehead. He took a drink of water, picked up his napkin and wiped his brow. 'It's warm in here,' he said.

'Are you okay, Freddie?'

'I'm fine.'

I forked some more salad into my mouth. The waitress came over and refilled my wine glass. I smiled at her. She walked back to the side of the conservatory, where she stood like a sentry on guard duty, surveying the room.

I picked up the wine glass, took another drink, held the glass in front of me and swirled the Muscadet. 'Perhaps this was a mistake,' I said.

He pushed his half-eaten plate of paté away from him. 'I'm sorry. I don't do this very often.'

'Just relax. Tell me about Becky. How often do you see her?'

'I haven't seen her for twelve years, not since Mum died.'

I waited, but that was it. He was looking around the room again. 'You must miss her,' I said.

'Yes,' he said. 'She died really quickly. Nothing they could do.'

'I meant Becky,' I said.

*

I had trout for the main course. My vegetarianism didn't include fish, much to Jason's disgust. 'You can't pick and choose,' he used to say. 'Yes, I can, and I'm choosing to eat fish.'

Freddie had stopped sweating, which was just as well because he'd gone for the goat curry, but he was still clinging onto his napkin, scrunching it up in his right hand. He kept touching the bridge of his glasses and pushing them back on his face. He told me about borrowing Jack's Mini for the evening, how he'd struggled to find the switch for the wipers. 'Typical Jack,' he said. 'He just expects you to know everything.'

'Good of him to lend you the car, though.'

'Yeah, I had to sell my car when the job went.'

'When was that?'

'About a year ago.'

'So you haven't worked for a year?'

'I've been looking,' he said.

We both forked a mouthful of our food. I took a sip of wine.

'Do you remember the bear?' I said.

He looked at me.

'The one you won at the fair.'

I reached down, picked up my handbag, undid the zip and ceremoniously fetched out the five-inches high teddy bear. I sat him in the middle of the table, leaning him against the water jug.

'You kept him,' he said.

'Yep,' I said. 'Carried him around all these years.'

Freddie picked up the bear and started to cry.

The waitress rushed over and asked if everything was all right. Freddie blew his nose into a napkin. The waitress and I averted our eyes. She asked if we wanted dessert. We said no and ordered coffee. She refilled my wine glass and walked away towards the kitchen. Freddie was still holding the bear.

'I didn't mean to upset you,' I said. 'I thought it would be nice.'

'It is,' he said. 'It's just, it's...'

The chipped-tooth smile, the downcast eyes, the little boy who'd stolen a toffee. He was back. For a split second my Freddie reappeared. I wanted to hug him. And then he was gone again. 'I'm sorry,' he said.

'Stop saying that,' I said.

Jo-Jo's Dream

I'm fist-banging on the front door.

'There's no one here,' I shout.

'There must be,' she says.

I hit the door again and step back, looking up at the windows, waiting for a sign of life. 'He's gone,' I say, falling to my knees. 'He's gone.'

'No,' says Amy. 'He's here somewhere. We have to keep looking.'

Two nurses look at each other.

'She's twitching a lot. Do you think she can hear us?'

'They say she can, but she can't.'

'It makes you shiver doesn't it? Imagine being like that.'

'It's not natural, keeping her alive in that state.'

'The daughter sits for hours talking to her.'

'Poor cow. Let's get her changed.'

I lie there listening, screaming at them from inside my paralysed body. 'I'm here. I'm here. I'm here.'

We keep searching. I pull Amy down a jet-washed cobblestone road, passing a line of Victorian terraced houses, conifer-lined driveways, lush green lawns, neatly trimmed privets, garden borders of rhododendron bushes and aphid-free roses. 'This isn't right,' I say. 'He won't be here.'

'Where did you meet?' says Amy.

'What?'

'Try to think about him, Mum. It might help.'

The doctor's back. He's talking to Amy.

'The stroke was too severe, Mrs Graham. It's been six months now. There's no sign of any brain activity.'

'What about the twitching, doctor? I'm sure she knows I'm here.'

'Involuntary, I'm afraid. There's no conscious movement.'

'Are you sure?'

'As sure as we can be. Your mum's not going to make any sort of recovery.'

'You mean, you want to turn off the machines?'

They do. Oh, my God. I need to find him. I need to find him now.

We carry on searching my head.

'This is hopeless,' I say.

'You can't give up, Mum.'

'What if he's not here?'

'He is. Tell me about his childhood. Where did he grow up? Did you visit?'

'It was so long ago.'

'Think. There must be something.'

'Yellow houses. I remember yellow houses.'

The nurses again.

'Matron told me they're going to switch off the machine tomorrow.'

'Sounds like the daughter's seen sense at last.'

'They should have done it weeks ago.'

'She seems a bit calmer today, less twitchy.'

We cross over the road and walk towards a circle of 1950s steel-framed houses, all painted buttercup yellow. There's a green in front of them with swings, a slide and make-shift goal posts. The smell of fish and chips and real coal fires lace the air. 'This is it,' I say.

'Which house?'

'I can't remember.'

She grabs my hand. 'Let's walk up and down until something clicks. Come on.'

We read the numbers as we walk: 46… 44… 42… I stop.

'What is it?' says Amy.

'There,' I say. 'The one with the Murano glass dogs in the window. We've found it.'

I can smell antiseptic wipes. They've already washed and changed me. Someone has switched on a radio. I can hear Chris Evan's breakfast show. I feel the nylon sheets being pulled back over my limp, helpless body, hear the door open, the footsteps of people walking towards the bed.

We look up at the house.

'I'm so scared,' I say.

'I know, Mum, but I'll be right here.'

I draw in a deep breath and walk up the driveway, the crunching gravel echoing inside my head. I reach the front door and single-press the bell. The hallway light comes on. The door swings open. I look back at Amy.

'Are you ready, Mrs Graham?'

'Can you give me a minute, doctor?'

'Of course.'

I feel Amy's warm breath and moist lips touch my forehead. 'I hope I'm doing the right thing, Mum.'

No. Not yet. Not yet.

I'm inside the house, walking slowly down the hall, passing Freddie's school photographs, him wearing a sky-blue uniform, shoulder-length dark black hair sticking out in all directions, the top two buttons of his shirt undone, his red check tie hanging loose in a wide knot.

I open the lounge door.

He's sitting on his mum's brown leather settee, his chipped front tooth smile beaming out at me. 'Hello, my darling. I've been waiting for you.'

I run over and hug him, his Kouros aftershave taking me back thirty-five years. I pull away, hold his face with both my hands and kiss him on the lips. 'Promise me you'll never leave me again. Promise me.'

'I promise,' he says, wiping tears from his face. 'I promise.'

Jo-Jo – May 1980

Going home day. I'd sent Freddie off to fill the Avenger with petrol. He'd left me three twenty-pound notes to pay Mr Lewis for our stay. I went downstairs, walked into the lounge and found Alison sitting on one of the sofas. She was crying. I rushed over and put my arm around her. 'What's happened?' I said.

She sniffed into a sodden paper tissue, which she'd curled up into a ball in her right hand. The tip of her nose had a red tinge. 'Ted's gone,' she said.

I pulled her closer. 'Have you had a row?'

She nodded and dabbed the end of her nose with the tissue. 'Last night,' she said. 'All I did was ask him to get the cases out of the wardrobe. He was watching some black and white film on the telly. You know what he said?'

I shook my head.

'In a minute. He's been saying it a lot lately. Everything's in a minute.'

She turned towards me, buried her face against my chest and sniffed into my new Adidas tee-shirt. I gently eased her away. 'He'll be back,' I said.

'No,' she said, lifting her head. 'He won't. I told him he was a lazy pig, shouted at him. I don't know where it came from. It's such a stupid thing to fall out over. He said I was boring. That the only thing I thought about was my tarot cards. It's not true. We do lots of things together. And then he slammed the door and left. All his stuff's still up there. He's taken the car.'

She put her head against my chest again. This time I let her stay. 'It's just a tiff,' I said, stroking her hair. 'It happens when couples go away together. Freddie and I are always falling out.'

'I don't know how I'm going to get home,' she said. 'All I asked him to do was get the cases out of the wardrobe.'

'It's okay,' I said. 'You can come back with us. He'll be waiting for you at home.'

She looked up at me with wide eyes like I'd suddenly rescued her from a burning building. 'Will he?' she said.

'Definitely,' I said, patting her leg. 'You just need a break from each other. Dry your eyes and fetch your bags.'

*

I tied the fluffy, yellow Snoopy to the interior mirror of the Avenger.

'Ah,' said Alison. 'He's sweet.'

She was sitting in the back seat and leaning through the gap in the front seats, talking to us, giving us the life and times of Ted and Alison: how they'd been together ten years, they didn't want any children, he was like a little boy really with his tantrums. She kept looking down and twisting the wooden buttons on her white Aran wool cardigan.

'You mean he's left you like this before?'

'He's always doing it. Sulks for days sometimes.'

'Why do you put up with it?'

'It's just how he is,' she said.

I looked at Freddie, wanting him to say something. He was chewing hard on his bottom lip. I tried to work out if he was annoyed. He'd hardly spoken all the way home. I'd have understood if he'd been angry. I'd inflicted Alison on him.

'It's not far from here,' she said. 'Take the next right.'

We pulled up outside a three-storey block of flats. I got out of the car and pulled the front seat forward to let her out of the back. She hugged both of us. Freddie fetched her case from the boot and got back in the driver's seat. He'd left the engine running.

'The car's not here,' said Alison, looking nervously up at the flat. 'He's still sulking. It's what he does.' She nodded at the Avenger. 'He didn't say much coming back.'

'He's fine,' I said.

She hugged me again, picked up her case and walked down the tarmac path. I got back in the Avenger, fastened my seatbelt and turned to wave, but she'd already gone through the entrance doors. Freddie U-turned the car and accelerated back towards the main road. Snoopy bounced against the window.

'He'd only do it once,' I said.

'You shouldn't get involved.'

'What was I meant to do? Leave her there?'

'I can't see what it's got to do with us.'

'She was stranded.'

'They'd have worked it out. He's probably still up there.'

'I can't believe she stays with him.'

'Jo-Jo, they've been together for ten years. If you ask me, they're as bad as each other.'

'You think that's a reasonable way for him to behave?'

'I'm just saying, she must know him by now.'

'Sulking. He's meant to be a man for God's sake.'

Jo-Jo – July 2015

I'd snapped at him again. I wanted my sweet, innocent Freddie, making me laugh, looking up at me like I'd fallen from heaven to bless his life. I could sense he was still in there, lurking beneath this fractured ghost sitting opposite me. 'You never got the tooth done then?' I said.

He touched his mouth. 'No. Never had the money. Does it bother you?'

'I've always loved it, Freddie. You know that. It makes you unique.'

He smiled. 'Never seen another,' he said.

'Remind me how you did it.'

'Showing off to some girls. You know this story, Jo-Jo.'

'Do I?'

'I dived in the shallow end of the swimming pool and banged my head on the bottom. Why are you laughing?'

'It's just so un-Freddie like.'

'Yeah, well, I was eleven, learned my lesson at an early age. Never try to impress women.' He wiped his mouth with the napkin. 'I'm disappointing you, aren't I?'

'No,' I said.

'Yes I am. I can see it in your face.'

'It's just… I didn't expect you to be so nervous. You never used to be.'

'That was a long time ago.'

'Maybe I should have left it where it belonged.'

'I'm still trying to work out why you didn't.'

'It felt like something I needed to do.'

He took a sip of water and looked around the conservatory. The older couple were having a break after their main course, the man had gone back to his paper, the woman was still searching for something in her handbag. 'It's a nice hotel,' said Freddie. 'Beats the curry Jack and I go for every month.'

'Perhaps we'd have been better in a nightclub.'

'Yeah,' he said, 'I could have nailed the Pac-Man record and you could have wowed them in your Go-Go boots.' He reached over and stroked the top of my hand with his right forefinger. 'I'm glad you decided to find me. Sorry I'm a bit of a wreck.'

'I wish you'd stop saying sorry,' I said.

*

We walked side by side into the hotel reception. It was empty, apart from the nervy receptionist, who was obviously working the night shift. He was trying not to look at us, busying himself with moving pieces of paper around his desk. I wondered what he was thinking. Madam and her strange man, a secret liaison, the fiery daughter nowhere in sight. I'd have imagined a thousand scenarios at his age.

Freddie's nerves were back. He was probably wondering whether to kiss me or to shake my hand. 'Thank you for coming,' I said. 'It was nice.'

'I'm not going to say sorry again,' he said.

'No. Please don't.'

'When do you leave for New Zealand?'

It was the first time either of us had mentioned my going away.

'I'm not sure. Amy's sorting it out.'

'Let me have your address,' he said. 'We can write, keep in touch.'

'I thought you weren't any good at writing.'

'Yeah, well. I've got better with age.'

It suddenly crossed my mind that Amy might be watching me. I scanned the reception area and into the conservatory. I'd told her to keep a low profile, but it wouldn't have surprised me if curiosity had driven her downstairs. I half-expected to see her striding over the carpet, hand held out, announcing herself as the daughter. I had this image of Freddie and the receptionist bolting for the hills. I couldn't see her. Freddie was looking at me.

'I'd like to kiss you,' he said.

'I'd like that too.'

He leaned forward. I closed my eyes.

*

An hour later, I lowered myself into the white porcelain bath, held my nose, submerged and resurfaced. I wiped my eyes and rested the back of my head against the non-tap end, watching the steam rise towards the ceiling of the hotel bathroom, coconut-smelling bubbles tickling my chin. The evening had ended okay. I wondered what he'd made of me. He'd remembered the boots, kept that memory with him all those years. He used to whimper slightly just before orgasming. What a thing to have in my head. The dance. I should have reminded him about our dance. Him trying so desperately to please me, to hold me properly, keeping his hands in the right places. He'd left before the hotel band had started. I'd imagined a dance, a last dance with my Freddie. At least he'd kissed me.

It started to rain as I pulled out of the hotel car park, turning into a full downpour as the journey progressed. I drove along the main road leading into the village, nearly back at my house, my eyes fixed on the shimmering tail-lights of a Ford Focus. I concentrated hard. Thank God I hadn't had a drink. The fuzziness of the beta blockers was bad enough. A lorry screamed past in the opposite direction, throwing up a splash of water, momentarily blocking out the world before the automatic wipers were triggered into a frenzy. A yellow haze from the street lights lit up a blurred bus stop queue, people standing in line, waiting patiently for the number 49, umbrellas drawn against the downpour. The brake lights from the Ford Focus lit up. 'Jesus,' I screamed, slamming my foot on the brake pedal, skidding the Mini to a stop. The engine stalled, honking horns sounded all around. I thumped the steering wheel. 'She must think I'm fucking mental,' I said.

Freddie – September 1980

I walked through the reception area of the Digbeth coach station and out into the empty main street. I stopped walking, looked up at the cloud-filled sky and drew in a deep breath. It was always going to happen. She was always destined to do something else, be somewhere else. I told myself how lucky I'd been to have her in my life for a short, glorious time. I'd tried to keep her, begged her not to go, but it was inevitable. She wouldn't expect me to phone. She'd meet new friends, intelligent, interesting, good-looking friends who could dance and knew how to use a knife and fork. Maybe it was time to let her go. I needed to talk to Jack.

Max's. 2.30 a.m. The lights had come up and everyone was making their way to the exit. Elaine Barber was slumped in a sofa, her wide eyes staring up at one of the mirror balls, a half-empty glass of Bacardi and Coke in front of her. One of the waitresses was shaking her by the arm. 'Time to go now, love.'

I knelt down in front of the sofa. 'Elaine?' I said.

'She with you?' said the waitress.

'I know her from school,' I said.

A memory – December 1971. The nativity play. We're on stage. I'm Joseph and Elaine is the Angel Gabriel. I kneel next to Sharon Clarke, who is playing Mary, in front of us a wicker basket brought in by Miss Balsam, our maths teacher, to be used as a makeshift cradle. Elaine stands behind us, holds her cardboard wand over our heads and gets ready to bless the baby Jesus. She's wearing a full-length white smock, polystyrene wings and a white tiara. 'You are truly blessed,' she says. 'The Lord is with you.' The audience gasps. My mum takes our picture from the back of the hall.

'Elaine?' I said again, this time gently squeezing her arm.

'She's well gone,' said the waitress. 'Been drinking that stuff all night. Blokes touching her up, getting a quick feel.'

Elaine looked at me.

'It's Freddie,' I said. 'From school.'

'Freddie,' she said, touching my cheek. 'Where've you been, Freddie?'

'It's time to go home,' I said. 'The club's closing.'

'I want another drink,' she said, reaching out for the glass of Bacardi. 'Get me a drink, Freddie.'

The waitress grabbed her arm. 'No more drinks, love. It's time to go.'

'Get off me, you cow. Tell her, Freddie. Tell her to get off me.'

Elaine slumped back in the chair again.

'You taking her with you?' said the waitress.

'I can't. I don't know where she lives.'

'I don't think she cares which bed she's in. Could be your lucky night.'

Freddie – July 2015

I saw this film once about a manic robot. They were going to melt him down, but they operated instead. A lab technician unscrewed the top of his head. 'The circuitry's burnt out,' he said. 'We'll have to rewire him.' A second technician leaned forward. 'Disconnect the blue wire,' she said. 'That should do it. Calm him down a bit.' I wanted that operation. I wanted to reach inside my head and unclip the wires.

I pulled up outside Jack's house and blew out a deep breath, pleased to get his car back in one piece. I'd told him I'd post his keys through the letterbox, but I really wanted to tell him what had happened, talk it through with someone, not just be left with my own thoughts rattling around my head. I got out of the car and looked up at the house. The curtains were drawn, but his lounge light was on. I looked at my watch. Nine-thirty. I thought it was later. I wondered if Bob might be there. He had a key. Why hadn't Jack told me about the key? Perhaps staying the night was a regular thing. I walked up the driveway, went to ring the doorbell, stopped and pushed the keys through the letterbox. I walked back down the path, hands in my pockets and headed home.

*

2 a.m. I was sitting at my kitchen table, staring at the framed Jack Nicholson poster on my wall. I'd bought it off eBay for

ten pounds and then paid two hundred pounds to get it professionally framed. It was a cinema promotion for the film *As Good As It Gets*, depicting a beaming Jack holding up Verdell, a Brussels Griffon dog, looking lovingly into each other's faces.

I wondered what Jo-Jo was doing. I'd kissed her. One soft, gentle kiss. Not long. I was conscious of not lingering. That would have been inappropriate. It was our first kiss in over thirty years. She'd closed her eyes. I'd kept mine open. There was no clumsiness. Muscle memory. Our lips remembered how we fitted. That's what it felt like.

I replayed the meal over and over in my head. I remembered sweating and shaking a lot, but it seemed to finish okay. She was pleased I'd remembered the boots. She'd blushed when I'd mentioned them. The Jo-Jo I knew never blushed. That was always my job. Vegetarian. How could you go from adoring a blood steak to eating green salad and, hang on a minute, fish? I smiled. That sounded like a rule bender to me. I made a mental note to say that when I next saw her. We hadn't agreed a next time. She'd said she was going away. That's what the kiss was. A goodbye kiss.

I picked up the phone.

'What time is it?'

'I need to talk to you.'

'It's two in the morning.'

'I know. I was going to knock the door when I brought the car back, but I didn't want to disturb you.'

'So you thought you'd wait until two in the morning?'

'No. It's just… I've been thinking and… are you on your own?'

'What?'

'I thought Bob might be there.'

'We really need to sort out that head of yours, Freddie.'

'Can I come round?'

*

3.15 a.m. I was back in Jack's lounge. He'd laid out the coffee before I arrived and greeted me with a 'this had better be good', when he opened the front door. That put me on edge. I didn't really know what I was going to talk to him about. I told him about the meal, about the kiss. It all sounded a bit "so what?" when I said it out loud.

There was a noise from the bedroom.

'It's the cat jumping off the bed, Freddie. He's wondering what everyone's doing awake in the middle of the night.'

'Sorry,' I said.

'What am I going to do with you?' he said, giving me a sad face look.

'I know. It's just, well, I needed to say it and you were the only one I could wake up at this hour.'

He laughed. 'I'm going to take that as a compliment.'

'Seriously, Jack, what should I do?'

'What do you want to do?'

'I don't know. She's leaving.'

'Maybe.'

'Her daughter's sorting everything out.'

He stood up, walked over to the lounge window and drew the curtains slightly to look out at the road. 'You'd better not have scratched the car,' he said.

'It's fine. You never told me how the wipers worked.'

'You can borrow it tomorrow if you want. I'm going to see Terry with Bob.' He turned and faced me. 'You need to tell her how you feel, Freddie.'

*

2.30 p.m. I pulled into the hotel car park, this time parking the Mini in one of the visitors' spaces. The security guard was still standing by the bins, watching me with his arms folded. I wondered if he'd been home or if he lived at the hotel. He was looking at me as though I was casing the place for a robbery. I was half-tempted to give him the finger, but I decided against it.

I'd napped on Jack's sofa, not able to face the anxiety of going back to my house, which meant I'd had to face it all this morning when I went home to feed the cats. I'd phoned Jo-Jo from Jack's and said I wanted to see her, talk to her. She'd sounded surprised, asked what it was about, said yes, of course, come over to the hotel at three. I gave a vague answer to the 'what is it about' question, said I needed to ask her something, but I didn't want to do it over the phone. Ask her what? It was okay Jack saying tell her how you feel, nodding, smiling encouragement all the way through the call, but all I really knew was I didn't want her to go. I wanted to keep her in my life. Perhaps that's what I should say, see how she reacted. She'd have to let me down gently, say her family were waiting for her in New Zealand. I hadn't exactly blown her away with my performance at the meal, but she had kissed me. Jack was right. I needed to try.

A woman walked out of the hotel exit, down the steps to the car park. She had bob-cut auburn hair and was wearing a light-tan leather bomber jacket, tight-fitting black cord trousers and a pair of sunflower-yellow pixie boots. She said something to the security guard, who nodded, and then she walked with confident strides across the car park towards the visitors' spaces. I looked each side of me, trying to guess which car she was heading for.

She opened the passenger door of Jack's Mini. 'Are you Freddie?' she said.

'Yes, but how...'

'I'm Amy,' she said. 'I think you're here to see my mother.'

She climbed into the passenger seat, shut the door, turned towards me and held out her hand. I stared at her nose freckles. She was still holding out her hand. 'Amy,' she repeated.

'I don't understand,' I said. 'I thought you lived in New Zealand.'

'I do. I've come to take Mum back with me. She told me you were coming, that she'd seen you last night. I've been waiting for you.'

I looked at the security guard.

'Mum doesn't know I'm here.'

'Right,' I said.

'I want to know what you're going to say to her. She said you'd phoned, that you had something to ask her.'

'That's between me and your mum,' I said.

'I don't want her upset. She's vulnerable.'

I looked at her. The daughter. The life without me. I couldn't imagine Jo-Jo vulnerable, but I did recognise this spit in your eye, bold as brass young woman as her daughter. 'You're so like your mum,' I said.

'What do you know about my mum?'

'Everything,' I said. 'And nothing. I probably don't know very much at all now, but I used to know everything.'

'Oh my God,' she said. 'You still love her.'

I looked out of the window. Neither of us said a word for a few minutes. I was listening to the birdsong from the surrounding wood, watching the still-vigilant security guard. Amy reached out and gently flicked Mickey Mouse, making him bounce against the air vent. 'He's nice,' she said.

'I need to go,' I said, looking at the clock on the dashboard. 'I told your mum I'd be there at three.'

'What are you going to say?'

'I don't know.'

'You do love her though? Don't bother answering. I can tell. I don't understand how you can still love someone after thirty-five years of not seeing them.'

'That's because you're young,' I said.

'You're not mentally ill, are you?'

I laughed. 'Maybe. What about you?'

'Mum said you have a daughter, but you don't see her.'

97

'That's none of your business.'

'I think it is if you're going to waltz into my life and take my mum away.'

'Take your mum away... Amy, we had dinner, most of which I spent sweating, stumbling over my words and trying to decide which fork to use. I'm here to say something I should have said years ago. I'll be lucky if your mum lets me finish the sentence before she sends me packing.'

'She won't send you packing.'

'Oh, I think she will. And she should. I've nothing to offer. I've never had anything to offer her.'

'She won't send you packing,' she said again.

This time I heard the certainty in her voice.

'Has your mum said something?'

'She doesn't need to say anything. When I ask about you she looks like you look when I ask about her. It's a bit nauseating actually.'

'No. You've got that wrong.'

'I thought you were going?' she said.

*

Amy left the car first, walked down the drive towards the main road, probably getting out of the way, not wanting to risk bumping into her mum in the reception area. I felt my heart rate increase, this time with excitement not anxiety, as it fought against the sedative effects of the beta blockers. Maybe I wasn't such a lost cause. 'Carpe diem, Freddie,' Jack had said as I left his house. I told myself to calm down. Amy had said what she thought her mum was feeling. Nothing more. And even if Jo-Jo had feelings for me, it didn't mean she wanted me in her life. It was something though. That and the kiss. It was something.

After Freddie had left the restaurant, I realised I'd forgotten to ask him why he hadn't phoned all those years ago. Ancient history, history that should have been forgotten, but I still wanted to know the answer. And now he wanted to ask me something. I looked at my watch. He'd be here soon. Knowing Freddie and his obsession for organisation, he was probably here already. I went over to the window in the reception area, my eyes scanning the car park for Jack's Mini. I spotted the car. The passenger door opened and Amy got out. She walked down the driveway. I could see Freddie still sitting in the driver's seat.

I walked, half-ran, outside and headed towards the car.

Freddie was walking towards me. 'Jo-Jo,' he said.

'Was that Amy in your car?' I said.

He looked back down the drive. 'I think she wanted to vet me before we met up again.'

'How did she know you?'

He nodded towards the security guard. 'I think Clouseau helped. He saw me last night. Did you tell her we were meeting today?'

'Damn cheek,' I said, looking at the security guard. 'I've a good mind to report him.'

'I don't think he meant any harm.'

'I'm cross with Amy too.'

'She asked me what my intentions were.'

I laughed. 'Your intentions? I don't think my dad ever asked you that question.'

'Thank God for that,' he said. 'Perhaps he should have. It might have woken me up a bit.' He held out his hand. 'Shall we go for a walk?'

Something had happened to him since last night. I held his arm and we walked across to the hotel gardens. We sat down on one of the benches underneath a eucalyptus tree, the smell reminding me of the Olbas Oil Dad used to put on our pillows if we had blocked noses and couldn't sleep.

'She's a romantic, your daughter.'

'She can get carried away,' I said.

'She reminds me of you.'

'Amy? She's nothing like me.'

'She's got your nose freckles.'

I reached up and touched my nose. I wondered where this was heading, what he was going to say next. I felt a roll of anxiety in my stomach. What had Amy said to him?

'Do you remember when we met?' he said. 'That dance. I always wondered why you asked me.'

'It's a good job I did. I'd still be waiting for you to ask me.'

'You were way out of my league, Jo-Jo.'

'You should believe in yourself more.'

'You sound like Jack.'

'And that makes Jack and me right.'

'I've missed you, Jo-Jo. All those years. I've never stopped thinking about you.'

'We were kids, Freddie. Things at that age matter more, stay with you longer.'

'I don't want you to go,' he said, blurting it out as though it was something he'd had wedged in his throat for decades. 'I don't want to lose you again.'

And there it was. We were back in my room, on my bed, lying underneath my Starsky and Hutch poster, Freddie asking me not to go, me not giving in, resisting his sulks, his emotional blackmail. I had ambition, hope and the rest of my life in front of me. I wanted to do something. Nothing was going to get in my way. He promised to phone. He was meant to phone.

Patrick Donovan, it said on the name badge hanging from the interior mirror of the black cab. 'You're my last fare,' he said. 'Be glad to get home and put me feet up. I've got a can of Guinness cooling in the fridge.' I told him the name of the road. 'Moor Park.' He told me about his family, his teenage daughters, what a handful they were. 'I bet you're the same. Giving your dad the run-around, driving him crazy.' I didn't answer. He stopped talking.

Twenty minutes later, he turned the taxi into a tree-lined avenue of 1950s council houses. 'Here we are, love, Moor Park. Worth a fortune, these. Where do you want me to stop?'

'Just here on the right.'

'What's this place then?'

He peered through the windscreen and read aloud the name inscribed on the stilt-mounted wooden sign at the front of the building: 'Faith Hill Clinic.' I watched him as he read, waiting for the realisation to dawn. His face crumpled. I could sense he was cursing himself for not realising. All that talk about his family, his children. He turned and faced me. 'You okay, love?' he said. 'Are you on your own?'

'I'm fine. How much do I owe you?'

'Sixteen eighty,' he said.

I handed him a twenty-pound note. 'Keep the change,' I said.

'You look after yourself, love.'

I climbed out of the taxi, clutching my mum's carpet bag, and walked up the gravel driveway. I took a deep breath and told myself again it was the right decision. I had the rest of my life to think about. I could feel the taxi driver watching me. I imagined him trying to guess my age, comparing me with his kids, hoping and praying they would never have to go anywhere near a place like this, not now, not ever. Maybe he would give them an extra hug when he got home.

A smiling receptionist, heavily made-up face, bright red lipstick, hair tied up in a bun. Waiting room. Cold blue plastic seats, contraception posters, coffee table magazines, *Woman's Own*, *Woman's Weekly*, *Woman's Realm*. Three other women. No one speaking. No one reading. Everyone staring straight ahead. Pale faces. Scared eyes. Form filling. Questions. Father's name. Unknown. Dry mouth. A sip of water.

More waiting.

The gown, the bed, the paper sheet. The doctor, the only man, looking down at me, softly spoken, Welsh accent, thin-rimmed spectacles precariously perched on the edge of his nose. Poke, prod, scratch. Counting down from ten, nine, eight, seven.

Darkness.

I could hear someone crying.

Wake up.

Pain. Painkillers. A cup of sweet tea. Leaflets. Counselling. Contraception.

Another taxi. Street lights. Stale tobacco smell. Traffic noise. Throwing up.

More crying.

Jo-Jo – A Memory

I'm six. Dad has bought a bright red swing from Woolworths and set it up in the centre of his newly laid lawn. I watch as Josh pokes a bamboo cane into the rhubarb patch, trying to annoy the wasps. 'All done,' shouts Dad. 'Who wants first go?'

'Me,' I shout, running over to the swing and jumping on the seat.

'That's not fair,' says Josh, throwing his stick up the garden. 'You're too old for swings.'

'You'll both get a turn,' says Dad. 'Hold on tight, young lady.'

He pushes me gently at first and then with more and more force.

'Higher,' I shout, the wind rushing against my face. 'I want to go higher.' I close my eyes and squeal louder and louder and louder. 'Higher. Higher. Higher.'

Dad runs to the front of the swing. He claps his hands and holds out his arms. 'Jump,' he says as I head skywards.

'I can't. I can't.'

He claps his hands again. 'Jump, my darling. Jump. I'll catch you. I promise I'll catch you.'

I shake my head and laugh as the swing goes back up.

'Jump,' he says again as the swing heads back towards him.

I let go. Two seconds flying through the air. He catches me, squeezes me close and slides me slowly to the floor. He kisses my forehead. 'Well done,' he says. 'My big, brave girl.'

'That was great, Dad. Can we do it again?'

'Of course we can.'

'My turn,' says Josh.

'Okay,' says Dad, ruffling Josh's hair. 'Let me check on your mum first.'

I look at Josh, who is looking at the floor. 'Come on,' I say. 'I'll push you until Dad gets back.'

Freddie – November 1980

7.30 a.m. We ran along platform two at Walsall railway station, drizzling rain and fog soaking into my bones. I'd forgotten my gloves and I could feel the ends of my fingers going numb.

We jumped onto the train. A whistle sounded and we hurried along the corridor, looking for an empty compartment. 'Here's one,' said Jack, dragging me inside.

Our black Adidas sports bags landed with a thud in the overhead luggage shelf and we dropped into the blue velour-covered seats, Jack sitting down diagonally opposite me and putting his feet up on the vacant seat at my side. I put my feet up on the seat next to him and flopped my head back, staring up at the white plastic ceiling. The train moved slowly out of the station. 'That was close,' said Jack. 'How come you were late?'

'I had to sort Mum's breakfast. You know what she's like.'

'Is she okay?'

'She'll be fine. We'll be back tomorrow.'

'I'll go round if you want to stay.'

I closed my eyes.

De-dum… de-dum… de-dum… de-dum.

The speed of the train increased.

De-dum… de-dum… de-dum… de-dum.

I felt Jack pat my leg and I opened my eyes. He was leaning forward in his seat. I sat up, dropping my legs to the floor. 'I was awake all night,' I said.

'I told you to phone.'

'I want it to be a surprise.'

'It'll be that all right. She's been up there a month and you've not even called.'

'I know. I needed to sort my head out.'

He smiled and patted my leg again. 'It'll be fine. Tell her it was the shock of her leaving.'

'I will. As soon as I see her.'

'You've got the address?'

I patted the pocket of my denim jacket. 'Thanks for coming with me, Jack. I need the moral support.'

'No problem. That's my job. What else was I going to do on a wet November day?'

A train sped past in the opposite direction.

'What's the plan when we get there?

I shrugged. 'Jump in a taxi, I suppose.'

He put his feet back up on the chair. 'I hope she's there,' he said. 'I'll wait for you at the station, grab a coffee or something. If you're not back in an hour I'm coming home.'

*

We walked into the greasy spoon opposite Lincoln station. It felt like we'd undulated our way across every inch of every one-horse town en route. Jack ordered a full English and a mug of tea. 'Extra black pudding,' he said to the pot-bellied, lank-haired man behind the counter. 'And he's paying.'

The tables were covered in fruit-patterned, wipe-easy tablecloths. We sat down at one near the window. Jack picked up a plastic tomato and squished red sauce all over his breakfast. 'Are you not having anything to eat?' he said.

'I can't. I need to get this over with.'

I left him to his double fried eggs, sausage, bacon, fried bread and extra black pudding and walked across the road to the taxi rank, climbing into the back of the first black cab. 'Dimbles Lane,' I said.

'Long road that, mate. You got a number.'

'Eighteen. How far is it?'

'Fifteen minutes.'

I settled back in the seat. The driver pulled his interior window across, not interested in any more chat, which I welcomed. I needed to get my head straight, think through what I was going to say. I asked myself again why I'd made it so complicated. We'd sorted it out. She'd sorted it out. I'd go up the following weekend and help her settle in. That's what we'd agreed. But I was never going to go. I'd closed her down in my head. She needed to move on. We'd done our time. It was Jack who changed my mind.

'Where are you going to meet someone else like her, Freddie?'

'That's the point. I'm punching above my weight. She'll realise that sooner or later.'

'Only one problem with that theory, dickhead. She seems to want you to stick around. God knows why. I'd have dropped you after that first dance.'

It took me two weeks of pondering, lying in bed for most of the day, thinking it through. Jack was right. Blackpool. Max's. Chatting. Laughing. Kissing. Making love. We fitted. But she'd still left me. Had she? "I have to do this, Freddie. It's only Lincoln. Come and help me settle in."

'Okay. I'll go and see her, but I want it to be a surprise.'

'Why?'

'I just do. I want to see how she reacts.'

'Jesus, Freddie. You can be such hard work.'

'Will you come with me?'

'I'm not talking to her for you. You can sort that yourself.'

The taxi came to a stop. 'Dimbles Lane, mate,' said the driver. 'I think eighteen's in there.'

I looked out of the window at the only block of three-storey flats. It was completely out of place in the long row of 1950s steel-framed houses, which were all painted buttercup yellow. It started to rain. 'Three fifty,' said the driver, clearly anxious to get on with his next fare.

I reached into the pocket of my jeans, mentally keeping a tab on how much this trip had cost me so far: Jack's train fare, his breakfast, the taxi.

The front door of the flats swung open and I heard Jo-Jo laugh.

She stepped out through the open door and opened up a pink umbrella. It was only spotting with rain, but she wouldn't have wanted to get her hair wet. A man walked out behind her, wearing a bowler hat, a full-length Crombie coat and red Doc Martens. He said something to Jo-Jo. She tapped him playfully on the back and then carried on wrestling the umbrella open. The man offered his arm, which Jo-Jo accepted, and they turned right, walking away from the cab – arm in arm, chatting, laughing.

'You okay, mate?'

'Yeah. I'm fine. I've changed my mind. Can you take me back to the station?'

Jo-Jo – September 1980

'What's with the hat?'

Shelley-man shrugged. 'It's a look,' he said, lifting up his right foot and tapping his red Doc Marten. 'And it goes with the boots.'

I laughed.

'Liam,' he said, holding out his hand.

'Jo-Jo,' I said.

'So, Jo-Jo, tell me what brings you on this coach.'

Liam. My university best friend, protector, counsellor and mentor. Sixteen years older than me, he used to work nights as a mortuary attendant, sitting with the dead, collecting them from the wards, helping put their organs back in the body, sewing up the carcass after the post mortem. One night, his radio came on all by itself. 'Three o'clock in the morning,' he said. 'I decided it was time to get out.' We sat next to each other in seminars and lectures, spent our time chatting about nothing and everything in the local pub over pints of Mackeson and Vimto, swopped books by Chekhov and Turgenev, which we read drinking vodka shots into the early hours of the morning, wallowing away long weekends in the company of princesses, duelling counts and innocent first love. We once spent a rainy Sunday reading Edith Wharton's *Ethan Frome*, him finishing first, lying on a battered leather sofa, pulling his bowler hat over his eyes and grinning at me as I worked my way through the last few chapters. 'Don't tell me,' I said, racing to the conclusion. 'I wouldn't dare,' he said, lifting up his hat and watching me closely, joy smothering his face as I gasped at the tragic ending.

I told him all about Freddie five minutes into the coach journey.

'You'll meet him next week,' I said. 'He's coming to visit.'

'Shame he couldn't help you settle in though.'

'Yes,' I said, looking out of the window.

Jo-Jo – December 1980

8 p.m. My second taxi of the day pulled up outside the block of flats, a mile from the university. Liam had rented a two-bedroom flat rather than stay on campus and had asked me to share with him. 'I'm not interested in a relationship, Liam.' 'Don't flatter yourself. I just need someone to share the rent.'

I pushed open the rear door of the black cab and vomited into the gutter.

'Shall I get someone?' said the driver, not moving out of his seat.

'How much?' I spluttered.

'What?'

'The fare. How much do I owe you?'

I thrust a twenty-pound note into his hand, grabbed my carpet bag, which I'd clutched tight the whole journey, and looked up at the second floor of the flats. The after-effects of the anaesthetic were blurring my vision, but through the haze of the December evening I could see there were no lights on. Good. Liam was out.

I tried to stand, but my right foot slid on the greasy pavement. I grabbed the door to steady myself. I heard the driver sigh.

He'd obviously looked at me, my age and decided I was drunk. I should have stayed overnight; they'd insisted I stay, but I'd told them I'd be fine. Yes, there was someone at home to look after me. Three hours they'd made me wait. I'd have sprinted out of the operating theatre door to get away, leave it all behind. I tried to stand again. The painkillers were wearing off. If I could only get up to the flat, get into bed.

'Jo-Jo.'

Liam ran up to the cab. 'What's wrong?' he said, grabbing my arm.

I dropped back down on the seat. 'I'm okay. Just get me in the flat.'

He grabbed my bag, threw it over his shoulder. 'Come on,' he said, putting his arm around my waist and helping me to my feet. He looked inside the cab at the driver. 'Prick,' he said.

'Nothing to do with me, mate. She should learn to hold her drink.'

'Please,' I said. 'Just get me inside.'

Jo-Jo's Dream

I throw the knife onto the draining board, drips of blood splash into the potato water.

'Are you okay?'

'I'm fine.'

'Let me see.'

'It's nothing,' I say, sucking the end of my finger.

'I want to meet him.'

'That's never going to happen.'

'How long?'

'Jason, please, I've told you everything.'

'How long were you seeing him?'

Silence.

'We'll go today.'

'It's over. I'm not going.'

I'm in the Mazda, outside the house, rain bouncing off the car roof. I turn towards the passenger seat. 'I was coming back to you. Why don't you believe me?'

'Was he better than me?'

Silence.

'I said…'

'I heard you.'

'Then why aren't you answering me?'

'Please can we go home?'

'I want to see him.'

'Why are you making me do this?'

'You know why.'

Silence.

I open the car door, step out into the storm, pull the hoodless anorak tight and crunch up the gravel path. The security light responds to my presence. I reach the front door and hesitate.

'Ring it. Ring it now.'

I press the bell, rain dripping off my face.

The house stays in darkness.

I press the bell again.

The hallway light comes on. My stomach drops. The door opens.

'Good God, Jo-Jo, you're soaked…'

'It's Jason,' I say.

'Jason?'

'He's here, Freddie.'

'Come inside, sweetheart. You'll catch your death.'

'You mustn't touch me. He's watching. Tell him. Please tell him.'

He pulls me close, kisses the top of my head. 'Jason's dead, sweetheart.'

I push him away. 'Don't say that. You must tell him.'

'I don't understand.'

'That I was going back to him. The night he died. The car crash.'

He hugs me, no resistance this time. 'You were never going back, my darling. It was over. Let's get you some dry clothes.'

'No,' I say, looking back at the empty car. 'That's not true.'

Jo-Jo – December 1980

I was sitting on the bed waiting for Liam to come back.

'Here,' he said, rushing into the room, a glass of water in one hand and a washing-up bowl in the other.

I took the glass, unzipped the side pocket of my carpet bag and fetched out a foil sachet. I popped two of the tramadol tablets clear of the foil, put them in my mouth, took a sip of water and swallowed. Liam was watching me. He was still holding the bowl. 'I don't think I need that now,' I said.

He put it on the floor next to the bed. 'Just in case,' he said, sitting down next to me and taking my hand. 'You going to tell me what's going on?'

'Not now. I need to sleep.'

'I only went out for a bottle of wine.'

'I'll stick with the morphine, if that's okay with you.'

He looked at the sachet. 'Jo-Jo,' he said.

'I'm fine, Liam. I just need to rest.'

His kindness over the days and weeks following my visit to that place cemented the foundation for our friendship. I worried about him being Irish, waited for some sermon on the rights and wrongs, but if he thought it, he didn't let it show. He served me breakfast in bed, two boiled eggs with bread and butter soldiers and a pot of tea. 'I'll get us a chicken for tonight,' he said. 'Mother always swore by a roast dinner to get you back on your feet.'

'I'm not six, Liam.'

'Course you're not,' he said, patting my leg. 'What vegetables do you want?'

Jo-Jo – January 1981

Liam and I had arranged to meet at the Three Chimneys pub, which was up the hill on the edge of the market, away from the centre of town and the regular student haunts. I was a bit early and, rather than walk inside on my own, I waited for him in a shop doorway. It was Mum's fault. Always let the man lead, she'd say, which was okay for her because she had Dad.

Liam appeared, swaggering his way through the empty square, his Crombie coat smacking against his legs, his closed umbrella held aloft in salute.

I looked around the empty stalls.

Two workmen, who had been sweeping up the discarded fish and chip wrappings, pizza boxes and crunched up Coca-Cola tins, were now leaning on their brooms and staring. Further along the pavement, a man and woman out walking their jack russell shook their heads and whispered something to each other.

Liam reached me. We hugged. 'Why didn't you wait inside?' he said.

I shrugged.

'It's not because you're a girl, surely?'

'No,' I said, hitting him on the arm.

He pushed the door and held it open, gesturing for me to walk across the threshold. 'Then lead the way. The first round's on you.'

I walked over the sticky blue carpet towards the bar, feeling every lift of my trainers as they sucked away from the nylon fibre. 10cc's 'Dreadlock Holiday' was playing on the jukebox, Liam was walking two paces behind me. I sat down on one of the worn leather stools and looked around, wondering why I'd chosen this sink pit of a pub. The place was empty apart from a man leaning against the far wall. He was picking at his fingernails, greasy hair matted to his scalp, a food-stained Led Zeppelin tee-shirt not quite covering his stomach paunch. My eyes fell on the line of black pubic hair poking out through the top of his tracksuit bottoms. I quickly looked away.

A smiling barmaid walked out from the back room. 'What can I get you?' she said, furrowing her brow and glaring at Liam.

I ordered a pint of lager and blackcurrant.

'Ah, my friend chooses a fine beverage,' said Liam, standing at my side. 'I'll have the same.'

The barmaid pulled the pints, all the time giving Liam a hard stare. 'Is he always like that?' she said.

I nodded, which prompted Liam to reach into his wallet and, as though he were a magician revealing shiny items from a top hat, he theatrically pulled out two one-pound notes and waved them in the barmaid's face. 'Keep the change,' he said, winking at her.

She took the money without a word and disappeared into the sanctuary of her snug.

'She thinks you're mad,' I said.

'Good,' he said. 'How tedious to be thought of as sane. Shall we move to a table?'

I took a sip of beer and we walked over to a small round table by the window. I could see the workmen still sweeping the streets. We sat down; the table rocked. I tore a beer mat in half and placed it under one of the legs. I could feel Liam watching

113

me. He kept touching the top of his nose stud. 'You okay?' he said.

'No,' I said. 'I miss him.'

Jo-Jo – April 1981

I went to a house party being thrown by someone in Liam's poetry circle. After about half an hour of smiling and pretending to socialise, I noticed a man about Liam's age sitting in a leather Sherlock chair, reading the *Guardian*. He wore a tweed suit and had hooded eyelids that reminded me of an eagle I'd seen at the zoo on a day trip with Dad. 'Night Boat to Cairo' by Madness was blasting out of the stereo and congaing students with glasses of Bacardi and Coke in hand were circling his chair. One of the lads flicked the newspaper and shouted, 'Come on, Professor. Let's see what you've got.'

'Who's that?' I said to Liam.

'He's one of the seminar tutors. He's a bit of an oddball.'

'Says the man in the bowler hat.'

'Touché,' he said, giving a full-length bow.

'He looks sad.'

'Sad? Not really thought about it.'

I looked around the room. 'Who's he here with?'

'No one,' said Liam, smiling. 'You really are a sucker for lost causes.'

'Shoot me. I like to see everyone happy. That's not a crime is it?'

'No. It's sweet. Shall I introduce you?'

Back at the flat, two weeks after Dad's funeral, Liam had cooked us ribeye steaks with mushroom sauce. Dirty pots and pans filled every work surface, which they always did when Liam cooked. His pièce de résistance was tiramisu, which he only ever made as a treat for me. 'It's not right, Jo-Jo. The coffee ruins a good trifle.'

We moved into the lounge, away from the dirty crocks – out of sight, out of mind – me carrying a bottle of Merlot, our second of the night. I'd already filled both our glasses. He stretched out on the cracked brown leather sofa and I dropped into the chair, draping my legs over the arm.

'You never talk about your family, Liam.'

He took a sip of wine. 'This is nice,' he said. 'Did you buy it from the supermarket?'

I shook my head. 'The shop on the estate. He's getting used to us now. Said he doesn't mind stocking it as long as it sells. You changed the subject.'

'It's complicated,' he said.

I'd tried a couple of times to have this conversation, to find out why a man in his mid-thirties had no past. I put his lack of interest in me down to our age difference, but there were plenty of women his age who'd have been interested and he never responded. 'You always say that,' I said.

'Let it go, Jo-Jo. It's private.'

'I thought we were friends.'

'We are… let's change the subject.'

'It's okay if you're gay.'

'Gay?'

'Yeah. It's no big deal these days. It doesn't bother me.'

'I'm not gay, Jo-Jo.'

'Okay. I'm just saying if you were, it wouldn't be a problem.'

He sat up and put his wine glass down on the coffee table. 'You're not going to give up on this, are you?'

'I'd like to know who I'm living with and, if we're friends, you should trust me. I tell you everything.'

He stood up and walked over to the door. 'It's not about trust,' he snapped. His face creased up and he burst into tears.

I rushed over to him and hugged him. 'Oh God, Liam. Ignore me. I'm just drunk and feeling sad about Dad… and I'm a nosy cow.'

He kissed the top of my head. 'You are a nosy cow,' he said.

'Let's forget I mentioned it. Go back to our wine. I'll never ask again.'

He shook his head. 'No. You're right. We're friends and we live together.'

'So what. Private is private. I don't want you upset.'

'I should talk about it, Jo-Jo, but I don't think you'll like me very much after I've told you.'

I stepped back. 'What do you mean?' I said.

He walked back to the sofa, took a gulp of wine and held out his glass. I fetched the Merlot from the side of the chair and filled the glass halfway. He shook it at me. 'Fill it up,' he said. 'I'm going to need it.'

I did as he asked. His hands were shaking, the blood had drained from his face.

I sat back down, filled my glass and looked at him expectantly. 'You're frightening me, Liam. What is it?'

'I'm not exactly the good guy in this story, Jo-Jo. So just let me tell it. No questions. And then we'll see how you feel about me.'

'Okay,' I said. 'If you're sure you want to tell me.'

He took another slurp of Merlot, put his glass down, leaned forward, gripping his hands in a prayer-like pose, the ends of his fingers anaemic, the blood draining away from the tips as he told his story to the carpet.

Married, Jenny, childhood sweethearts, little girl, Rosie, five years of age. And then he met her. The other woman. The cliché. I gulped down a mouthful of Merlot. He looked up at me. 'I know what you're thinking.'

'I'm not thinking anything. I'm listening.'

The lie was obvious. I tried to push away the disapproving look I could feel on my face, tried to smile reassuringly, but it was forced, hard. He looked at the carpet again. I had to say something. 'Who was she?'

'No one.'

'I don't understand.'

'It doesn't matter who she was.'

'You're not making sense, Liam. If she broke up your marriage...'

'My wife and daughter are dead.'

He said the sentence as though he was on speed, the words falling out of his mouth in a lump, a tumour. 'Dead? My God. What happened?'

'I killed them,' he said.

My stomach dropped. It flashed across my mind that I didn't really know him. He was still leaning forward, hands clasped, staring at the floor. I looked towards the lounge door. It was behind the sofa, behind Liam. I looked at him. He was staring at me through tear-filled eyes; his whole face had crumpled in on itself.

'I don't mean literally, but I might as well have done.'

I stood up, walked over to the sofa, sat down and put my arm around him. 'Just tell me what happened.'

He looked at the carpet again. 'I was with her. Some run-down hotel that lets you book rooms by the day. We'd used it a couple of times before. Jenny followed me. I thought we'd been careful.'

'Your wife came to the hotel?'

'Came up to the room. I opened the door in a dressing gown. She had Rosie in her arms. Never said a word. Looked at me, looked at the crumpled double bed and just walked off down the corridor.'

'What did you do?'

'I went after her, but she was like a zombie, staring straight through me. Rosie was crying. Everyone was staring at us in the reception area. I asked her to wait while I got dressed, but she strapped Rosie in her seat, got in her car and drove off.'

He stopped talking. I hugged him closer, waiting for him to carry on, dreading what was coming next. 'I never saw them again,' he said. 'Not alive.'

He finished the story quickly, taking big gulps of air to help him through. Jenny's car ploughed into a combine harvester about a mile away from the hotel. She'd just overtaken a cyclist along a narrow country lane. The cyclist escaped with minor injuries; the driver of the combine harvester was treated for shock. Jenny and Rosie died instantaneously.

'She never drove like that. It was me. I killed them.'

I hugged him to me. I couldn't think of anything to say.

Jo-Jo's Dream

A prism of white light falls into the bedroom, hanging from the ceiling like a stalactite about four foot away from me. Something moves inside the frosty veneer.

'What is that?'

'It's your audience.'

I stare hard. Dad's woman stares back through the white light, but it's a three foot puppet version secured to the sides of the prism, strings attached to each of her limbs, pulling her arms and legs up and down in a slow dance, a ghostly waltz. I reach out a hand.

'She can't hear or see you.'

'But what's she doing here?'

'She needs your forgiveness to set her free.'

'She'll be dancing a long time before I forgive her.'

Freddie – August 1981

I bumped into Alison in the Telford shopping centre. I saw her walking out of Boots as I was heading towards HMV. I dropped my eyes, but it was too late. 'Freddie,' she shouted. I smiled and she came over. I looked behind her, expecting to see Ted. 'Hi,' I said. 'Fancy seeing you here.'

'I'm with my mum,' she said. 'This is the only town round here with a Debenhams. Where's Jo-Jo?'

'University. She's in Lincoln.'

'That must be hard.'

'We split up. I miss her.'

'You must,' she said, touching my arm and dropping her bottom lip. 'You seemed so close.'

I realised it was the first time I'd said I missed Jo-Jo out loud. I'd refused to talk to Jack about it since we'd come back from Lincoln and had spent most of the year staring at the Artex swirls on my bedroom ceiling, thinking about what she might be doing, the guy I'd seen her with, trying to convince myself it was no big deal, people split up all the time. All I needed to do was move on with my life. But I hadn't. I'd stayed with her in my head, spooling the memories over and over and over, and now it was all on the verge of pouring out... to Aran-wool-cardigan Alison... here in the town centre. 'Where's Ted?' I said, trying desperately to change the subject.

'We split up as well,' she said.

Alison and I saw each other for about two months, me talking about Jo-Jo, her telling me about Ted. It felt like a healing, cathartic process for us both, interrupted by occasional bouts of tension-relieving sex. When we'd finished talking about loss, when the grieving had come to an end, the relationship fizzled out like flat pop. She stopped calling. I stopped calling. The next thing I knew six months had gone by and we hadn't spoken. Alison got me away from the Artex, and I went back to Max's with Jack.

Freddie – May 1985

I started working nights in one of the local care homes. One of the staff had left to have a baby and I got the job. 'It'll be good to have a man,' said Matron. 'Someone to change the light bulbs.'

Most of the care staff were middle-aged women, but I was paired with Lorraine because she was closer to my age, only ten years older than me. She had tightly cropped, bleached blonde hair and olive skin, which I found out later was a gene present from a Maltese great-grandfather. Her red dress uniform fascinated me, with its purple press studs running down its full length. She wore it just above her knee, leaving the last two studs unfastened. One night, about two in the morning, the home was graveyard quiet and we made a cup of coffee, pulled a couple of lounge chairs together and sat with our feet up, listening out for any call bells or Matron sneaking up from the sleeping-in room to try and catch us asleep. Lorraine caught me staring at her legs. 'You see anything you want?' she said. I lowered my eyes, my cheeks on fire. She stood up and turned my head back towards her. 'Ask me?' she said.

'Ask you what?'

She reached out and guided my hands to the hem of her uniform. 'Open it,' she said.

I gently pulled and two of the studs popped open. I could see the top of her stockings and the start of bare flesh.

'Open the rest, Freddie,' she said.

We had sex every night we worked a shift together, usually in one of the empty rooms, lying down on the unmade bed in the cocoon of the home, neither of us saying a word, her dress open, my shirt unfastened, our bare flesh making forbidden contact. Her cold marriage made her cry. 'He's a pig and he's not shy of giving me a back-hander.' I kissed her tears, told her over and over I'd look after her, it would all be okay. I had no idea what that meant, but it seemed like the right thing to say. The Commodores' 'Night Shift' became our song. We never saw each other outside of work.

And then she told me she was pregnant.

'It can't be his. He never touches me.'

Freddie – October 1985

Lorraine. The Lost City girl. She'd learned to swim in the canal, had cousins who were roaming gypsies, and she could ride a horse bareback by the time she was ten. Everyone owned a horse. They were tethered on every spare patch of grass. People rode them to the White Swan, the estate pub, and tied them to the wooden pole outside. Pony and trap races were commonplace down the main street, crowds gathering to place their bets.

She told her husband, Keith, about us and, fuelled by Johnny Walker, he walked up to the home in the middle of the night and backheeled his Doc Martens into each of the door panels of my Ford Fiesta. It had taken me months of working overtime to save for that car. The police arrested him, kept him in a cell overnight. 'You're welcome to her,' he shouted at me as I arrived for work one evening.

'He doesn't love me,' said Lorraine. 'I think the pregnancy's upset him.'

Keith told everyone. 'God knows who was looking after the residents while they were at it,' he said. Matron called us into the office. 'I need to put you on different rotas.' We knew that wouldn't work. She didn't have that many staff. Lorraine shrugged. 'I'll have the kid soon. I can't work then anyway.' I hadn't thought about that.

We found a maisonette for rent and moved in together. Lorraine cooked us a full English breakfast, including black pudding and bubble and squeak, which we covered in brown sauce and ate in bed. We slept until the middle of the afternoon, took a bath together and went back to bed until teatime. I fetched a Chinese takeaway and we watched Miami Vice on a black and white portable television I'd brought with me from my mum's. We went to work at ten o'clock. Straight from affair, to pregnancy, to living together, sleeping with each other every day, working together at night. Five months in, the pregnancy started to show, the morning sickness kicked in and Lorraine went off on maternity leave.

'You're going be a great dad, Freddie.'

Dad. I was seven years old when he left me. I knew what a mum was, but I had no idea about being a dad.

Freddie – A Memory

We're in the delivery room. Lorraine is two weeks overdue and the hospital staff have made the decision to break her waters. 'No epidural, Freddie. I want it to be natural. That's what we deserve.' I nod sagely as though I understand every word. I'm fully gowned up, a paper mask covering my mouth. Lorraine is squeezing my hand tighter and tighter with every contraction. She screams at the nurse for something to take away the pain. The nurse nods and fetches the doctor. Two hours go by and the top of Becky's head enters the world. 'Would Dad like to see?' All eyes face me, everyone's waiting for me to react. Black matted hair, blood and mucous is what I see. I look back at Lorraine. 'It's a baby,' I say, trying to sound proud. The nurse grins. 'Thank God for that,' she says. 'Get ready to cut the cord, Dad.'

Freddie – February 1986

We'd all gathered for visiting time on the second-floor maternity ward at New Cross hospital. Lorraine's bed, the last in a row, overlooked a wood and there was lots of birdsong drifting in through the draughty full-length window. I looked around the bed at my ready-made in-laws.

Doreen. The mum. Black-framed NHS bifocal spectacles perched on the end of her nose, receding ginger hair parted in the centre, thick black tights, laughing at her own jokes, worshipping Black Country food, grey peas, faggots, jellied eels, pig's tails and trotters. 'You can eat anything off a pig.'

Pete. The dad. Elf-like face, false teeth too big for his mouth, beaming out a fixed, slightly unsettling smile, rarely uttering a word, always wearing a paisley cap, even indoors. He rode a bike everywhere, wobbling in the middle of the road on his way home from the pub, occasionally falling off it, finishing up under a hedge or on a front lawn, a phone call to Doreen who'd get one of the boys to go and fetch him home.

Ryan. The youngest brother. Body builder, sweat vest, eagle tattoo on the bicep of his right arm, dealing in scrap metal, a wad of cash held together with an elastic band, peeling off notes like a croupier dealing cards in a game of pontoon, most of his adult life spent with Social Security on his case, father unknown written on the birth certificates of his three kids.

Stuart. The middle one. A red eye patch covering his left eye. Someone fired a pellet into it when he was a kid, making him a nightmare driver, throwing his pick-up around corners, drifting over to the wrong side of the road or up the kerb. He laughed at everything – inappropriate affect the doctors called it – and couldn't sit still, up and down to the window. 'For Christ's sake, sit down, Stu,' snapped Lorraine.

Doreen looked over her glasses at me, pausing as if trying to remember something. 'Freddie,' she said, looking relieved. 'Is your mum not coming?'

'Not tonight.'

She smiled and went back to looking at the baby.

'I saw Keith in the pub last night,' said Ryan.

'Ryan,' said Lorraine, pulling the baby closer to her and nodding at me.

'He doesn't mind. Do you, mate?'

'Of course not. Why should I?'

'Have you thought of a name?' said Doreen.

'I can't decide,' said Lorraine.

'Becky,' said Pete.

We all looked at him.

'Nice name, Becky,' he said.

Freddie – February 1989

I'd attended a care conference in Leeds and had booked to stay in one of the local bed and breakfast places five minutes' walk away from the university campus. I always hoped Lorraine would try and persuade me to drive home from these things, say Becky would miss me, but she never did. 'You should stay. Get to know people.' She was right. She was always right.

I should have called, shouldn't have popped up out of the blue, disrupting her plans, but I wanted to surprise her, and the last session had been cancelled. 'You're too predictable, Freddie.

I know everything you're thinking and doing.' She would never have expected me to drive home, not without calling first.

I turned into the driveway, pulled up behind Lorraine's yellow Mini, which meant she was in, but there were no lights on in the house and all the curtains were drawn. The curtains didn't bother me, but no lights was unusual. Perhaps she'd gone to bed, had one of her migraines. I told myself to be careful, not to wake her, not to wake Becky.

I eased out of the car, crunched my way as softly as I could up the gravel driveway, put my key in the lock, opened the front door and stepped into the house, gently closing the door behind me. I heard the toilet flush, which made me look up the stairs at the bathroom door directly in front of me. The door opened and Keith appeared, wearing nothing but boxer shorts. He looked straight at me. 'Lorraine,' he said. 'Lover boy's back.'

She'd been seeing him for months, taking Becky to stay at her parents. I think she was relieved when I found out. She appeared next to him, still pulling on her dressing gown. 'Freddie,' she said. 'You should have called.'

Jo-Jo – July 2015

Jason used to enjoy his candy time. That's what he called it. Candy time. 'You mean you want to screw me.' 'Don't say that.' 'Why not? It's what you want to do.' Screw was exactly what it was. Him grunting through ten minutes of exertion, racing to his climax, falling on top of me, rolling off me like I was radioactive, no kissing, no tenderness, no cuddling, walking the few steps back to his bed, facing the wall, asking me if I'd come as an afterthought. 'Yes. Thank you.' That annoyed him. Me thanking him in the same voice I used when he'd done the washing up. I'd wipe him away in the toilet, flush him down the drain, go back into the bedroom, put the light on and change the sheet. 'Do you have to do that now?'

And then I'd lie there, listening to his snoring, telling myself it would get better, having a child was going to make it all okay, give me a purpose. I tried to imagine what Mum's life had been like. Schizophrenia, split mind, shattered thoughts, disembodied voices. 'I talk back to them, Jo-Jo. They're like my friends.' 'They're not real, Mum.' 'Of course they are, sweetheart.' The tranquillisers numbed her, sucked her away, turned her into a zombie.

Freddie and I were still sitting on the hotel's garden bench.

'Why didn't you phone me, Freddie?'

'When?'

'When I went to university. You said you'd call, wait for me, and then you didn't.'

He let go of my hand and looked at the ground. 'I thought that was what you wanted. To get on with your new life. It was for the best, Jo-Jo.'

'The best?'

'That's what I thought. Like I said, you were way out of my league.'

'But not to call, not to say goodbye. That was cruel. You just left me.'

'You could have called me,' he said.

'It wasn't that simple. It got complicated.'

'I was going to call when your dad died, but I didn't think you'd want me to.'

'You're right, by then it was too late, but at the beginning... when it really mattered...'

I could feel the adrenaline pumping through my veins, hear my heartbeat in my head. I didn't want to have this conversation. My plan was to see him one last time, make sure he was okay, bury the demons, say goodbye. Closure. Not this. I didn't want to talk about this.

I stood up and walked away from the bench.

'Jo-Jo,' he called.

I stopped walking.

He came to my side. I was crying.

'I'm sorry,' he said. 'But I didn't think you wanted me. I never thought I was good enough for you. If I'd have known.'

'I needed you so much, Freddie.'

He gently lifted my chin and looked into my eyes. 'I love you, Jo-Jo. I've always loved you. Please don't go.'

I touched him on the cheek. 'It's too late, Freddie. We were so good, but you should have called.'

I walked out of the garden. I didn't look back to see if he was following me. I ran up the steps to the hotel entrance and, forcing myself to stop running, walked through the doors into the lobby. The receptionist lifted his head in greeting and then dropped a concerned look on his face when he saw me. 'Are you okay, madam?'

'I'm fine,' I said, without looking at him. 'Just in a hurry.'

I turned back towards the entrance doors, half-expecting to see Freddie walking up the steps, coming to find me. I looked across the car park and spotted him walking towards Jack's Mini with his head bowed, hands in his pockets. He got in the car, started the engine and drove away down the tree-lined hotel exit route.

'Mum.'

Amy was at my side.

'I thought you'd gone for a walk,' I said.

'I changed my mind. I've been waiting for you in the conservatory. Have you been crying? Where is he?'

'He's gone, sweetheart.'

'Gone? What did he say?'

'That he loved me. That he'd always loved me.'

'And?'

'He doesn't want me to go. He wants me to be part of his life.'

127

She threw her arms around me. 'Oh Mum, that's great. And don't worry about New Zealand. We'll sort that out. Maybe you can rent somewhere here for six months or a year. See how it goes with this Freddie. I'll call the estate agents.' She was rubbing my back. I could smell her leather jacket.

'You don't understand, Amy. I need to come with you.'

Freddie – July 2015

Back at my kitchen table, I looked again at the picture of me and Jo-Jo.

Maybe I should have followed her into the hotel, told her about my going to Lincoln, seeing her with the bowler hat man, but all I could think about was that I'd made her cry. What was the point of raking over old ashes? We'd both had lives. She'd been married, had a family. If I could turn the clock back, I'd call, help her settle in, wait for her, but at the time, it felt right. She was moving into a new circle, a circle that I didn't and could never fit. And now she was moving on again, emigrating.

Another photo dropped into my head. A two-year-old girl. Her hair in pigtails, wearing a white dress with a navy blue trim, black leather buckled shoes and short white socks that were pinching her legs. She was smiling. Forty minutes it had taken us to get that smile – forty minutes of treading on eggshells, pulling faces and waving her teddy bear. A year later she was gone, out of my life, a new dad, a new city.

I shook my head and turned the packet of beta blockers over and over in my hand. The kitchen walls were closing in on me, a feeling of nausea dropped into my stomach like a lead weight.

A memory. I look in the rear-view mirror. There's a flash of light. It could have been the sun. I flick the indicator to turn right. 'What are you doing?' 'Turning round. I need to check something.' 'Not this again, Freddie. Becky needs her tea.' I drive back towards the speed camera. There's another one on this side of the road, trapping me in both directions. I check the speedometer. Thirty miles an hour. I feel pressure on my right foot. I want to press harder. *Go faster. Go faster.* 'Can we go home now?' she says, looking at Becky asleep on the back seat. I turn the car around and drive back towards the first camera. The pressure's back on my foot. Another flash of light. It is the sun. Thank God.

It wasn't about thirty-five years ago. It was about now. When I'd said I loved her, didn't want her to go, that's when she'd got upset. Panicked. Didn't know what to say. All she'd wanted was to say goodbye and I'd made it complicated. She'd needed an escape route. That was it.

I dropped my head on the kitchen table and sobbed.

Jo-Jo – July 2015

Amy put her arm around me and walked me quickly across the hotel lobby, up the two flights of stairs and into my bedroom. She shot the receptionist a glare as we walked by. He lowered his head and went back to looking at his computer screen. 'It'll be okay, Mum,' she was whispering over and over as we walked. I was holding a balled-up tissue that I'd found in my handbag. I could feel my head filling up with fluid, ready to gush out if I lost my *"I don't want to cry"* concentration. It crossed my mind that Amy was embarrassed, trying to get me out of sight. Her mother having a breakdown in public was not a good look.

We reached my room. She sat me gently on the bed, walked over to the minibar and pulled out two miniature bottles of Jack

Daniels. She blew the dust out of two tumblers, like they do in the cowboy movies, poured a full bottle of whisky into each glass and thrust one in my hand. 'Drink it,' she said.

'I don't like whisky.'

She put her hand under my glass and nudged it gently towards my mouth. 'It's medicinal, Mum.'

I took a sip of the Jack Daniels and swallowed, wincing a little as it burned the back of my throat.

She nudged the glass again. 'And another.'

I did as I was told, this time taking more of a slurp than a sip. Amy did the same.

'He seems nice, Mum. I think he still loves you.'

'I know, darling. I know.'

She hugged me close. 'One day you're going to tell me the full story. We'll sit in the garden and work our way through a bottle of New Zealand Chardonnay.'

'I'd like that,' I said. 'I'd like that very much.'

Freddie – July 2015

I walked to the station, my head bowed, hugging into my leather jacket, my eyes on the pavement. It was drizzling with rain and the wind was getting up. I quickened my pace. A couple walked past me, but all I saw were their shoes. A bus sloshed by, workmen were drilling the road, surrounded by traffic cones. I reached the station, walked past the ticket operator and looked up at the departures board. I looked at my watch.

I headed for the platform.

'Nasty day,' said an old man huddled on one of the wooden benches. I smiled but said nothing. He scowled at me, muttered, 'Manners,' and went back to his book.

The train came into view.

I removed my Ray-Ban spectacles and put them in my coat pocket.

I stared at the track for a few seconds and then looked again at the old man.

'Freddie.'

It was Jack. He was running towards me.

The train had nearly reached me.

'Freddie,' Jack called again.

Part Two

Dancing in the Dark

Jack punched me on the arm as the train sped past. 'You scared the shit out of me,' he said. 'A text. Is that it? Is that all I get?'

'I didn't know what else to do,' I said.

'You could have phoned me.'

'It felt pointless.'

'It is, Freddie. It is pointless.'

He started walking away from me.

'Jack,' I said.

He stopped walking, turned to face me and held out his hands. 'What? What do you want me to say?'

'I want you to help me. I need you to help me.'

*

An hour later, I was sitting in the Next bucket seat in Jack's lounge, trying to distract myself by singing along in my head to Joan Armatrading's 'More Than One Kind of Love'. It wasn't working – the volume on the Bose sound-dock was so low I couldn't hear the words. I thought about the old man at the railway station and tried to remember the name of his book.

'Are you going to talk to us?' said Jack. 'Or shall we just sit here and stare at you.'

'This isn't really any of my business,' said Bob, standing up. 'I'll leave you to it.'

'No,' I said. 'I'd like you both to stay.'

I looked past them and stared out of the bay window. A sparrow was pulling at the tiny leaves on the tall, thin Cypress tree Jack had planted when he'd first moved in ten years ago. He'd fretted about it ever since, worried that the tree was too close to the house and it would block out the light. The book title dropped into my head. *My Face for the World to See* by

Alfred Hayes. I liked the cover. A girl asleep in bed, her blonde hair flopped over her face, a naked man standing in a doorway staring at her. I hadn't read it.

Bob walked over to my chair, knelt down and hugged me. It felt nice, warming. I could smell his Jean Paul Gaultier aftershave. He pulled away from me and sat down on the floor. 'Tell us what happened,' he said. 'We want to help.'

'She doesn't want me,' I said. 'I told her I wanted her in my life, that I'd always loved her, that I didn't want her to go to New Zealand, but she said it was too late, that I should have called.'

'When?' said Bob.

'When she went to university. She said I'd promised to call and didn't.'

'Did you tell her you went up there?' said Jack. 'That you saw her with that guy?'

'I didn't get the chance. She started to cry and ran into the hotel.'

'And you just got in the car and drove away?'

'I'd upset her. I didn't want to upset her anymore.'

'Hang on a bit,' said Bob. 'All of this is about something that happened when this girl went to university?'

'Yes,' said Jack. 'Freddie fucked up thirty-five years ago and we're still paying the price. I can't believe you just drove away. Why didn't you follow her into the hotel and sort it out?'

'She'd already told me it was too late.'

'Oh, for Christ's sake,' said Jack, standing up and walking over to the window. 'You're doing it again. I can't believe you.'

'Who was this bloke?' said Bob. 'The bloke you saw her with all those years ago.'

'He doesn't know,' said Jack. 'He ran away then as well.'

*

136

Jack had made more coffee, Joan had moved on to 'Drop the Pilot' and Bob was still sitting on the floor next to my chair. He was holding his warm coffee mug against his cheek. My eyes fell on a vase full of daffodils on the oak shelf over the cast-iron log burner. The vase was covered in raised oriental figures in different meditation poses. It was the only ornament in the room. 'That's new,' I said.

'It's mine,' said Bob. 'Mr OCD relented and let me bring a little colour into his life.'

'Must be serious,' I said. 'He gets twitchy if we keep our shoes on.'

'Tell me about it. The smell of bleach is about as aromatic as it gets.'

'When you two have finished,' said Jack. 'We were in the middle of Freddie's psychoanalysis session.'

'I'm not crazy, Jack.'

'Of course not. Jumping under a train is rational behaviour.'

'I wouldn't have jumped.'

'You've always been obsessed with death, Freddie. Remember your ten best ways to commit suicide?'

'That was just kids' stuff.'

'Kids play marbles, hide and seek, run about a lot. Not think about killing themselves.'

'Only in Enid Blyton's world,' said Bob. 'Is that what you were like as a kid?'

'No,' I said. 'He spent most of his time fancying girls. How did that turn out, Jack?'

'We're not talking about me. We're talking about you and your crazy head.'

'So,' said Bob, giving Jack a hard, wide-eyed glare, 'you and this Jo-Jo had a thing when you were kids. Why has she reappeared now?'

'She's emigrating,' I said. 'She wanted to let me know she was going away.'

'But you haven't seen her for over thirty years?'

'No.'

'And she doesn't want to get back with you?'

'That's what she said.'

'You do know that doesn't make sense?'

'I've told him that,' said Jack. 'Why would she do that, Freddie?'

'She's like that. She hates loose ends.'

'You're one hell of a loose end, Freddie,' said Bob. 'Three decades' worth. It can't be that simple.'

'What is it then?' I said.

'We don't know,' said Jack. 'You ran away and went to jump under a train.'

Jo-Jo – July 2015

I'd finished my Jack Daniels, but I was still swirling my empty tumbler and staring at the Lowry picture on the hotel bedroom wall. The toilet in the en suite flushed and I heard the sink tap run for a moment. The door opened and Amy walked back into the bedroom. 'You okay, Mum?' she said, looking down at my glass. 'Do you want another drink?'

'I can't believe I drank the first one,' I said. 'I can't stand whisky.'

'I told you, it's medicinal.'

'I was thinking about New Zealand,' I said. 'Getting everything sorted.'

'That's easy. I'll call Dan. He'll make the arrangements. When do you want to go?'

'You put on that husband of yours too much.'

'He's okay about it. He likes to feel useful.' She came over to the bed and sat down next to me. 'You're thinking about Freddie, aren't you?'

'I can't believe how long that man has stayed in my head,' I said.

'I think he loves you, Mum.'

'But why am I thinking about him so much? He's never been good-looking, his dress sense is appalling, he's unemployable, a bit of a nervous-wreck-car-crash and his best friend's named after a pirate. What's wrong with me?'

'I don't know, Mum. I don't get it either.'

I handed her my empty glass. 'I think I need that drink.'

She took one of the miniature bottles out of the minibar, unscrewed the cap, poured the whisky into the tumbler and handed it to me. I took a gulp. It made me cough. Amy rubbed my back. 'Thank you, sweetheart,' I said. 'I'm glad you're here.'

'Are you sure about New Zealand, Mum, about leaving this Freddie behind?'

Jo-Jo – November 1979

Max's nightclub. Blondie's 'Dreaming' started up. I took a deep breath and walked across the dance floor towards him. I'd noticed him at the bar earlier, pointed him out to my best friend, Karen. 'Him?' she said. 'Why? Look at his hair.'

'Jet-black, gypsy hair. What's your point?'

'He needs it cut, and his front tooth's chipped.'

'He's cute. Look at that smile.'

I'd tried to meet his eyes as he'd walked past us clutching a Bacardi and Coke, but he was looking at the floor. 'There's no way he's going to ask you,' said Karen. 'Not in his wildest dreams would he think that was possible.'

I reached him as Debbie Harry was telling everyone that dreaming is free. His mouth fell open when I asked him to dance. He looked at his mate, stared at me for a few seconds and, just as I was about to turn and walk away, he said yes. We walked under the mirror balls to the dance floor. He made a nervous joke about gangly men and disco dancing. The music changed to Dr Hook, 'More Like the Movies', followed by the Commodores, 'Still' and Exile, 'Kiss You All Over'. I could feel his concentration, his hands barely touching my back, as though he was frightened of the intimacy, of overstepping the mark. I felt like I was made of glass. The lights came up, he waved goodbye to his mate and then walked me home, held my hand all the way, didn't try to kiss me, waited for me to kiss him on the cheek. He watched me walk up my path and into my house, making sure I was safe. Sweet.

I closed the front door behind me and peeped through the rippled pane of glass. He was still standing under the oak tree, looking at the house. After a few seconds, he turned up his jacket collar and walked around the corner. I smiled at the collar. I'd told him it was too cold, not to walk me all the way, but he'd insisted. Lower Farm. He'd have to walk back on himself to get home. I smiled again. Really sweet.

'Is that you, Jo-Jo?'

I popped my head around the lounge door. Dad was standing in front of the fire, hands in his pockets, his empty whisky glass on the hearth shelf. I wanted to go over and get one of his bear hugs, comfort-hugs that had kept me safe all of my life, but his woman in the park two years ago had changed all of that.

'I'm tired, Dad. I'm going to bed.'

'Don't go, come and talk to me.'

'I thought you didn't want to talk.'

'Not about that,' he said. 'But I miss our chats.'

I walked into the room. 'Is Mum okay?'

'She's asleep. Went to bed about nine. I watched Minder. It was good.'

I looked at the empty glass.

'I've only had one,' he said, sitting down in his cottage-suite chair, the one next to the fire, facing the telly. 'Come and sit with your old man for five minutes.'

'I don't know, Dad. I don't want us to fall out anymore.'

'Who's the young man?' he said, nodding at the lounge window.

'Someone I met at the club. Were you watching us?'

'I was waiting for you to come back. I saw you under the tree with him.'

'We didn't do anything.'

'I know. You kissed him on the cheek.'

'Yeah, and then he went home.'

'I didn't mean anything. He seems nice, walking you home, gentlemanly.'

'Unlike you, in the park, snogging your tart's face off.' I spat it at him with all the toxicity I could dredge up from my gut. He crossed his legs, uncrossed them, stood up, turned to the hearth and picked up his empty glass. 'I think I'll have another drink,' he said, walking over to the sideboard.

'Yes,' I said. 'You probably should. I'm off to bed.'

*

I reached the landing and heard a clink of bottles downstairs. I guessed it was the whisky bottle catching on Mum's Courvoisier as Dad lifted it out of the cupboard – her Christmas Day drink that had stayed untouched for four years. I felt guilty for snapping. I looked across at Mum's room. Her door was open, the bedside light was on. I walked over and leaned against the door frame, looking at the lump of her body under the duvet. I could hear her gentle snore, almost a purr. I was pleased she was asleep. I wondered if her voices bothered her dreams. I hoped not – even they must need a break from their constant chitter-chatter. She'd seemed better of late, a stronger prescription dampening her split mind, but she slept most of the time now, real life unnoticed as she lay consumed with the everyday battles going on inside her head. She muttered something and rolled over under the duvet. I could see Dad's bowl of water at the side of the bed and his ever-ready flannel on the bedside cabinet, waiting for him to mop Mum's forehead as he whispered words of comfort when it all became too much. I turned to go back downstairs, but the scar of his woman in the park came back to me. Him leaning his umbrella against the bench, walking, nearly running to meet her, kissing her, holding her, laughing with her. Mum waiting for him at home. I walked into my bedroom and closed the door.

*

Two days later, Karen and I were in the outdoor of the Saddler's Arms. One of the pub's regulars, Ginny, short for Virginia, a Minnie Caldwell lookalike, was sitting at the two-seater table underneath the cigarette machine, sipping her stout and watching us with a knowing grin. She had a tiny little voice that you struggled to hear, but a dirty titter that gave you the impression she'd lived a life. She'd bought us a drink a couple of times, always a made-up snowball – a mixture of Warninks Advocaat, soda water and lime juice, finished off with a glazed cherry on a stick. 'I bet you girls have the boys drooling.' I'd told her about Freddie, our nervy dance at Max's, him walking me home. 'Sounds like a catch, dear. You'd best keep him. They don't grow on trees.'

I picked up the payphone receiver.

'Go on then,' said Karen.

'What if he's not there?'

'You can phone him back.'

'His mum might answer.'

'So? Leave him a message.'

'I should have given him my number, got him to call me.'

'But you didn't. I don't know why you want to call him. He didn't do it for me.'

'There's something about him. Something sweet.'

'For Christ's sake, Jo-Jo. You've made him wait two days. Call him.'

I dialled the number. He answered on the third ring. The pips sounded.

I pushed in a two-pence coin.

Jo-Jo – November 1992

Saturday in Cannock. Me and Karen were standing on the top of the steps at the back of the shopping centre, looking down on the bus station. 'This is her bus,' I said.

'Bang on time,' said Karen.

'Thank God. You know what she's like. Let's hope she's on it.'

The bus came to a stop at one of the shelters.

'There she is,' I said. 'Last one off as always.'

Mum stepped off the bus onto the tarmac. She straightened the collar on her grey raincoat and pulled her light-tan leather shopping bag into her body. I'd made her buy the bag on our trip to Stafford the year before – 'It's too expensive, Jo-Jo.' 'There are no pockets in shrouds, Mum.' She waited next to the bus, looking as though she'd done something wrong, as though she was considering getting back on and going home. She saw us and smiled. We waved and walked towards her. She hugged Karen first.

'Thank you for coming,' she said. 'I don't know why you bother.'

'Because you're my mum and I love you.'

'It's still good of you though.'

She walked in the middle of us, me carrying her shopping bag, Karen linking arms with her and chatting away. 'How are things at your scheme?'

'Oh, they're okay.'

'Is that neighbour still sending you flowers? Frank. Didn't you say his name was Frank?'

'Oh, him. I put a stop to that. Knocked on his door, gave him his flowers back, told him to send them to someone who'd appreciate them.'

'I thought you liked him,' said Karen.

'You've got to be careful,' said Mum. 'There's always a price to pay with men.'

We reached the entrance to Taylor's tea-rooms.

'You go first, Mum. I'll be behind you.'

'Yeah,' said Karen. 'We'll catch you if you fall.'

Mum started to hobble up the stairs, wincing as the arthritis in her knees caught her by surprise. 'Have you taken your painkillers?' I said.

'They make me drowsy,' she said, limping up the next step.

I rolled my eyes at Karen.

We reached the landing, went through the double entrance doors into the restaurant and waited next to the function room for the waitress to come over and show us to our seats. 'I always feel like I'm coming to the Ritz here,' said Mum.

'It's a nice tea-room,' I said.

'The best,' said Karen. 'Makes you feel like royalty.'

A waitress in a black skirt, Persil-white top and frilly bow-tied apron came over and showed us to a table in the window. Through the net curtain we could see the war memorial with its red poppy remembrance wreaths covering the steps. Mum studied her menu as though she was reading a holy parchment. Karen and I waited.

'I'll have fish and chips, two slices of bread and butter and a pot of tea.'

'We'll have the same,' I said. 'But we want the tea in separate pots.'

Mum smiled. 'Those pots are so cute,' she said.

Karen and I laughed.

The waitress returned, carrying a silver tray with three white ripple-patterned ceramic pots and three blue willow china cups and saucers. Mum served us, putting a spot of milk in each cup. 'Always put your milk in first,' she said. 'Don't show your ignorance.' She lifted the lid off each pot and mashed the tea bags. 'Leave them for a few minutes. Let them stew a bit.' Her hands shook as she poured the tea. 'I'll play Mum.' She lifted her cup, pursed her lips and blew gently. 'They always make it too hot.' 'You could put more milk in, Mum.' 'Oh no. I can't stand baby tea.'

The waitress appeared again with our food, which she laid out in front of us. 'Goodness. I'll never eat all that.' 'Leave what you don't want, Mum.' We made fish and chip butties with Lurpak butter, cutting the sandwich into four triangles. 'Shall we have pudding?' said Mum. I waved at the waitress. Back she came, this time wheeling the sweet trolley – strawberry trifle, Victoria sponges, chocolate eclairs, fruit scones.

'I'll have the trifle,' said Mum.

'We'll have the same,' I said.

After trifle we ordered another pot of tea each and listened to Karen telling us about the latest drama in her love life.

'You have three men?' said Mum.

'They're not all in my life at the same time,' said Karen.

'I'm lost,' said Mum.

'Me too,' I said.

'It's easy,' said Karen, holding up the salt pot. 'This is Tony, my soul mate. He's married, but we know we're destined to be together eventually.' She put the salt pot down and picked up the pepper pot. 'This is Jake, my bloke. We go out to the pub, the theatre, meals, but it's short-term, companionship really.' She picked up the mustard pot. 'And this is John, my ex-husband. I'll never stop looking after him. I see him for a meal every Friday.'

'Isn't he living with someone else now?' I said.

'I'm the wife though,' she said. 'We never got divorced.'

'It all sounds very complicated,' said Mum.

I lined up the salt, pepper and mustard pots. 'Tony, Jake and John,' I said, tapping each one in turn. 'Do they know they're part of a condiment set?'

Mum and Karen laughed.

After lunch we walked around Cannock centre. Mum liked to go to the indoor market, looking for a bargain. One year she bought a red Regatta coat, reduced from eighty to twenty pounds. It was two coats in one, a rain mac and a fleece. She never wore the mac, didn't like the colour, but she loved the fleece. 'So you've paid twenty pounds for a fleece.' 'Still a bargain, sweetheart.'

We walked past Preedy's newsagents in the high street, the shop where Freddie had worked as a trainee manager after he'd left the timber yard. One Saturday he'd taken me to meet Mavis, the manageress, who was renowned, locally and nationally, for her prize-winning window displays. She was a five-foot-four-inches rocket of a woman with a jet-black beehive hairdo. 'You're his girl, are you?' she'd said as we walked into the shop. 'I can see why he's always talking about you.' Freddie had blushed from the neck upwards and stared at the floor. 'Oh, bless him. I've embarrassed him again.'

'Wait for it,' said Karen as we walked past the shop.

'Isn't that where your young man worked?' said Mum.

'Freddie,' I said.

'Love of her life,' said Karen. 'I still can't believe you asked him to dance.'

'I liked him,' said Mum.

I'm walking past a coffee shop in Walsall high street and I see him. He's sitting at a table in the al fresco area at the front of the shop, drinking cappuccino and eating a slice of Bakewell tart. She's opposite him with her back to me. His woman, his knock-off, his bit on the side. They're laughing. He squeezes her hand. She touches his face. I walk up the path, stand right next to their table. 'Dad,' I scream. 'Dad.' He turns to face me. 'I still love your mother,' he says. 'I still love your mother.' I spit in his face. He groans and wipes his cheek with a serviette. His skin is peeling away, his hair is falling out – his flesh drops with a splat on the table. 'Dad,' I scream. 'Dad.' He stops wiping and looks straight at me. His woman turns away and retches bile onto the coffee shop floor. Dad's skull gives me a rictus smile.

Tap, tap, tap.

I opened my eyes and rubbed them.

Tap, tap, tap.

I peered at the clock. 12.30 a.m.

'Who is it?' I called.

'Mum. It's me. You awake?'

I pushed the duvet back and rolled out of bed. 'For God's sake, Amy, it's after midnight.' I stumbled over to the door and opened it. 'Are you okay?'

She pushed past me into the room and sat down on the bed. 'He wants to meet you, Mum. He wants to explain everything.'

I closed the door, walked over to the bedside table, picked up my glass of water and took a gulp. 'Who?' I said. 'What are you talking about?'

'Freddie,' she said.

I sat down next to her and had another gulp of water. 'You've seen him? I don't understand. When did you see Freddie?'

'He called. I asked him to come to the hotel.'

147

'He called you?'

'No. He called you, but I asked the receptionist to put your calls through to me. I didn't want you upset.'

'You did what?'

'I thought you'd be pleased.'

'Pleased that you met my ex-boyfriend and sorted out my love life. At what point did I become the child in our relationship?'

'You're not listening. Freddie wants to meet you. He wants to explain everything.'

I stood up, walked over to the window and opened the curtains. Night had fallen like a blackout sheet. I could see a half moon and a sky full of stars. 'Go to bed, Amy.'

'I said you'd meet him.'

'You meet him. Tell him I've checked out and I don't want to see him again.'

'Why would you do that?'

'It's all too late.'

Amy joined me at the window and put her arm around me. 'What's wrong, Mum? I can't help if you don't tell me. He loves you and you clearly love him.'

'What makes you say that?'

'The way you talk about him. You never talked about Dad in that way.'

'I never felt that way about your father.'

'What's the problem then?'

'Freddie doesn't know everything that happened.'

'He said he came to find you a couple of months after you went to Lincoln. He came up on the train with Jack, got a cab out to your place.'

'That's not true. I didn't have any contact from him.'

'He saw you with another guy who had his arm around you. He assumed you'd moved on, told the cab driver to take him back to the station.'

'Liam,' I said.

'So you had moved on?'

'Liam was a friend, nothing more. When was this?'

'He couldn't remember exactly, but he thought it was about November time.'

I stared out of the window again. 'That could have changed everything,' I said.

*

Amy had gone back to her room. I was thinking about Liam. Chicken dinner, Merlot-drinking, bowler-hatted, umbrella-swinging Liam. I wished he'd reappear like a genie out of a bottle and cosset me in our little rented student flat, shutting out the rest of the world, rescuing me as he'd saved me from the ten, nine, eight, high-pitched screaming in my head, one man, a doctor, paper sheets, waiting, judging eyes, more waiting, painkillers, taxi-ride-crying, vomiting, black hole-nothingness.

Freddie – July 2015

Bob's iPhone rang. 'Terry's dead,' he said, dropping his phone on the settee, tears already welling in his eyes. Jack and I went over and put our arms around him, the three of us scrummed in the centre of the lounge. 'I want to see him,' said Bob.

We crawled over the village speed bumps in Jack's Mini Cooper, heading for the main road, splodges of rain bouncing off the windscreen, tributaries spreading out and joining up to create a hazy film. I thought about the drooling, food-stained man I'd seen on my one and only visit to the care home, his communication limited to a gentle squeeze in his right hand. Bob was staring out of the passenger window. I wondered what he was thinking. Jack had his hand on Bob's leg, only moving it to change gear. No one spoke. I had no idea what to say.

We reached Bluebird Lodge and Jack reversed the Mini into one of the parking spaces. A man and a woman got out of the BMW parked next to us. The woman searched her handbag, pulled out a folded-up daffodil-yellow umbrella and pressed a button on the handle to make the umbrella spring into life. They carried on walking, the man hugging the woman close, holding the umbrella over them both. 'I'll wait here,' I said.

Thirty minutes later, I saw the care home's entrance doors swish open. The Jam's "A' bomb in Wardour Street' was banging out of the Mini's CD player – Rick Buckler's drum beat ricocheting around the car. Bob stepped through the doors first. Jack was behind him. They said something to each other and then hugged before walking across the car park and getting into the Mini. Jack turned off the music.

'You okay?' I said.

'He looked like he was asleep,' said Bob.

'Has someone phoned his family?'

'Matron,' said Jack. 'The daughter's on the way. Fucking hypocrite. She hasn't spoken to him for twenty years.'

'She's still family,' said Bob. 'Terry would've wanted her there.'

Jack faced him. 'You're his family,' he said.

Bob stroked Jack's face. 'Let's go home,' he said.

Freddie – July 1997

Sitges. The piano bar was starting to fill up. A man, woman and two kids walked in, all of them red-faced from the sun. We'd chatted to the woman by the pool, found out they were from Dudley. The man was always rushing into dinner at the last minute, his family already halfway through their main course, the woman sighing as he explained about his day on slow trains trekking across Catalonia to visit all the religious sites. They perched on the bar stools next to us. The man handed the son, who looked about thirteen, a brown paper bag. 'I bought it today,' he said. 'Go on. Open it.'

The boy sighed, reached into the bag and pulled out a white tie. 'You're rubbish at presents, Dad.'

'Look at the front,' said the man. 'It's Bogie. Isn't that cool?'

'Who?'

'Humphrey Bogart.'

'Never heard of him,' said the boy, putting the tie back in the bag.

'You couldn't have loved each other,' said Terry, taking another sip of his San Miguel. 'Not if you let university pull you apart.'

I looked at the picture of the bull and matador on the wall behind the bar. 'I still think about her most days,' I said. 'That's a bit odd, don't you think?'

'Not really. You should try and find her.'

'No point. She's with someone else. She had lots of dreams and a family was one of them.'

'You should look her up. At least you could put her memory to rest.'

'What about you?' I said. 'You and Bob seem pretty good together.'

'Another beer?' he said, nodding at my empty glass.

The barman came over and picked up the three torn beer mats. 'This you?' he said to me.

'Sorry,' said Terry. 'I get this nervous twitch around beer mats.'

The barman wiped the bar, removed our empty glasses, put down fresh mats and started filling up two pints of San Miguel.

Jack walked up to the bar. 'Make that three,' he said.

'You're late,' I said.

'I've told you before, Freddie, you and I aren't married. How's it going, Terry? You okay?'

'Getting better the more of these I drink,' said Terry, lifting up his frosty refilled glass.

Jack and I did the same and we clanked our glasses together.

'So,' said Jack, 'half an hour with Freddie. That must have been fun. What's he been telling you?'

'I am here you know.'

'We've been talking about love,' said Terry.

'You've been talking to Freddie about love. Don't tell me. Jo-Jo. You've been telling him about Jo-Jo.'

'Is that her name? The girl who disappeared to university.'

'That's her,' said Jack. 'It's always her.'

'We decided he needs to find her,' said Terry. 'Check out if it's the real thing.'

Jack looked at me. 'Haven't we done that already?'

'I didn't say that,' I said to Terry. 'I said I think about her most days.'

'What's the point in thinking about her if you're not going to do something about it?'

'Because that's what Freddie's good at,' said Jack. 'Thinking about stuff.'

'And what about you, Jack? I'm sure we'd all love to hear your views on love. Tell us about your last or any relationship you've had.'

Terry glugged down what was left of his beer. 'I'm going to find Bob. Let you two get on with your domestic. Good chatting with you, Freddie.' He dropped down from the stool and walked out of the bar.

'Well done, Jack. You know how to clear a room.'

'Nothing to do with me,' he said. 'You always get prickly when Jo-Jo gets a mention.'

I picked up one of the beer mats and tore it in half.

'You know what I find really strange?' said Jack.

'Go on,' I said. 'I'm sure you're going to tell me anyway.'

'You never mention the mother of your child. You were with her for longer. You had a daughter with her. And yet you never mention her. It's always Jo-Jo.'

'You two want more beers?' said the barman.

'Not for me,' I said.

'I'll have one,' said Jack.

The barman refilled Jack's glass and put a new beer mat on the bar. He glared at me as he picked up the ripped mat and placed Jack's replenished pint in front of him.

'You know what it was like with Jo-Jo,' I said.

'She's gone, Freddie,' said Jack. 'You've got to let her go. Get on with your life.'

'Maybe Terry's right,' I said. 'Perhaps we should try and find her.'

'What do you mean, we?'

'Come on, Jack. We're inseparable. You'll always need me to make you look wonderful.'

'That's true,' he said, putting his arm around my shoulder and hugging me. 'Everyone needs a mate who's slightly less good-looking than they are.'

I punched him on the arm. 'You can be a real prick sometimes.'

'You serious about finding her?' he said, taking a sip of his beer.

'Not really. Like you said, we've been there and it didn't get me anywhere.'

'We need to find you someone,' he said. 'Come on, let's go out.'

I shook my head. 'I'm not in the mood for your gay bars.'

'You could try your straight ones. Oh, hang on a minute, you don't go anywhere apart from with me.'

Freddie's Avenger. Driving past the Saddler's Arms, down the lanes, past a waving Sam the gypsy, winding the window down, stopping for a chat, stroking his greyhounds, driving past our middle of the night lay-by, getting to Fishley Driving Range. We'd buy a bucket of balls for fifty-pence, rent two clubs, a seven iron and a putter, play nine holes of pitch and putt, no one else around, make love on the fourth green. Playing golf in a storm, the ball hitting the phone lines running the length of the second hole. Freddie getting a hole in one on the seventh. Freezing cold, a Mars bar and a hot chocolate to warm us up. Bucket after bucket after bucket of balls on the driving range.

'Where to now?' said Freddie.

'Is your mum in?'

'She's at work until five.'

'Let's go to yours then. We can curl up in bed for the afternoon.'

Walking into Freddie's house. A blue nylon carpet in the hallway covered in dog hair from his incontinent bull terrier, a faint smell of ammonia hitting my nostrils. 'Why don't you get rid of her? Have her put to sleep.' Him looking at me like I'd suffocated a new-born lamb. Up to Freddie's bedroom. A single bed, a wardrobe, orange curtains, a poster of Debbie Harry onstage at CBGB music club in New York, a walnut-veneer telly at the foot of the bed, precariously balanced on a narrow pine coffee table, a coat hanger acting as a makeshift aerial. We stripped each other naked, climbed under the sheets and blankets, cuddled up, feeding off each other's body heat, me nuzzling into his black chest hair, him kissing the top of my head.

We were playing darts in the working men's club in New Invention with Jo-Jo's cousin, Mark, and his girlfriend, Kerry, all of us drinking pints of Mackeson and Vimto. Mark was still gloating after winning the last game, humming along to his Thin Lizzy treble-play-jukebox-reward – 'The Boys Are Back in Town', 'Whisky in The Jar', 'Waiting for an Alibi'. Kerry was chalking up the score on the blackboard. Mark had his arm around her. They smelt of patchouli oil and were wearing leather biker jackets covered in heavy rock band badges. 'Your go, Freddie,' said Mark.

'What do we need?' I said.

'A hundred and fifteen,' said Jo-Jo.

First dart, a five.

Jo-Jo squeezed my arm. I took a deep breath, lifted up my black pork-pie hat, ran the tip of my next dart around the rim and put the hat back on my head. I looked again at the board. 'Good luck, sweetheart,' whispered Jo-Jo.

'A hundred and ten left,' said Mark.

Second dart, treble twenty.

Jo-Jo kissed me on the lips. 'You need the bull,' she said, her eyes sparkling with excitement.

'Are we playing darts or snogging?' said Kerry.

'We can do both,' said Jo-Jo. 'You two should try it.'

I took aim, conscious of the two old men sitting at the table behind me. One of them had a mouthful of broken, yellow teeth, the other had no teeth at all. 'Gummy,' his mate called him. I could smell their cigarette smoke. I blinked. Blurred vision. I blinked again.

'Oh,' said Mark. 'He's hesitating. That's a bad sign.'

Jo-Jo slapped him on the shoulder. 'Ignore him, sweetheart. You can do it.'

I refocussed on the board and touched my hat with the final dart. Jo-Jo was nodding at me. I let go of the dart. It hit the red centre and quivered against the wire. I held my breath. It stayed in. 'Bullseye!' shouted Jo-Jo, throwing her arms around my neck. 'Our turn to choose the music. What shall we have?'

*

We walked over to the jukebox and studied the song choices. Jo-Jo bit her nail on the forefinger of her right hand as she pondered the cards. 'We should go for the Beatles,' she said. 'They've got most of the *Hey Jude* album on here.'

'Is that the hats and beards one?' I said.

She nodded. 'Dad loves it. The last photo of the Beatles together. Bushy beards, hippy hair and black, wide-brimmed hats – Fedoras, I think.'

'Your kin and his girlfriend won't be impressed.'

'Who cares? You've already ruined his night with that bullseye.' She squeezed me tight around the waist. 'What did I do to deserve you? Mr Arrow Man.'

'It was a good shot, wasn't it?'

'It was wonderful,' she said. 'And our reward is hats and beards. Your choice, but you've got to have that one… that one… and that one.'

I pressed the buttons. The jukebox clunked into life. 'The Ballad of John and Yoko', 'Revolution', 'I Should Have Known Better'.

*

As we walked back from the jukebox to the sound of John Lennon standing in the dock at Southampton, I could see Kerry and Mark sitting at the table, their half-empty pints in front of them. They were holding hands. Mark was saying something to her. Kerry had her head on his shoulder. She said something back and Mark kissed her on the lips. The old man with no teeth, Gummy, turned to his mate and pouted. I nudged Jo-Jo. We stopped walking.

'Go on, my son,' shouted the man with broken teeth.

'Get your tongue in there,' said Gummy.

Kerry and Mark pulled back from each other and looked round, their faces pumped with blood. They looked like they'd just walked out of a sauna.

'You want to get a room, lad,' said broken teeth man.

'Yeah, do it properly,' said Gummy.

Mark stood up.

'Leave it,' said Kerry, pulling at his arm. 'They're not worth it.'

Jo-Jo walked over and stood between Mark and the two men. 'What are you doing?' she said to Mark.

'I'm going to punch that bloke behind you,' said Mark. 'Knock his teeth out so him and his mate are a matching set.'

'And what do you think that's going to look like?' I said, walking over and standing next to Jo-Jo. 'Punching a defenceless old man.' I sat down and took a sip of my Mackeson and Vimto. 'Sit down for God's sake. Kerry's right. They're not worth it.'

Jo-Jo sat down and took a sip of her beer. Kerry did the same. We all looked up at Mark who was still glaring at the old men. Gummy pouted at him, broken teeth kissed the back of his hand three times and then licked his lips. Jo-Jo laughed. 'Sit down, Mark, and drink your beer,' she said. 'You look ridiculous.'

Mark sat down.

'I know I said snog him, Kerry, but I didn't think you'd do it here,' said Jo-Jo.

'Why not?' I said. 'If the urge takes you.'

'You're right,' said Jo-Jo, pulling me towards her.

The old men cheered. Mark and Kerry laughed. John Lennon told everyone him and Yoko were getting married in Gibraltar and honeymooning down by the Seine.

Mum was in bed. Me, Freddie and Dad were in the front room watching the *Eurovision Song Contest*. Dad had let me and Freddie curl up on the settee. I was lying in between Freddie's legs, my head rested against his chest, and he was massaging the top of my arm. Prima Donna, 'Love Enough for Two' was the United Kingdom entry, but everyone wanted Ireland's 'What's Another Year?' by Johnny Logan to win.

After Johnny had performed, Dad gave us five pounds to fetch steak and kidney pies and bottles of Dandelion and Burdock from the Saddler's outdoor. We got back just as the voting started. Terry Wogan was trying to keep the excitement out of his voice as Ireland took the lead. Germany caught up, picking up twelves, Ireland picking up eights and sevens. Each country was phoning into the arena to have their calls answered on different-coloured phones by the presenter on stage, who looked relieved when the scores were delivered in English. Belgium cast the final set of votes. The camera panned to Johnny, who held up three fingers to indicate what he needed. He got twelve.

'Good song that,' said Dad. 'It deserved to win.'

'Sax solo that did it,' said Freddie.

'What?' I said.

'The sax solo,' he repeated. 'Have you never heard that quote? "All they wanted was the sax". It wins every time.'

'I think I'll make some tea,' said Dad, getting up and walking into the kitchen.

'Oh, God,' said Freddie. 'I can't believe I said that in front of your dad.'

I laughed. 'He is over twenty-one, Freddie.'

I jumped off the number thirty-two bus from Bloxwich, blew on my hands and pulled up the collar on my full-length donkey jacket. I walked down Corporation Street, under the railway bridge, turned right onto Queen Street, past the Robin Hood pub, crossed over the road, up the ramp, through the only entrance to the sawmill, and into Mac's posh wood warehouse with its mouldings, skirting, architraves, dado rails, handrails and beadings. Mac looked up from his workbench, down at his watch and then back at me. 'You're late,' he said.

Mac: brother-in-law of the owners, Neville and Simon, colloquially known as snitch, grass, plant, arse licker. He wore pull-on navy blue overalls, thick-framed spectacles and had a bald head with wisps of hair on each side, which he combed religiously. His Scottish drawl was confused with tinges of an Aynuk and Ayli Black Country accent.

'The bus was late,' I said, walking past him.

He looked at his watch again. 'Better hurry up before Neville catches you.'

I nodded and carried on walking through his warehouse, slowing my pace, knowing he'd tell the owners and I'd be docked a quarter anyway. I walked into the open yard, past stacks and stacks of rough-sawn stock, pallets, floorboards, decking. I carried on up the ramp into the main warehouse, past the saws, the planers, the drills, the ladder leading up to the carpenters' loft space, walking through sawdust, the smell of burned wood invading my nostrils, and into the shack – a wooden shed with a couple of portable heaters, benches on either side and a pine dining table in the centre. It was the only refuge from the bitter cold of the open yard, the biting wind that blew in through the ever-open warehouse doors, and the only hiding place from the owners.

Snap Break: Time to run my YOP boy errand to the local café for breakfast, claiming my free piece of toast and Cadbury's creme egg while I waited. Ten minutes later I was back at the shack, clutching greaseproof paper sandwich bags with an order scribbled on each one in blue ink – bacon and egg with brown sauce, sausage and tomato, bacon with tomato sauce, sausage; variations on the same theme, everyone waiting for me, machines silenced, mugs of coffee and tea in front of them.

Alan – a timber yard veteran, two missing fingertips on each hand, the ex-son-in-law of the owners whose wife had left him and his alcoholism ten years into their marriage. He wore a black beanie hat and was always in recovery, always relapsing, always going on benders. His steroid-inflated face had tiny blue veins pulsing in its cheeks. He ate cheese and onion sandwiches for breakfast and refused to drink the machine coffee, bringing in his own filter coffee in a red flask, chucking the dregs out of his plastic cup at the end of break.

Ronnie – our pallet gun expert. He used to fill the yard with Ian Dury songs, changing the words to relieve the boredom – 'Hit me with your shovel, Mick. Hit me. Hit me. Hit me with your rubber prick. Hit me. Hit me'. He was heroin-thin with a full body twitch, twitch, twitch, constantly knotting his legs together, folding and unfolding his arms, and chain smoking filter-free Woodbine cigarettes. A Baggies fan, he loved Laurie Cunningham, Cyrille Regis, Willie Johnston – 'They call him Willie, Willie. Faster than lightning' – and told us tales of his bedroom: 'Me and the wife had a good go last night. You'd have been proud of me, lads.'

Kenny – AKA Doody. He had a Tom Selleck moustache, pursed his lips as he drew on a Benson and Hedges Silk Cut, screwing his eyes tight at the smoke, telling us tales of Northern Soul nights at the Camelot nightclub, singing Frank Wilson's

'Do I Love You? (Indeed I do)' as he strutted around the yard talking to anyone who'd listen about martial arts films – 'Did you know Bruce Lee died of an aspirin overdose?'

The card game had started. They grabbed their orders off me and ripped open their bags. 'You took your time,' said Ronnie, still looking at his cards.

I slid onto the bench and watched in silence.

'Twist.'

Three of clubs.

'Twist.'

Queen of hearts.

'Shit,' said Ronnie, throwing his cards on the table. 'I'm bust. This game's fucking fixed.'

'No,' said Mac, gathering up the cards to start a reshuffle. 'You're an arrogant prick that pushes his luck too far.'

'Piss off,' said Ronnie, pulling his black donkey jacket tight and slumping back on the wooden bench.

Alan nudged me and nodded down at the open page of his newspaper – page three of the *Sun*. 'You don't get many of them to the pound,' he said.

I looked at the picture.

Donna, nineteen, from East London, was beaming out at the world, licking her lips. She was standing in front of set-up foliage. Her ambition was to deliver worldwide peace and love. I felt the flush start to rise from my neck. 'Ah, bless,' said Mac, still shuffling the cards. 'He's blushing again.'

'You not had any yet, Freddie?' said Ronnie. 'I thought you had a woman now.'

'He's not still a virgin?' said Kenny.

They were all looking at me, cards lowered, newspapers folded.

There was still ten minutes left of the break.

It was the third Monday in the month. General staff meeting time in the day centre of Baytree House Care Home. 'Smokers' Break' was the main item on the agenda.

'I'm sorry,' said Barbara, fiddling with the key worker badge on her navy blue smock top, 'but they get more breaks than us.'

'And what about you and your chocolate?' said Tim, a twenty-a-day Benson and Hedges chef, still in his whites and hat. 'For every hour I work, you waddle around doing half as much.'

'Piss off. For every ten minutes I have, you have fifteen. And you have twice as many to feed your filthy addiction.'

'Now, now,' said Val, deputy manager, fake tan, bottle-topped glasses, red dress uniform. 'There's no need for that. I think we need to move on.'

I looked around the room. There were three rows of chairs. Val was sitting at the front, facing everyone. All of the seats were occupied, people sitting together in comrade groups – morning staff, afternoon staff, night staff, cleaners and kitchen staff. Most of the faces I recognised, but there were a couple of new reliefs at the back. A man, older, probably in his fifties, wire-thin body, broad smile, was chatting away to the woman next to him – the other new face. She looked about my age, a mole on her right cheek, brown eyes, black hair tumbling to the middle of her back. She caught me looking at her and smiled. I smiled back and nudged my afternoon co-worker, Dot. 'Who's that?' I said. Dot leaned into me, conspiratorial fashion. 'Poonam,' she said. 'She started last week. Done a couple of shifts so far.' I met Poonam's eyes again. She was still smiling at me.

*

First Date – Poonam and I were sitting on a cold, wet bench next to a lake. We were wearing big coats, woollen scarfs, and blowing out frosty breath. I poured steaming coffee from a two-cup thermos flask into my Jamie Oliver slogan mugs and we sipped in silence, cuddling, holding hands, watching an obese Canadian goose as it waddled along the bank after his mate. There was a bevy of swans on the water, tugging gently at the grasses, their backsides pointing to the heavens, and a flock of small birds were hunting gnats, waiting in the trees, tranquilly pouncing to secure their breakfast. It felt like the world was on pause. I leaned across and kissed Poonam gently on the lips. She pulled back, flashing an anxious look around the park.

'It's a bit public here, Freddie.'

'It's just a kiss.'

Our eyes met. We held our gaze for a few seconds. She pulled me towards her, and we kissed again.

*

More Dates – I reversed my Ford Focus into a parking bay on the far side of the empty pub car park, facing the exit, ready for a quick getaway. There was a wood behind me, lots of birdsong. Birdsong relaxed Poonam, but the dog walkers made her jittery. I looked at my watch. 9.05. I checked my phone. No text. A spasm of uncertainty turned my stomach. Fashionably late or not coming? I was never sure. My phone pinged. 'Be there in twenty.' I wanted to drive off, show her she couldn't take me for granted, couldn't treat me like a royal servant waiting to be nodded at by the Queen. 'I was a princess in a former life,' she'd say. 'I had an army of lovers carrying me about on a red velvet sedan chair.' I switched on the CD. Stevie Wonder's *Songs in the Key of Life*. I switched off the CD. My brain felt full of syrup. The memory of her face dropped into my head. She was looking up at me from a pillow, her black hair covering the Egyptian white cotton. Wide eyes, moistened lips.

There was a flash of lights. Poonam's Citroen pulled centre stage into the car park. She parked up next to me. I got out of my car and walked around to open her driver's door. She stared straight ahead, white-knuckled hands gripping the steering wheel. 'I'm okay,' she said, giving me a sideways look. 'Have you checked the wood? He might be watching me.' She turned out of the seat. I knelt down and hugged her to me. 'All I ever need is for you to hold me,' she said.

I fetched my ever-ready duck-feather duvet from the boot of my car and went through the ritual we'd repeat again and again in pub car parks, lay-bys and country lanes. Sometimes she'd point out places as we were driving. 'I want you to make love to me there,' she'd say. I'd pull over, remove the parcel shelf, flatten the back seat, pull the front seats forward and lay out the duvet. She'd wait. 'My princess,' I'd say. 'Your love shack awaits.' She'd climb in through the rear passenger door, clutching her purple throw, always giggling. We'd undress each other, gasping as bare flesh touched bare flesh.

On rare occasions, she'd follow me to my house, park at the end of the cul-de-sac, walk up the path clutching a tin of Cadbury's chocolate biscuits and a bottle of Merlot from Waitrose. She'd hand them over in the hall and burst into tears. 'I'm sure I was being followed. I can't believe I'm here.' She'd take my hand. 'Take me to bed,' she'd say. She never sat down in my lounge or entered my kitchen. We'd go from the hall, up the stairs, across the landing and into the bedroom, her Marks and Spencer chenille blanket ready to wrap around her naked body whenever she went to the bathroom.

1 p.m. In bed. Her sitting astride me, throwing her head forward, brushing my flesh with her tumbledown hair. Lots of tears. Life with her OCD husband dominating the conversation – tales of towels hung in symmetry on a heated rail, cans of beans stacked uniformly on a larder shelf. 'Have you seen the

film *Sleeping with the Enemy*? That's him.' Me telling her about Jo-Jo – the ever-present Jo-Jo.

10.30 p.m. Alone. Tinges of her Beautiful perfume on the edges of the duvet. It seemed like thirty seconds ago she was here, next me. We'd kissed for twenty minutes without a break. Our lips pumped, gorging, hungry for the physical contact. I reached out and touched the rumpled, empty pillow. I could still smell her, taste her.

11.30 p.m. Needing contact. Text first. 'You awake?' Gentle prod. Nothing. Press her number. Risky. Four rings. Voicemail. End the call. Lie back and look up at the ceiling. Imagining what she was doing, doing with him. I closed my eyes. I'm walking into a river. Treacle-black, icy-cold water moving up my body. And then the drop. Submerge. I hold my breath, fight against my bursting lungs, force myself to stay under, pray someone will look after the cats. I opened my eyes, looked at the phone. Nothing. Stupidity, vulnerability, regret. I felt like a fucking idiot. Bet she knew it was me, smiling as my name came up. Ignoring me. Laughing. Screwing him. What a loser. I closed my eyes again. Back to the river.

Freddie – December 2005

I was lying in bed, watching the red digits on my alarm clock tick away the night and thinking about my year of serving Poonam. She'd taken my sanctuary and used it as a crutch to prop up her bloodless marriage – that's how it felt. Starry skies and magic carpets were what we wanted. What we got was hurried back-seat car sex under a stained duvet, texts from her prayer room at six o'clock every morning, e-mails from her Hindu temple in the middle of high worship – forbidden communications to an illicit lover from a holy place.

Jo-Jo's face dropped into my head. Her auburn hair, her nose freckles. I wrapped my arms around my body and hugged myself tighter.

Freddie – July 2015

We were back in Jack's lounge. I was sitting in the bucket seat, thinking about Terry, about his years of living a lie, about his advice to find Jo-Jo. Jack and Bob were sitting side by side on the leather sofa. Bob was lying down, legs curled up underneath him, his head on Jack's chest. Jack was cuddling him and comfort-stroking his hair, occasionally kissing him lightly on the top of his head. They were locked in their private world, like I wasn't in the room.

'It was a blessing in the end,' said Bob.

'I can't believe he's dead,' said Jack. 'Will you go to the funeral?'

'I doubt I'll be welcome.'

'You were with him for years. He loved you.'

'We'll see. You okay with me going?'

'You should be there.'

'I'm going home,' I said. 'Let me know if there's anything I can do.'

'You should call her,' said Bob, his head still on Jack's chest. 'One of Terry's biggest regrets was leaving it too late before he was honest with himself.'

'He told me.'

'When?'

'In Sitges. He said he should have told his family earlier. Are you two okay?'

'Yes,' said Jack, kissing the top of Bob's head again. 'We're sad about Terry, but I think we're in a good place.'

'Me too,' said Bob, looking up at him.

*

An hour later, I was sitting at my kitchen table, a picture of Mum on the wall in front of me, next to the poster of Jack Nicholson's film, *As Good As It Gets*. Mum's photo was taken in the restaurant of the hotel we'd stayed in on our last holiday to the Isle of Wight. I have my arm around her. She's wearing her best dress, her rare outing-after-dark dress. I looked down at the oak table, a strip of my purple beta blocker tablets in front of me, next to them a torn-out page from a notebook on which Jo-Jo had written her contact details. I felt my mood drop off a cliff as I read her married surname. Coulman. She was my Jo-Jo. No one else's. I turned my mobile phone over and over in my right hand, remembering her nose freckles and the mole above her bellybutton. I pushed the tablets to one side and punched the number into the phone.

'Good evening. Hotel Rushmore. How can I help?'

Nothing. The words wouldn't come. I could hear them in my head. 'Can you put me through to room 242?' 'I'd like to speak to Mrs Coulman in room 242.'

'Hello. Hotel Rushmore. Can I help?'

'Yes,' I stammered. 'Mrs Coulman.'

'Is that a guest, sir?'

'Yes.'

'Do you have a room number?'

'242.'

'One moment. I'll check.'

I could feel the beads of sweat on my forehead, my tongue sticking to the roof of my mouth. I wondered if I should have left the call until tomorrow, but I remembered what Bob had said. 'Don't leave it until it's too late.'

'Hello.'

'Jo-Jo.'

'It's Amy. Is that Freddie?'

'I wanted to speak to your mum.'

'She's upset. What do you want?'

'To talk to your mother.'

'Are you messing her about?'

'I want to explain, to apologise.'

'You can explain to me.'

'I want…'

'You're not speaking to Mum until I'm happy you're not going to hurt her. Come to the hotel in an hour. We'll talk in the car.'

The line went dead.

I looked at the phone and then back at the beta blockers. I called Jack. He answered on the third ring. 'The daughter wants to see me.'

'When?'

'Now. She said to get to the hotel in an hour.'

'Do you want to borrow the car?'

'I want you to come with me, Jack.'

'I don't think that's a good idea. You need to sort this yourself.'

'I'll mess it up. I always mess it up.'

'You want her in your life, don't you?'

'More than anything.'

'Just be honest. I'll bring the car and get Bob to give me a lift back.'

*

I recognised her this time as she ran down the hotel steps and strode towards Jack's Mini. She was still wearing the tight-fitting black cord trousers and sunflower-yellow pixie boots, but the light-tan leather bomber jacket had been substituted for a blue cowboy denim jacket. I couldn't see her nose freckles from the

168

distance she was away, but I knew they were there – a gene present from her mum that made my heart melt. She waved at the parking attendant and I wondered what he was thinking of all this toing and froing. Perhaps it happened all the time, was an occupational hazard in all hotels – English eccentrics and their strange ways. At least he'd been saved the job of guiding me to the visitors' spaces. I'd learned the drill off by heart.

Amy opened the passenger door and glared at me. 'My mum was really upset after you left. What did you say to her?'

'I'm sorry. I didn't think she'd react like that.'

She sat in the seat and slammed the door shut. 'How was she meant to react? I'm still trying to decide if you're bonkers.'

'I love your mum. I always have.'

'And I think she loves you,' said Amy. 'That's why I'm talking to you.'

I stared out of the window at the security guard, who was still looking over at the car. 'That bloke is really getting on my tits,' I said.

'To be fair,' said Amy, 'this has become a bit of an *EastEnders* episode. He must be wondering what's going to happen next.'

'I think he's a nosy twat.'

'You could be right.'

'Will she see me?'

'I don't know.'

'She doesn't know I'm here, does she?'

'Not yet. I want to hear what went on between you and then I'll ask her. I can't promise anything.'

'I told her I wanted her in my life and she said it was too late, that I should have phoned.'

'When?'

'When she went to university.'

'You mean, you dumped her?'

'Not really.'

Freddie had taken me on a tour of his street, showing me the little green where he'd played marbles, the big green where he'd played British Bulldog, the house where Jack lived with his army of fifteen siblings, the house two doors away with its family of seven brothers, the Tolleys, whose dad used to chase them around the block in his slippers, the house next door to that where Mrs Hedges, a widow with one arm, lived, everyone fascinated because she could still peg her washing out, and we were now standing in front of a privet hedge, which was tall enough to shield us from Freddie's mum's three-bedroom, steel council house.

'Are you sure about this, Freddie? We've not been seeing each other that long.'

'Yes,' he said. 'She wants to meet you.'

He pulled me up the tarmacked drive. In front of us a pair of white double gates and a bay window. A woman with black shoulder-length hair was looking out of the window. She waved. 'What have you told her about me?' I said.

'That I like you.'

'She's probably met all your girlfriends.'

'You're the first,' he said, holding my hand as we walked up the drive.

The front door opened.

'Mum. This is Jo-Jo.'

The woman smiled. I felt like I should be curtseying. There was a panic going on inside my head about what to say, what to call her. I finished up saying nothing, just returning her smile. She stood to one side and gestured for us to come into the house. 'It's good to meet you, Jo-Jo,' she said. 'Freddie's told me all about you.'

We walked through the hallway, past three rows of Freddie's school pictures, hung side by side on the flock wallpaper. I guessed they were in date order, from infants, through junior and up to senior school. In the earlier ones, he wore burgundy roll-neck jumpers, his shoulder-length hair was neatly combed into a forced parting and his perfect front teeth protruded out of his mouth, until, in one, the chipped tooth appeared. In the last two, the parting had gone, the hair, which was still shoulder-length, was dishevelled, the jumper had been replaced by a black plastic bomber jacket, acne spots covered his chin, and the smile of the earlier photos had been substituted with a horse-length frown. 'These are good pictures,' I said.

'Yes,' she said. 'He's so handsome, isn't he?'

We came out of the hall and into the kitchen. Three Royal Doulton china cups and saucers were already laid out on the walnut work surface, and a teapot, which was wearing a brown ribbed cotton cosy, was perched on a cast-iron stand, a matching milk jug and sugar bowl at its side.

'Tea, Jo-Jo?'

'Yes please,' I said, repressing a desperate urge to giggle. It really felt like I'd been granted an audience at Buckingham Palace.

'Go through,' she said, pouring the tea and nodding in the direction she wanted me to go.

I walked from the kitchen's red-tiled floor into the floral-patterned carpet of the adjoining room. A coal fire danced away in the hearth; next to it was an oak sideboard, its top covered in Murano glass animals and a pink dish with a dancing nymph as its centrepiece. I looked through the window and saw a dog kennel at the bottom of the garden. I sat down on the two-seater sofa, expecting Freddie to sit next to me, but he flopped into the green velvet-covered rocking chair. His mum came through carrying a tray, which she placed on the dining table at the end of the room. Freddie jumped up, walked over and picked up two of the cups and saucers. He handed one to me and sat back down in the rocking chair. His mum, clutching the third cup and saucer, sat down next to me. She stirred her tea. She smelt of lavender oil. 'I expect you want to know all about Freddie,' she said. 'Where shall I start?'

'Jo-Jo doesn't want to hear about me, Mum.'

'Of course she does. Don't you, dear?'

She didn't wait for me to answer.

'Well,' she said, taking in a deep breath. 'He played Joseph in the nativity play. The kid across the road played the Innkeeper. I said to his mother, what sort of a part is that? And then there was the time he sang in the school choir at Walsall Town Hall. He's got a lovely voice. Gets it from his dad. His poor father. Been gone ten years now. Freddie was only seven. He took his dad's death badly, locked himself away with his Cowboys and Indians, used to talk to them for hours, making up his stories. All that time on his own, muttering away to himself. A creative mind, the doctor said. And then there was the time his dad bought him a puppy. It weed all over him when we fetched it home in the van. She's in the kennel. He'll show you later.'

I looked at Freddie. 'You didn't tell me you had a dog,' I said.

'Didn't I? I must have forgot.'

'What sort of dog is it?'

'A bull terrier. Tina. She's gorgeous.'

'Six weeks old when he had her,' said his mum. 'Saved his life after his dad died. She's getting old now. She likes the kennel. A bit of peace and quiet for her.'

'She should come in more,' said Freddie.

'Yes, well, it's not you who has to mop up after her, is it?' said his mum. 'Remember the budgie? You never cleaned him out.'

'I was only four.'

'You cried like a baby when that bird died. You weren't four then.'

'You put him in a sugar bag and chucked him in the bin.'

'You make too much fuss. He was only a budgie.'

'The bin was full. I could see the sugar bag every time I went out.'

'You're always crying. You cried over the rabbits.'

'The ones you let die of thirst.'

'We lost the key to the garage. That's not my fault.'

'You never looked for it. Three days they were shut in there, in the middle of summer.'

I coughed, making their ping-pong conversation come to an emergency stop. His mum put her cup on the floor. 'You can take your young lady outside and show her the dog now,' she said. 'I've got work to do.'

*

The bespoke wooden kennel was built in between the house and the small garden wall that separated the concrete patio from the well-manicured lawn. It had a pitched felted roof and was more like a planked log cabin than a kennel. Freddie pulled the bolt free and opened the door. The inside was separated into two areas: a toilet area, which was spotlessly clean, and a sleeping area, which had a wicker basket in the one corner. Lying in the basket on a thick woollen blanket was Tina, a black brindle bull terrier with grey hairs all over her face. 'Come on, girl,' said Freddie, patting his right thigh. The dog jumped up at the sound of Freddie's voice and ran towards him, her tail wagging.

'She's smaller than I expected,' I said.

'Everyone says that. I think she might have been the runt of the litter.'

The dog was jumping up and weaving in and out of Freddie's legs. Freddie was patting whatever he could catch. He knelt down. 'Calm down, girl,' he said, making the dog sit. He started massaging her head. Tina closed her eyes and turned her head up towards him, nudging his hand with her chin if the massaging pace slowed. Freddie looked up at me. 'You going to say hello?'

I stroked the dog's back. 'She is a lovely dog,' I said.

'She's old now, nearly thirteen.'

'You obviously love her.'

'Mum was right about her saving me.'

I could see tears welling in his eyes. I touched his arm and he smiled.

'We nearly lost her a couple of months ago,' he said. 'She got out of her kennel. Mum found her sitting outside the fish and chip shop. She used to go there when she was a puppy, run in and steal a Pukka pie if the guy left his store gate open.'

'Clever dog,' I said.

'She is, but she has to be quick and get back over the main road sharpish. When Mum called her, she ran into the road without looking and a car nearly hit her. Mum couldn't look. She came back here in tears, felt a nudge on her leg and there's Tina looking up at her, moist eyes and wagging tail. God knows what we'd have done.'

Freddie's Recurring Dream

Treetops wine bar in Bloxwich. ABC's 'All of My Heart' is playing full volume on the MTV channel. I can see her, she's at the bar, but the place is ram-packed with Friday night punters. 'Jo-Jo,' I call. 'Jo-Jo.' I nudge the bloke in front of me, trying to ease him out of the way. He stumbles into the guy next to him who spills his lager. 'Fucking hell, mate.' 'Sorry,' I say. 'I'm trying to get through.' 'Join the club,' he says. 'We're all trying to get served.' 'You don't understand,' I say. 'I'm trying to speak to that girl.' I point. She's gone. I'm back in my kitchen. We've booked a holiday, but she doesn't know. I need to talk to her, tell her the details, the plane leaves at three o'clock. I look at my watch. Twelve thirty. I scroll down the contacts on my Windows phone, looking for her number. A blurred screen. 0771... I squint. I can't see it properly. 0771... I strain my eyes. The screen's too blurred, the last set of digits are fading in and out. I'm back in the wine bar. She's on the other side of the room, chatting to two girls, holding a Bacardi and coke. 'Jo-Jo. Jo-Jo.'

Jo-Jo's Recurring Dream

I am standing in a glass top of the world atrium, looking out at an orbiting carpet of ocean-blue and flame-red planets of different sizes, all interspersed with a sprinkling of diamond-encrusted stars. I look expectantly at the Astrologer, who removes a telescope from his right eye, concertinas it together and furrows his brow. He steps closer to the observation window, the blue satin tunic covering his pot belly almost touching the glass. I take a step towards him. 'Well, Professor. What's the planet called?'

He hesitates, reaches into his red satchel and brings out a glass sphere, which he throws upwards along a straight vertical. It shoots out of view. Seconds later a bang echoes in the atrium summit and purple rain begins to fall, some of the droplets sticking to the window on their descent. He pulls a magnifying glass from his pocket and starts to examine the bubbles of liquid.

I walk to his side. 'What's this telling us?'

'It's a name grid,' he says. 'The planet is called Annexe Five. Better known as Fate in the old scriptures. It's heading our way, travelling at quite a speed. I must get back to the observation gantry.' He throws the satchel over his shoulder and sprints out of the room.

I watch the fireball planet edge its way across the sky, getting closer and closer to the glass atrium, the white heat-tails of two meteors circling its surface. I touch the glass. The sound of a single cough makes me look around. 'Professor,' I say. 'What have you discovered?'

'It is Fate,' he says. 'We must try to make contact. Find out what they want.'

'I think I know,' I say.

'He's coming back for you,' says the professor.

'You know about him?'

'Everyone knows about him, Jo-Jo.'

Jo-Jo – July 2015

The brass bell over the coffee shop doorway sounded and in walked Freddie. We'd arranged to meet at two o'clock, but I'd got there early, knowing he'd be bang on time. I wanted to prepare myself, be ready for the conversation. I couldn't believe I was sitting there, back in the place where a few days ago I'd re-emerged into his life clutching a black and white photo booth picture and three-decades-old memories. He saw me and smiled – that chipped-tooth grin, the always looking at the ground blue eyes, the hesitancy, the sense of no harm and, yes, sweetness. The old man with the stick, who'd spoken to us on my last visit, was sitting at the table in the window with his wife. I saw him tap the woman's arm.

'Hello, Jo-Jo.'

Freddie was standing next to the table, the waitress from behind the counter at his side. 'I didn't know if you wanted something to drink,' he said.

'Cup of tea,' I said. 'I'll have a cup of tea.'

The waitress nodded. 'Pot of tea for one and a skimmed milk latte,' she said.

'No,' said Freddie, sitting down opposite me. 'I'll have tea as well.'

'Are you sure?' said the waitress. 'I can put in an extra shot of coffee if you want.'

'Two teas, thank you,' I said.

The waitress walked away.

'That'll be the talk of the village,' I said.

'Oh, I think the village have something better to talk about,' he said, nodding at the old man, who was trying not to look like he was watching.

'Is this a good place for us to talk?'

'As good as any. Anyway, we've ordered tea now.'

The waitress returned and laid out a pot of tea, two china cups and saucers, and a small churn-shaped jug containing the milk. She looked at Freddie as though she was expecting him to realise his mistake. 'Thank you,' I said.

'Sugar's there,' she said, nodding at the bowl of brown and white lumps in the centre of the table before walking away.

I lifted the lid on the pot and swirled the teabags with one of the spoons. 'Milk?' I said, picking up the churn.

Freddie nodded. I splashed some milk into his cup and then some into mine. 'We'll let it brew for a few minutes,' I said. 'Nothing worse than baby tea.'

'I've missed you, Jo-Jo,' he said, putting his hands on top of mine.

I was distracted by two women walking past our table. One of them was carrying a light-tan leather shopping bag similar to the one Mum always carried around with her. 'Do you remember the day Mammy had her leg off?' the woman with the bag said in a Northern Irish accent. 'I do,' said the other woman. 'What a sad day that was for Daddy.' They carried on walking out of the shop.

Freddie laughed. 'I love the way you people-watch,' he said. 'You make it an art form.'

'You're not too bad yourself if I remember rightly. All those stories you used to tell.'

I took a sip of my tea.

'I'm glad you came,' he said.

'I don't know what I'm doing here.'

'I'm hoping it means you must have some feelings for me.'

'Yes,' I said. 'It appears I still do.'

He looked down at the table. 'I thought I wasn't good enough for you. That's why I didn't call.'

'I never know what you mean by that, Freddie.'

'I mean you needed a proper man, someone to take care of you.'

'You're saying I couldn't take care of myself.'

'No. I'm saying you deserved to be taken care of.'

'You think too much. You always have. You still do.'

'I couldn't see how the future would work out for us, Jo-Jo.'

'Why should you? No one knows, unless you're clairvoyant. You're not, are you?'

'I wanted it to be certain. That's why I walked away.'

'It's still not certain, Freddie. If anything, it's less certain now than it was then. We've had lives. There are complications, emotional baggage for both of us.'

'I know, but I love you, Jo-Jo. Let's go away.'

'What? Where?'

'Devon. A cottage for a few days. See how we get on.'

'I don't know...'

'Just say yes.'

'I can't get over how you just left me.'

'It was so long ago,' he said.

'But it could happen again,' I said. 'Your head. You must have been planning to leave when we made our way to the coach station. You had no intention of calling me, even though you promised.'

'I came looking for you.'

'Two months later, and then you didn't hang around.'

'I thought you'd moved on. You and that guy looked close. He had his arm around you.'

'He was a friend. Nothing more. You must have known how I felt about you.'

'Let's go away.'

'I don't know if I want to open up my feelings for you again. I'm too old for all that.'

'If you still feel the same after our time away, we'll say our goodbyes. Don't you want to find out? You were the one that started all this by looking me up after thirty-five years.'

'Ghosts,' I said. 'That's the reason I came to look for you. I wanted to settle ghosts.'

Jo-Jo – October 1979

Me and Karen were at Wolverhampton Civic Hall. Elkie Brooks wasn't due on stage until seven thirty, but I'd been sitting in my seat for twenty minutes, staring at the bass guitar, drums and keyboards, all waiting to be claimed and brought to life by the band. I could hear the hall filling up behind me. I was thinking about Dad, him singing 'Love Potion No 9' and 'Honey Can I Put On Your Clothes' as we listened to the *Two Days Away* album, him showing me the cover, Elkie on the phone, panda eyes, wearing only a nightshirt, behind her a lit-up Empire State Building viewed through the open door to the apartment balcony, him telling me about Vinegar Joe, the Robert Palmer connection and the Janis Joplin comparisons.

'We must be the youngest ones here,' said Karen, still standing and looking around the ram-packed three-thousand-seats venue.

'Sit down,' I said, pulling at her arm. 'It's nearly time.'

She dropped into her seat and put her feet up against the wall of the stage, the hall lights glistening off the top of her monkey boots. 'I can't believe you've made me come to this,' she said. 'She's not Blondie, is she?'

I pinched her leg. 'Stop being an ungrateful bitch. You didn't have tickets to see Blondie. What else would you be doing tonight?'

The lights dimmed and I felt goose bumps rise all the way up my arms. I squeezed Karen's hand. She smiled at me. A drum roll started. 'Ladies and gentlemen, Elkie Brooks.'

Two hours later, the stage smoke had disappeared, the lights had come up, but the crowd were still stamping their feet and shouting, 'More, more, more.' Karen was screaming at the top of her voice. 'She's been back twice,' I said. 'She won't come out again.'

'I don't think this lot are ready to go home yet,' said Karen.

The lights went down. Elkie walked onto the stage, punching the air as she strutted over to the mike. 'Okay,' she said, running her hand down her red silk dressing gown. 'We'll have to do this one without the band.' She leaned into the mike and purred the opening lines of 'He Could Have Been an Army.'

Jo-Jo – August 2015

I could see him through the double entrance doors of the hotel reception. He was parked in one of the visitors' spaces on the far side of the car park in Jack's Mini Cooper, drumming his fingers on the steering wheel. The security man in his high-vis jacket was watching him from his sentry position by the three industrial bins. I hoped I was doing the right thing. Three days away with a man I hadn't been intimate with for over thirty years. I didn't think he'd find a cottage, but he had; I didn't think Jack would lend him the car, but he did. Amy had asked the killer question. 'Where are you going to sleep, Mum?' She'd rolled her eyes when I didn't answer. 'Mum, he's a man. You need to have the conversation before you go.' I'd spent all night turning that question over and over in my head.

I walked outside, clutching Mum's geisha girl carpet bag, the bag that I'd taken to Blackpool on my last trip away with Freddie. I smiled at the memory of my teenage self, running down the front path of my parents' three-bedroomed semi-detached house, throwing the carpet bag on the rear seat of Freddie's new Chrysler Avenger.

I stopped for a second and took a deep breath. It was already quite warm, and I could smell the eucalyptus trees from the hotel gardens. The Mini pulled out of the parking space and parked up again in front of the concrete steps leading down from the block-paved patio to the car park.

Freddie jumped out of the car and walked up the steps towards me. He'd left the engine running. 'Lovely day,' he said, holding his hand out for the carpet bag.

'How many bedrooms are there in this cottage, Freddie?'

'One,' he said, still holding his hand out for the bag. 'But I'll sleep on the couch.'

'I'll hold you to that,' I said, walking down the steps, still clutching the carpet bag.

*

We'd pulled out of the conifer tree-lined exit road of the Hotel Rushmore, made our way through the country lanes and turned right onto the main road heading for the motorway. Neither of us had said anything for about five minutes. Freddie's face had dropped, the chipped front tooth smile had disappeared. I felt guilty for snapping.

'You did well to find a cottage,' I said. 'I thought you'd struggle in August.'

'I got lucky,' he said. 'The third place I called had a cancellation.'

'And Jack doesn't mind you borrowing the car?'

'He said he needed it for work, but I told him how important it was. Anyway, it was his idea that we should talk.'

'Oh, it was Jack's idea.'

He looked at me, taking his eyes off the road. 'Jack just woke me up. I want to spend some time with you.'

'I want to spend some time with you as well,' I said.

He faced the road again. His chipped-tooth grin reappeared.

*

The bungalow cottage was on its own at the end of a dirt track in the middle of an eco-friendly park. It was surrounded by lush woodlands and there was a lake with a boathouse at the bottom of its garden, a single rowing boat with no oars moored alongside the jetty. We walked down the steep slope from the car park to the back door, trying to maintain our balance as our feet squelched into the soggy ground.

A man, sitting on one of the green metal patio chairs, waved at us as we got closer to the bungalow. He looked like he lived permanently outdoors. He was wearing grey hiking shorts, heavy walking boots and thick grey socks. His skin was a dirty tan colour, like it had never been properly cleaned. 'Derek,' he said, standing up. 'I'm the park caretaker.'

We shook hands and introduced ourselves. I looked at the clipboard Derek was holding. 'Health and safety briefing,' he said, tapping the board.

'Oh, there's no need,' said Freddie.

'There's every need,' said Derek. 'I have to make sure you're fully briefed.'

Freddie and I looked at each other and smiled.

'Let's start with the keys,' said Derek, walking off towards the cottage. 'The Yale one is for the back door, the other one is for the front. I know most people have their Yale lock on the front door, but we don't. It's simple enough when you get used to it.'

Freddie laughed.

Derek stopped walking, turned around and looked at us. 'I'm just trying to save you a mix-up when it's dark and you can't find your key.'

'Sorry,' said Freddie. 'You're right. It is simple once you know.'

'Thank you,' I said, squeezing Freddie's hand. 'That's really helpful.'

Derek opened the back door. 'I've chopped you some logs for the wood burner,' he said, pointing at a wheelbarrow.

'Oh, I don't think we'll need them,' said Freddie. 'Not in this heat.'

'No,' I said. 'Logs are good. We'll use them.'

Derek grinned and walked into the cottage. 'Let me know if you need any more.'

We stepped into the hallway, which was actually part of the lounge.

Derek tapped his clipboard again and launched into his safety briefing, working his way down his checklist of items, most of which were backed up by laminated signs: how to change the toilet roll, how to use the space-age shower, how to use the space-age shower's remote control, which was covered in icons, a standing woman, a sitting woman, head spray, side sprays, digital temperature, how to use the extractor fan with its piece of blowing tissue sellotaped on the end to let you know it was working, how to use the cooker, the fridge, the washing machine, the television.

'Do either of you row?' said Derek, looking up from his clipboard.

'I don't think we'll be getting that energetic,' said Freddie.

'I row,' I said. 'I saw the boat on the lake. Are we okay to use it?'

'I'll need to instruct you first,' said Derek. 'Make sure you're up to scratch before I issue the oars.'

*

Derek left us, satisfied we'd been fully inducted. I looked around the cottage and Freddie went up to the car to collect our bags. He brought my carpet bag first and two fully loaded Sainsbury's carrier bags. 'What's this?' I said.

'A few essentials,' he said. 'It'll save us having to find a shop.'

I unpacked the shopping, holding up each item as I fetched it out of the bag: skimmed milk, gluten free bread, cream biscuits, crumpets, a box of organic porridge oats, organic runny honey, Lurpak butter, Clipper teabags, Kenco Colombian coffee, toilet rolls, washing-up liquid, washing tablets, softener, gluten free pasta and pesto, four bottles of Muscadet, and three Jamie Oliver wine tumblers. 'Jesus, Freddie,' I said. 'We're only here for three days. And what's with the gluten free?'

'It's better for you,' he said. 'Less calories. If we run out, there's a pub a mile away that's got good food reviews. We can get a cab.'

'A cab? We're walking if it's a mile away.'

'Walking?'

'That thing you do with your legs. Remember?'

'I usually get cabs.'

'Not if you're with me. And I know it's a stupid question, but why three wine tumblers?'

'Just in case we break one. What do you think of the cottage?'

I grabbed his hand and pulled him into the bedroom. 'That bed is enormous, emperor size. And have you seen the bath?' I pulled him into the bathroom. 'That is the biggest bath I've ever seen, and pear shaped. It's gorgeous.'

'You like it then.'

'I love it.'

'The couch isn't very big though,' he said, dropping his head and looking like the little boy who'd been given the smallest ice-cream.

'Okay,' I said. 'We'll share the bed, but only because it's so big. Come on. I want to have a closer look at the lake now clipboard man has gone.'

'Why did you ask him to leave the logs? We won't need them in this heat.'

'You think I'm going to pass up the chance of having a real fire in this setting? We'll leave the doors open.'

*

12.30 a.m. I could hear Freddie breathing, could sense that he was awake. He was lying right at the opposite edge of the emperor bed. I turned on my back and stared up at the ceiling, thinking about our evening. He'd cooked pasta with pesto, we'd opened a bottle of Muscadet, which he'd chilled in an ice bag from the freezer, and we'd reminisced about Max's, Sam the gypsy, Blackpool. After the meal, we'd taken our drinks onto the patio and stared up at a cloudless night sky and an endless universe of stars. We'd leaned back, back, back and made more and more stars come into view. I was going to ask him to lie on the grass and then I remembered it was damp. I turned on my side and faced the place in the darkness where Freddie was lying. I thought of Dad and the telescope he'd bought me when I was a little girl. He would have loved this place. Magic carpets and starry skies. I sighed, expecting Freddie to respond, but he didn't say anything.

And then I heard him roll over, and then, crash.

'My God,' I said, reaching up and pulling the cord for the bedside light. 'Are you okay? Where are you?'

He groaned and I rolled across the bed to look over the edge.

'Jesus, Freddie. What happened?'

'I think I've broken my leg,' he said.

I got down beside him on the floor.

'Careful,' he said. 'It really hurts.'

There was a duck-egg lump on his shin.

'I banged my head as well,' he said.

I looked. A graze, no blood.

'You've caught the bed frame as you rolled out. What were you doing?'

'Trying not to touch you,' he said.

I sat on the edge of the bed and he sat up, holding the back of his head. I laughed, leaned forward and kissed him lightly on the lips. 'This is absurd. Only you could fall out of a bed this big.'

*

The next morning, I persuaded Freddie to come rowing with me. 'Don't we need the oars?' he said. 'You'll have to convince clipboard man that you're worthy.'

I hadn't thought of that. 'How difficult can that be?' I said.

We walked past the log pile, up the dirt path to the eco-park entrance. I rang the front doorbell of the main house. A woman with a sparrow face and a 1970s curly perm opened the door. She was wearing a full housecoat and holding a feather duster. 'We're staying in the cottage,' I said. 'We've come to see Derek.'

'He's not here, love, off on one of his trips, won't be back until this evening. Can I help? I'm Rose, his wife.'

'We were hoping to use the boat. He said he'd let us have some oars.'

'Can you row?' she said.

'My dad taught me,' I said, nodding.

She reached around the back of the door, grabbed two oars and handed them to me. 'Can you row?' she said to Freddie.

Freddie shook his head.

'Best leave your good lady in charge then.'

'Thank you,' I said.

We turned and walked back down the path.

'He'll be furious,' said Freddie. 'I expected an exam or something.'

'Remember what Rose said. We're okay as long as I'm in charge.'

*

I rowed us gently around the lake, occasionally lifting the oars out of the water to manoeuvre the boat through a cluster of lily pads. Freddie lay back in the passenger side and watched the trout bubbling their way to the lake's surface. 'City boy,' I said, kicking his foot. 'Are you going to have a go at rowing?'

'No chance,' he said, draping his hand lazily in the water.

'Probably best,' I said. 'I'd like us to stay afloat.'

'There's Gordon,' he said, pointing out the biggest fish.

'Gordon?' I said.

He shrugged and then serenaded me with all the words to Jilted John's 'Gordon is a Moron', which I realised halfway through I also knew off by heart. 'I'd forgotten that song,' I said.

After about an hour, I rowed to the mooring point and held my breath while Freddie negotiated the tension-filled short step to dry land. He tied up the boat and held it steady for me. I jumped ashore and looked around. There was a man in a floppy straw hat and baggy blue walking shorts sitting on one of the wooden benches on the opposite bank. I'd seen him earlier walking around the lake, resting in between benches. I wondered where he was staying, who he was with, why he was on the bench on his own. He was looking away into the distance, staring at the four cows and their three calves on the hillside. I took Freddie's hand and we walked up the hill towards the cottage, carrying an oar each in our free hands, using them as walking sticks to propel us forward.

'Shall we open some wine when we get back?' he said. 'I've got some CDs with me as well.'

'Are you trying to seduce me, Freddie?'

He stopped walking and pulled me towards him. 'Of course I am,' he said.

Freddie – August 2015

Jo-Jo was lying on my chest, curling my grey chest hair as we watched the fire that she'd made when we came back from the lake. I was mesmerised by the yellow and blue dancing flames, the white heat spot, the world of fairy-fire-folk that I imagined inhabited a burning universe inside the log burner. We'd left the front and back door open to keep the heat down. The whole cottage smelt of charcoal. I thought about the last time Jo-Jo and I had made love, over thirty years ago.

'Are you okay?' she said.

I kissed the top of her head and hugged her closer to my body. 'I was just thinking about the last time we slept together. I can't remember where that was.'

'Probably in my bed the night before I went off to university.'

'Underneath your Starsky and Hutch posters.'

'God, I'd forgotten about those.'

I picked up our glasses of wine from the bedside table and handed one to Jo-Jo. 'Shall I put some music on?'

'What have you brought?'

I slid out of the emperor bed, opened the wardrobe door and reached into my black Adidas holdall. I pulled out a purple CD storage wallet and handed it to Jo-Jo. 'Take your pick. There's over fifty CDs in there.'

She laughed. 'You must be one of the last people in the world to carry music around on CDs. Is there even a CD player in this cottage?'

'I checked before we came,' I said. 'It's part of the TV system.'

'Of course you did,' she said, handing me back the wallet. 'I don't mind. You choose.'

I took the wallet and walked into the lounge, conscious of being naked and the front and back door being open. 'This wouldn't be a good time for Derek to arrive and take you to task about those oars,' I said.

'No,' she said. 'But it is quite a nice view from where I'm lying.'

I unzipped the wallet, pushed a CD into the player and pressed the play icon on the remote control. I walked back into the bedroom and got into bed. Jo-Jo rolled over and snuggled into my chest again. 'I'd forgotten how cuddly you are,' she said.

I slid down the bed until we were face to face.

Her expression changed, became more intense.

'What's wrong?' I said.

'I'm frightened you'll disappear again, turn into the nervy guy from the hotel restaurant the other night.'

Eddi Reader's *Simple Soul* album started to play.

I kissed her and pulled her closer. 'How's your stamina?' I said.

*

We sat up in bed and grabbed our wine glasses. Eddi Reader had reached 'The Girl Who Fell in Love With the Moon'. 'I thought desire was meant to diminish with age,' said Jo-Jo.

'We've got a lot of catching up to do,' I said.

'I don't think I can manage thirty-five years' worth in one long weekend, Freddie.'

Simple Soul restarted as the CD slipped into repeat mode.

'Dance with me, Jo-Jo.'

'What?'

'I want to dance with you.'

She lifted up the duvet. 'We're naked.'

'I know.'

'Okay,' she said.

We walked into the lounge, put our arms around each other, me with a mile-wide grin, Jo-Jo trying to suppress a laugh. We started to sway to the music. 'I can't believe I'm doing this,' she said. 'The front and back door are still open.'

'I've waited a long time to ask you to dance,' I said, closing my eyes and remembering our dance in Max's when I'd held her for the first time. And now she was back with me, dancing to Eddi Reader. I started to think about all the wasted years, the what if and the if only, but pushed the thoughts away to suck in the memory of now, the cottage, in front of the log fire. *Simple Soul* and Jo-Jo's warm, bare flesh against mine.

She reached up and touched my forehead. 'What are you thinking about?'

'Our first dance,' I said. 'I'm glad I asked you this time.'

'So am I,' she said, snuggling back into my chest. 'I'm glad you're back in my life, Freddie.'

'Me too. Let's make it forever.'

Jo-Jo – August 2015

I woke up in a state of panic. The fire had gone out, the room was in full darkness and, for a moment, I didn't know where I was. Freddie was lying on his side, facing me, with his left arm under my neck and his right arm and right leg draped over my body, like he was afraid I was going to run away during the night. I remembered our love-making, the closeness, the gentleness, the passion. And then I remembered what he'd said just before we'd finished dancing. I didn't know what he meant by 'forever' and the more I thought about it, the more it bothered me. He'd re-emerged as my Freddie, but I didn't know anything about his life away from me, his daughter, and he'd barely asked about Jason or Amy. It felt like we were locked in a thirty-five-years-old time bubble, but we weren't. Life had happened for both of us and I still hadn't told him about the clinic. I felt the panic rise again in my stomach.

'Cheese and wine,' he said. 'Cheese and wine.'

I couldn't believe he still talked in his sleep.

'Cabbages and beans. We need cabbages and beans.'

I closed my eyes and snuggled into him. 'Of course we do,' I said. 'We'll get some tomorrow.'

He turned over, releasing me from his legs and arms. I needed to talk to him, be honest with him. The last twenty-four hours had been wonderful, a reminder of how good we were together, but I didn't want us to get carried away without me telling him the whole story.

'Cabbages,' he said.

I shuffled over, pressed my body against his back and kissed him on the shoulder. 'Oh, Freddie,' I whispered.

*

The following day, Sunday, I decided we were going to the Junction Inn pub for lunch. 'I've Googled them and you're right, they do good food.'

'I'll book the cab,' he said.

'I've told you, we're walking. You said it was only a mile.'

'But it is a mile, Jo-Jo. I'll pay for the taxi.'

'We're walking, Freddie.'

I loaded the route into my Samsung phone, Freddie put his arm around my shoulder, I put my arm around his waist, and we set off up the dirt track.

'We should have got a taxi,' he said, five minutes into the walk.

'It's not far,' I said, staring at my phone. 'Just around the corner and up the hill.'

'And then we have to walk back.'

'Stop moaning. Think of all the calories you're burning.'

We walked up the hill, past a dormer bungalow with an open plan front garden. There were three mature fruit trees growing in the centre – the first two were apple, the last one was a pear tree. All of them were laden with fruit. 'Let's rest here a bit, Freddie.'

'I thought you said it wasn't far,' he said.

'It isn't, but I want to check something.'

He looked at the bungalow and gave me a puzzled look. 'What are you up to, Jo-Jo?'

'When did you last go scrumping?' I said.

'We can't do that. What if we get caught?'

'Where's your sense of adventure?'

He hesitated, looked again at the bungalow and its trees. 'Apples or pears?' he said.

'Both. You get the apples off the second tree, I'll get the pears. Two of each.'

'Are you sure about this?'

'I double dare you,' I said, running off towards the last tree. I could hear Freddie running behind me. We reached our trees and started pulling at the fruit. There was a knock on the bungalow window. I started to run up the hill, my heart pumping adrenalin at racing car speed. Freddie caught up with me. He was gasping for breath but laughing at the same time. I looked behind.

'Is anyone coming?' he said.

'No, I think we're safe. Did you get them?'

He grinned and held out his hands, an apple in each.

'Me too,' I said, showing him the pears.

'God that felt good,' he said.

I put all of the fruit in my bag and we carried on walking, I had to move my bag off my left shoulder so I could cosy into his body. There was no path, and the road was quite narrow. We were walking against the traffic and every so often we had to go single file as a lorry or van screamed by. We came back together again as soon as it was safe, him on the outside, me on the inside. I could feel him squeezing me against him and I squeezed him back – it felt comforting.

'There it is,' I said, pointing at the white building at the top of the hill. 'I hope they've got a table. Perhaps we should have booked.'

We reached the pub, climbed the steps and walked into the lounge. It was about half full of people already tucking into their Sunday lunches. The lounge door closed behind us with a slam and the gossipy chatter died to a silence. There was a crackle of tension in the air, and for a second I wanted to turn around and walk back out. Freddie grabbed my hand and we walked to the bar, everybody in the pub looking at us; some had stopped eating mid-fork to mouth. I could hear the sound of my shoes from every step I made on the beer-stained carpet. I felt a desperate urge to order a Babycham, replicating the 1970s advert of the posh couple going into a working men's club.

'Yes?' said the barman, looking us up and down.

'We'd like to see the wine list,' said Freddie.

I could have kissed him.

The conversations at the tables started back up.

'Of course,' said the barman, handing the menu over. 'Would you like to see the food menu as well?'

'I think I'm going to go for the carvery,' said Freddie.

'Pork, beef or chicken?' said the barman.

Freddie chose the chicken, which I remembered he always used to have in Max's. I asked what the vegetarian option was, thinking it was going to be nut roast, but was pleasantly surprised when the barman handed over another menu. 'My wife's a vegetarian,' he said. 'You two staying at Granny Mary's cottage?'

'No,' I said.

'I thought everyone who comes visiting stays at Granny Mary's.'

'We're not,' I said, still looking at the menu. 'What's the red dragon pie like?'

'Really nice. One of the wife's favourites. She puts extra soy sauce in to spice it up a bit.'

'I'll have that,' I said.

The barman closed his notebook and walked away down a corridor at the back of the bar, which I assumed led to the kitchen.

'Who do you think Granny Mary is?' I said to Freddie.

'I have no idea,' he said. 'But she sounds like a character from a Stephen King book.'

Freddie – August 2015

It was after midnight by the time I dropped Jo-Jo at the hotel and I was struggling to keep my eyes open after the drive back from Devon. I managed to get the car back to Jack's house, park it on his drive and post the keys through his letterbox. I then walked home, my head bursting with Jo-Jo and our weekend. I felt like making an announcement in the coffee shop, shouting it out over the coffee grinder, the steamer and the gossipy chatter, telling everyone about our new memories – the lake, the boat, Gordon the Trout, Muscadet, Eddi Reader, the village of the damned pub, my clumsy fall out of bed.

Jack texted me the next morning to say he'd pick me up at twelve thirty and he was taking me to the Mason's Arms for lunch. He pulled up outside the house bang on time and beeped the horn. I went through my leaving the house checks, starting in the kitchen, room to room, plugs out, taps off, making sure the curtains were equidistant each side of the windows, locking and unlocking the back door, counting, one, two, three, four, moving the handle up and down after each turn of the key, same routine with the front door, one, two, three, four.

'Your mum has a lot to answer for,' said Jack as I climbed into the passenger seat.

'You can't help who you are,' I said.

'Hang on a minute,' he said, turning to face me. 'You've had sex. I can tell by the look on your face. I thought you were on the sofa.'

'So did I.'

I told him everything about the weekend on our way to the pub. One glorious sentence rolled into another, and another, and another. I had to force myself to take a breath. 'It was wonderful,' I said. 'We just fitted.'

'You always did,' he said. 'You just needed to get that head of yours sorted.'

'I can't believe we've wasted so many years.'

'I'm happy for you, Freddie. It's felt like the longest running soap opera of all time, but at least you got it together eventually.'

'Where's Bob?' I said. 'I thought he'd be with you.'

'He's meeting us there. There was no way he was going to miss this lunch.'

*

Bob was sitting in one of the three red leather Sherlock chairs, which were positioned in front of the fireplace next to the bar. It was a prime spot in the winter with the coal fire blazing but hardly ever used during the summer. On the wall there were framed pictures of ex-Wolverhampton Wanderers footballers, some of them signed – Derek Dougan, Phil Parkes, Derek Parkin. The pub was quiet, just a couple of pot-bellied regulars standing in front of the games machine. There were usually four of them playing the *Who Wants to Be a Millionaire* quiz, whooping at correct answers,

195

chastising each other for stupid ones, drinking pints of real ale and dipping into a jumbo bag of cheesy Quavers ripped open on a table in front of them. Jack could never resist making his hygiene alert – 'I bet none of them washes their hands when they go to the toilet, which means that bag of Quavers is being seasoned with all of their urine, and worse.'

'You look like you've been here a while,' I said to Bob.

'Ten minutes,' he said. 'I wanted to hear about your Don Juan adventures.'

'Freddie as Don Juan,' said Jack. 'Now there's an image.'

'I'll get some drinks,' I said.

'Just a coke for me,' said Jack.

Bob nodded. 'I'll have the same.'

I turned to the bar, but the barman was already pouring the drinks. 'And I'm guessing you'll have a Dandelion and Burdock,' he said. 'You three really are the last of the big spenders.'

'Remind me why we come here again?' said Jack.

'You like the atmosphere and the politeness of the staff,' said the barman. 'Do you want these on a tab?'

I nodded. 'We might get some food later.'

'I won't hold my breath,' he said, lining the drinks up on the bar.

*

'So, how was it?' said Bob. 'I can tell you've had sex.'

'I said that,' said Jack. 'It's so obvious.'

'It was perfect,' I said.

'Please,' said Jack. 'Once is okay, Freddie, but I don't want to hear it all again.'

'I haven't heard it,' said Bob.

'That's right, Jack. Bob hasn't heard it.'

'Okay,' said Jack, holding up his hands in mock surrender. 'Tell it all again, but the big question is, what next?'

196

'I'll call her I suppose.'

'You mean you haven't agreed anything?'

'About what?'

'You've had a perfect weekend, Freddie. When are you seeing her again?'

'I don't think we actually said.'

'I can't believe you,' said Jack. 'You describe a weekend straight out of Ali MacGraw and Ryan O'Neal's *Love Story* and then you walk away without knowing when you're going to see her again.'

'It didn't come up.'

'Not everyone's as pushy as you,' said Bob. 'He's playing it cool.'

'No he isn't,' said Jack. 'You weren't, were you? You just forgot.'

'I'll call her,' I said. 'I'll go outside and call her.'

Jo-Jo – August 2015

I walked through the hotel reception and smiled at the man behind the desk. It was the same man who always called me madam and wore an expression like he was about to be held up at gunpoint whenever Amy walked towards him. I'd sent Amy a text on our journey home to let her know when I was getting back and not to wait up. She'd replied saying she wanted to meet up for breakfast. Her text had two big smiley face emojis at the end.

The next morning, I walked into the conservatory. Amy waved at me from one of the wicker chairs next to the yellow daisy-patterned jardinière, which was home for a well-established citrus tree – we'd discovered the tree was lemon by rubbing the leaves and releasing the aroma of its oils. 'I've ordered your tea,' she said as I sat down. 'How was the weekend?'

'It was lovely. We had a lovely time.'

'Did you share a bed?'

'That's none of your business.'

'That means yes.'

I smiled and looked down at the glass-topped cane table. 'That waitress always takes her time bringing the tea.'

Amy squeezed my leg and laughed. 'Good for you, Mum. When are you seeing him again?'

I felt the smile slip off my face. 'I'm not sure.'

'It did go well though?' said Amy.

The waitress walked over carrying a tray. 'Earl Grey, madam?'

I nodded and she placed the teapot, one cup and saucer and a jug of milk on the table. I lifted the lid off the pot and started swishing the bag around with a teaspoon. It always reminded me of Mum and our trips to Cannock. I replaced the lid and poured the tea. 'It went very well,' I said. 'A bit too well if I'm honest.'

'I don't understand.'

'He was wonderful, the old Freddie, my Freddie. It made me remember how much I loved him, realise how much I still love him.'

'That's good, isn't it?'

'In a way, but it came back so easily, so quickly. I need to think about it.'

'There's no rush, Mum. Enjoy it, take in every second. He's not putting pressure on you, is he?'

'No. I'm putting pressure on me. I never expected to feel like this again. It's, well, you get used to being...'

'Alone. You're going to say alone, aren't you?'

'It's not just that. There are things he doesn't know. Things I need to tell him.'

'You don't have to tell him anything. I'm sure he's lived a life as well.'

'I mean things that involve him. From when we were kids.'

I took a sip of my tea.

'Mum, tell me what happened. I think I can guess.'

'You can't. Not about this.'

'Sometimes we have to do things we don't want to do,' she said. 'At the time it's the right decision, but it doesn't mean you don't regret it later. You were eighteen and on your own.'

The image of her, seven years old, playing with her Sindy doll and Eagle Eyes Action Man, marrying them off in a wedding ceremony, standing them up against her My Little Pony cushions, filled my head. 'They're going to love each other forever, Mummy.'

'How on earth did you get so wise?' I said, reaching out and touching her face.

'It's ancient history, Mum. Let it go.'

'I need to be honest with him.'

'Is that why you went looking for him?'

'I never expected to still have the same feelings, to still love him, but he still has a right to know.'

'How do you think he'll react?'

'I don't know. His relationship with his daughter isn't good.' I took another sip of my tea. 'I thought you might have reacted differently. You could have had a brother or sister.'

'Can you really imagine me sharing you?' she said.

Jo-Jo – December 1979

Freddie walked around the corner into my street, past the oak tree and the wooden bench, which had been the view from my bedroom window all of my life. He raised his hand when he saw me on the doorstep. I pulled the front door closed behind me, ran across the road, grabbed his hand and hurried him back to the tree. We sat down on the bench. 'I thought I was meeting your mum and dad,' he said.

'I need to talk to you, tell you about my mum.'

'You don't think I'll be good enough for her.'

'What? No. I mean, yes. What makes you say that?'

'I've been awake all night, thinking about it. They're going to hate me.'

'I'm not worried about you. It's Mum. She's not well.'

The smile disappeared from his face. He looked like he'd done something wrong, which made me feel sad. 'I can't believe I'm having to tell you this,' I said.

'Tell me,' he said, putting his arm around me.

I snuggled into his hug, enjoying the comfort. 'She hears voices,' I said. 'They scare her. She's better with her medication, but most days she can't get out of bed.'

'Jesus. That sounds like a nightmare.'

'Not really. We're used to it. It's embarrassing more than anything. I'd understand if you didn't want to meet her.'

He stood up and pulled me to my feet. 'She can't be any nuttier than my mum,' he said.

*

I closed the front door behind us. We could hear Genesis' 'Follow You, Follow Me' coming down the stairs from Josh's bedroom. 'My brother,' I said. 'He's obsessed with Phil Collins.'

Dad stood up as we walked into the lounge and held out his hand. 'It's nice to meet you, Freddie,' he said. 'I hope you're going to look after her.'

'Always,' said Freddie, shaking Dad's hand.

'This my mum,' I said.

Mum was lying on the sofa, her eyes squeezed shut, muttering to herself. Dad had stacked the coal fire so it was roaring like a blast furnace up the chimney, but Mum was still wrapped from head to toe in a green and white striped woollen blanket. 'I feel the cold, Joseph. You know I feel the cold.' Freddie crouched down and stroked Mum's hand. 'It's lovely to meet you,' he said. Mum opened her eyes and smiled – a behind the eyes smile.

'I'll make some tea,' said Dad, walking towards the lounge door. He stopped when he reached me, met my eyes and mouthed, 'He'll do.'

Freddie was still holding Mum's hand. She was still smiling.

Jo-Jo – April 1981

Madness were beating out their nutty boy sound as Liam and I cut across the path of congaing students and headed towards the Sherlock chair, Liam brushing people out of our way with his bowler hat. 'Why's he here,' I said. 'At a student's party.'

'No idea,' said Liam. 'He just sits there reading his *Guardian*. Do you still want to meet him?'

'Definitely,' I said. 'I'm intrigued.'

We reached the chair and Liam gently flicked the broadsheet. 'Hi Prof,' he said. 'This is Jo-Jo. She wants to know what you're doing here.'

The man looked over the top of his paper. 'I imagine you wanted him to put that more delicately,' he said. He leaned forward to the coffee table and stubbed out his filter-free cigarette in a blue Whitefriars bubble glass ashtray.

I felt the blush rise from my neck and across my face. 'I was just... well, you do look a bit out of place, and I'm interested in people...'

'She means she's a nosy bitch,' said Liam.

The five-person conga-train went past and a girl at the back with red hair flicked an air kick in Liam's direction. 'I love this song,' I said, desperately trying to change the subject. 'Night Train to Cairo.'

'You know it's not called that, don't you?' said Liam.

'Yes it is.'

'And how exactly does a train make its way down the River Nile?'

'Sounds better though,' said the professor.

'Yes,' I said. 'That's what I thought.'

'Right,' said Liam. 'Makes absolutely no sense with the lyrics, but it sounds better. I think I'll leave you two alone. You deserve each other.'

The conga-train went past again and Liam joined the back, putting his hands on the hips of the red-haired girl. She smiled at him and he said something to her which made her laugh. The opening line of 'One Step Beyond' reverberated around the room. 'Sit down,' said the professor, patting the leather sofa next to the Sherlock chair.

I flopped into the seat. 'He's right,' I said. 'I am a nosy bitch. What brings you to a student party?'

'Would you believe the company?'

'You must have better places to hang out.'

He folded up his newspaper, crossed his legs and looked around the room. 'And which of these young men is lucky enough to have you on his arm?'

'None of them,' I said.

'You're single.'

'I am now.'

The image of the waiting room landed with a thud inside my head – the receptionist with the bright red lipstick, the accusing whispers of the nurses, the sobbing, the pain, ten, nine, eight, seven, six…

'Are you okay?' he said, reaching forward and touching my hand.

'I will be,' I said. 'What about you? Are you married?'

'For ten years. I lost her to breast cancer five years ago. It was too late by the time they found it.'

'I'm sorry,' I said. 'You must miss her.'

'I miss her laugh the most,' he said. 'One of the best memories I have is her challenging me to a race on our way home from the pub. She hoisted up her black dress, the one with the zip down the front, freed up her stockinged legs, took off her high-heel shoes and sprinted away from me. I can still hear the sound of her belly laugh in the early morning silence of the streets. I never want that memory to leave me.'

I looked at him. He'd drifted off into another world. I put my hand on his hand, which he'd rested on the arm of the Sherlock chair. 'What's your name?' I said.

'Jason,' he said.

Jo-Jo – July 1983

Karen and I were sitting at the window table in the Three Chimneys pub in Lincoln, looking out at the derelict market stalls, the vendors having packed up and gone home for the day. She'd come up on the train from Walsall and was staying over at the flat for a few days to help me get things sorted for the big move-out. We were drinking pints of lager and blackcurrant. 'I can't believe how quickly it's gone,' she said. 'I never thought you'd stick it out.'

'Me neither,' I said.

'And now you're a graduate. Well done, you.'

She hugged me again. It was the third time she'd congratulated me since we'd sat down with our drinks. 'Are you okay?' I said.

'I'm good,' she said. 'Rob's dumped me, but I'm glad. It wasn't going anywhere.'

'Oh, Karen, I'm sorry. When did this happen?'

'A couple of months ago. He's shacked up with some nurse now.'

'You should have called me.'

'It's no big deal. Same old story. I pick rubbish men. That's what I do.'

We took a sip of our pints. A man in a brown wool Crombie coat and red Doc Martens came into the pub. Him and his coat looked like they needed a good wash. He had a skinny lurcher on a lead walking at his side. 'You can't bring him in here,' the barwoman shouted across the lounge. 'I've told you before.'

The man muttered something, patted the dog's head and walked back outside where he tied the lead to the concrete wastepaper bin. The dog lay down on the pavement, put his head on his paws and yawned, looking as though he was used to the routine. The man walked back into the pub and up to the bar. I stared at the lurcher through the window. It had been three years since Freddie had said, 'You'll forget about me, Jo-Jo,' made his guilt trip proposal of marriage, delivered his no-show phone call, and then the clinic, Dad's death, Liam. The dog closed his eyes.

'What next?' said Karen. 'You coming back home?'

I lifted up the pint glass and glugged at the lager. 'No,' I said, putting the drink back on the table. 'Jason's asked me to move in with him.'

'Jason. You mean the old guy?'

'He's not old,' I said.

'He's a lot older than you. I thought he was just your "sleep with the teacher" moment.'

'He's nice, lonely. Anyway, the other option is to go back home. Dad's dead, Josh has moved out and I'd be left with Mum and all the weirdness coming out of her schizophrenia-addled head. I don't exactly have many choices here, Karen.'

'Yeah, but moving in with an old guy you hardly know. Is that a good idea?'

'He's okay. I'll be okay.'

'Where's he live?'

'He's got a detached house on the outskirts of Lincoln.'

'The one he lived in with his dead wife?'

'She wasn't dead when she lived there.'

'It wouldn't do for me,' she said, feigning a full body shiver. 'I couldn't stand her ghost rattling around in my life.'

'You do say the strangest things,' I said. 'I won't be there long. It's only until I get sorted.'

*

'We can do want you want with the house,' said Jason. 'It hasn't been decorated since Tanya died.'

'Let's see how it goes,' I said.

He walked over to the fireplace and picked up one of the six Whitefriars red bubble glass dilly ducks and turned it over in his hand. 'I want you to be comfortable here,' he said. 'Make this your home.'

'It's not really my home, Jason. It's your home.'

He put the ornament back on the shelf and faced me. 'Couldn't it become ours?'

'Like I said, let's see how it goes. I've only been here a couple of weeks.'

'I talk about Tanya too much, don't I?'

'We've both got pasts.'

'But mine's in this house. Is that it?'

'Partly,' I said. 'But it's also me. I don't want to rush into anything permanent.'

'I see,' he said. 'It's the age difference then.'

'No. It's nothing to do with you. It's me. Let's just enjoy what we have and see what happens.'

He walked over to me, put his hands on each side of my face and kissed me. 'You're right,' he said. 'Thank you for being here. You've changed my life.'

'I just want to clear my head,' I said. 'Work out what to do next.'

I heard the window cleaner lean his ladders against the front of the house and, clump, clump, clump, he climbed up the steps to the bedroom, which was always at the start of his job. It would take him a while to work his way around to the bathroom, but I stood up and pulled down the blind. I sat back down on the toilet lid and looked again at the white plastic stick. The indicator was still blue. 'My God,' I said out loud.

Ten, nine, eight, seven, six...

I flushed the toilet, went out onto the landing and walked downstairs. Jason was sitting on the sofa, reading his *Guardian*. I walked into the room and sat down in the armchair opposite him. I could hear the Seiko wall clock ticking away the minutes from its position on the wall behind me. He dropped his newspaper and looked at me. 'Are you okay?' he said. 'You're as white as a ghost.'

'I've got something to tell you,' I said.

He put the newspaper on the seat next to him. 'You're leaving me,' he said.

'No, Jason. I'm not leaving you, but I am...'

'You're pregnant.'

I looked down and realised I'd unconsciously had both my hands on my stomach. 'Yes,' I said. 'I'm pregnant.'

He jumped up, walked over to the chair and kissed me. 'That's wonderful,' he said. 'Just wonderful.' He was crying. 'A baby. I'm going to be a dad. Oh, Jo-Jo, that's wonderful.'

'It's going to change everything, Jason.'

'I know,' he said. 'We'll have to, well, I assume, we'll get married.'

'Married?'

'That's the right thing to do, isn't it? For the baby.'

'Is it right for us though?' I said.

'I love you,' he said.

The squeaky sound of the window cleaner's chamois leather as he rubbed away on the glass made us both look across at the bay window. The window cleaner waved. Jason waved back.

Jo-Jo – May 1984

The clock ticked over to five o'clock, triggering the bell to mark the start of visiting time. Our Hattie Jacques lookalike matron opened the double entrance doors to the ward and Jason walked, almost ran, down to my bed, which was about four beds along, clutching his two red roses. Wendy, the woman in the bed next to mine, who'd given birth to a twelve pounds, three ounces boy, leaned towards me and said, 'He always looks so happy your husband. Your first is it? He's my fourth. I can barely get my old man away from the footie.'

Jason handed me the flowers. 'One for each of you,' he said, before turning to the foot of the bed and leaning down to the cot. 'She's so perfect. Aren't we clever?'

'Yes,' I said. 'She is perfect.'

'They let me cut the cord,' he said. 'I didn't even know you could do that. I thought the dads had to wait outside.' He was still looking down at the cot.

'You back again, love,' said Wendy. 'I was telling this one, she's lucky to have you.'

Jason smiled at her, walked up the side of the bed and sat down in the armchair. 'I've been thinking about a name,' he said. 'I'm not sure how you'll feel about this.'

'It's not going to happen, Jason.'

'You don't know what I'm going to say yet.'

'You want to call her Tanya.'

'Well, yes,' he said. 'I thought it would be nice.'

'You want me to call our baby after your dead wife?'

'I wish you wouldn't talk about her like that, Jo-Jo. She's...'

'We're calling her Amy,' I said.

'Amy?'

'It's my mum's middle name. I've always loved it.'

Jo-Jo – July 1987

'Do we have to go out tonight? There's a documentary on telly I want to watch.'

He was standing behind me. I was sitting cross-legged in front of the dressing table, halfway through putting on my thick black mascara. I paused the brush mid-way and glared at him through the mirror. 'We're going, Jason,' I said. 'I don't see Karen half as much as I should and the baby-sitter's booked.'

'You could go,' he said. 'You don't need me there.'

'She's bringing her new fella. She wants us to meet him.'

'I never feel comfortable with your friends. They make me feel old.'

'Oh, for God's sake. Not this again. I thought you liked Karen.'

'I do. It's just, well, our age difference is obvious.'

'No it isn't. Only in your head. Anyway, we're going.'

'And then there's him?'

I put the brush on the dressing table. 'Who?' I said, facing him. 'Karen's boyfriend? You've not met him yet.'

'Not him. You know who I mean.'

'You mean Freddie. Is that who you're talking about?'

'I don't like the idea she might be comparing us.'

'You think Karen's comparing you with Freddie. That's ridiculous.'

'I would. And what chance do I stand against him? You were the same age. Your first love always has a bigger impression. She saw you together, saw what you meant to each other. There's never going to be anything like that for you.'

'You mean like you and Tanya?'

'We're not talking about me.'

'We are now. I have to live with that bloody woman every second, breathe the same air in every room in this house. And the biggest thing you've got is having dinner with my best friend who happened to know my first boyfriend.'

Jo-Jo – November 2006

Our neighbours, Alex and Julie, had descended on us for a ritual Saturday night game of Monopoly. I threw the dice. They landed against my wine glass, which I'd placed on the carpet next to me. A three and a two. I picked up the iron and bounced it slowly across the board, watching Jason out the corner of my eye. Mayfair, my four green plastic houses and one red hotel already cramming up the purple-headed square.

'I'll buy a hotel,' I said.

'Jammy sod,' said Alex, picking up one of the cheese and pineapple sticks I'd laid out on the coffee table. 'I've never known anyone have two hotels on Mayfair and four houses on Park Lane.'

'It was an illegal throw,' said Jason.

'What?'

'Your dice didn't stop rolling. They hit your wine glass.'

'Seriously?'

'There's no point in playing if you're not going to play properly.'

'But you could say that about every throw. The carpet slows the dice down.'

'It's not an obstacle you can avoid. You can avoid your wine glass.'

'Really, Jason,' said Julie. 'It's only a game.'

'It's cheating. She needs to take the throw again.'

I picked up the dice. 'Where would you like me to put these?'

Alex and Julie laughed.

'Just throw them on the carpet,' said Jason.

I rattled the dice in my hand. I could feel the silent tension oozing out of Alex and Julie. Jason was wearing his lording it over everyone grin, the one that always made me want to slap him hard. I threw the dice, one roll, two, three, they came to a stop against the white sheepskin rug in front of the gas fire. A two and a one. I smiled. Alex clapped his hands. I moved the iron slowly, coming to a stop on Park Lane. 'I'll buy a hotel,' I said, peeling a £200 note from my stash of money.

'Another illegal throw,' said Jason. 'The roll was stopped by the edge of the rug, which you could have avoided.'

'You don't think you're taking this a bit too seriously?'

'It's the rules.'

'Fuck your rules, Jason,' I said, picking up the bottle of Muscadet and filling my glass to the brim. I offered the bottle to Alex and Julie, who nodded. I filled their glasses and held my glass out. 'Fuck Jason and his rules,' I toasted.

*

We undressed in silence, me getting into my bed, Jason into his.

'Well, another evening spoiled,' I said.

'By me, I suppose,' he said.

'Who else? You and your stupid rules.'

'I don't see the point in playing if we're not going to follow them.'

'You were just pissed off because I landed on those squares. You don't like me winning.'

'That would make me really childish, Jo-Jo.'

'You said it.'

Silence. I turned off my bedside light. Jason turned off his. I stared at the ceiling, waiting for it. A part of me enjoying the moment. Saturday night rituals, his vulnerability, his weakness. 'Jo-Jo,' he said.

'You've got no chance, Jason.'

*

Breakfast – I bounced his fry-up plate in front of him. Bacon, sausage, eggs, beans, tinned tomatoes and fried bread. 'You could cook that yourself, you know. Just for a change.'

'I don't do it as well as you.'

'Must be the practice I get.'

'You're still annoyed about last night.'

'Not really. You can't help what you are.'

'Too old for you. Too set in my ways. I told you that when we first met.'

'We've been married for over twenty years, Jason.'

'Doesn't make it any less true.'

'It's got nothing to do with age.'

'You like the money though, don't you?'

I carried on buttering my toast. I could feel him looking at me, waiting for a response. 'You're Amy's dad,' I said.

'Yes,' he said. 'And that's the only reason you've stayed.'

I met his eyes. 'You were kind when I met you.'

'You needed me after him. That was all there was to it.'

'I can't believe you still talk about him. I wish I'd never told you.'

He picked up his knife and fork, cut the end off one of his sausages, and dipped it into the egg yolk. 'Hard not to talk about him,' he said. 'He's been here every day of our marriage.'

'You can't let go of the past, can you?'

He put the knife and fork down. 'Face it, Jo-Jo. I was just your rescue dog.'

'You're Amy's dad.'

'He even beat me there. She's not exactly your first, is she?'

'Why are you mentioning that?'

'It's why we're here isn't it? Me rescuing you from your termination. You finding a daddy to balm your conscience.'

'You really hate me, don't you?'

'No, I really don't, Jo-Jo.'

He folded up his newspaper, stood up and walked into the lounge.

I stared at his uneaten breakfast, yellow streams of disturbed egg yolk running through the blood-coloured gunge of the tinned tomatoes. My eyes landed on Amy's graduation picture, which hung on the dining room wall – her face-filling smile, a tilted mortar board on her head, a faux parchment tied with red ribbon clutched in her hands, her life ahead of her.

Jo-Jo – October 2008

It was sunset time on our last trip to the Maldives. I was sitting on a swing and looking out at the talcum powder beach and the azure blue sea of the Indian Ocean, thinking about my early morning snorkelling trip. I'd seen a pod of dolphins bobbing up and down on the tide, but they'd disappeared as I was trying to reach them. That's when I'd felt a nudge in my back. I'd spun round in the water and a solitary dolphin was staring at me, our eyes meeting momentarily before it glided away from the coral and out into the ink-purple deep. He'd waited for me – that's what it felt like. This was the sort of thing I'd experienced with Amy, but without her the excitement deflated like a punctured Lilo. 'I never know why you want to come,' I'd said to Jason on the seaplane. 'You can't swim and it's always too hot for you.' 'I like the solitude,' he'd replied. And he did. He'd sit in the shade, next to the swimming pool, wearing a straw hat, suit trousers and a long-sleeved shirt, and he'd read, read, read. His only concession to the tropical climate was the absence of socks underneath his Jesus sandals. Our worlds never collided. I lived in the ocean, snorkelling along the reef, gasping at the marine life, paddle-boarding through the surf, canoeing to the sandbanks, swimming with the fishes, catamaran sailing in search of turtles.

The sun finally fell into the sea, sending a fireball splash of colour across the sky and turning the clouds into horizon plops of gassy islands, the whole view dropped into silhouette. One of the cloud clusters started to break up, morphing from a Popeye image into a Desperate Dan figure. It reminded me of Freddie and our field by the driving range. I hoped he was okay.

Jo-Jo – February 2014

A niggling cough, chest pain on exertion, shortness of breath. Six weeks later we were sitting in front of a Harley Street consultant getting the results of his MRI scan. 'I'm afraid it's spread to the brain,' said the surgeon.

'We'll get a second opinion,' I said. 'There must be something they can do.'

'How long?' said Jason.

'Months at most,' said the surgeon, 'but more likely weeks.'

'For God's sake,' I said. 'There must be something...'

'It's okay,' said Jason, squeezing my hand. 'I'm ready to go.'

Three weeks later he was dead.

Amy sobbed like a baby when I told her. 'Oh God, Mum. What are we going to do without him?' 'Let's just get through the funeral,' I said, not knowing what else to say.

I felt sad for Amy, but my overriding emotion was apathy. A chance meeting at a student party over a quarter of a century earlier had morphed into something so malignant, it needed cancer to pull our lives apart – that's how it felt. One of Jason's last requests was to have Tanya's family at his funeral. They all came, but none of them acknowledged me. Whatever afterlife Jason had travelled to, he'd be searching for Tanya. And that was okay. Tanya was his soul mate. We all had them.

Freddie – September 1971

I was lying on my side, rubbing my forefinger and thumb in a one, two, three, four rhythm across the brushed cotton sheet. The breeze from the open window was cooling the sweat on my forehead, but I snuggled deeper under the two woollen blankets to ease the shivering that was overtaking my body. I kept my eyes on the silhouetted wooden tallboy in the corner of the room, which was lit up by the bathroom light spilling across the landing. 'Leave the light on, Mum. Please leave the light on.' I quickened the rubbing across the crisp dry sheet. One, two, three, four. I could smell pineapple chunks and see air bubble fairies at the foot of my bed, streaming their way from floor to ceiling. 'Dad,' I said. One, two, three, four. Bang. I was standing on a tower block, the ground looming up at me. Mum was at my side. She was trying to pull me towards the edge. 'I don't want to jump. You can't make me jump.' 'It's okay, Freddie. I'm here.' Bang. Blackout. I opened my eyes. Mum was holding me, mopping my forehead with a warm flannel. 'I've called the doctor,' she said. 'I want Dad,' I said. She started to cry.

Two members of staff, one of the bar workers, a man, mid-fifties with a Kevin Keegan hairdo that he'd dyed blonde, and one of the kitchen assistants, a woman, early twenties, anorexic-thin with jet-black hair pulled into a tight ponytail, were sitting on the metal patio chairs. They were smoking cigarettes and chatting. I nodded at them as I walked across to the far side of the beer garden, clutching my mobile phone and cursing my stupidity.

The evening had ended with us kissing goodnight in the car on the hotel car park, the parking attendant watching us from his sentry position by the bins, arms folded tight across his chest. Jo-Jo had got out of the car and run up the hotel steps, disappearing through the reception doors and into the lobby. I'd selected Springsteen's *Tunnel of Love* album from the iPod Shuffle connected to the Mini's entertainment system and drove out of the car park with 'Ain't Got You' playing through the speakers. Arranging to see her again had not crossed my mind.

I pressed her name on my Windows phone.

'Hello.'

'Jo-Jo.'

'Freddie. I was just about to call you.'

'You were?'

'Of course. Are you okay?'

'I've just realised we haven't arranged to meet up again.'

There was a pause, a nanosecond, but definitely a hesitation, enough to roll my stomach and dry my mouth. 'Jo-Jo,' I said.

'We need to talk, Freddie.'

'I know. There's so much we…'

'No,' she said. 'I need to talk to you. We need to meet and talk.'

I walked back into the pub. Jack and Bob were staring at me like expectant fathers. 'Well?' said Jack.

'We're meeting up tomorrow. She sounded strange. Maybe she's changed her mind, maybe the daughter's put her off me.'

'You're overthinking it,' said Bob.

'Only one way to find out,' said Jack, taking a sip of his coke.

Jo-Jo – August 2015

'That pause was a bit obvious, Mum.'

'I know. I'm not sure what I'm going to say to him.'

'Like I said, you don't have to tell him anything. It's ancient history.'

'He was the father, Amy.'

'And he'd walked out of your life. It was your decision.'

'I wish I'd known he'd come to find me.'

She reached across and put her hand on my knee. 'You didn't, and he didn't try again. He jumped to conclusions. You were kids.'

'I wonder every day if it was a boy or a girl, but I couldn't get out of that hell-hole quick enough.' I looked at her; tears were streaming down her cheeks. 'Oh God,' I said. 'I'm an insensitive cow. This has got nothing to do with you, sweetheart. You are the best thing that's ever happened to me.'

She reached into her Gucci handbag, pulled out a paper tissue and blew her nose. 'That's not why I'm crying, Mum. I wish I'd been there for you. You were all alone. It sounds like a nightmare.' She hugged me and whispered in my ear, 'You should have told me years ago.'

'It's not the sort of thing you say to your daughter,' I said into her neck.

Jo-Jo had asked me to meet her on the wooden bench by the oak tree, opposite the house she'd lived in when we were seeing each other thirty-five years ago. I got ready early, went through my leaving the house ritual and decided to road trip the Mini around my old estate, reliving some of the places from my childhood. Down Severn Road where my mum and dad had lived, past the greens where Jack and I had played marbles with ironies and fobbers, past Dad's white double gates, still standing nearly five decades after his death, past Green Rock Primary School where me and Nigel Hale had collected insects in jam jars, down Wye Road where Mickey Lawton had lived – he'd thrown a house brick at my leg when I was seven and Dad had got out of bed, come down to the lounge in his pyjamas and looked at the bruise. 'You should have thrown one back.' It was the year Dad died. The year I was fractured.

I parked up outside the shops on Lower Farm estate and was astonished at how little it had changed. The newsagents, the hairdresser's, Saddler's Arms, King George's park where Jo-Jo and I used to kiss for hours, putting our freezing cold hands inside each other's coats, desperately seeking body warmth. I got out of the car and walked across the road to the Buxton Road street sign. I looked on the back of the wooden board and felt my heart jump – our initials inside a love heart, scratched there three decades ago, covered in layers of paint.

I looked at my watch. I had five minutes to walk to the bench.

I could see the oak tree and the bench as I walked down Buxton Road. I was thinking about Karen – us at twelve years of age with

Charlie Brown and Snoopy Dog posters covering our bedroom walls; us at fifteen years of age walking out of the back entrance to T.P. Riley wearing our thigh-length navy blue school uniform skirts and, inspired by the TV show *FAME*, black leg warmers. We had an inch of leg flesh on show, enough to make Rob and Nigel, our boyfriends at the time, stare open-mouthed as we headed down the slope towards them. I hoped Karen was okay. The last I'd heard she was married to an Army guy who was a bit of a control freak.

I reached the bench, sat down and looked at my old house – the house where Mum's schizophrenia had lived with us like a squatter, but I'd found an order to accommodate her craziness, her voices, her paranoia, her lethargy; the house where Dad's affair had made him human, taking away my big hugs God of a dad and leaving me with something common; the house where Freddie was my Sir Lancelot, my big-hearted, sweet Freddie who'd rescued me, given me hope. And then he hadn't phoned.

'Jo-Jo.'

I turned at the sound of his voice.

I still hadn't worked out what I was going to say to him.

He hugged me and sat down on the bench. 'You okay?' he said. 'I've been for a walk around the estate, parked the car up by the shops. Hardly anything's changed. We should go down the lanes, see what's replaced Sam's caravan.'

'You don't think he's still there, do you?'

'I'm damn sure he's not. He was in his seventies when we knew him.'

'Yes,' I said. 'Of course.'

'The house is still here then,' he said, nodding across the road.

'Still here,' I said. 'I wonder who lives there now.'

'We could knock the door and ask. Perhaps they'll let us have a look around, see what's changed.'

'It's just a house, Freddie.'

He went quiet. I squeezed his knee. 'It was a nice thought though,' I said.

'You wanted to talk,' he said. 'It sounded serious. I thought Devon went well. Have I done something wrong?'

'It's not about Devon,' I said. 'It's about Lincoln, something that happened in Lincoln.'

'Lincoln? When you were at university?'

'I did something, Freddie. Something awful that I think you'll hate me for.'

He touched my face. 'I could never hate you,' he said.

'Promise you'll just listen to me,' I said. 'It's too painful to drag it out.'

'If it's about you and that bloke I saw you with...'

'Promise me, Freddie.'

'I promise,' he said, holding my hand.

Freddie – August 2015

I could feel she was waiting for me to say something, but my body and brain had gone numb as soon as she'd said the word. I had so many questions, not least what she'd told them about me, but it was another lifetime ago.

'I thought you'd gone, Freddie,' she said.

'A baby,' I said. 'You and I could have had a baby?'

'That's the point. There was no us. I thought you'd gone.'

I realised that I'd let go of her hand. I held it again and she smiled at me.

'You should have told me,' I said. 'Got in touch. I could have helped.'

'I know. Years later, I knew, but it was too late. I was married, Amy came along...'

'I mean at the time, Jo-Jo. I'd have come back.'

I let go of her hand again.

'You'd left me, Freddie. I thought you'd gone for good.'

'You should have contacted me,' I said.

We stared at the house in silence.

I felt Jo-Jo take my hand.

'What happens now?' she said.

'I need to think,' I said.

Jo-Jo – August 2015

Amy was waiting for me when I arrived back at the hotel. We walked across to the gardens and sat down on the bench underneath the eucalyptus trees. I sniffed at the menthol aroma from the trees, closed my eyes and sucked in the birdsong and the woo wooing of the pigeons. 'He needs to think?' said Amy.

'It's the shock. He'll be talking it through with Jack.'

'It's about time he grew up. Did he ask about you? How did you leave it?'

'He said he'd call.'

'I can't believe him. It was thirty-five years ago. I'm going to phone him, ask him what he's playing at.'

'Leave him alone, Amy.'

'I can't believe you're so calm. I'd be steaming at him.'

'To be honest, I'm relieved he knows.'

'And what about next? Do you still want to be with him?'

I opened my eyes. 'I think so. I never expected it, but I still love him.'

'Oh, Mum, what a mess.'

'I'm fine, darling. I'm fine now I've told him.'

She put her arm around me and hugged me into her shoulder. 'I think we deserve a stiff drink,' she said.

'I'm not drinking any more of that bloody awful whisky,' I said.

Part Three
Last Dance

I was sitting on a bench in the gardens of the Hotel Rushmore, sipping my peppermint tea and thinking about the thirty-five-years-ago clinic with its paper sheets, omnipresent antiseptic, pain, vomit and black-hole nothingness. I placed my hand on my stomach and sighed. 'Oh, Freddie,' I said.

The French door to the hotel restaurant opened and Amy walked out, closed the door behind her and strode across the lawn. She sat down next to me and squeezed my knee. 'You okay?' she said.

I nodded, my hand still on my stomach.

'Dan's booked the flights, Mum. We leave the end of the week. If that's what you still want.'

'It's been three days, Amy. He's not going to phone.'

'Dan thinks you should call him.'

'You've discussed this with Dan?'

'He is your son-in-law. He cares about you.'

'I did wonder about calling Jack,' I said. 'But it feels like I'm a stalker. And if Freddie's made his decision…'

'Didn't all this start with missed phone calls? Don't let pride get in the way.'

'You're right,' I said, reaching into my bag and pulling out my Samsung phone. 'Jack must have spoken to him.'

'I'll get us some more tea,' said Amy, picking up my cup and saucer from the lawn. She stood up and walked off towards the hotel.

I scrolled down my contacts list and tapped on Jack's name.

*

We had a full view of the car park through the glass doors of the hotel reception area. Amy was picking at her fingernails. It was something she did when she was concentrating. I'd spent most of her childhood trying to stop her, but that just made her anxious. I was churning over the possibilities of what might have happened. Jack had sounded serious, but he didn't want to give me the details over the phone. 'I wonder why Jack didn't call me earlier,' I said.

'Perhaps he felt a bit awkward,' said Amy.

'Or perhaps something's happened today.'

'That would be a huge coincidence, Mum.'

'He's here,' I said, nodding towards the car park.

Jack's Mini was reversing into one of the visitors' bays.

*

Amy linked her arm in mine, and we walked out of the reception and onto the hotel patio. Jack ran up the concrete steps and hugged me. 'This is my daughter, Amy,' I said.

'Hi,' said Jack, shaking her hand.

'Is Freddie okay?' I said.

'Let's go and sit in the garden,' said Amy.

We reached the bench and sat down. Amy had filled the short walk across the lawn with small talk, asking Jack if he'd found the hotel okay, saying how much she loved his car. Jack had kept his eyes on the grass, nodding occasionally, muttering monosyllabic answers, all of which raised my anxiety. 'Isn't this garden lovely?' said Amy.

'What's happened to Freddie, Jack?' I said.

'He's okay,' he said. 'But he took your news pretty badly.'

'It wasn't an easy thing for Mum to tell him,' said Amy. 'I told her not to. It's nothing to do with him really. After what he...'

'Tell me what's happened,' I said.

'You know what he's like,' said Jack, tears welling in his eyes. 'He blames himself for everything.'

'You're a good friend,' I said, squeezing his hand. 'You always have been.'

He returned my squeeze and met my eyes. 'He fell in love with you the moment he saw you, Jo-Jo. You do know that, don't you?'

'Yes,' I said. 'And I've never stopped loving him. Tell me what's happened.'

'He's okay.'

'You've said that already.'

He looked at the grass again.

'She needs to know,' said Amy.

*

An hour later, Jack had left us sitting on the bench. I was trying to clear my head, create a distraction by thinking about something else. Lawrence Coulson's *Midnight Chimes* picture, a moonlit sky, clouded over and sucking you into the canvas through different hues of blue into darkness, moonbeams reflecting off a lake, shadows of a hilly landscape, a brick tower with a pinprick of yellow electric light escaping from its attic. I tried to focus on the light, let it fill the void in my head, let everything else blur out of existence. I wondered what the room looked like inside, a barred window, limestone walls covered in lichenous fungi…

'I need to see him,' I said.

'Is that a good idea? I know he wants to see you, but Jack said he's still in a bad way.'

'I can't just walk away from him.'

'This isn't your fault, Mum. None of this is your fault. You've just told him something you felt he had a right to know. There must be something wrong with him.'

'He's always been vulnerable,' I said.

'And you haven't seen him for over thirty years. You don't owe him anything.'

'I need to make sure he's all right.'

'Okay,' she said. 'But I'm coming with you.'

225

One, two, three, four. I moved the front door handle up and down. It's locked. No it isn't. One more time. One, two, three, four. I could feel Mo, my neighbour, watching me through her grey net curtains. One, two, three, four. Check it again. I heard a car turn into the street and drive past the house. I turned to walk away from the door. It's still open. No it isn't. Yes it is. I turned back. One, two, three, four. 'Freddie.' An arm dropped around my shoulder. 'Come on, Freddie. Let's go back to mine.' I looked at him, tears dripping off my face, snot bunging up my nose. 'I can't lock the door, Jack. The bloody thing won't lock.' 'Leave it,' he said, prising my hand off the handle. I looked at him again. 'I should have been there,' I said. 'Come on,' he said, hugging me to him and walking me to the car.

*

The car park of the boatyard take-out point in Ironbridge was empty and a mid-afternoon tarpaulin of hush had dropped over the day's activities. We were going to sit in our usual thinking place on the concrete steps leading into the River Severn, but the overnight rain had submerged four of the six steps and Jack led me to the top of the grassy embankment. We sat down on a bench and stared out at the fast-flowing current. A raft of ducks, two adults and four ducklings, sped past us, carried along at breakneck speed, casting ripples of motion across the surface of the water, the lead duck honking loudly out of exhilaration or possibly fear. Neither of us had said a word during the ten-minute car journey. 'You okay?' said Jack, finally breaking the silence.

'I can't believe it,' I said.

'Believe what? You still haven't told me what's happened.'

I looked at him. 'I thought Jo-Jo had called you. What made you come round?'

'Your neighbour phoned me. You'd been on that doorstep for half an hour. What's wrong, Freddie?'

I regurgitated the three-decades-old news. It felt like someone else was telling the story, like I was eavesdropping on the conversation, the emptiness in my stomach growing by the second as though some vital organ was being sucked out of me. I felt Jack's hand on my leg. 'I should have been there,' I said.

'How could you have been? You didn't even know.'

'But I shouldn't have walked away in the first place.'

'You can't do anything about that now. You've got to deal with the present. Leave the past where it belongs.'

'But we could have had a baby. That would have made all the difference.'

'And it could just as easily have pulled you apart. You don't know how it would have worked out.'

I looked at the river. The ducks had disappeared, but further along the bank a man was screwing together two halves of a fishing rod. He reached into a wicker basket and fetched out a pencil-case-sized wooden box. It looked like it was made out of rosewood and, I guessed, contained his bait. He made his selection, fixed a shimmering blue fly to the end of the line and cast off into the water. The line landed with a plop, bobbed up and down for a few seconds before he reeled it back in and cast off again. It re-landed in pretty much the same spot, but this time he left it, secured the rod into a bank stick and sat down on a green canvas picnic chair. 'Why do fishermen do that?' I said.

'What?' said Jack.

'Cast their line a couple of times before they're happy. It always seems to land in the same place.'

He shrugged. 'I guess they know what they're doing,' he said.

The fisherman reached into the wicker basket again and fetched out a red Thermos flask. He unscrewed the lid, filled up

227

a plastic cup, held it against his face cheek for a few seconds before blowing on the contents and taking a sip. He stared at the bobbing float, waiting for a sign that he'd tempted something to take a bite. 'Bob does that,' I said. 'Holds his cup against his face.'

'Does he?'

'Whenever he takes a drink. It must be a comfort thing. Haven't you noticed?'

He looked at the fisherman. 'You need to talk to her, Freddie.'

'I can't,' I said.

'She did what she thought was right. You can't blame her for that.'

'I don't blame her. I blame me.'

He stood up and brushed the step dust off the back of his jeans. 'Let's go for a walk,' he said.

We walked side by side through the park, past the craft centre and onto the narrow path of the high street, the River Severn on our right-hand side as we headed up the hill towards the bridge. We stopped at a wooden bench to read the inscription on the seat – *In loving memory of Terry. I hope you enjoy the view as much as he did.* 'Not our Terry,' said Jack. 'Nice gesture though. We should talk to Bob about getting something done.' A man and a woman came towards us, walking a black labradoodle. Jack stepped into the road to let them by. The dog looked up at him, the expression on his face saying, 'I should think so too,' as he plodded past. There was no one else around, which was unusual for such a nice day in August. I looked at my watch. 'It's only seven thirty,' I said.

'You've probably been up for hours. Did you get any sleep last night?'

'Not much. I kept playing it over and over in my head.'

'I know it's hard, Freddie, but it was a long time ago. You got on well in Devon, didn't you?'

'The best.'

'There you are then.'

We walked past the café in the square, where we'd stop sometimes and have a cafetière of Jamaican Blue coffee and a slice of homemade Victoria sandwich. We stopped on the bridge and stood peering down through the railings at the river. 'I wonder how many lovers have stood here,' I said.

'Thousands, I should think,' said Jack. 'It's two hundred years old.'

'And I couldn't wait for three. That's all she was asking, time to do her degree, but I chose to walk away from her and the baby.'

'You didn't know about the baby. You've got to stop punishing yourself for something you can't change, enjoy the fact you've got a second chance.'

'Maybe,' I said. 'But it all feels like such a waste.'

'Then don't waste any more time. Call her.'

Freddie's Dream

'Wake up.'

The voice is soothing. I want to obey, but my eyelids feel stitched shut. I lift my right arm and touch my face. My skin feels cold. 'Wake up.'

'Who are you?'

I'm surprised to hear my own voice. I'd made the words sound demanding. Be careful, I tell myself. At least until you know where you are. A smell, laundered clothes straight off the washing line, a tinge of something else, cut grass. 'Wake up.' I lift my eyelids. White light pain. I squeeze them shut. 'Jesus,' I say.

'Don't be afraid. You're running out of time. Your eyes will adjust.'

Not enough time. I open my eyes again. Sting, sting, sting, blink, blink, blink, a stream of tears, blink, blink, blink. The pain eases, the room comes into a hazy view. More blinking, more tears. I sit up and look around. All I can see is white, the walls, the ceiling, the floor, the couch I'm lying on. I'm tired. I need to sleep. I lie down again and close my eyes. The room feels warm, a safe cocoon, eiderdown duvet soft. I can feel myself floating.

'Wake up. Wake up.'

Freddie – June 1980

We were on our way to Dudley Zoo with Stuart and Louise, our first outing as a foursome. The upstairs of the bus was empty, so we piled on the back seat, me and Stuart with our feet up on the crappy brown upholstery, our backs pressed against the window, Jo-Jo and Louise in the middle, lying in between our legs. We could see the conductor standing halfway up the stairs, watching us through the viewing mirror. A stench of cigarette smoke and dirty clothes pervaded the air like mustard gas. Stuart coughed. 'Jesus,' he said. 'It stinks back here.'

'I bet it was that four bellies bloke who got off in Bloxwich,' said Jo-Jo.

'Four bellies?' I said.

'Yeah, he barged past us. Don't tell me you didn't see him. He was as big as a tank.'

'I saw him. I've just never heard anyone get called four bellies before.'

'She's being kind,' said Louise. 'I'd have said six.'

'Did you see the way he was walking?' said Jo-Jo. She rolled off the seat, stood up and penguin-walked halfway up the bus. Louise stood up and followed her. They turned, puffed out their cheeks and wobbled back – their bloated faces rocking under the weight of supressed laughter.

'You two are mad,' said Stuart.

'And gorgeous,' I said, pulling Jo-Jo towards me and kissing her on the lips.

Louise glared at Stuart. 'Why couldn't you say that?' she said.

'I was just about to,' he protested.

*

We took our place in the long entrance queue. I sighed. 'I can only just see the ticket office,' I said.

Jo-Jo squeezed my hand. 'Stop moaning,' she whispered. 'It'll be worth it.'

We juddered along as though we were on a faulty travelator. I could feel droplets of sweat popping on my forehead; my Adidas tee-shirt was sticking to my back. A boy and a girl in front of us, each of them eating an ice-cream, started tapping each other and giggling. Their mum leaned down, took them both by the arm and said, 'If you don't behave, I'm going to feed you to the tigers.' Jo-Jo and I laughed. The children glared at us. We reached the ticket window. 'Morning,' said the rosy-cheeked woman behind the counter. 'Lovely day, isn't it?' 'Gorgeous,' I said, handing her a ten-pound note. She took the money and gave me two tickets, nodding at the two children we'd queued behind for the last twenty minutes. 'I'd get one of those ice-creams if I were you,' she said. We walked through the turnstile and waited for Stuart and Louise to pay their money.

'Shall we?' said Jo-Jo.

'What?' I said.

'Get an ice-cream. You do look hot.'

Stuart and Louise joined us. 'Where shall we go first?' said Louise.

'Freddie wants an ice-cream,' said Jo-Jo.

'Jesus,' said Stuart. 'How old are you, mate? Six?'

'It's to cool him down,' said Jo-Jo. 'Don't you want one?'

'Of course he does,' said Louise, taking Jo-Jo's arm, the pair of them walking off towards the pink and white Mr Whippy van.

*

We huddled around the site map with our 99s. I'd eaten half of my chocolate flake, pushed the rest down into the bottom of the cone and was now lightly licking my way in clockwise concentric circles around the vanilla ice-cream. 'How can you eat that so slowly?' said Jo-Jo.

'I'm making it last,' I said. 'You've just munched yours to death.'

'It's an ice-cream, Freddie. It's meant to be munched.'

I took another slow lick with the tip of my tongue, this time staring straight into Jo-Jo's eyes. 'Yummy,' I said.

She laughed.

'Shouldn't you two be getting a bed?' said Louise.

'Not when there's elephants to see,' said Jo-Jo, pointing straight in front of us.

'You didn't need to tell us,' said Stuart. 'You can smell them from here.'

Jo-Jo grabbed Louise's arm and they ran over to the elephant enclosure. Stuart and I walked over and joined them. We stared in silence through the wire net at the two elephants and their two calves. One of the elephants reached up and pulled hay out of a basket strung high from a wooden pole. Her mouth was wide open, revealing fold after fold of fresh pink flesh, hay being dropped in from her trunk and munched to mulch before she swallowed. The other female was standing by the man-made pool, flicking up squirts of water to clear the chalky dust from her head. The calves ambled over to join her, the baby nudging his sibling closer to the pond. 'Oh God,' said Jo-Jo. 'He's trying to push him in.'

'Here's the male,' I said.

The bull elephant charged across the dusty ground towards his herd, his gleaming tusks leading the way. He reached his family, barged straight through the middle of them, almost knocking over one of the calves, and then stood perfectly still for a few seconds, looking at the fence. Finally, he lifted his trunk to the azure sky and trumpeted his arrival. 'Pity you can't do that,' said Jo-Jo, squeezing me around the waist.

'What makes you think I can't?' I said.

'I've not seen it so far,' she said.

'I can do that Clyde thing,' said Stuart.

We all looked at him.

'You know, the orangutan in the Clint Eastwood film.'

'You mean where he swings from the hotel bedroom light?' I said.

'That's the one,' said Stuart.

'Looks like you're in for treat,' Jo-Jo said to Louise.

'Yeah,' said Louise, looking nervously at Stuart. 'I'm glad he's warned me.'

'Shall we go and see the giraffes?' I said.

Jo-Jo and I walked off towards the giraffe house, which, according to the map, was the next stop en route and right next to Monkey World. I put my arm around Jo-Jo and squeezed her into my body. 'Your mate's a bit awkward,' she said.

I looked behind us. Stuart and Louise were following, but slowly, and walking apart from each other. 'I don't think they've been together that long,' I said.

'How do you know him?'

'From school. Jack knows him better than me.'

We reached the giraffes just as two of them were lolloping out into the sunshine from their covered wooden enclosure. One of the giraffes rubbed himself against the wall of the building, stretching his neck almost to the tin roof, and then started chewing on a long willowy branch that had been tied there by the keepers. The second giraffe seemed to realise he was missing out, turned around, walked back to the building and started munching on the bark. They looked like they were kissing the wood in a slow, seductive mating ritual. Stuart and Louise joined us at the fence.

'They are ugly creatures,' said Stuart. 'It's like God had lots of bits left over and said, what do I do with these?'

'I think they're gorgeous,' said Louise.

'Me too,' said Jo-Jo. 'They're so different. That's what makes them beautiful.'

Stuart looked at me in desperation.

'I don't mind them,' I said. 'At least they've got a bit of character.'

'I need the loo,' said Louise.

'I'll come with you,' said Jo-Jo.

Stuart and I leaned on the fence and watched Jo-Jo and Louise walk away towards the toilets. 'You two okay?' I said.

'No idea. I don't seem to be able to say anything right.'

'You seemed fine earlier.'

'I know. She went all frosty after I said how I envied you being with Jo-Jo.'

I stood up and looked at him.

'I didn't mean anything by it,' he said. 'I just meant you make a good couple, but I think she took it the wrong way.'

'A bit like most people would,' I said. 'Maybe you should apologise.'

'Yeah, sorry, mate.'

'Not to me. To Louise.'

'Maybe,' he said, looking back at the giraffes. 'Do you really like those things?'

I pushed my strawberry lip gloss into the tight pocket of my blue denim Levi shorts and stared at myself in the mirror. We'd left Freddie and Stuart watching the giraffes. I wondered what they were talking about. Freddie wasn't great at man-talk and I'd got the impression Stuart was a bit of a lager lout. I couldn't imagine him being Jack's friend. Perhaps I didn't know Jack well enough. The toilet flushed behind me. Louise came out of the cubicle, walked over and stood by me at the sink. She started washing her hands. I looked at her through the mirror. 'You okay?' I said.

She nodded, turned off the tap, pulled a green paper towel out of the holder, the kind that always reminded me of school, and dried her hands.

'How long have you and Stuart been going out?'

'A few weeks. How about you and Freddie?'

'It feels like forever. But we only met last November.'

'It's obvious you love each other. I don't think Stuart and I will last much longer.'

'Have you had a row? We couldn't help noticing there was an atmosphere.'

'Not really. He's just… well, compared to you two, we're not… he's not what I'm looking for.'

I waited for her to elaborate, but she scrunched up the paper towel, lobbed it into the bin and started to walk towards the door. 'We can head home if you want,' I said.

'Not before I've seen the monkeys. It'll give that prat a chance to see a real orangutan.'

I laughed. 'I think he's a bit nervous. I don't think he was serious about swinging from a light.'

'That's a pity,' she said. 'I was looking forward to that bit.'

We rejoined Freddie and Stuart just as the giraffe herd were lolloping back inside their covered enclosure. 'I think it's too hot for them,' said Freddie.

'Shall we head to the monkey house?' I said.

'Good idea,' said Stuart. 'They're my favourites.'

Louise and I looked at each other and burst out laughing.

'What?' said Stuart. 'They are.'

'Come on, mate,' said Freddie, putting his hand on Stuart's back. 'I think it's a private joke.'

*

The queue to get inside the monkey house ran along the wire net fence, which meant we could pass the time by watching the tribe of six chimpanzees lying moribund on the grass in the midday sun. One of them, it looked like the alpha male, was flat on his back, slightly apart from the rest of the group, arm over his eyes, one leg raised and the other crossed over it. We could hear him snoring and breaking wind. 'Looks like he's sleeping off last night's beer,' said Stuart.

'Typical man,' said Louise. 'One sniff of the barman's apron, a bit of sun and he's good for nothing.'

'Could be worse,' I said. 'You could be lying next to him.'

The queue edged forward, the pong of ammonia raising up in notches of pungency as we moved closer to the door. Two of the chimpanzees lifted their heads at exactly the same time, threw their arms around each other, cuddled and stroked each other's faces. One of the other chimps sat up, edged over to the cuddling pair and flopped on her back in submissive pose with her legs up and wide open.

'Okay,' said Freddie, a toothy grin spread across his face. 'It feels like we should stop watching now.'

The queue moved forward just as the cuddling two were separating and eagerly moving towards the legs-up monkey. I looked at Freddie. 'There are children watching,' I whispered.

'Some of them are taking pictures.'

'They probably think it's a game,' he said. 'Which it is, sort of.'

I turned around to look at Stuart and Louise. Stuart was rubbernecking to see the monkeys, the movement of the queue having stolen his vantage point. Louise was staring at me, her cheeks flushed. 'He is so embarrassing,' she said.

'What?' said Stuart, turning back towards us. 'You've got to admit it's funny. You can't take your eyes off them. Dirty buggers.'

Louise slapped him on the arm and laughed. 'You needn't get any ideas,' she said.

*

As we walked into the monkey house, I grabbed Freddie's arm and pulled him back towards me. He gave me a quizzical look and I nodded at the young couple in front of us who were posing against the viewing glass, arms wrapped around each other, for their picture to be taken by an older man who was wearing a tweed flat cap. 'You nearly walked across their shot,' I said.

'Sorry,' said Freddie, putting up his hand to the couple. 'She's always telling me off for that.'

'Not that he takes a blind bit of notice,' I said.

'Jesus,' said Stuart, walking up behind us. 'It stinks of piss in here.'

'What did you expect?' said Louise.

'Yeah,' said Freddie. 'They don't exactly have en suite.'

'Mind you,' I said, 'that's a bit out of order.'

All their eyes followed my gaze towards the ceiling of the first enclosure where a red-haired orangutan was hanging upside down from a tyre and urinating a golden shower onto the concrete floor below. The urine splashed and pooled, narrowly missing a troop of gambolling and grooming chimpanzees.

'It's never ending,' said Louise.

'How great would that be?' said Stuart. 'Just pissing on everyone from the roof.'

'I'm not sure that bus conductor would be impressed,' said Freddie. 'He wasn't happy with us putting our feet on the seats.'

The shower stopped and the orangutan let out a scream. He turned the right way up, grabbed one of the ropes hanging next to the tyre and swung across to the other side of the roof, where he perched on one of the many branches fixed by the keepers to the walls of the enclosure. He reached over his shoulder with his lanky arm and scratched his back.

'He looks pleased with himself,' said Freddie.

'Yeah,' I said. 'He's not hung around the scene of the crime for long though.'

'You should never shit on your own doorstep,' said Stuart.

'It all looks really sad,' said Louise. 'Concrete floors and nailed-on branches. Where's nature in all of that?'

'They look happy enough,' said Stuart.

'They've not got much choice,' said Freddie.

'Come on,' I said. 'Let's see what's next door.'

Me, Freddie and Stuart walked forward, but Louise didn't move. She was still staring into the enclosure. I looked at Stuart. He turned back to Louise and put his arm through hers. 'He's fine,' he said, nodding at the grinning ape.

'There's a donation box at the entrance,' she said. 'It might help.'

'Okay,' he said, smiling. 'We'll sort it on the way out.' He put his arm around her, and they joined Freddie and me at the next enclosure.

'Macaque monkeys,' said Freddie, reading from the wooden plaque screwed to the wall. 'I can't see them,' he said, peering through the glass.

'Me neither,' I said. 'How come there are so many bushes and plants in here and next door was like a cell?'

'I guess it's because these are a bit timid and like to hide,' said Freddie. 'Whereas your man next door doesn't care who sees him.'

'There they are,' said Louise, pointing to the top of the enclosure.

I looked up. There were two black monkeys cuddled together high in the branches, their wide, dewy eyes staring straight back at us. 'Oh God,' I said. 'They look terrified.' One of the monkeys shifted position slightly, pulling apart from the other, and there, suckling a nipple on the second monkey's chest, his eyes closed to the world, was an infant. The first monkey seemed to realise his mistake and moved back into his original position, cuddling the second one close, hiding the baby from view once more.

'That is so sweet,' said Louise.

'Yes, it is,' said Stuart. 'They're almost human.'

Jo-Jo – June 1989

We were in the Saleem Bagh curry house in Cannock. I ordered a vegetable bhuna, Stuart had the beef madras and Louise had the tandoori mix with lamb, chicken and seekh kebabs. 'It's a pity Jason couldn't make it,' said Louise, tearing off a piece of her garlic naan bread.

'Not unusual though,' said Stuart. 'We've only met the bloke once and that was accidental when we were out shopping. I don't think he likes us.'

'It's not you,' I said. 'He's shy. He doesn't mean anything by it. Anyway, someone's got to look after Amy.'

'Yeah,' said Louise. 'Not everyone's as full of themselves as you.'

'It's only a curry,' said Stuart, wiping his forehead and blowing his nose on the white cloth napkin.

'How come I always finish up apologising for you?' said Louise.

'How old's that sprog of yours?' said Stuart, totally ignoring the question.

'Five,' I said. 'They grow up so fast, don't they?'

Louise glanced nervously at Stuart.

'You're not, are you?' I said.

'Yep,' said Stuart, squeezing Louise's hand. 'It finally happened.'

I stood up and hugged them both. 'Oh God,' I said. 'I'm so pleased for you. I know how much you've wanted this.'

'We're not there yet,' said Stuart. 'We've got to wrap her in cotton wool until Superman arrives.'

'Her?' said Louise. 'Who's her? The cat's mother?'

'You. I mean you. You know what I mean.'

'And what's with the Superman. I'm having a Superwoman.'

I laughed.

'What?' said Louise.

'You two,' I said. 'You bickered like that the first time I met you.'

'At the zoo,' said Stuart. 'You were with Freddie. Do you ever hear from him now?'

'Do you?' I said. 'He was your mate.'

He shook his head. 'I saw Jack a few years ago.'

'You know,' said Louise. 'I'd have put my house on you and Freddie making it. We were gobsmacked when you split up.'

'Me too,' I said. 'These things happen I suppose.'

'His loss,' said Stuart, mopping up the madras sauce with his chapatti.

'Yes,' I said. 'His loss. I'll tell you one thing, I wouldn't have bet a dog kennel on you two making it through the trip to the zoo, let alone beyond.'

'Me neither,' said Louise, glaring at Stuart. 'Do you have to eat like that?'

240

'Like what?' he said.

'Slapping your chops. No one wants to see inside your mouth.'

Jo-Jo's Affair – February 1990

I was in a wine bar on a rare night out with Karen. She was slow-dancing with a bushy-bearded Australian waiter who'd been chatting to her between orders all evening. He'd finished his shift an hour ago and in that time they'd consumed most of the bottle of Merlot he'd brought with him when he'd perched on the stool next to her. Phyllis Nelson's 'Move Closer' had started up, which prompted Karen to scream, 'Oh, I love this song,' and drag him onto the dance floor. I was watching them dance, their legs interlocked, slow rhythmic swaying from the hips. They were standing up, with their clothes on, but definitely making love. The couples around them were giving out nervous sideways glances. Some stopped dancing and went back to their tables. 'Your friend looks like she's enjoying herself,' said a voice beside me. I turned around.

'Scott,' said the man sitting on the stool next to me. 'Can I get you a drink?'

I pointed at my wine glass, which was over half-full. 'I'm good, thanks,' I said.

He nodded at the dance floor. 'How about a dance?'

'I'm married,' I said, holding up the third finger on my left hand to show him the eighteen carat gold band.

'Does that stop you dancing?' he said, holding out his hand.

That's when I should have made my excuses, but I hadn't been out in months. I looked at him, Scott, my new bar companion. He was clean shaven, which bucked the trend of the designer stubble doing the rounds, had blonde shoulder-length hair, blue eyes, and was dressed in what looked like a very expensive navy blue suit, probably designer, with a white shirt. He reminded me of Joey out of the sitcom *Bread*. 'Just one dance,' I said, taking his hand.

We walked onto the dance floor as Phyllis was fading out and Rod Stewart's 'First Cut is the Deepest' started up. We started swaying to the music, his hands resting gently on the bottom of my back. I could smell his Kouros aftershave. 'I know it's only one dance,' he said, 'but do I get to know your name?'

Jo-Jo – April 1990

It was eleven o'clock in the morning and we were lying in bed, our third time at the same hotel, staying in what Scott called a day room. 'Hotels let you do that?' I'd said when he suggested it. 'Of course. Wedding parties do it all the time.' 'But we're not a wedding party. Have you done this sort of thing before?' 'No. But I've got friends who have.'

We used to meet on the car park at eight forty-five exactly, ready to occupy our nine to five room, the hotel staff smiling at each other knowingly as we booked in, taking full payment on arrival. Scott used to come prepared with what he called his Scooby snacks – first time, ham and tomato sandwiches, until he found out I was vegetarian and then he brought tuna to go with the plain crisps, tomato juice and a flask of coffee.

'I don't get why you can't leave him,' he said, repositioning his pillow and sitting up against the headboard.

'I can't just walk out, Scott. What about Amy?'

He looked up at the ceiling, his one hand behind his head. I lifted myself up and put my head on his hairless chest. I didn't know men could have bald chests. I assumed it was something to do with him being blonde. 'You could take her with you,' he said.

'He'd never let that happen. Anyway, I couldn't break up her family.'

He sighed, rolled from underneath me and got out of bed.

'You okay?' I said.

'I need the loo,' he said, walking off towards the bathroom.

I wondered, not for the first time, what I was doing, risking everything for a day-room liaison and now he was talking about going away for a weekend to Oxford. I'd get caught. People who have affairs always get caught. I heard the toilet flush and he walked out of the bathroom and climbed back into bed. He squeezed me close. I felt a tingle of electric charge shoot through my body. His touch, being held by him, it was something I hadn't felt since...

'You know,' he said. 'We could make this work.'

'What do you mean?'

'Take it to the next level, turn us into a proper couple.'

'We're okay, aren't we, as we are?'

'I'm just saying if you ever wanted to.'

I lifted my head, pulled myself up his body and kissed him on the lips. 'Let's just have some fun for a while, see what happens.'

He returned my kiss. 'Talking of fun,' he said.

Jo-Jo – May 1990

We were sitting on a public bench opposite the entrance to Magdalene College, eating cheese and pickle sandwiches, drinking tomato juice, watching the cyclists and walkers, who we assumed were students, as they rushed past us and into the college, most of them travelling in pairs. 'First thing you do, I guess,' said Scott.

'What?' I said.

'Find yourself a lover when you get to university. Makes the time go quicker.'

'Is that what you did?'

'I didn't go. Not something you did where I come from.'

'I went and it wasn't the first thing I did.'

'You went to uni?'

'You don't have to sound so surprised.'

'Sorry, it's just, well, like I said, not many people from my background do. What did you study?'

'English Lit. I went to Lincoln. That's where I met Jason.'

'Proves my point.'

'He wasn't a student. He was one of the lecturers.'

'You had an affair with your teacher?'

I could feel a growl of irritation starting in my stomach. Sometimes, outside of the hotel bedroom, being with him felt like I was out with a child. We were the same biological age, but there was an aeon of maturity gap. I looked at him, his face smeared in a smutty grin. I imagined a Sid James laugh reverberating around his head. I was starting to feel like his mum, which, given what we'd been doing an hour ago, felt wrong. He saw the expression on my face and stopped smiling. 'I met him at a party,' I said. 'He didn't teach on my course and neither of us were in a relationship. His wife had died years earlier. He was kind at a time when I needed someone to be kind.' I could hear the tone of my voice, clipped, like Miss Moir, my senior school deputy headmistress.

'Sorry,' he said. 'I didn't mean to annoy you.'

'You haven't,' I said, squeezing his hand. 'It's just, it was a bad time in my life. I don't how we got onto the subject.'

'Lovers at university. I didn't know you'd met Jason there. He must be a lot older than you if he was a lecturer. That explains a lot.'

'It doesn't explain anything. The age difference isn't what's wrong with our marriage.'

I parked up in a lay-by, just along the lane from the church in Buildwas. Scott pulled his car behind my Nissan Sunny and flashed his lights to announce his arrival. I watched him through the door mirror. He got out of his car, locked it and walked up to my car. I wound down my window. 'Your car or mine,' he said.

'My car or yours for what?'

'You know. To get comfy. We could use the Cortina. The seats go right back.'

'Sounds like you're an expert.'

'No, it's just…'

'There's no way I'm having cramped sex in a car, Scott.'

'That's not what I suggested.'

'It's what you meant though.'

I wound up the window, got out of the car, locked it and walked off across the lane. 'Let's go for a walk.'

'A walk?'

I turned around and held out my hand. 'Yes, a walk.'

'Oh, I get you. A walk.'

We climbed over the three-bar, ranch-style fence and walked through the trees, emerging into a farmer's field. We stood and stared at the openness, which stretched out and out and out to the horizon. 'Imagine owning all of this,' said Scott.

'It's beautiful,' I said. 'Uncluttered. Helps you clear your head. Come on. Let's lie down over there. I want to look at the clouds.'

'Course you do,' he said.

I lay on the grass. Scott knelt beside me. I put my hand behind my head and looked up at the sky. He leaned down and went to kiss me. I put my finger on his lips. 'I really do want to look at the clouds.'

He sighed and lay down.

'Now,' I said. 'You need to look for a cloud that looks like a face and say which celebrity it reminds you of.'

'Do we have to do this, Jo-Jo?'

'Yes, it's fun. Look. That one over there. It looks like Freddie Mercury. Don't you think?'

'No. It looks like all of the other clouds.' He sat up again. 'I'd really like to kiss you,' he said.

'Okay,' I said. 'If you're not going to play my cloud game, you can kiss me.'

Jo-Jo – August 1990

We were walking along Cleethorpes beach, the air filled with screeching gullies looking for chips along the prom. Scott squeezed my hand and nodded towards the horizon. 'That beach goes on forever. Do you think the sea's still there?'

Two women walked past us, heading in the opposite direction, roll upon roll of fat squeezed up, out and over their boob tubes and tight-fitting beach shorts. They smiled at Scott over their 99 ice-creams and then giggled to each other as they passed us. 'Looks like you've pulled,' I said.

'Did you see the state?' he said.

'Fat lasses. They need the layers. It gets cold up here in the winter.'

We carried on walking. A blonde-haired girl, aged about seven, in a bright pink swimming costume, and a man in swim shorts covered in penguin motifs came towards us, the man in front, the little girl stepping out behind. 'What are you doing, Chloe?' said the man, turning his head. 'I'm walking in your footsteps, Dad,' she said. 'But your strides are so big.' It resurfaced my memories of Dad, his bear hugs, his sixth sense that always told him where I was, how I was feeling, but that had all changed with his tart. I focussed on the horizon, trying to push everything else out of my head.

Scott stopped walking, pulled me towards him and kissed me. 'I think I love you, Jo-Jo.'

I took a step backwards. 'Where's that come from?' I said.

'I've been wanting to tell you for a few weeks, but I was waiting for the right moment.'

I looked down at the sand. 'I'm married, Scott. I have a child. You know I'm not going to walk away from that.'

'You don't have to. Being with me doesn't mean being without Amy.'

'It means Amy not having a proper family, being without her dad. I can't do that to her.'

'Don't you feel anything for me?'

'We're good together. Can't we just have some fun for a while?'

'Is that all you want?'

'It's all I can have.'

'I was hoping for more.'

I met his eyes. It felt as though a full stop had been jabbed in place. I looked at the horizon. The sea had reappeared. 'Tide's coming in,' I said.

Jo-Jo's Letter to Jo-Jo

Dear Jo-Jo,

Scott's Dear John arrived today, the one you've been expecting since Cleethorpes.

He's right when he says it was always going to end this way. You've always been honest with him, but he thought if he kept saying what he wanted it would come true, like unicorns or fairies. But everyone has to grow up sometime and he heard the clang of certainty in your voice on the beach.

You'll be fine. That's the word. Fine. You'll be fine on your own. That's a truth you slammed in place years ago. You'll concentrate on Amy, that's the right thing to do, and try to ignore the mood-sucking misery of your marriage. It wasn't as though Scott was the one, your soul mate, but you'll miss the warmth, the way he looked at you, the way he wanted you, the way he cuddled you. You'll be fine though. You'll suffocate the emotion, bury it so deep even you can't find the key. That's what you do.

Scott's going to be fine as well. You'll see him at a train station five years from now, he'll smile at you from the opposite platform, you'll put up your hand, but he'll have already turned away and walked back to a woman sitting on a bench with a toddler at her side. The little girl will jump on his lap, the woman will lean over and kiss him on the cheek. He'll have found a new story, and you'll walk off the platform in search of a coffee. No one will notice you're late home. Amy will be at school. Jason will be in his study.

Everyone will be fine.

Take care of yourself.

All my love.

Jo-Jo Xxxx

Freddie – August 2015

I'm clutching a bottle of Jack Daniels in my left hand, the steps of the ladder are blurring in and out of view, tears stream down my face, my nose is bunged with snot, my head feels as though it's cracked across the scalp. I flick on the light switch, dump the uncapped whisky bottle on the boards and haul myself inside the loft, spittle dripping from my mouth. I look around at my setup. A cottage oak dining chair, Edwardian antique, really uncomfortable to sit on, a polyester rope hanging down next to it, already secured to the beam. I take a last swig of whisky, climb onto the chair and place the noose around my neck. I hesitate and draw my hand across my face to wipe away the sweat and sobs. I pull the knot tight and start to shuffle on the chair, one rock left, one rock right, backwards, forwards. I can feel the chair going from under me…

Springsteen's harmonica.

For a moment I stayed in the dream – the whisky, the noose, the rocking chair. I could feel my heartbeat in my ears. I opened my eyes, reached over, turned off the alarm and lay back with my hands behind my head and stared at the Artex ceiling. 'Jesus,' I said.

Tai, my little black cat, who was lying at the end of the bed, lifted her head and blinked at me. 'I've got no choice,' I said to her. 'You'll be okay with Jack.' I turned out of bed, surprised at how calm I felt, and walked out of the bedroom, across the landing to the shower.

Half an hour later, I was sitting at my kitchen table, a cold mug of coffee pushed to one side, four boxes of the ten milligram propranolol in front of me, a glass of water already poured. I'd popped sixteen of the round purple tablets from the two strips in the first box. I picked up my phone. I realised I should call Jack, say goodbye properly, but I didn't know how to start the conversation. I put the phone down and reached for the tablets.

*

'Freddie. Freddie.'

Jack's voice. He was shaking me. I wanted to wake up, but my eyelids wouldn't lift.

'Freddie. Freddie.'

His shaking was getting harder. 'Wake up. For God's sake. How many of these have you taken?'

I opened my eyes. It felt like I was looking through slits. He was leaning over me. I raised my head, which felt too big for my shoulders, and wiped the saliva from the corner of my mouth. I felt drunk. 'I'm not sure,' I mumbled, staring through fog at the tablets.

'Jesus,' he said.

I dropped my head back on the table and closed my eyes again. Seconds later I heard him say, 'An ambulance, please. I think my friend's taken an overdose.'

'I want to die, Jack,' I said.

Freddie – June 1970 – Cowboy Dreams

We were lying on the grass in King George's park – John Wayne and Audie Murphy. I spat once, pushed my black Stetson back on my head and squinted into the distance. I mimicked a gunshot, threw a puffball of dust behind us and pushed him to the ground. 'I thought you said they were miles away,' I said.

'We're too open here,' he said.

'Over there. That cabin.'

'It's too far. I'm not moving.'

I rolled to his side. 'We owe it to the others, partner. Where's your loyalty?'

'I don't want to die.'

'You think they did. Staying here we die.'

I whistled another bullet and pushed him down again. 'They've found their range. We need to go now.'

'Okay. I'll follow you.'

'That clump of conifers, first base.'

I bounced to my feet and started running, head down, weaving left, right, left, my toy Colt 45 still in my holster.

I stumbled, went onto my knees, got back up and danced a cowboy hop across the grass, sounding death-warrant bullets, pretending they were pinging at my shiny plastic cowboy boots. I skidded a dust slide into the trees, panting, my heart banging out of my chest. 'Come on,' I shouted. 'Get out of there.'

He appeared, the brim of his hat pulled low, his gun drawn, firing bullets out of his Colt like a demented wasp.

'For God's sake, run. What the hell are you shooting at?'
He fell.

'No,' I screamed, getting onto my knees.

'I'm okay,' he shouted, getting back on his feet, his gun lost, weaving like a gazelle outthinking a lion. He was nearly there. Another ping, another, another. He skidded beside me. A Cheshire-wide grin. 'God, that felt good,' he yelled to the sky.

'What were you shooting at?' I said.

'Anything. Didn't feel right just running.'

'But they're too far away.'

'They're shooting at us.'

'With rifles. It's different.'

I looked at the horizon, mimicked a hail of bullets and pushed him to the ground. 'I think we might have wound them up a bit, but we're nearly at the cabin. We can regroup there.'

'That might be pushing our luck.'

'We have no choice, brother.'

'It's all right for you,' he said, patting his stomach. 'I'm not exactly built for speed.'

'You'll be fine.'

'Famous last words. It's always the chubby guy who gets it.' He rolled onto his back and puffed out his cheeks. 'I've done my bit. I need a horse.'

'Do you see any horses?'

'Yeah, well...'

'Hang on a minute. Why have they stopped shooting?'

We made another scan of the horizon.

'You see it?' I said, the sun stinging my eyes.

'I see it.'

'How many?'

'Six or seven. Riding hard.'

'This is our chance.'

'They'll have left a gun on us.'

We looked at the sanctuary of the bandstand, five hundred yards of open ground away. I whistled the sound of a bullet zinging into the bushes and we hit dirt again. 'They can't have left more than one, two at the most.'

'I've already told you, I don't want to die.'

'We'll run together. They're getting closer by the second. There's rifles in the cabin.'

'I've got a wife and kids.'

I patted him on the back. 'And you'll see them again, my friend, if we keep our nerve.'

'You'll stay with me?'

'Every step.'

He looked up at the cloudless sky, crossed himself and squeezed my arm. 'Let's do it.'

'After three...'

'Run. For God's sake, run.'

A ping off a rock, another off a fallen branch, another...

He crumpled. 'I'm hit.'

I skidded to a halt, turned back. 'I'm coming, buddy. Hold on.' I reached him. 'You okay?'

'My arm.'

Two more shots. He grabbed his thigh, screamed, and looked at me. 'I'm bleeding bad,' he said. 'Leave me. Save yourself.'

I dragged him to his feet. 'Come on. We're nearly there.'

Ping, ping, ping...

We put our arms around each other, limping and weaving. 'Come on, man. We can do this.'

Ping, ping, ping…

He fell, pushed me forwards. 'Go on. Leave me.'

'No chance.'

I dragged him up again, more limping, more weaving, nearly there, nearly there. We jumped onto the bandstand, dropped to the floor and laughed. 'That was brilliant,' I screamed.

'Best yet.'

'What was all that about your wife and kids?'

Jack lifted his hat and wiped his brow. 'It's what cowboys say, partner.'

Freddie – August 2015

'So, he's going to be okay.'

'He's going to be fine. Just sleepy for the next twenty-four hours. He's only taken about eighty milligrams. Some people take that every day.'

I could hear the conversation, machines were beeping. I could smell antiseptic. Someone was holding my hand. 'Jack,' I said, opening my eyes. He let go of my hand.

'I'll leave you to it,' said the nurse. She turned to me. 'I'll come back and check you later.'

'Thank you,' said Jack.

'She seems nice,' I said.

'She's pissed with you. They've got enough to do with people who are ill. What were you thinking of?'

'I wasn't.'

'It's becoming a habit, Freddie. First the train, now this…'

I started crying. 'It's all right for you, Jack. With your perfect life.'

He held my hand again. 'It's okay,' he said. 'We'll talk later. Let's get you out of here and back to mine. At least if we're under the same roof I can keep an eye on you and not feel the need to pop round every five minutes to check you're still breathing.'

I closed my eyes again.

*

I was lying in a single bed in Jack's spare room, snuggled under a white Jeff Banks duvet – the cat's room, he called it. On the walls were the framed pictures that Jack had said he couldn't hang anywhere else in the house – a framed copy of John Lennon's *Shaved Fish* album, 'Woman is the Nigger of the World' jumping out of the track list. Even in the early seventies, Lennon was pilloried for using the N word, but he brushed it off, saying only the white 'right on' people were getting offended. Next to that was an original framed *Pulp Fiction* film poster that Jack had tracked down on eBay and bought from a cinema in Copenhagen – the headline said, 'simpelthen et mestervaerk' (simply a masterpiece). The picture was Uma Thurman drawing on a cigarette and holding a smoking gun.

The bedroom door opened. 'Oh good,' said Jack. 'You're awake. I've brought you a cup of tea.'

I sat up and rested the back of my head against the headboard.

He put the tea on the bedside cabinet and sat down on the edge of the bed. 'How are you feeling?' he said.

'Knackered.'

'I'm not surprised. You slept okay though?'

'Yeah. This bed's really comfortable. No wonder the cats like it.'

'Do you feel up to talking?'

I was surprised he'd held it inside for twenty-four hours. Neither of us had said a word on the way back from the hospital, but you could feel the tension of the unanswered questions simmering away inside the Mini. 'I don't know what to say to you, Jack.'

'You could start by telling me why. I thought you were okay after we'd talked at the boatyard.'

'So did I, but I couldn't see any other way.'

'Killing yourself isn't the answer. I thought we were friends.'

'We are, best friends, but you've got Bob and, well, I just keep fucking everything up.'

'What am I going to do with you?'

'Give me a best friend hug.'

'I ought to punch you.'

'I'd prefer the hug, and you are a social worker.'

'Okay,' he said, smiling. 'But this doesn't mean I fancy you.'

'You've already told me that.'

He gave me a puzzled look.

'When I asked you to kiss me in Sitges.'

'Jesus, Freddie. That was years ago. And you were drunk.'

'You turned me down.'

'Well, I've always had my standards,' he said, pulling me towards him and hugging me close. 'Call me next time. I don't want to lose you.'

Something splattered against the bedroom window. Jack let go of me, stood up and walked over to look down into the back garden. 'A crow,' he said. 'Damn thing's landed on the patio. I'll have to get it up before Boris skins it and leaves it on the lounge carpet.' He looked back at me. 'What do you want to do about Jo-Jo?'

'I can't imagine she'll want to see me now.'

'Do you want to see her? After what she told you?'

'I keep telling you, Jack. It's not her fault. It's mine.'

'It's just life, Freddie. Do you want to see her?'

'I can't call her.'

'You don't have to,' he said. 'She called you. She's coming round tomorrow.'

'You've spoken to her?'

'I went to see her this morning. Her and Amy.'

'You've told her what happened.'

'She has a right to know, Freddie. You just left her. She was worried about you.'

'I don't know if I can speak to her.'

'No choice, mate. Listen, I'm going to sort that bird.'

'I am sorry, Jack. You must think I'm a right pain in the arse.'

'Same as it ever was,' he said, walking out of the bedroom.

Jo-Jo – August 2015

A memory – It's mid-November and I'm lying in bed listening to Mum and Dad talking in low-pitched voices on the stairs. 'Come back to bed, love. It's two o'clock in the morning.' 'But he's out there, Joseph. I can hear him. He needs me.' I creep out onto the landing and sit on the top step, my back against the wall. I can see Dad's pyjama-covered back and feel the cold draught blowing into the house through the open front door. 'There's no one there, love,' pleads Dad. 'Come inside. You'll catch your death.' 'No,' screams Mum. 'He's here on the front lawn. He's lost his mummy. Don't you care? What's wrong with you?' Another evening, around the same time, Mum gathers us around the kitchen table and tells us about a man, dressed in a suit and tie, who had visited her in the middle of the night, sat at the end of her bed and told her fairy tales about children being cut in half by slathering ogres and flea-ridden witches. Dad stands up halfway through the story. 'Come on,' he says to me and Josh. 'No, Joseph,' says Mum. 'They need to hear this. He's coming back.' 'No, they don't,' says Dad, pushing us out of the kitchen.

'Your destination is on the right,' said the Mazda's sat nav.

'It means left,' said Amy, pointing at Jack's Mini. 'There's number twenty-two. You'll have to park over the road.'

I pulled into the only space, turned off the engine and looked at the house with its lush, perfectly mown front lawn, red-rosebed borders, all in perfect bloom, not a hint of greenfly in sight, all edged to slide rule standard. I smiled. Jack's OCD was still alive and kicking.

'You ready?' said Amy.

'I just hope he's ready for us.'

'Jack said he wanted to see you.'

'I'm not sure he'll want the audience though.'

'You think I should wait in the car.'

'No. I want you with me. At least to start with. Let's see what Jack does.'

She hugged me. 'It'll be fine,' she said.

We unfastened our seatbelts, got out of the car and walked across the road hand in hand. As we reached the pavement, the front door opened. Jack smiled at us from the step. 'You found it okay then,' he said.

'The joy of sat nav,' I said.

'Freddie's in the lounge. I've bunked him up in the spare room for a few days.'

'Mum was wondering if we ought to leave them to it,' said Amy. 'Perhaps you and I should go out.'

'We don't want to throw you out of your own house,' I said.

Jack laughed. 'Happy to go for a coffee, Amy. If you fancy it.'

'Will you be okay, Mum?'

'Of course,' I said. 'Me and Freddie need to talk.'

Jack grabbed a denim coat off one of the hooks in the hallway and offered Amy his arm. 'There's a good place not far away,' he said. 'We can walk there.'

Amy hugged me again. 'I'll be back in an hour,' she said.

'The lounge is on the left,' said Jack as they walked down the path. 'I've made the coffee. Freddie knows where everything else is.'

I closed the door behind me, took a deep breath and walked down the hallway.

Jo-Jo – December 1979

Me and Freddie were lying on my bed, underneath my Starsky and Hutch Gran Torino poster. Freddie was turning a 'Love Is' statue over in his hand, a naked boy and girl kissing. The inscription on the base read, 'Love is being together... or being with you.' 'Who gave you this?' he said.

'It's not mine. It's Josh's. Some girl in the year below him left it on his desk. It's cute.'

'It's vomit inducing.'

I held out my hand. 'Hand it over, philistine. You have no soul.'

'I have class,' he said, handing me the statue. 'That's why I chose you.'

'Oh, you chose me. I seem to remember it was me that asked you to dance.'

'Yeah, well, I'd have got there eventually.'

'So you say. I think I'd still be waiting, waiting for Christmas.'

'Talking of Christmas...'

'We've already had this conversation, Freddie. I can't organise your Christmas afternoon. What's your mum going to say?'

'She's never bothered, not since Dad died. She cooks the dinner and goes to bed early. It's a bad day for her.'

'Mine's not much better,' I said. 'Dad tries his best, but Mum's a bit, well, you know, and Josh stays in his room, playing his Genesis albums.'

'So let's do something at mine. Even if it's just you and me.'

I looked down at the statue. 'Are you sure your mum will be okay about it?'

'She'll be glad. She might even stay up for a bit.'

'You need to ask her, see what she says.'

'I've already asked her. She's fine with it.'

I looked again at the statue. 'Okay, but we'll keep it simple. Wine. We'll have wine, Merlot, everyone likes Merlot, and trifle, the Bird's Eye one, covered in hundreds and thousands sprinkles. What about a tree?'

'We don't normally bother?'

'You can't have Christmas without a tree, Freddie. Come on.'

'Where are we going?'

'To get a tree.'

'They do some cheap ones in Woolworths.'

'There's no way we're having artificial. That greengrocer in Bloxwich is selling real ones.'

*

We dragged the seven-foot Christmas tree one and a half miles through the slush of melted snow and back to Freddie's house. His mum was looking out of the bay window, waiting for us. She opened the front door. 'It's huge,' she said. 'Where are we going to put it?'

'I thought we'd put it in the front room,' said Freddie.

She looked at the tree and then at me. 'Is that what you'd do?' she said.

'No. I'd put it in the room you sit in the most.'

'But that's the dining room,' said Freddie. 'It's nowhere near big enough.'

'It is if we move the sideboard,' said his mum. 'Come on. You'll need a pot to put it in.'

Freddie followed her through the white driveway gates. I sat down on the doorstep, thinking I'd get a chance for a breather, but they returned minutes later. Freddie was carrying a turquoise ceramic plant pot, which had gold stars around its centre and handles on each side. 'Will this do?' he said.'

'Course it will,' said his mum.

'It's wonderful,' I said.

'Now,' said his mum. 'I've got some decorations out of the loft. We haven't used them for years.'

'We've bought some…'

'That's great,' I said, cutting across Freddie's sentence. 'Did you bring a shovel, Freddie?'

'What for?' he said.

'You need to fill the pot with dirt.'

'You can get some from there,' said his mum, nodding towards the border under the privet hedge.

Freddie walked off again through the white gates.

His mum laughed. 'Looks like he's met his match,' she said.

*

We waited while Freddie's mum cleared the ornaments from the top of the oak-veneered sideboard. Most of them she carried into the kitchen and stood on the work surface, but she clutched the pink dish with a dancing nymph statue as its centre piece. 'His dad bought it me,' she said when she saw me looking. 'He was drunk when he bought it, but I've had it a long time.' With the top cleared, me and Freddie moved the sideboard about three foot along the wall. 'There,' said his mum. 'You can put your tree in there. I'll wait until you've finished before putting the ornaments back.' She looked at Freddie. 'I know how clumsy you are.'

We'd left the tree, now planted in the ceramic pot, in the hallway. We stood each side of it. I couldn't see Freddie because the tree was in the way. One of the branches was brushing against my face. I could smell the pine needles, some of them had already shed into the dirt. 'We'll have to water this,' I said. 'But let's get it in place first.'

'Are you walking backwards or shall I?' said Freddie.

'Definitely you,' I said.

'We haven't got much lift leeway,' he said.

I looked up. 'We've got enough,' I said, grabbing the handle. We grunted as we lifted the tree off the floor, the top brushing against the Artex of the hallway ceiling. 'Drop it down a touch,' I said. 'Okay. Ready. Walk.'

We shuffled along the hallway, me nervously watching the ceiling.

'Waddle, waddle, waddle, waddle.'

'What are you doing?'

'Keeping myself motivated. Waddle, waddle, waddle, waddle…'

We carried on shuffling; Freddie carried on with his waddle chant.

'Waddle, waddle, waddle, waddle.'

I laughed. He laughed.

'You're nearly there,' said his mum.

I felt my cheeks flush. I'd forgotten she was watching.

*

We were sitting on the floor unravelling tinsel. Freddie's mum was sitting in the rocking chair, pulling decorations, one by one, out of a brown hessian sack, which had Freddie's name embroidered across the front in red cotton. 'He's had that since he was born,' she said. 'His Aunt Floss made it for him.' The champions of the bag were dusty 1950s baubles, mainly gold and blue, and a set of ten hand-carved wooden soldiers dressed in red uniforms and wearing Foreign Legion hats, which looked like fezzes but with a veil down the back and a wide-rimmed peak. 'I can't remember where we got those from,' said his mum, holding up one of the models.

'Aunt Jess,' said Freddie. 'She gave them to us after Dad died.'

'Oh yes,' said his mum.

'That was Dad's sister,' Freddie said to me.

'Still is,' said his mum. 'But we've not seen her since the funeral.'

They exchanged glances, making me feel like I was intruding on some dark family secret. 'Anyway,' said his mum, 'I'll make some tea. Put some music on, Freddie.'

'Music?' he said.

'Yes. Pop that ABBA LP on you bought. I like them.' She walked into the kitchen and we could hear her filling the kettle and humming 'Dancing Queen'.

'I don't know what you've done to her,' said Freddie. 'She never wants the record player on.'

He stood up, walked over to the Ferguson cabinet record player, selected the ABBA *Arrival* LP out of the storage rack, a picture of the band in a helicopter on the front cover, and pulled the record out of its sleeve. He dropped the black vinyl onto the turntable, lifted up the stylus arm, which triggered the turntable to start revolving, and placed the needle on the far edge of the record. The crackling sound of 'When I Kissed the Teacher' started up through the single built-in speaker. 'Turn it up,' shouted his mum. 'I can hardly hear it.'

Freddie did as he was told and sat down next to me on the floor. 'This is all your fault,' he said, kissing me.

'Me. What have I done?'

'Being so gorgeous. She clearly likes you.'

His mum came back into the room, carrying a silver tray loaded with a teapot, three cups and saucers, a milk jug and a sugar bowl. Freddie jumped up and grabbed the tray. 'You should have called me,' he said.

'I'm quite capable of carrying a tray,' she said. 'Put it down on the table and I'll pour. You two can start putting the decorations on the tree.'

'We need to get it the right way first,' I said.

'What do you mean?' said Freddie, still holding the tray.

'I mean we need to turn it to different positions, see what looks best.'

'It's a tree, Jo-Jo.'

'You just do the turning, Freddie. Your mum and I will tell when it's right.'

'Best put the tray down and listen to her, son,' said his mum. 'She knows what she's doing.'

*

Christmas Day – Me, Freddie and his mum settled down for dinner, which we ate on our laps in front of the Christmas tree. His mum had cooked roast beef, homemade Yorkshire pudding, sprouts, cabbage and mashed potatoes, all smothered in gravy that made my mouth salivate to bursting point. 'This gravy is delicious,' I said.

'Perhaps I'll show you how to make it,' she said.

I smiled and looked at the tree. We'd wound his mum's pink and white candle lights around its branches, used hardly any tinsel and placed a peg fairy in a white ballerina dress on the tree's summit. At the bottom of the tree, there were four wrapped presents, one from me and Freddie to each other, one from us to his mum, and, most intriguing of all, one from Freddie's mum to us. 'What's she bought us?' I said when I saw it under the tree. 'I have no idea,' he said. 'But it's making me very nervous.' On a small coffee table next to the tree, his mum had placed a wooden model of a church with a red roof, which was lit up. Before we started our meal, she wound up the key on the back of the church and it played 'O Little Town of Bethlehem'. 'It's beautiful,' I said. 'It was his dad's,' she said.

Once we'd finished dinner, Freddie stacked up the plates from the table and disappeared into the kitchen. His mum rolled her eyes. 'He's been waiting to deliver this all day. Men. They always make a mountain out of a trifle.' I laughed as Freddie came back into the room, carrying a glass dish as though he were serving it to a maharaja's banquet. 'Tara,' he said, laying the dish in the centre of the table. 'The pièce de résistance.'

'Freddie,' said his mum. 'It's a trifle.'

'No,' he said, sitting down. 'It's a trifle made by me.'

'We'll need some dishes if we're going to enjoy your great work.'

'Oh yeah,' he said, going to stand back up.

'Stay there,' she said. 'I'll get them.'

She rubbed the top of his head before walking off into the kitchen. Freddie beamed after her.

'She's lovely,' I said.

'You're good for her,' he said, squeezing my hand. 'Was your dad okay with you coming here today?'

'He seemed to be. Mum's in bed and Josh has gone to his mate's.'

'So your dad's on his own. He could have joined us.'

'He can't. He needs to stay with Mum.'

'It must be lonely for him with the way your mum is.'

I felt an itch of irritation creep under my skin. Dad's woman in the park dropped into my head. 'That's what being married means, isn't it? Better or worse.'

'I suppose so. I just meant you've got to admire him. The way he...'

'He's not a saint, Freddie.'

He put his hand on top of mine. 'I didn't say he was. Are you okay?'

'Yeah, sorry, it's, well, me and Dad don't get on these days.'

His mum walked back into the room, holding three pudding dishes and three spoons, which she set out in front of us. 'What are you two looking so serious about?' she said.

'Oh, nothing,' said Freddie. 'I was just telling Jo-Jo about the secret ingredient in the trifle.'

'Secret ingredient?' she said.

'Navy rum,' he said. 'I slopped a couple of glasses in with the jelly.'

*

I was conscious all the way through eating my trifle of the unfinished conversation. Side one of the ABBA album ended with 'Knowing Me, Knowing You' and Freddie stood up, walked over to the music system and turned the record over. Side two started up with 'Money, Money, Money'.

'Well, I have to say, for a packet trifle, that was delicious,' said his mum, placing her spoon back in her now empty dish.

'It was lovely, Freddie,' I said.

'Shall we open the presents?' his mum said.

Me and Freddie looked at each other.

'Do you want to open my present first?' she said.

Freddie grabbed it from under the tree and handed it to me like it was a live grenade.

'It's okay,' she said. 'It won't bite.'

I looked at the card and showed it to Freddie. 'May these keep you safe, wherever life takes you. xx'

'What is it?' said Freddie.

'Well, if you open it, you'll find out.'

I started to unpick the wrapping paper. I could feel straightaway there were two ring boxes inside. I looked at Freddie's mum. 'What?' she said.

A lump wedged in my throat at the thought of what she might have bought, what she might have assumed. We'd only been together a matter of weeks. I pulled the red velvet boxes free of the wrapping.

Freddie looked horrified. 'Mum,' he said. 'What...'

'The pair of you needn't look so worried,' she said. 'Open the boxes.'

I opened the lid on the first box and smiled. 'A St Christopher,' I said.

'There are name labels in the lid,' she said.

I looked. The label in the box I'd opened said Freddie. I handed it to him and opened the second box. A matching St Christopher, gold, about the size of a sixpence.

'I've guessed the length of the chains,' she said.

I undid the clasp, put the chain around my neck and fastened it. The medallion sat just below my collarbone. 'It's perfect,' I said.

Freddie put his on. 'They're wonderful, Mum,' he said.

I hugged her. 'Thank you. I'll keep it with me always.'

*

Me and Freddie washed up, him washing, me drying, while his mum snoozed in the rocking chair. She'd protested about us doing it, but only half-heartedly.

'Do you want to tell me about your dad?' said Freddie as he washed the meat dish.

'He had an affair,' I said, not looking at him, concentrating on drying the plates. I waited for a few seconds for him to say something, but then realised I might have said it too sharply, as though it was none of his business. 'It's nice to be able to tell someone,' I said.

'Who was she?'

'Some woman he used to meet in the park. I saw him on a bench with her.'

He stopped washing up, dried his hands and hugged me. 'That must have been awful.'

'Yes,' I said. 'It was.'

'Does your mum know?'

'Dad never told her, and I've never had the guts.'

'He stayed though.'

'He said he loves Mum, but I think he just feels sorry for her.'

'I think he loves her from what I've seen.'

'What he did with his tart wasn't love.'

'No,' he said, turning back to the sink.

I rubbed his back. 'Let's not talk about it anymore. I don't want Dad spoiling our day. Do you think your mum will have a drink with us?'

'No idea. She's a different woman round you.'

'Let's go and ask her then.'

His mum opened her eyes when we walked in from the kitchen. 'What have you got there?' she said to Freddie, who was carrying a bottle of Pernod and a bottle of Crème de Menthe, which he put down on the dining table. 'We thought we'd have a drink, Mum.'

'Unless you want Advocaat,' I said. 'We've bought some soda water and lime juice so I can make snowballs if you like.'

She sat up in the rocking chair. 'Isn't that an old woman's drink?'

'You like Advocaat, Mum.'

'I'll have what you're having,' she said, looking at the bottles.

Freddie shrugged and fetched three whisky glasses out of the sideboard. I opened the Crème de Menthe, splashed a measure in each glass and then put in double the amount of Pernod. I handed Freddie's mum one of the glasses, picked up one myself and Freddie picked up the third. 'Happy Christmas,' said Freddie, holding his glass out in front of him. We clinked our glasses together and took a sip.

'It tastes like the gob-smackers we used to have as kids,' Freddie's mum said, curling her legs underneath her and taking another sip. 'It gets nicer the more you drink.'

'We get through a fair few in Max's,' I said. 'Be careful though. They say Pernod makes you drunk from the legs upwards.'

'Time for *Top of the Pops*,' said Freddie, switching on the television and flopping down next to me on the two-seater settee. He squeezed my hand, the theme music to *Top of the Pops* started, Peter Powell and Kid Jensen appeared on screen. 'You don't have to watch this, Mum.'

'Oh, I like him,' she said. 'Don't they call the other one 'Puffter' Powell?'

'Mother.'

'Everyone says he looks gay,' I said.

'That's it,' said his mum.

Boney M opened the show with 'Mary's Boy Child', the band dressed in white fur coats with hoods. B.A. Robertson did 'Bang Bang', Legs and Co danced to Anita Ward's 'Ring My Bell' and Blondie did two songs, Debbie Harry dressed in her *Parallel Lines* dress, sunglasses on for 'Sunday Girl' and off for 'Dreaming'. 'That's our song,' I said when 'Dreaming' started up. 'I asked him to dance when that song was on.'

'You asked him to dance?'

'She beat me to it by seconds,' said Freddie, putting his arm around me.

'You never were very quick off the mark,' she said, without taking her eyes off the television. 'Me and his dad had the Beatles.'

'Really,' I said. 'My dad loves them. What's your favourite?'

'"All My Loving",' she said, emptying her glass and looking at Freddie. 'I don't think I've ever told you that.'

'No, but it's nice to hear you talk about Dad.'

'These are all miming,' she said, looking back at the television.

'I think they have to,' I said.

'I'd like to have seen them tell John Lennon that. Are we going to have another drink?'

I cuddled Jo-Jo into my chest and we knotted our bodies together on the two-seater sofa. *Top of the Pops* had finished, we'd turned off the telly and Mum had gone to have a lie down. 'I'll be back for *The Poseidon Adventure* though,' she'd said as she left the room. 'And if you make a cup of tea, bring me one up.'

'You're quiet,' said Jo-Jo, pinching my arm.

'I was thinking about my dad,' I said.

She lifted her head and looked at me. 'You don't talk about him much,' she said.

'Not much to say. I don't really remember him.'

'If you ever do need to talk, I'm a good listener.'

'I know. I'm glad you came round today. You're good with her. I've never seen her like that. It's usually all doom and gloom.'

'Well, she's had a tough life. It can't have been easy, him dying so young.'

I kissed the top of her head. 'How did you get so wise?'

She kissed me on the lips. 'Shall we have another drink?'

'We could, but I've suddenly got a very urgent urge.'

'Really,' she said, smiling. 'And what urge would that be?'

'Oh, I think you know. And it's probably a life or death scenario.'

'Your mum's upstairs.'

'She won't come down.'

'Okay,' she said, pulling me towards her. 'If it's life or death, we'd better see if we can sort this urge of yours.'

*

We ended up on our backs, lying side by side on the carpet, looking up at the ceiling, the cushions off the sofa scattered around us. 'Jesus,' I said.

'My thoughts exactly. That was quite an urge you had.' She turned over and dropped her head on my chest. 'Your heart's racing.'

'I'm not surprised. Do you think Mum heard anything?'

'She might have heard that whimper you do.'

'I don't whimper. When?'

'Just before, you know, it's cute, but it's quite loud.'

I sat up and looked at her. 'I whimper?'

'Sort of, like you're clearing your throat, but a bit higher-pitched. Don't you know you're doing it?'

'If I was going to choose a noise, it would be something a bit more manly than a whimper.'

'Like what?'

'I don't know, a roar maybe.'

'Go on then. Let's hear it.'

I roared three times.

'I prefer the whimper. And you only do it once.'

'Oh, that's okay then. You're enjoying this, aren't you?'

She whimpered.

'Stop it,' I said, kissing her lips.

She whimpered again, this time muffled and into my mouth.

'You are completely bonkers.'

'And you, mister, have got to make your mum a cup of tea.'

'I can't go up there. What am I going to say to her?'

'You should have thought about that when you had your urge.'

*

I made the tea, left Jo-Jo tidying the room, and walked upstairs and into Mum's bedroom. She was lying on top of the duvet, fast asleep, still wearing her moccasin slippers. The curtains were half closed, putting the room in semi-darkness. I placed the tea on her bedside cabinet, next to the wooden cottage jewellery box I'd bought her two Christmases ago. 'Mum,' I said. 'I've brought your tea.'

'Freddie,' she said, opening her eyes.

I sat down on the side of the bed and held her hand.

'I was fast asleep,' she said. 'It must be that drink you gave me.' She sat up and reached for the cup and saucer.

I picked it up for her and put it into her hands.

'That's nice,' she said, taking a sip.

'The St Christophers are lovely, Mum.'

'Does Jo-Jo like hers?'

'She loves it. She's put it on already.'

'She's a nice girl. You really like her, don't you?'

'She's perfect, Mum.'

'Then make sure you don't lose her. Take it from me, perfect doesn't happen that often.'

'Dad was perfect, wasn't he?'

'He had his moments, but I never wanted anyone else from the day I met him. Why are you asking?'

'I was thinking about him. I don't really remember him.'

'I can see him in you.'

'I'm not perfect.'

She took another sip of her tea. 'You're perfect enough. You just need to realise it. Now, let me drink my tea in peace and I'll come down and watch that film with you.'

I stood up and walked towards the door.

'Freddie,' she said.

I turned back towards her.

'You could have closed the lounge door, you know.'

Jo-Jo – August 1980

Me and Freddie kissed our goodbye outside the chip shop in Bloxwich, him having walked the twenty-minute journey from his house to mine so we could catch the bus together. We'd already been into Woolworths to get my quarter pound of liquorice comfits to help get me through the shift. 'Last day,' I said. 'I can't wait to get away from that cow.'

'And I get you to myself on a Saturday.'

'Until I go to uni. I can't believe that's only weeks away.'

'I'm still hoping you might change your mind.'

'I'm not going to change my mind, Freddie. We've talked this to death.'

He dropped his gaze into the gutter. I lifted his head. 'What are you going to do with yourself today?'

'Wait for you to finish work.'

'Can't you go to Jack's?'

'He's studying. I'll be fine. I'll crash out in King George's.'

'Sounds better than my day.'

'It'll go by in a flash,' he said.

I kissed him lightly on the lips, squeezed his hand and then walked away along the high street, leaving him outside the chip shop. I could feel him watching me, making sure I was okay. I smiled to myself. Sweet.

I reached the M.E.B., turned and waved. He waved back. I looked down the alleyway at the side of the shop. There were three overflowing grey metal bins in front of me, a mound of used tea leaves spilling out of the first bin, its lid plonked precariously on a heap of rubbish. The stench of rotting fruit and food waste invaded my nostrils as I walked, trying to hold my breath, to the fire escape stairs halfway down the alley. I climbed the rackety metal steps, feeling them swaying underneath me, and opened the door to the hairdresser's, which occupied the top floor.

Roma was sitting in one of the black leather barber's chairs, facing the mirror, drinking a mug of coffee. 'You're late,' she said as I walked through the door.

'The bus was late,' I said.

She placed her coffee cup on the floor, leaned forward to look in the mirror and started pinching and stretching the skin at the side of her eyes. 'Do you think I'm getting wrinkles?'

I stood behind her, looking over her head at her face in the mirror. 'No,' I said.

'Liar.'

'I'm not lying.'

'It'll come to you one day,' she said, still looking in the mirror, still pulling at the skin on her face. 'Look at these hands. You see that, there, I swear that wasn't there last week.' I looked at the spot on the back of her right hand, which she was jabbing with her left forefinger. There was a faint brown stain about the size of a halfpence piece. 'It's there, isn't it?' she said.

'I can't see anything.'

'Age spots. My mother had them all over her body. They give you away. Especially on your hands. You'll find out.' She sighed, stood up and walked over to the small kitchenette at the back of the shop. She opened one of the cupboard doors over the sink and looked inside. 'I could have sworn we had some biscuits. That Rob's probably nicked them.'

'Nicked what?' said Rob, walking into the shop.

'Biscuits,' I said, raising my eyebrows.

'Just what she needs with that gut,' he said.

'What?' said Roma, still looking in the cupboard.

'I said I'll pop out and get some later,' said Rob, winking at me.

'Oh, you're here,' she said, turning to face us.

'Charming,' he said, pulling at the blonde highlights in his feather-cut hair. 'I can always go again if you want.'

'You know she's going today, don't you?'

'I don't blame her, the way you talk to her.'

'She's a Saturday girl. That's what they're for.'

'I'll get the biscuits,' I said.

'No,' said Roma. 'You can sweep the floor. You're already late. I need some fresh air.' She walked out of the shop. We heard her heels clattering as she descended the steps.

'By fresh air she means a fag,' said Rob. 'She needs fresh everything.'

'I shan't miss her,' I said. 'She's never liked me.'

'It doesn't help you being so gorgeous. You still seeing that Freddie bloke?'

'Yes,' I said, feeling my cheeks flush. 'He's meeting me later. You're not going to stay here, are you?'

'What, with old iron-drawers? What would she do without me? Better the devil you know, I guess.'

'She needs a man,' I said.

'Maybe not say that to her,' said Rob, hanging up his coat. 'I know it's your last day, but I'm assuming you don't want to spend it in casualty.'

'Don't worry. I asked her once and nearly lost my head. You've never told me what happened with her husband.'

'Usual story. He dumped her for a younger model. I know it nearly finished her off.'

'And she never had anyone else. That must have been years ago.'

'Some things you never get over. He was a shit, but she loved him.'

'I hadn't realised,' I said, sadness suddenly smothering me like an old grey overcoat.

'Why would you? They were kids when they met, about your age. She thought they both wanted to change the world, went off to a kibbutz in Israel, but it turned out he wanted to let her do all the work while he spent their money on booze and slept it off on the beach.'

'And she still married him?'

'Yep. Kidded herself she could change him. They dragged on for ten years, broken promise after broken promise, until the money had gone and he pissed off, leaving her with the debt. He still lives round here, turned up at the shop about five years ago, drunk, broke, on his own, begging her to take him back. I had to call the police.'

'Jesus. No wonder she's bitter.'

'Lesson for us all,' he said, grinning at me. 'Be careful of young love. It's not always what it seems.'

I heard Roma's heels coming back up the stairs.

'Better get sweeping,' said Rob.

*

Late afternoon, Rob had finished his shift, the blue rinse brigade had all been sated, and I was sweeping up the last of the, mainly grey, strands of hair. 'You'll be wanting this,' said Roma, opening the till, lifting the spring on one of the drawers and pulling out a brown pay packet. 'Not that you deserve it.'

I stopped sweeping, stood the brush against the wall and took the envelope from her. It had Jo-Jo written in capital letters across the front in red ink. 'Thank you,' I said.

'You think I'm a cow, don't you?'

'It doesn't really matter now,' I said.

She laughed. 'I don't suppose it does,' she said, closing the till drawer.

I folded up the envelope and pushed it inside my skirt pocket. 'You never seemed to like me very much. I'm not sure what I did.'

'You didn't do anything,' she said, flicking through the pages in the appointments book. 'You shouldn't be so touchy.'

I walked to the top of the stairs. I could feel her watching me, could sense that she was going to say something. 'Jo-Jo,' she said.

I stopped walking and turned back towards her.

'Do you need a reference?'

'No thanks. I'm off to uni in a couple of weeks.'

'Let me know if you do.'

'Can I ask you something?' I said.

'That depends what it is.'

'I was just, tell me to mind my own business, but, well, I've never heard you mention your family.'

'That's because I don't have any.'

'What, no one?'

'I have a sister, but she lives back in Liverpool. We don't get on.'

'And there's no one else?'

'You mean a man?'

'You're right, it's none of my business. I'm just being a nosy cow.' I went to walk down the stairs.

'Hang on,' she said, closing the appointments book and walking from behind the till. 'This young man of yours.'

'Freddie,' I said. 'What about him?'

'You love him, don't you?'

'I think so. Why are you asking?'

'I don't know really. It's just, don't let him become everything. If he loves you, he'll understand.'

'He does understand,' I said. 'That's why I'm going to uni.'

Freddie – August 1980

I watched her as she walked down the high street, her blue denim miniskirt and white cheesecloth top showing off her tanned skin. She reached the alleyway, turned and waved. I waved back. She walked out of view and I stood, confusion knotting my stomach, looking at the space she'd vacated. This was what it would be like without her. I'd be left with her ghost and, even worse, three years of futile hope that she'd come back to me – a death of a thousand cuts. From that first dance in Max's, I'd known she was out of my league. I still didn't get why she'd asked me to dance, why she'd stayed with me for nearly a year.

A bus screeched to a stop outside the chip shop, passengers chattering as they disembarked, jolting me out of my head space. I shoved my hands inside the pockets of my jeans and walked down the Stafford Road, heading for the park. I missed the Avenger, not because of the walk, but because it meant I wouldn't be able to park up in King George's, lie on the grass with the door open and listen to Springsteen tapes. It was okay though. I needed to save the petrol if we were going to New Invention later to play darts with Jo-Jo's cousins.

I reached the gates of the park and walked along the driveway towards the open fields. It was only ten o'clock, but I could already smell the burned charcoal of the local neighbourhood's barbeques, a sticky haze smothering the landscape like a honey and mustard dressing. The park was deserted. Normally there was a football match being played, but I remembered it was a break in season.

I turned right at the top of the drive and headed up the hill towards the deserted cottage, the one Jack had convinced me was haunted. 'Seriously, Freddie. It belongs to a bloke whose bride-to-be dumped him on their wedding day. He's probably still hanging in there.' The dirty white building was hidden from view by wild bramble bushes and feral roses. Its windows had been boarded up recently by the council, but for years it had sat with broken panes of glass, shivering cobwebs hanging out of every orifice. I lay down on the grass in front of the bushes and looked up at the sky. If Jo-Jo had been there we'd have been looking at the clouds, the sun drawing out her nose freckles as we searched the heavens for famous faces.

'Freddie.'

I lifted myself up onto my elbows. Nicki was walking towards me, her pet dachshund, Sacha, trotting on a lead at her side. I put up my hand, hoping she'd walk straight past, but she walked over, unclipped the dog's lead so he could sniff along the bushes and then sat down beside me on the grass. 'You okay?' she said. 'Still with, what's her name?'

'Jo-Jo,' I said. 'And yes, we're still together. What about you? Still with…'

'Tommy,' she said. 'No. We called it a day. I couldn't cope with all that Navy rubbish.'

I smiled.

'No need to look so pleased,' she said.

'You did dump me for him. I never understood what you saw in a bugle player from the sea cadets.'

'Hey, he's an excellent bugle player. He can play Reveille all the way through.'

'I wouldn't have thought there was much call for that in Walsall. We've all got alarm clocks.'

She laughed. 'You're probably right. Anyway, I did you a favour from what I can hear.'

'And what have you heard?'

'That she's gorgeous, that you're inseparable, that you look at her with puppy dog eyes.'

I felt the blood fill my cheeks.

'Oh God,' she said. 'It's true. Freddie's in love.'

I looked around at the bushes. Sacha had found himself a stick to gnaw on. 'You've still got the dog then?'

'Stop changing the subject. I'm pleased. You deserve someone to look after you.'

'She's off to uni soon.'

'Brains as well as beauty. What does she see in you?'

'My thoughts exactly.'

She gave me a hard look. 'I was joking, Freddie. You're not overthinking this, are you? You know what you're like.'

'I was right about you and the bugle player.'

'That was my mistake, not yours.'

'It still happened though.'

Sacha came bounding over and nudged at Nicki's elbow. 'Listen, I've got to go,' she said, patting my leg. 'But call me if you need to talk.'

'Thanks,' I said. 'I will.'

'There is one thing this Jo-Jo can't claim,' she said, standing up and reattaching Sacha's lead.

I gave her a puzzled look.

'Your virginity. That was me on my mum's sheepskin rug. Don't tell me you've forgotten.'

'I haven't forgotten,' I said. 'It's a pity I couldn't play the bugle. We could have played Reveille afterwards.'

She laughed and walked away towards the entrance gates, Sacha's stunted legs sprinting hard to keep up.

Freddie – May 1980

Blackpool. Early morning. I could hear Jo-Jo breathing next to me. There was a cock crowing somewhere close, perhaps next door to Mr Lewis's B and B. The bedroom smelt of sleep and sex. A gentle breeze from the open window was cooling my face. Tap, tap, tap. Anxiety, the voice that kept me awake at night, was knocking out its rhythm inside my head. *She's too good for you.* Turn off my brain, turn off my brain. *You're not good enough for her.* I moved closer and eased myself against her body. She muttered something and threw her arm across me. The heat glow from her naked skin was comforting, like the afterglow of a hot chocolate drink on a zero degrees winter's day. *She not going to stay.* Shut it out, shut it out. *You know what's going to happen.* I cuddled her closer. She rolled over and turned her back on me. Don't go. Don't go. Don't go. The cock crowed again.

I could hear them talking in the hallway, but their voices were whisper level and I couldn't make out what they were saying. I tried to concentrate on Elton John's *Blue Moves*, which was playing at low volume out of the Bose sound dock, but Amy's voice was distracting me. I'd suspected she would come, but the reality of Jo-Jo and I talking in front of her ratcheted up my pulse rate and churned my stomach. I could have done with a propranolol to settle my nerves, but that wasn't possible now. *Of course she wants her here*, I said to myself. *She probably thinks you're mad and she needs a chaperone.* Jack had said he'd go out, but, covering all the possibilities, he'd laid out four cups and saucers alongside the coffee percolator, milk and sugar bowl on the glass-topped table in front of me. I suddenly realised he hadn't given us any teaspoons. I ticked off the mistake in my head – Jack not getting it one hundred per cent right proved he was human. I stood up, ready to go into the kitchen to fetch the spoons, but I heard the front door close. I sat back down in the Next bucket chair and waited. The lounge door opened.

'Hello, Freddie.'

I burst into tears and Jo-Jo rushed over to me. 'I'm so sorry,' I said as she hugged me to her.

She squeezed me tighter. 'So am I,' she said. 'So am I.'

*

Our hug started to feel tense after a few seconds, the initial relief ebbing away and bringing us back into the confusion of the real world. We came apart and Jo-Jo sat down on the other bucket seat and crossed her legs. I blew my nose into a paper tissue.

'Jack said you're going to stay here for a few days,' she said.

'He thought it best. I think he's worried about what I might do next.'

'You can't blame him, Freddie.'

'I know. I've messed it all up again.'

'You mustn't say that.'

'It's true though.'

A silence descended. I looked at the floor.

'I need to know why,' she said.

'I don't know. When you told me about the baby, it all seemed, I couldn't stop thinking about it and…'

'I wanted to be honest with you, Freddie. I've held that guilt inside for thirty-five years.'

I lifted my head and met her eyes. 'I should have phoned you, should have been with you. I should have, I don't know, I wish we could go back to the beginning.' I started crying again and she came over and knelt in front of me, stroking my hair.

'Everyone wants that,' she said. 'It wasn't anyone's fault. You've got to stop blaming yourself for everything.' She pulled a fresh tissue out of the Kleenex box at the side of the chair and handed it to me.

'We were good,' I said, taking the clean tissue from her and blowing my nose again.

'Yes,' she said. 'But we were kids.'

'I mean in Devon. It was still there, wasn't it? Tell me you felt it as well.'

'Of course I did.'

'Then we can make it right, can't we? Even now we can make it right.' I hugged her to me, sniffing in her white musk perfume, which always took me back to Max's and our first dance. 'Tell me it's all going to be okay,' I whispered.

I had my hands on his shoulder blades. He felt bony. He'd lost weight in the few days since I'd last seen him and he seemed older, shrunken; the nervy Freddie from the hotel meal was back, not the Devon Freddie, certainly not the Max's Freddie, not my Freddie. He was squeezing me tight. I eased myself away from him. I noticed he wasn't wearing his Ray-Ban spectacles. Crow's feet wrinkles had spread their reach from the corners of his eyes and onto his cheeks, and patches of grey beard stubble were dotted across his face and neck.

'It is going to be okay, isn't it?' he said.

'I don't know,' I said.

'You don't love me.'

'I've never stopped loving you, Freddie.'

'That's okay then. We can work all of this out.'

I started to think about Mum, her schizophrenia, how it had smothered Dad's existence, driven him to an affair with his tart. 'It's not that simple,' I said. 'You frighten me when you react like this.'

'I'll change. You can help me change.'

'It's not about me. First the train, now the tablets. You need to get well.'

'Who told you about the train?'

'Jack. He was worried about you. What you did isn't normal.' I realised what I'd said as soon as the words tipped out of my mouth. His face crumpled. He looked like I'd punched him on the nose. 'I didn't mean that,' I said.

He stood up and walked over to the bay window. 'When do you go to New Zealand?' he said.

'Come and sit down, Freddie. Come and talk to me.'

'You should go,' he said, turning to face me. 'I'm still not sure why you came looking for me in the first place.'

I stood up, walked over to him and went to touch his face. He turned his head away. 'Please, Jo-Jo. Leave me alone.'

'I don't want us to finish like this.'

'What do you want?' he said, his voice bubbling with emotion. 'We finished thirty-five years ago, but you decided to start it all again.'

'I know and...'

'And what? You came away to Devon knowing how I feel about you.'

'I felt the same.'

'And then you decided to tell me about the baby.'

'I thought you had a right to know. I didn't expect you to react like you did.'

'Why? You know me better than anyone. How could you not know how I'd react?'

'I thought I was doing the right thing.'

'I love you, Jo-Jo. You say you love me, but you're going to walk away.'

I went to touch his face again.

'Please go,' he said.

The lounge door opened. 'Mum,' said Amy. 'Are you okay?'

I hadn't realised, but I'd started crying. 'No,' I said. 'We need to go.' I turned and walked out of the lounge, pushing past Amy and Jack who were standing side by side in the doorway.

Freddie – August 2015

'What have you said to her?' said Amy.

I was still standing by the window, but I'd turned back towards the street. I saw Jo-Jo walk, half run down the garden path. She pressed her key fob and the Mazda's lights flickered twice. She opened the driver's door and got into the car. 'Nothing,' I said.

Jack walked across the lounge and put his arm around me. 'You okay, mate?' he said.

'She thinks I'm mad, Jack.'

'Well...' said Amy.

Jack glared at her and she stopped whatever it was she was going to say.

'I'm going to check Mum's okay,' she said and walked out of the lounge.

'Come on,' said Jack. 'Let's sit down.'

He guided me back to the bucket chair. I felt as though I was in a trance, being led back to my seat by Matron on the psychiatric ward.

Jack knelt in front of me. 'What's happened?' he said.

'She's going to New Zealand. She always was.'

'Is that what she said?'

'I think I've frightened her.'

'You frightened all of us, bud.'

I suddenly realised how he was talking to me, carefully, thinking about what he was saying, no sarcasm, no edge. Not Jack. 'Do you think I'm mad, Jack?'

'No,' he said. 'But you need some help. We can't ignore what's happened. What you tried to do.'

'I don't want to see her again.'

'You don't mean that.'

'I do, Jack. I can't bear the thought of her seeing me like this. Why did she come back?'

'To see you.'

'And the baby, I didn't need to know about the baby. We could have left it all in the past.'

'She hasn't seen you for over thirty years. I don't suppose she'd thought any of it through any more than you had. I think Devon took her by surprise.'

'What do you mean?'

'Come on, Freddie. It must have surprised you how easy it was for all those feelings to come back. It's not going to be any different for her, is it?'

'She's still leaving me though.'

Jo-Jo – August 2015

Amy opened the passenger door and dropped into the seat.

'Is Freddie okay?' I said.

'No,' she said. 'But Jack's with him. What did he say to you, Mum?'

'He told me to leave him alone.'

'Why?'

'I said something stupid and upset him. I told him he needed to get some help, that what he'd done wasn't normal.'

'Sounds pretty spot on to me.'

'I don't know what to do, Amy. I should go back inside and make sure he's okay.'

'I don't think that's a good idea, Mum. Not today.'

'I can't leave it like that.'

'You don't have to. We don't fly until Friday. Let Jack sort him out first.'

A silver Ford Fiesta pulled up in front of us. A nurse in uniform got out of the car and ran up the path of the house opposite. I remembered Jack saying one of his neighbours was expecting her third child. A few spots of rain landed on the front windscreen of the Mazda. I pressed the power button and dabbed the accelerator with my right foot. The engine purred into life. 'You're right,' I said. 'Text Jack and tell him I'll call him tomorrow.'

Jack's ginger tomcat, Boris, slid around the lounge door and sat on the carpet looking at me. I patted the front of the chair to call him over, but he stood up and walked back out into the hallway, his tail pointing at the ceiling. Jack walked into the lounge carrying two mugs, one full of coffee, which he handed to me, and the other, I could smell, full of liquorice tea. He sat down in the opposite chair.

'You're not still drinking that stuff, are you?' I said.

'It's good for me,' he said, taking a sip and grimacing.

'That must be why you always pull that face when you drink it.'

He took another sip, scrunched up his face again and put the mug down on the glass coffee table. 'You okay?' he said, crossing his legs.

'I'd be better if you stopped asking me that, Jack.'

'You can't expect us all just to forget what you did.'

'I don't expect that, but you're not my counsellor. I just want to get back to normal. I fucked up, but you going all Nurse Ratched on me isn't going to help. You'll be playing Mozart at a low hum next and calling me up for medication time.'

'Fuck off,' he said.

'That's better.'

He uncrossed his legs and sat forward in the chair. 'If you want the truth, I'm pretty pissed off with you. You want to get back to normal. None of us know what that is with you. We're circling you on tiptoes, trying not to say the wrong thing in case you top yourself. No wonder Jo-Jo's leaving. I'm thinking of going with her, but I don't think it'll be far enough away.'

'Don't let me stop you.'

'No point. You'll probably follow me. That's what you do, isn't it? Something dramatic and wait for someone, usually me, to pick up the pieces. Any decisions to be made, and you run and hide. You've never been any fucking different. What did you expect Jo-Jo to do? Fall into your arms and play happy families. She's probably packing right now.'

'I don't need any of you.'

'You need all of us, Freddie. You're useless on your own.'

I stared at the blank television screen, the word useless spooling over and over inside my head. Jo-Jo had said I wasn't normal. No. She'd said what I'd done wasn't normal. She'd looked at me differently, though, like I'd crossed a line, become someone she needed to worry about. She used to say that's what she found attractive, my vulnerability, and even now she kept coming back. I wanted to be different, to be a better man for her, but maybe it was too late, maybe too much time had passed, maybe the train and the tablets were the final fracture. I felt Jack watching me. 'Why did you tell Jo-Jo about the train?' I said.

'I'm not a robot, Freddie. I needed help.'

'But she hates me now.'

'Jesus,' he said. 'You're such a fucking idiot.'

Jo-Jo – January 1980

We'd just watched Eddie Charlton beat Ray Reardon in the *Pot Black* final when Dad made his big announcement. 'We're going to have a birthday tea for your mother tomorrow.'

'No, Joseph,' said Mum from her usual spot on the sofa, smothered in an eiderdown duvet. 'I don't want a fuss.'

'It's all arranged,' said Dad. 'I've asked Arthur to come with his latest.'

'That's a great idea,' said Freddie, who was sitting on the opposite chair with me on his lap. 'We'll come.'

I looked at Dad. 'Yeah, of course we will,' I said. 'If that's what Mum wants.'

'I don't feel well enough,' said Mum.

'You'll be fine,' said Dad. 'You don't want to let Arthur down, do you?'

Dad's trump card. I always thought Mum had a crush on Arthur, Dad's eldest brother. He used to pick them up in his saloon car and escort Mum arm in arm down the path, opening the back door for her and wiping the seat with his ironed white cotton handkerchief, like she was the Queen Mum. 'For you, my lady,' he'd say. She'd giggle and flush like a sixteen-year-old on her first proper date. 'You shouldn't make a fuss of me, Arthur.' 'I'll make a fuss of who I want. And he'd better treat you right or I'll whisk you away from him.' Dad would smile through pinched lips, as though he wasn't quite getting the joke. When they reached the club, Arthur would run around the car and open the door for Mum to get out. She would always sit there and wait for him.

'No,' said Mum, as the *Pot Black* credits rolled up the screen. 'I wouldn't want to let Arthur down.'

*

The next morning, me, Josh and Dad were sitting at the dining table in the kitchen, eating breakfast, when Mum walked in fully dressed. Most mornings Dad had to spend a couple of hours persuading her to get up and, on the days she relented to move downstairs, she'd keep her dressing gown wrapped tight around her body, regardless of the weather, and swap one lying under the duvet place for another by flopping on the settee in the lounge, waiting for Dad to bring her a cup of tea.

'Morning, love,' said Dad when she walked into the kitchen. 'You okay?'

'Of course I'm okay,' she said. 'I'm going to cook some boiled eggs.'

I looked at Josh and we both looked at Dad who stood up, walked over to Mum and tried to guide her towards the lounge. 'I'll do it, love. How many eggs do you want?'

Mum pushed his hand away. 'I'm perfectly capable of boiling some eggs,' she said. 'Now, where did I put that saucepan?' She walked over to the larder cupboard, opened the door, slammed it shut, then the cleaning cupboard, then the fridge. She turned and faced Dad. 'You've hidden them. Why would you do that?'

'Nobody's hidden anything,' he said. 'They're in the cupboard here, where we've always kept them.' He reached into the cupboard next to the sink and pulled out one of the stainless steel saucepans.

Mum ran over and grabbed it out of his hand. 'You're always trying to make me look stupid,' she said.

'Oh, for God's sake, Mum,' I said.

'And you,' she said, glaring at me. 'You're as bad as he is.'

'Calm down, love,' said Dad, putting his hand on her arm.

'I am calm,' screamed Mum.

'Dad's only trying to help,' I said.

'Help. You'd all starve if I wasn't here.'

I laughed. Dad put his other arm around Mum's shoulder. Mum swung around and hit him square in the forehead with the saucepan.

*

Two hours later, me and Josh were sitting on the settee in the lounge, listening to Dad on the phone in the hall.

'That's right, Arthur. She's gone down with a tummy bug. We're going to have to do it another day.'

'Yes. I'm looking after her.'

'Yes. I'll call you tomorrow and let you know how she is.'

'Thank you, Arthur. I'll tell her.'

He hung up the phone and walked into the lounge.

I could see a lump in the middle of his forehead. It was already turning blue. 'You should get that looked at,' I said.

'It's fine,' he said, sitting down in his chair.

'How's Mum?' said Josh.

'She's asleep,' said Dad. 'I managed to get some tablets down her. I don't know what set her off.'

'Apart from being bonkers,' I said.

'You shouldn't say things like that, Jo-Jo.'

'Why not? That's what she is.'

'I'm going out,' said Josh, standing up and walking out of the lounge.

Dad and I flinched as we heard the front door slam behind him.

'What a family,' I said.

'We never used to be like this,' said Dad.

'No...'

'Please don't say it, Jo-Jo. Not now.'

'What? Mention your tart, you mean.'

He held his head in his hands. 'I'm trying my best,' he said.

Jo-Jo – August 2015

The rain started to fall heavily as we drove back to the hotel, the Mazda's automatic windscreen wipers struggling to keep pace with the downpour. Telephone poles and trees whizzed by as the car's wheels hissed through the road puddles. We passed a wind farm, five turbines staggered across a field, their blades rotating at Billy Whizz speed as the breeze geared itself up a few notches. I'd not noticed them before and for a second I wondered if we'd taken a wrong turning. 'Is this the right way?' I said.

'Yes,' said Amy. 'I think so.'

I focussed on watching out for the sharp left turn into the hotel's driveway. I'd sped past it a couple of times on previous journeys and had to do a U-turn.

'We're nowhere near yet,' said Amy, noticing the car slowing down.

'I do know,' I said and then realised I'd snapped. 'I'm sorry. It's this rain. It's making me nervous.'

'He'll be okay with Jack, Mum.'

'I wish I hadn't upset him.'

'You told him the truth.'

'Perhaps he didn't need me to do that today. I'll call him. I don't want to leave it like that.'

'I'm not sure what you're wanting out of this,' said Amy. 'You seem to keep changing your mind. When you came back from Devon you seemed happy, and then you were really sad when he didn't contact you. And now...'

'He's just so frail, Amy. It's like he's two different people. First the train, now the tablets.'

'Neither of them were serious. Jack said he was already stepping back from the edge of the platform when he got to him, and as for the tablets, he hadn't taken more than some people take as a daily dose. It was all pretty half-hearted.'

'So why do it?'

'To get a reaction off you probably.'

'That's madness.'

'That's what he is, isn't it? A bit bonkers. I spotted that after meeting him once. He thinks you're going to leave him. He told Jack everyone leaves him in the end, something to do with his Dad dying. But you still love him, don't you?'

I concentrated on the road and thought about Mum. All those years I'd spent telling myself, I must try harder. I must try harder. The rain had slowed down so I pressed my foot on the accelerator. Freddie's face dropped into my head, his broken tooth, his blushing cheeks, his looking-down-at-the-floor gaze, his little-boy-who'd-stolen-a-toffee expression. I must try harder. I must try harder.

'You've missed the turn,' said Amy.

Jo-Jo – November 1974

Me and Dad were in the kitchen, sitting at a pine dining table. In front of us were two bamboo sticks, which Dad had already cut to size and tied together to form an X, and two front pages of the *Daily Mirror* newspaper. One of the pages carried the headline, 'Where Did He Go?' and a picture of a moustachioed Lord Lucan who was wanted by the police for the murder of his children's nanny; the other page showed a picture of President Nixon, arms aloft, climbing up the steps of Air Force One with the headline, 'Goodbye America'.

'Watch carefully,' said Dad. 'You might have to do this with your kids one day.'

'I'm watching, Dad,' I said.

He squeezed a line of Golden Gum glue down the side of one of the pages, biting his tongue all the way through to aid his concentration, making sure to get an even spread out of the red rubber-spouted lid. Satisfied, he placed the edge of the other page over the line of glue and rubbed his finger all the way along the join, making sure it had stuck firm. Next, he put a blob of glue in each corner of the now joined together pages and glued the X-shaped bamboo sticks in place. He picked up a pair of scissors, punctured two pinprick holes through the centre of the newspaper and then threaded through the start of a ball of string, which he tied to the centre cross of the bamboo sticks. 'There,' he said, turning the paper over. 'We have a kite.'

'That's great, Dad. Can we go out and fly it?'

'Best let the glue dry first,' he said. 'Let me take your mum a cup of tea and then we'll try it out.'

An hour later, I climbed into the passenger seat of Dad's Volvo. I was wrapped up tight in my Parka coat, scarf and fingerless gloves. I placed the kite on the back seat. 'I don't know why Josh didn't want to come,' said Dad. 'It's a perfect day for kite flying.'

'You know what he's like,' I said. 'I think he's allergic to the outdoors.'

'Takes after his mum,' said Dad.

'And I take after you,' I said.

He smiled, started up the engine, pulled the car away from the kerb and headed towards the Arboretum.

*

The Arboretum in Walsall was our family go-to place for bonfire night. Dad would gather us at the side of the lake, me and Josh staring open-mouthed as the rockets spat and flared skywards, exploding over the water, showering anyone too close with falling fragments of ash. We'd munch on our steaming jacket potatoes bought from the chuckling stallholder, Cyril, who Dad vaguely knew from the Saddler's pub, but who treated us like he was our closest relative – 'Got them kids out again, Joseph. You're lucky. I can't get mine from in front of the telly.' Mum would glare at Cyril like he was something she wanted to scrape off her shoe. 'Who is that awful man, Joseph?' 'Just some bloke from the pub, love.' We used to cheer when two men doused petrol around the base of the fire stack and dropped lit torches to ignite the whoosh towards a doomed, and slightly dejected looking, Guy Fawkes. I always felt sad, almost tearful, when the flames finally consumed the paper-stuffed effigy. Dad would put his arm around me. 'You okay, love?' I'd nod and squeeze him back.

We had our choice of parking bays in the visitors' car park. I retrieved the kite from the back seat and we waded through the piles of autumn-shed leaves yet to be swept by the whistling gardeners, the trees shivering in the breeze. At the end of the path, we turned a corner to be greeted by an expanse of undulating field at the back of the lake. I grabbed Dad's hand. The wind notched up its force and made a snatch and grab raid on my breath. I pulled on my faux fur-trimmed hood and squeezed Dad's hand tighter. 'Do you think the kite's strong enough, Dad?'

'It'll be fine,' he said. 'Let's go to the top of that hill.'

We wheezed our way up the steep incline. From the hilltop we could see the whole park yawning to the horizon. 'Isn't it wonderful,' said Dad.

'Perfect,' I said.

'Let's get this baby flying,' he said, holding the kite up in front of him.

The wind started biting at the *Daily Mirror*, trying to wrench it from Dad's grasp. 'Unwind the string a bit,' he said.

I grabbed the ball of string with both hands and walked backwards.

'Ready,' said Dad.

I tightened my grip. 'I'm ready,' I shouted into the wind.

Dad let go of the bamboo sticks and I jolted forwards as the kite pulled on the string, trying to make its escape. Dad grabbed the string as well. 'Roll it out some more,' he shouted.

I took a few more steps backwards, the ball unravelling in front of me. Dad let more of the string pass through his hands, the *Daily Mirror* soaring further and further away. Finally, Dad reached me, there was hardly any string left on the ball. 'Are you strong enough to hold it?' he said.

I nodded and gripped the ball even tighter.

'I'm going to let go after three. One, two... three.'

I was yanked forwards as he released the string. I thought I was going to slip on the dewy grass. I dug my heels in, regained my balance and looked upwards. The kite seemed miles away, on its way to space, backdropped by a thick grey sky and tug, tug, tugging at my arms. 'This is great,' I shouted.

Jo-Jo – August 2015

I pulled the Mazda into its usual parking space in the hotel's car park, pressed the power button to turn off the engine and unfastened my seatbelt. Amy unfastened hers and put up her hand to the hotel security guard, who was waving at us from his usual sentry point by the grey industrial-size bins. 'I wonder what he's making of this,' said Amy.

'Yes. I'd wondered that myself.'

'Makes his day a bit more interesting I suppose. He probably goes home and tells his wife about the mad woman and her daughter who've moved into the hotel and their strange goings on.'

'We have been here a long time, Amy. A couple of months now. Is Dan still okay with that?'

'I've told you, Mum, he's booked it at corporate rates for us. He'll sign it off as a tax loss anyway. Stop worrying. You've got enough to think about.'

'I think I'll go and sit in the garden for a bit, clear my head.'

'Well, I'm going to have a soak, try out that new bath bomb I bought. I'll see you at teatime.'

I put my hand on her leg. 'Thank you for coming with me today, sweetheart. I'm afraid your old mum's gone a bit bonkers herself at the moment. Don't give up on me though. I'll work it out.'

'You've always been bonkers,' she said, reaching over and hugging me. 'But it's nice to have a mum who's a bit different.'

We got out of the car. Amy walked off towards the hotel entrance and I walked to the bench underneath the eucalyptus tree and sat down. A red squirrel suddenly ran out from underneath the bushes, stopped in the centre of the lawn, caught my eye for a second before sprinting off, rustling through the long grass in front of the huge oak tree and emerging to scramble up the trunk and into the sanctuary of the upper branches. I looked up into the tree, but the squirrel was well hidden in the canopy. 'If only it was that simple to escape,' I muttered to myself.

Freddie – February 1980

I walked behind Jo-Jo down the spiral staircase leading from Max's games area to the dance floor, slowing my descent as she carefully placed out the high heels of her yellow Go-Go boots on every step. I could see a gang of lads at the bar, looking up at Jo-Jo and then at me as I turned the corner. Jo-Jo tugged down the hem of her black and white polka-dot Twiggy dress and looked back at me. I smiled and she carried on walking. John Lennon's 'Imagine' started up.

Jo-Jo looked relieved as we reached the bottom of the stairs. She pushed her way through the crowd, heading for the second spiral staircase on the far side of the dance floor, leading to the restaurant. I started to follow her, but one of the lads from the bar, glazed eyes, blonde hair, Tom Selleck moustache, top button open on his white shirt, tie loosened off, stepped out in front of me, his three mates leaning in over his shoulder. 'You jammy bastard,' he shouted in my ear, trying to make himself heard over the music.

I went to walk past him, but he put his hand on my chest. 'How much?' he said.

I looked at him quizzically.

'For the girl. You must be paying her.' He took a sip from his pint of lager and turned back towards his mates. 'Told you she was on the game, lads. I might have a go next week.' They all laughed.

I carried on walking. I could see Jo-Jo waiting for me. I stopped walking, my head was pounding, stuffed with blood. I turned around and walked back towards the bar, my fists squeezed together, my heart racing. One of Tom Selleck's mates saw me and nudged Tom. I squeezed my fists tighter. I felt someone grab my arm. I spun around. 'Freddie,' said Jack.

'Jesus, Jack. I nearly punched you.'

'I could see you were going to punch someone.'

I looked towards the bar. Tom was grinning at me, chewing on the rim of his beer glass, two of his mates had their arms around his shoulders. 'He asked me how much I was paying Jo-Jo.'

'Him. He's a prick.'

'I'm still going to kick his head in.'

Jack laughed. 'How long have I known you?' he said.

'All my life.'

'And when did you last have a fight?'

I looked at Tom again. Lennon asked everyone to imagine all the people living life in peace. I laughed. Jack put his arm around me. 'Let's face it, Freddie, you're more a lover than a fighter.' He turned me back towards the restaurant and we started walking. We reached Jo-Jo, who was standing at the top of the second staircase. 'Everything okay?' she said.

'Yeah,' I said. 'It's just...'

'Blame me,' said Jack. 'I thought we knew that bloke at the bar.'

'Right,' said Jo-Jo. 'Can we eat now?'

'I'm starving,' I said, grabbing Jo-Jo's hand.

Third day at senior school. Me and Jack were leaning against the gym wall, staring at the grey industrial rubbish bin being rocked from side to side by four laughing fifth-formers, a group of eight or nine older boys standing next to them, clapping, cheering, chanting – 'Rock, rock, rock. Rock, rock, rock' – the screams from inside the bin echoing off the classrooms and offices of the Victorian courtyard. A bin rocker pointed at me and ran a finger across his throat. 'You're next,' he shouted. Jack and I dropped our eyes.

At that moment, Barrett-Simpson, science teacher, pinstriped suit, straight back, protruding chest, no neck, strode across the courtyard ringing the end of break-time bell. Rumour had him enjoying the corporal punishment a bit too much, slipper for the boys, spanking hand for the girls. 'Get back to your class,' he screamed.

'Thank God,' I said.

'There's always tomorrow,' said Jack. 'We might as well get it over with.'

The fifth-formers walked away, pulling on their too-small blazers, patting each other on the back and laughing. The bin rocked gently to a standstill and an ashen-faced, tear-stained eleven-year-old, who looked like he needed a mum, any mum, climbed out. 'You okay?' I shouted. He nodded and ran his arm across his face, snot smearing his cheek. 'You been done yet?' We shook our heads. 'It's fucking terrifying,' he said.

Back in the classroom, 1H chalked on the blackboard, Mr Bloor, our form teacher, tracksuit, trainers, was standing at the front of the class. 'Get used to me,' he said. 'We've got each other for five years. No slackers. I want us to be the best.'

'Jesus,' I whispered. 'You're going to have to help me get through this, Jack.'

'We'll survive,' he said.

I looked at Mr Bloor again. Five years. I couldn't imagine surviving the rest of the day in this hellhole. Jack squeezed my arm and grinned at me.

Freddie – August 2015

I was in Jack's garden, sitting on the park bench that he'd bought from the local charity shop. I'd gone with him to collect it and twisted my back as we were loading it into his Dad's Ford Focus. 'Jesus, Jack. What's this thing made of?' 'It's bomb-proof, mate. It'll outlive me and you.' I looked around the garden and started counting how many different sorts of conifer he'd planted over the last ten years. I'd reached twelve, including the one that crept across the ground, which he'd proclaimed to be rare when he saw it in the garden centre, when the patio door opened and Jack emerged with Bob closely behind him. They each grabbed one of the folded-up wooden patio chairs. Bob smiled at me as he walked across the lawn, Jack kept his eyes on the ground. They reached me, unfolded the chairs and sat down. 'How's it going Freddie?' said Bob, dropping his red Panama hat on the grass.

I looked at Jack. 'I suppose you've told him about Jo-Jo.'

'He's told me,' said Bob. 'The question is, what are you going to do next? We're on your side here, Freddie.'

'There's nothing I can do.'

'You could stop feeling sorry for yourself,' said Jack.

'She's going, Jack. I think I've finally killed it off.'

'Look,' said Bob. 'If you want my opinion as someone who's sort of on the outside...'

It took me a second to realise he was waiting for an answer. 'Which I do,' I said.

'Okay. What you did was stupid.'

I shifted a little on the bench.

'It was, Freddie. There's no point beating about the bush. I know you were upset about the baby, but what you did…'

'You don't have to say it again,' I said.

'The point is,' said Bob, 'Jo-Jo came to see you already knowing what you'd done…'

'She felt sorry for me. That's all. It's what she does. Makes sure everyone's okay.'

'Maybe. But she's going to call you tomorrow. She doesn't have to do that.'

'Amy sent a text,' said Jack.

'She keeps coming back, Freddie,' said Bob. 'Despite you making it really easy for her to walk away, she keeps coming back. Don't you think it's worth one last shot?'

'Maybe it's all best left where it belongs,' I said. 'I keep getting it wrong.'

'So stop doing that,' said Jack, leaning forward in his chair. 'She threw you a curve ball with the baby, but you know that now. Meet her, be honest with her, tell her how you feel.'

'You've got nothing to lose,' said Bob.

'I'm not sure,' I said. 'I don't think I'm up to it.'

'Bloody hell,' said Jack.

I started to cry.

Jack dropped off the chair, knelt in front of me and hugged me. 'It's okay,' he said. 'You don't have to do anything you don't want to do.'

'I want to, Jack, but it tears me apart when it goes wrong. I don't think I'm strong enough. Not now.'

Amy and I were in the hotel conservatory, sitting in our favourite spot next to the yellow daisy-patterned jardinière, home for a well-established citrus tree, waiting for our gin and tonics that had become our pre-evening meal ritual. We were alone apart from the Captain Birdseye lookalike and his foot-shorter wife, the couple Amy had said looked like a ventriloquist and his dummy on a works outing. 'They've been here as long as we have,' I said.

'I wonder what their story is,' said Amy.

'It can't be any more colourful than the one we're living.'

The waitress walked over, carrying a tray. 'Two gin and tonics, madam?'

Amy nodded and she put the two glasses on the wicker table, handing Amy a slip of paper and a pen. 'You did ask for the Copperhead gin, madam?'

'That's right,' said Amy, signing the paper and handing it back.

The waitress walked away and I lifted up the glass and took a sip. 'I know this gin's expensive,' I said, twirling the ice and lemon around, 'but it is gorgeous.'

Amy picked up her glass and clinked it against mine. 'We deserve it,' she said. 'After the day we've had.' She took a sip of the G&T and leaned back in her chair. 'What are you going to do, Mum?'

'I don't know. It's all such a mess.'

'It needn't be.'

'I know, but, well, we're not exactly straightforward, are we?'

She took another sip of her gin. I took another sip of mine.

'I'll call tomorrow,' I said. 'Make sure he's okay.'

'I wonder what it would have been like,' she said. 'If you and him had stayed together. If he'd waited for you, phoned you. Do you think it would have worked out?'

'Who knows? We were young. We failed the first test, me going off to university, so we couldn't have been that special.'

'Maybe that's the problem,' said Amy. 'The fact that it ended before it began. It's a bit like those film stars who die young – they become legends. And Princess Diana. Who knows what she'd have turned out like, but we all worship her now.'

'You're comparing me and Freddie with Princess Diana.'

'You know what I mean. Maybe you've romanticised it, turned it into something it never really was.'

'If only it were that simple. I feel something caressing me whenever I think about him and a huge chasm opens up inside when I think I'm not going to see him again. It's always been the same.'

'I envy you. I've never felt like that about anyone.'

'It's a curse,' I said. 'And it makes it so hard to walk away.'

'So you are walking away.'

'You never met your granddad, Amy.'

'That would have been hard. He died before I was born.'

'But I've told you about him, about how he cared for your gran.'

'What's that got to do with Freddie?'

'Nothing really, except, well… he is fragile.'

'You're worried you'll have to care for him.'

'I feel awful for thinking it, but I saw what it did to your granddad, what it meant for him, and your Uncle Josh had to do it afterwards. I tried, but I never really got it. I stayed away mostly.'

'That's a bit of a leap, Mum. Gran had schizophrenia. Freddie's just a bit needy.'

'But look at how he reacts to things, what he does. I'm not sure I want that worry or if I can give him what he needs.'

'It all went okay in Devon, didn't it?'

'It's perfect when he's like that, but his head, when he starts overthinking. You're never too sure what he's going to do, what you're going to get.'

'Sounds like you're scared, Mum, but none of us know what the future holds. I guess it comes down to how much you love him.'

'I'm not sure that's enough.'

'And being without him again. You've just said about the emptiness that will leave.'

'I don't know what to do, Amy.'

She put her glass on the table, reached into her bag and fetched out her phone.

'What are you doing?' I said.

'You need to talk to him, tell him what you've just said to me and then see how you feel. You'll always wonder if you don't.'

'I can't do that over the phone. And phoning him tonight's not a good idea after this morning.'

She turned the phone over in her hand. 'Tomorrow then. I'll text Jack to say we're coming back tomorrow to get this sorted once and for all.'

Freddie – August 2015

Bob had fetched a box of Kleenex from inside the house and was sitting on the patio chair, waiting to hand me another one. 'I feel like I might have been a bit hard on you,' he said.

'No. You're right. What I did was stupid. I'm cross with myself for crying.'

'At least you're giving me a chance to play nurse,' said Jack, smiling.

'Seriously, Jack, if I ever need a nurse, I hope she's a lot better looking than you.'

I blew my nose. Bob handed me a fresh tissue. Jack's phone pinged.

'It's a text from Amy,' he said, looking at the screen. 'They want to come back tomorrow to try and sort everything. I'll go and see them and explain.'

'I should be the one explaining,' I said.

'You're not really up to it, are you?'

'What will you say to her?'

'I was hoping you might help me with that.'

I searched my head for a response, but white noise bounced back at me – leaving her at the coach station, not phoning, the baby, the train, the tablets, the years without her. I wanted it to be okay, to switch off my head for the rest of my life, for Jo-Jo to say it was all going to be okay, to tell me what to do. 'I don't know,' I said. 'It depends on what she says to me.'

Boris came meowing out of the bushes, a crow hanging from his mouth.

'Bloody cat,' said Jack. 'He's dug up that bird I buried yesterday.'

Freddie – August 1980

Me and Jo-Jo walked in front of Jack and Karen, down Baslow Road, across the green and, after climbing over the padlocked back entrance gates to T.P. Riley School, up the dirt track slope to the hidden sanctuary of the white pebble-dashed walls of the English Language teaching blocks – our regular Sunday evening snogging retreat.

'I'm not going to kiss you,' Karen said to Jack as we approached the building.

Jack shrugged. 'Don't worry,' he said. 'You really don't do it for me.'

'I'm not sure this a good idea,' said Jo-Jo.

'It's the last chance we've got before you go away,' I said.

'He wants ownership papers,' said Karen. 'I'd tell him to piss off if I were you.'

'It's sweet,' said Jack. 'Shows he cares.'

'I love you,' I said to Jo-Jo.

'Oh my God,' said Karen. 'I think I'm going to vomit.'

Jo-Jo looked nervously at Karen and then back at me. 'Does it really mean that much to you?' she said.

I held her hand. 'I want us to declare our commitment to each other before I lose you for three years.'

'You're not going to lose me, Freddie.'

'You know what I mean.'

'We're fine, aren't we?'

Karen went to say something, but Jo-Jo glared at her.

'It just feels like something we should do,' I said. 'Makes us official.'

Jo-Jo looked at Karen and Jack. She turned back to me. I was still holding her hand. 'Why are these two here?' she said.

'To witness me giving you the ring.'

'You've bought a ring?'

I let go of her hand, reached into the pocket of my jeans and pulled out a red velvet ring box.

'Oh,' said Karen. 'You didn't tell me you were getting a ring.'

'Can you afford this?' said Jo-Jo, taking the box from me.

'I've been saving up. Mum helped a bit. She guessed your ring size when you tried on that ring of hers.'

She opened the lid, fetched the ring out of the box and looked at me. 'It's gorgeous,' she said.

'It's a DEAREST ring,' I said, taking the nine carat gold ring from her, holding it up to the early evening summer sky, and naming each stone across the front of the band. 'Diamond, Emerald, Amethyst, Ruby, Emerald, Sapphire, Tourmaline... DEAREST.'

'Tourmaline?' said Karen.

'They needed a T,' said Jack and they both sniggered.

'It is lovely, Freddie,' said Jo-Jo.

I took her left hand, held it out in front of me and pushed the ring onto the third finger. 'For all eternity,' I said, looking into her eyes. 'I will love you for all eternity.'

Freddie – August 2015

Jack beeped the Mini's horn as he drove the car away from the kerb.

'I won't be long,' he'd said as I got out of the car.

'I just need to get some fresh clothes, Jack, and to make sure the cats are okay.'

'They're fine. I've been popping in every day.'

'I know. I just need to see for myself.'

I closed the front door, walked down the hall into the kitchen and threw my keys on the table. The only sound was the tick, tick, tick of the Seiko wall clock. Jack had washed up the dirty crocks, four ceramic cat dishes, a single mug, cereal bowl and cutlery, and left them on the work surface next to the sink, probably not sure where I kept them. There was no sign of the propranolol. I guessed he'd flushed them down the toilet, used the quickest route to get them out of the house. I thought of my secret stash in the attic, safely stored away in the front of the house soffit space, hidden under old jumpers and tee-shirts in a battered copper chest.

I sat down on one of the oak dining chairs and put the tin foil-wrapped sandwiches on the kitchen table. Jack had handed them to me just as we were leaving the house. 'Tomato,' he'd said. 'And I've put some fresh milk in your fridge.' I unwrapped the foil and smiled. Tomato with lots of salt. It reminded me of Shirley the Greek, a Dolmio Mamma, who used to be my work partner in one of the care homes. She used to charge one of the octogenarian residents, Henry, a couple of pounds to put his hand inside her bra and squeeze her breast. 'Puts a smile on his face,' she'd say. 'What else will he spend his money on?' The only thing Henry would eat was tomato sandwiches.

A memory: Jo-Jo and I are on our way to Blackpool in my Chrysler Avenger. Springsteen's *The River* is playing on the car's cassette player. Jo-Jo opens the lid on a Tupperware sandwich box. 'Mum made us a snack,' she says. I take my eyes off the M6 for a moment and look at her. 'Your mum, not your dad?' 'Yep. She must like you. Dad supervised, but I think she did most of it.' She fetches out a piece of fruit cake. 'Oh dear,' she says. 'What?' I say, slowing the car down. 'It's a bit overcooked,' she says. I look at the cake and laugh. 'Overcooked. It's cremated.' 'You've got to try it,' she says, holding it towards my mouth. 'I'm not eating that, Jo-Jo.' She pulls her face into a pained expression. 'I can't believe you'd disrespect my mother.' She brings the cake closer to my mouth. 'Just try a little bit,' she says. 'Just for me.' The first thing I taste is charcoal, like it's been scraped off the bottom of a wok. I try to bite it. 'Jesus,' I say. 'I think I've broken my tooth.' 'I know,' says Jo-Jo, laughing and closing the lid on the sandwich box. 'Mum's cake is as hard as the knockers of hell. I've never known anyone try a piece before.'

I pushed away the tomato sandwich and picked up my phone.

Jo-Jo – August 2015

I was back in my hotel room, lying on the bed, clutching a black velvet drawstring bag, which was about the size of a soap bag. I untied the string and pulled out two red satin boxes, which I laid side by side on the white duvet. I opened the lid of the first box and touched the gold St Christopher, which was slotted into the black sponge base, its chain neatly folded out of sight. Freddie's mum's face dropped into my head, her beaming smile as we realised what she'd bought us, me telling her it would stay with me always. And here it was. Nearly forty years later. Not for the first time, I wished I'd seen more of her, had her in my life for longer. I smiled at the memory of Freddie's blushed cheeks when he'd realised she'd heard us making love, how he couldn't look at her when she came downstairs to watch *The Poseidon Adventure* on that Christmas Day evening in 1979, how she'd kept tutting at him, but smiling and winking at me when he wasn't looking. I touched the St Christopher again and then opened the lid of the second box.

A memory: I'm on my own walking barefoot across the beach in the Maldives. There is a full moon, the beams on the Indian Ocean making it look like the sea has frozen silver. I suddenly realise there is something bobbing all over the surface of the water. Luminescent algae. It looks like the stars have fallen out of the sky. Another memory: I'm walking back on my own from the restaurant when I notice three couples and the manager from the hotel reception crouching down in a small huddle at the top of the beach, all of them looking closely at a metal cage that's nestled in the white sand. I walk over and reach them just as the manager lifts the cage to one side and gently starts to scoop the sand underneath. 'What's happening?' I say. 'Turtles,' says the manager. 'We've been waiting for them to hatch for weeks.' I crouch down as well. There's a movement in the sand. The manager stops scooping. A flipper pokes out, flicking the sand aside, closely followed by a turtle head. The baby turtle frees itself and then there's another one, and another one, and another one, scurrying out of the nest and scuttling down the beach towards the sea. More follow, until there are about sixty baby turtles crawling across the white sand, some of them starting to go the wrong way, but quickly realising and joining the race to the sanctuary of the water. We walk slowly behind them and watch as they morph from clumsy land dwellers to Olympic swimmers, disappearing into the aqua blue tide.

I pulled the DEAREST ring out of the second box and slid it gently onto the third finger of my left hand. 'For all eternity,' I whispered.

My phone rang. Freddie's name came up on the screen.

Stephen Anthony Brotherton grew up in the West Midlands and spent over thirty years working as a Social Worker. He now lives in Shropshire with his two cats, Boris and Tai. *Fractures, Dreams and Second Chances* is his first novel.